BEE AND PUPPYCAT™

VOLUME ONE

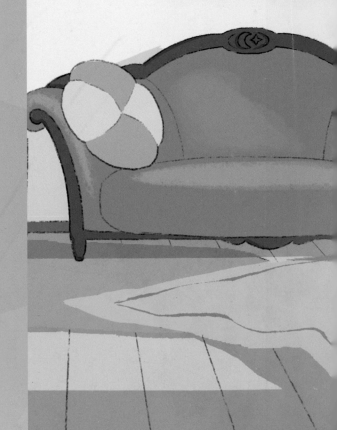

ROSS RICHIE *CEO & Founder*

MARK SMYLIE *Founder of Archaia*

MATT GAGNON *Editor-in-Chief*

FILIP SABLIK *President of Publishing & Marketing*

STEPHEN CHRISTY *President of Development*

LANCE KREITER *VP of Licensing & Merchandising*

PHIL BARBARO *VP of Finance*

BRYCE CARLSON *Managing Editor*

MEL CAYLO *Marketing Manager*

SCOTT NEWMAN *Production Design Manager*

IRENE BRADISH *Operations Manager*

CHRISTINE DINH *Brand Communications Manager*

DAFNA PLEBAN *Editor*

SHANNON WATTERS *Editor*

ERIC HARBURN *Editor*

REBECCA TAYLOR *Editor*

IAN BRILL *Editor*

CHRIS ROSA *Assistant Editor*

ALEX GALER *Assistant Editor*

WHITNEY LEOPARD *Assistant Editor*

JASMINE AMIRI *Assistant Editor*

CAMERON CHITTOCK *Assistant Editor*

MARY GUMPORT *Assistant Editor*

KELSEY DIETERICH *Production Designer*

JILLIAN CRAB *Production Designer*

KARA LEOPARD *Production Designer*

DEVIN FUNCHES *E-Commerce & Inventory Coordinator*

AARON FERRARA *Operations Assistant*

JOSÉ MEZA *Sales Assistant*

MICHELLE ANKLEY *Sales Assistant*

ELIZABETH LOUGHRIDGE *Accounting Assistant*

STEPHANIE HOCUTT *PR Assistant*

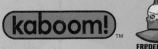

BEE AND PUPPYCAT Volume One, April 2015. Published by Ka-BOOM!, a division of Boom Entertainment, Inc. Based on "Bee and PuppyCat" © 2015 Frederator Networks, Inc. Originally published in single magazine form as BEE AND PUPPYCAT No. 1-4. ™ & © 2014 Frederator Networks, Inc. All rights reserved. KaBOOM!™ and the Ka-BOOM! logo are trademarks of Boom Entertainment, Inc., registered in various countries and categories. All characters, events, and institutions depicted herein are fictional. Any similarity between any of the names, characters, persons, events, and/or institutions in this publication to actual names, characters, and persons, whether living or dead, events, and/or institutions is unintended and purely coincidental. KaBOOM! does not read or accept unsolicited submissions of ideas, stories, or artwork.

A catalog record of this book is available from OCLC and from the KaBOOM! website, www.kaboom-studios.com, on the Librarians Page.

BOOM! Studios, 5670 Wilshire Boulevard, Suite 450, Los Angeles, CA 90036-5679. Printed in China. First Printing.

ISBN: 978-1-60886-487-4, eISBN: 978-1-61398-341-6

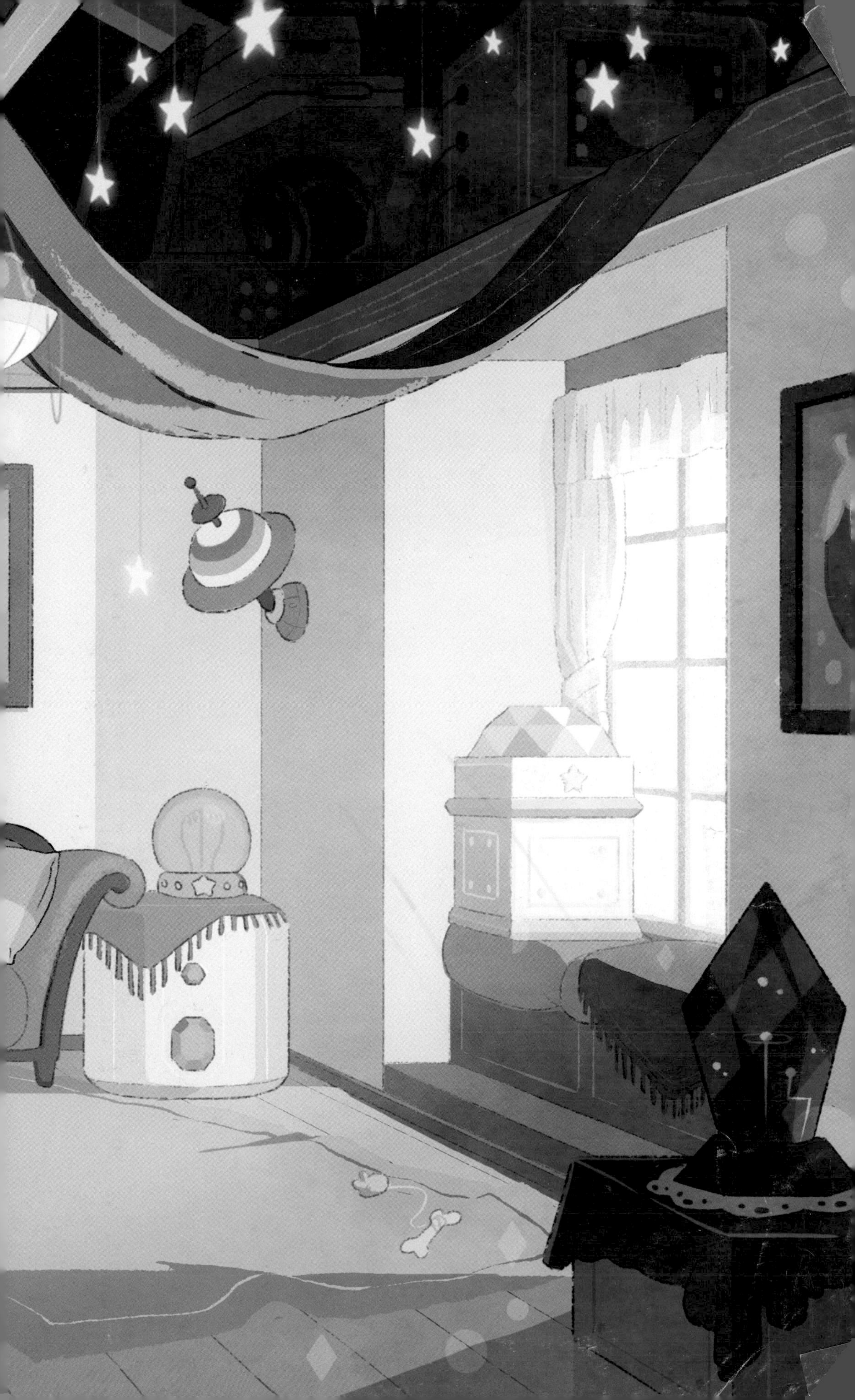

Created by

Natasha Allegri

Written by

Natasha Allegri
& Garrett Jackson

Illustrated by

Natasha Allegri

with additional colors by Patrick Seery

Letters by

Britt Wilson

Cover by

Natasha Allegri

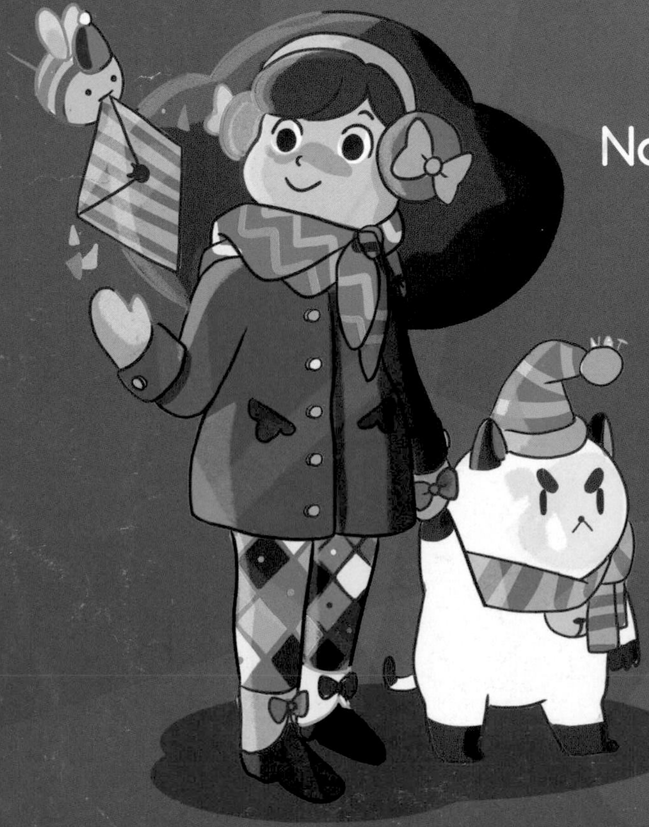

"What Happened"

Written and Illustrated by
Madeleine Flores

"A Fighting Spirit"

Written by
Frank Gibson

Illustrated by
Becky Dreistadt

"A Nice Day Off"

Written and Illustrated by
Anissa Espinosa

"Clean Up"

Written and Illustrated by
Tait Howard

Letters by
Aubrey Aiese

"Dumguy"

Written and Illustrated by
Ian McGinty

Colors by
Fred Stresing

"The Package"

Written and Illustrated by
T. Zysk

"Plantsapalooza"

Written and Illustrated by
Mad Rupert

Colors by
Whitney Cogar

"Play the Game!"

Written and Illustrated by
Coleman Engle

"The Perfect Sandwich"

Written and Illustrated by
Aimee Fleck

"Hungry"

Written and Illustrated by
Pranas Naujokaitis

Colors by
Whitney Cogar

Collection Designer Kelsey Dieterich

Assistant Editor Whitney Leopard

Editor Shannon Watters

With Special Thanks to Eric Homan, Fred Seibert
and all of the classy folks at Frederator Studios.

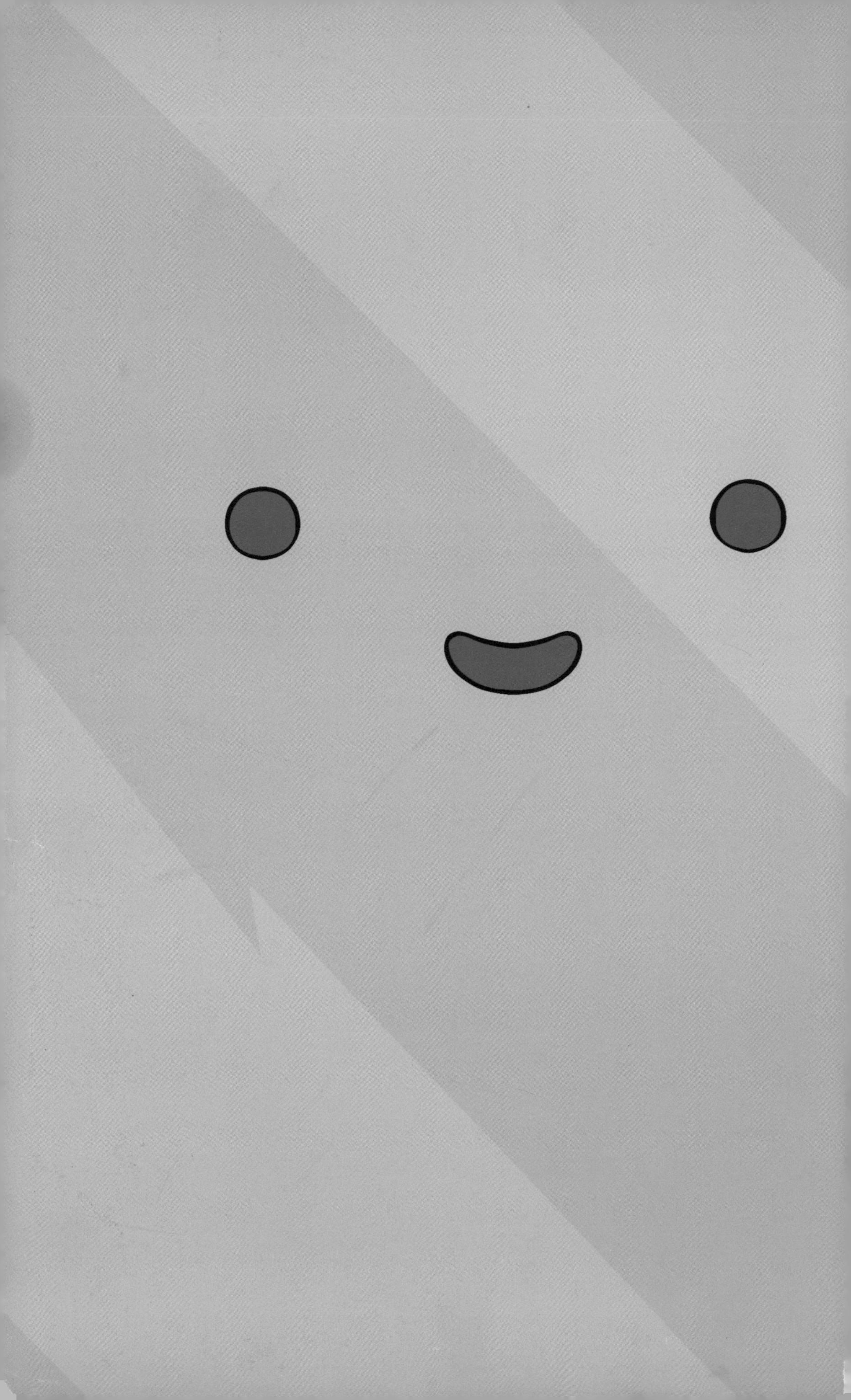

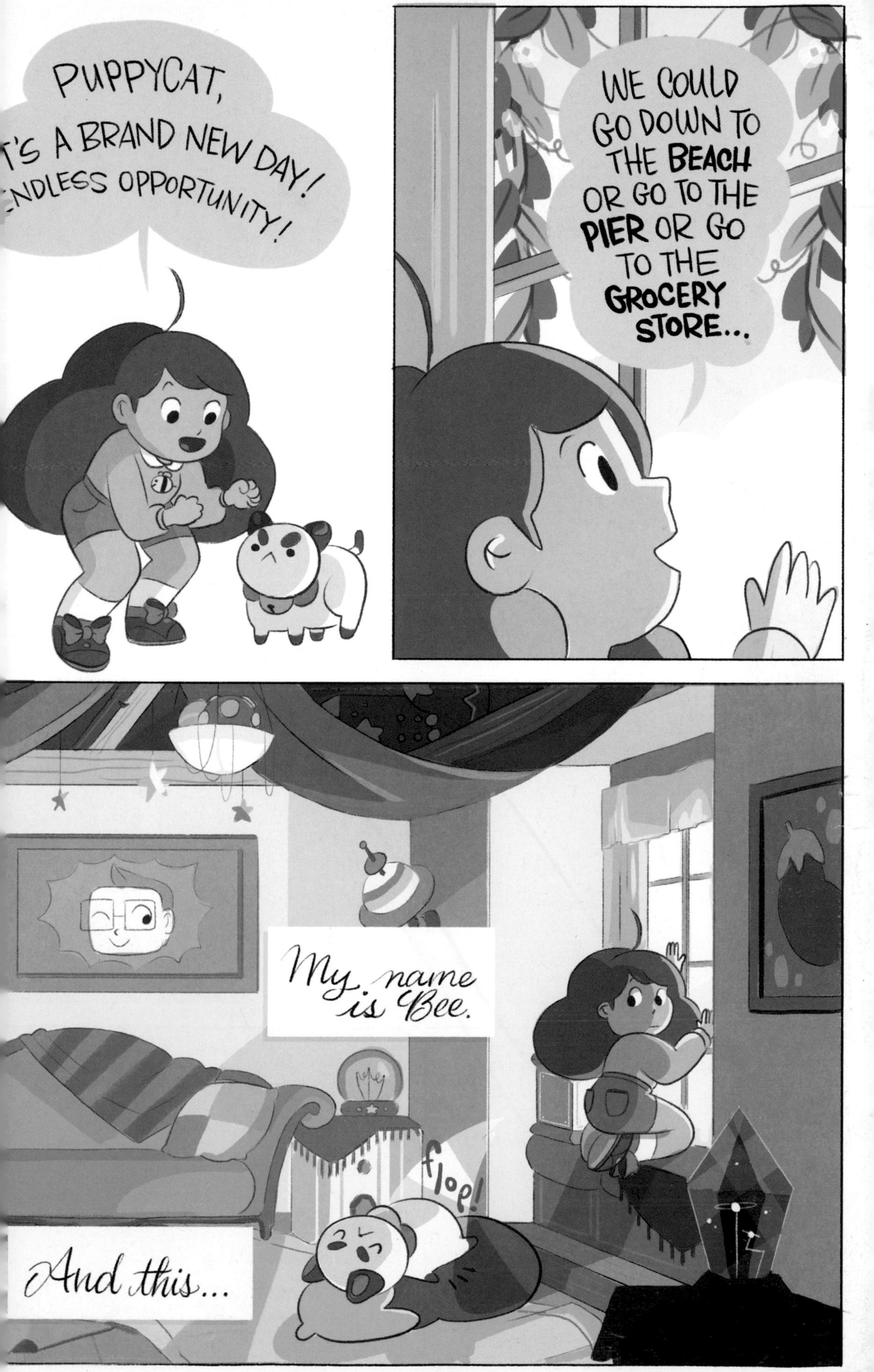

PUPPYCAT,
T'S A BRAND NEW DAY!
NDLESS OPPORTUNITY!
WE COULD GO DOWN TO THE **BEACH** OR GO TO THE **PIER** OR GO TO THE **GROCERY STORE...**
My name is Bee.
And this...
floe!

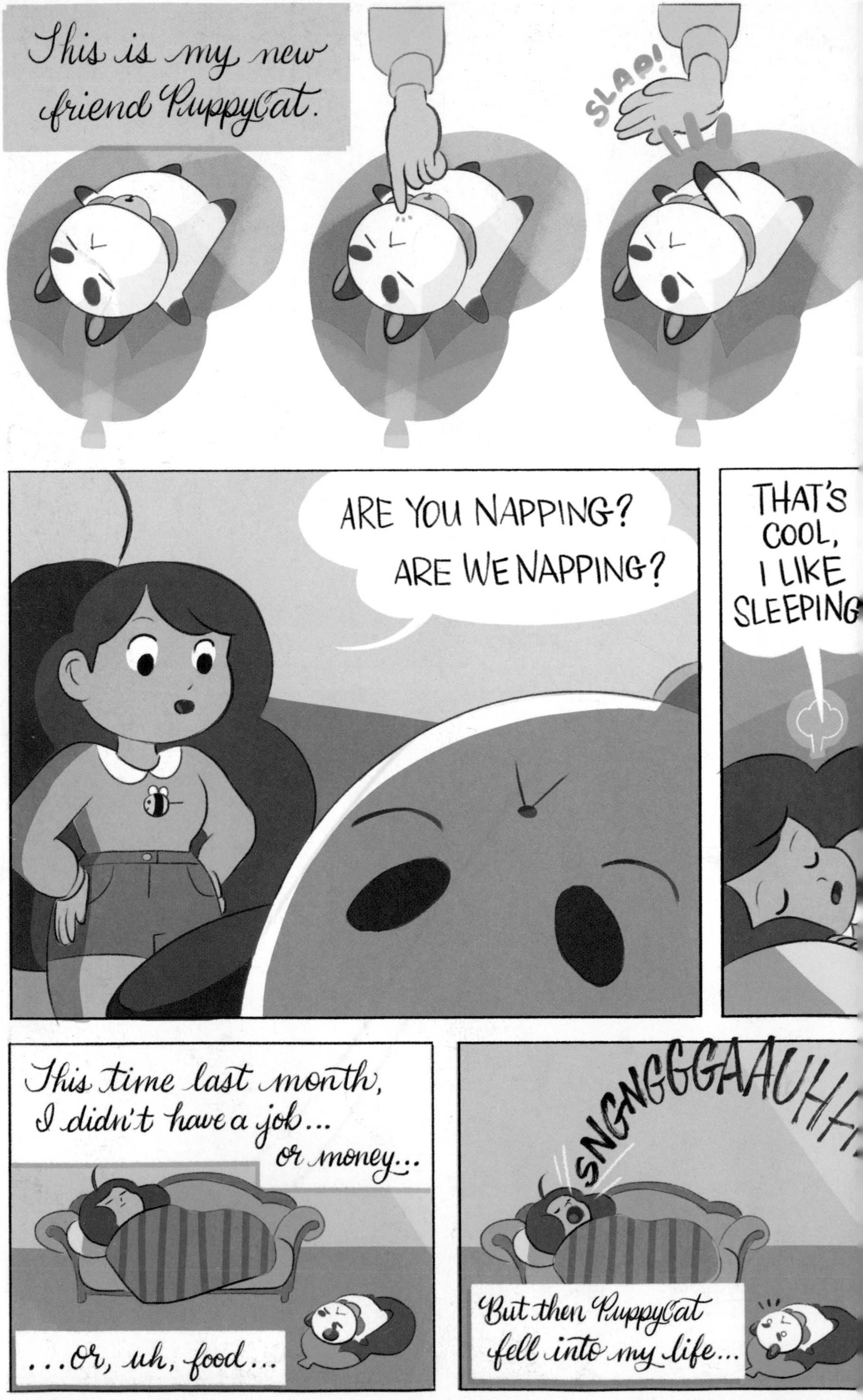
This is my new friend PuppyCat.
SLAP!
ARE YOU NAPPING? ARE WE NAPPING?
THAT'S COOL, I LIKE SLEEPING
This time last month, I didn't have a job...
or money...
...or, uh, food...
SNGNGGGAAUHH
But then PuppyCat fell into my life...

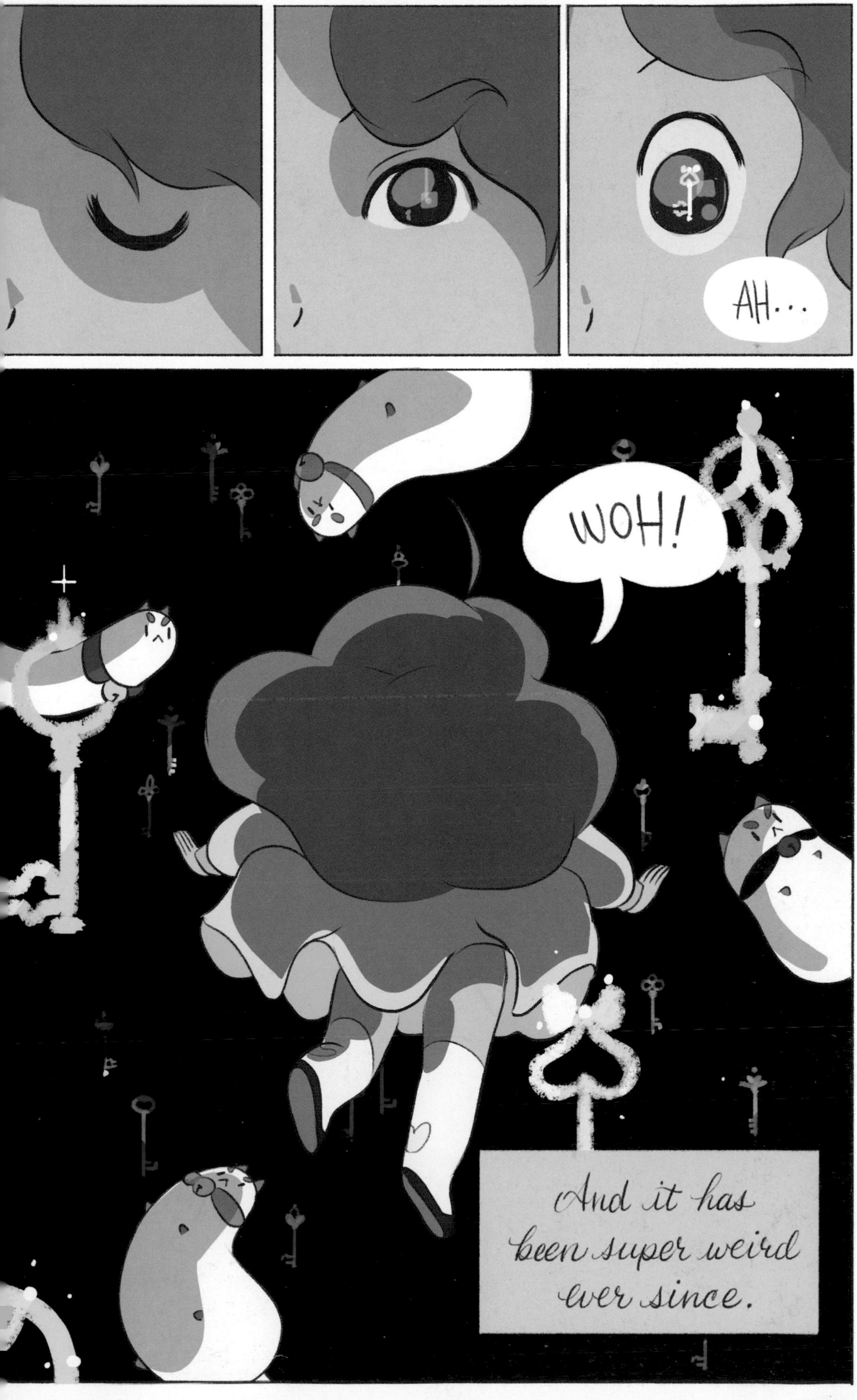
AH...
WOH!
And it has been super weird ever since.

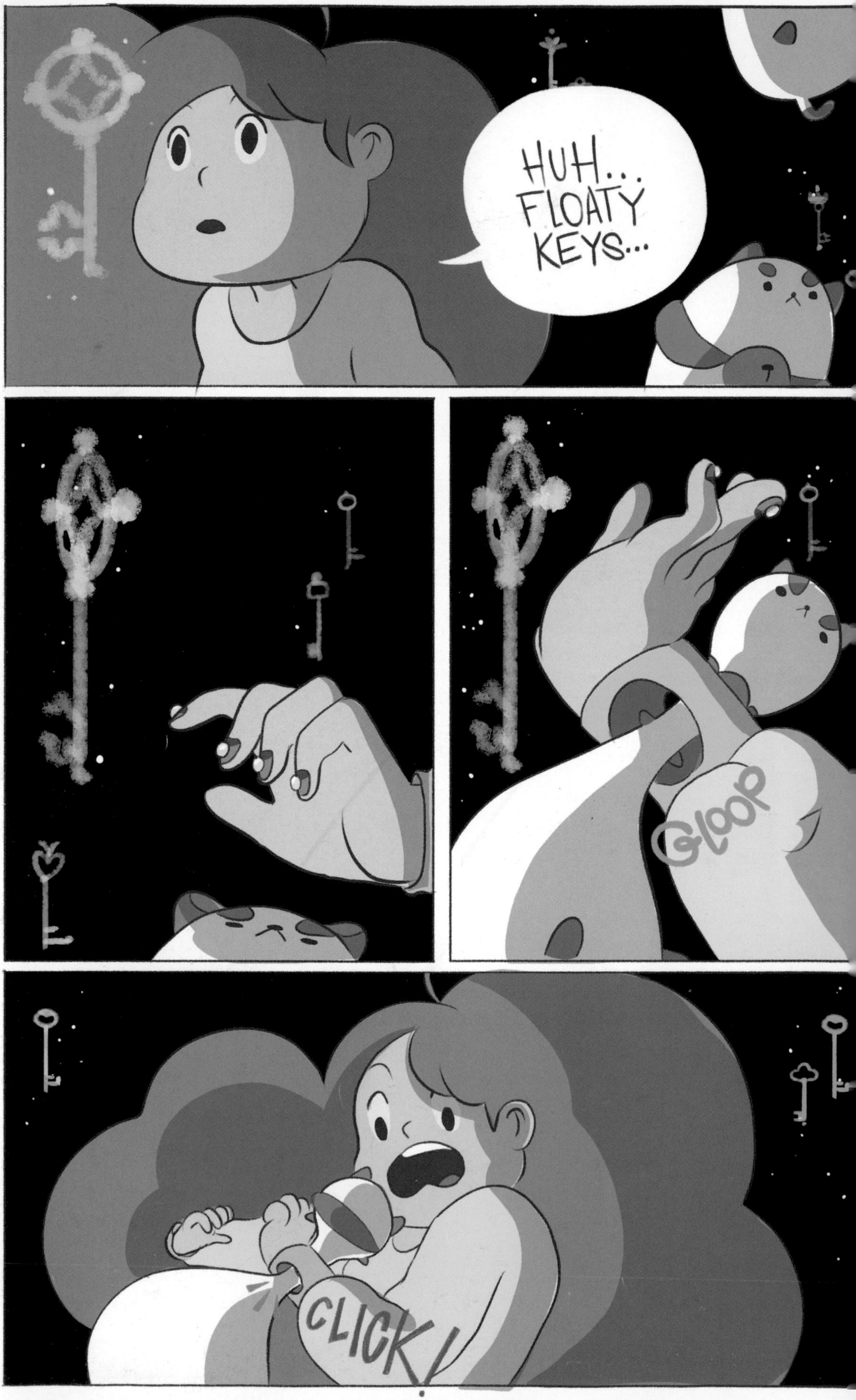
HUH... FLOATY KEYS...
GLOOP
CLICK!

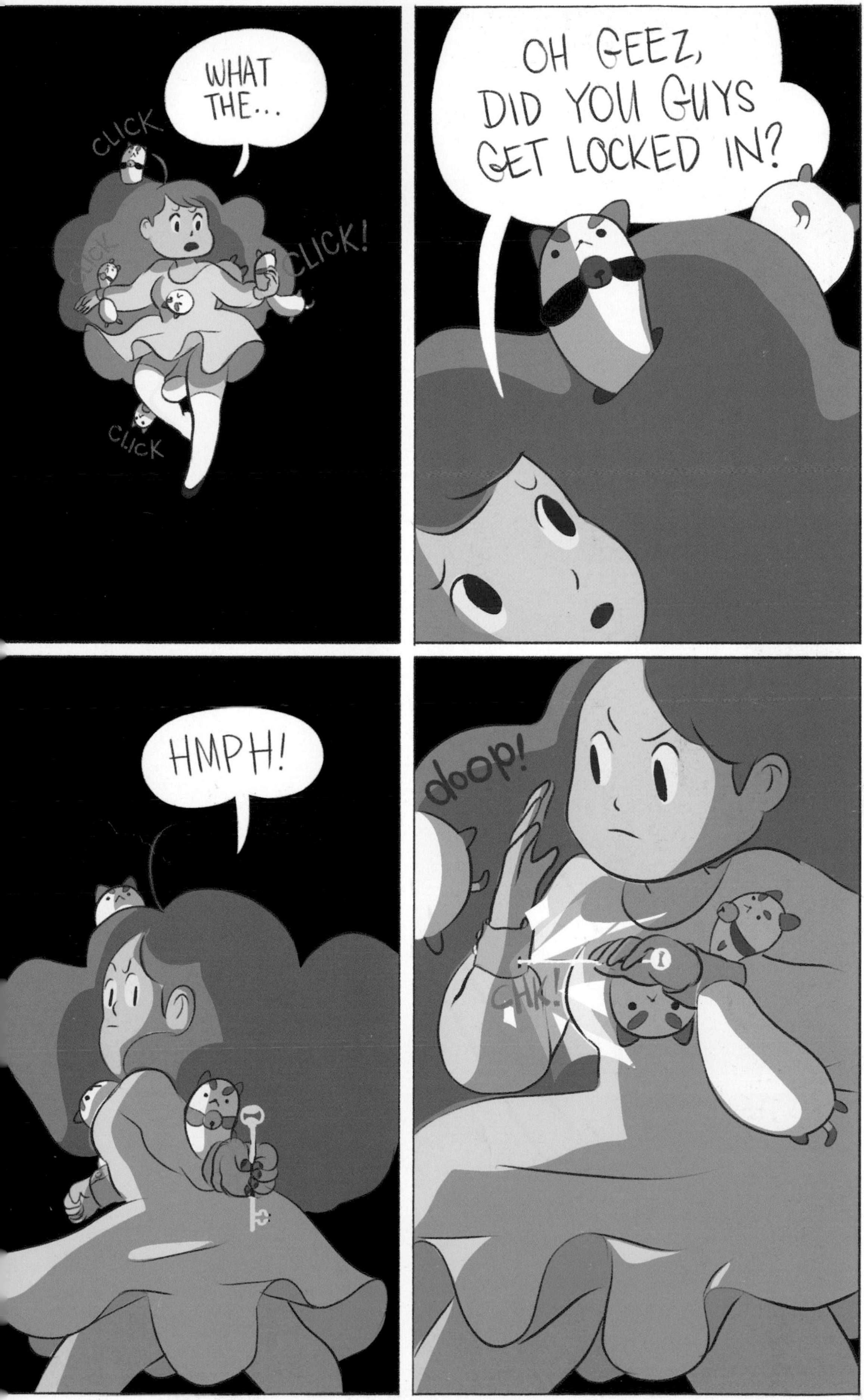

WHAT THE...
CLICK
CLICK!
CLICK
CLICK
OH GEEZ, DID YOU GUYS GET LOCKED IN?
HMPH!
doop!
CHK!

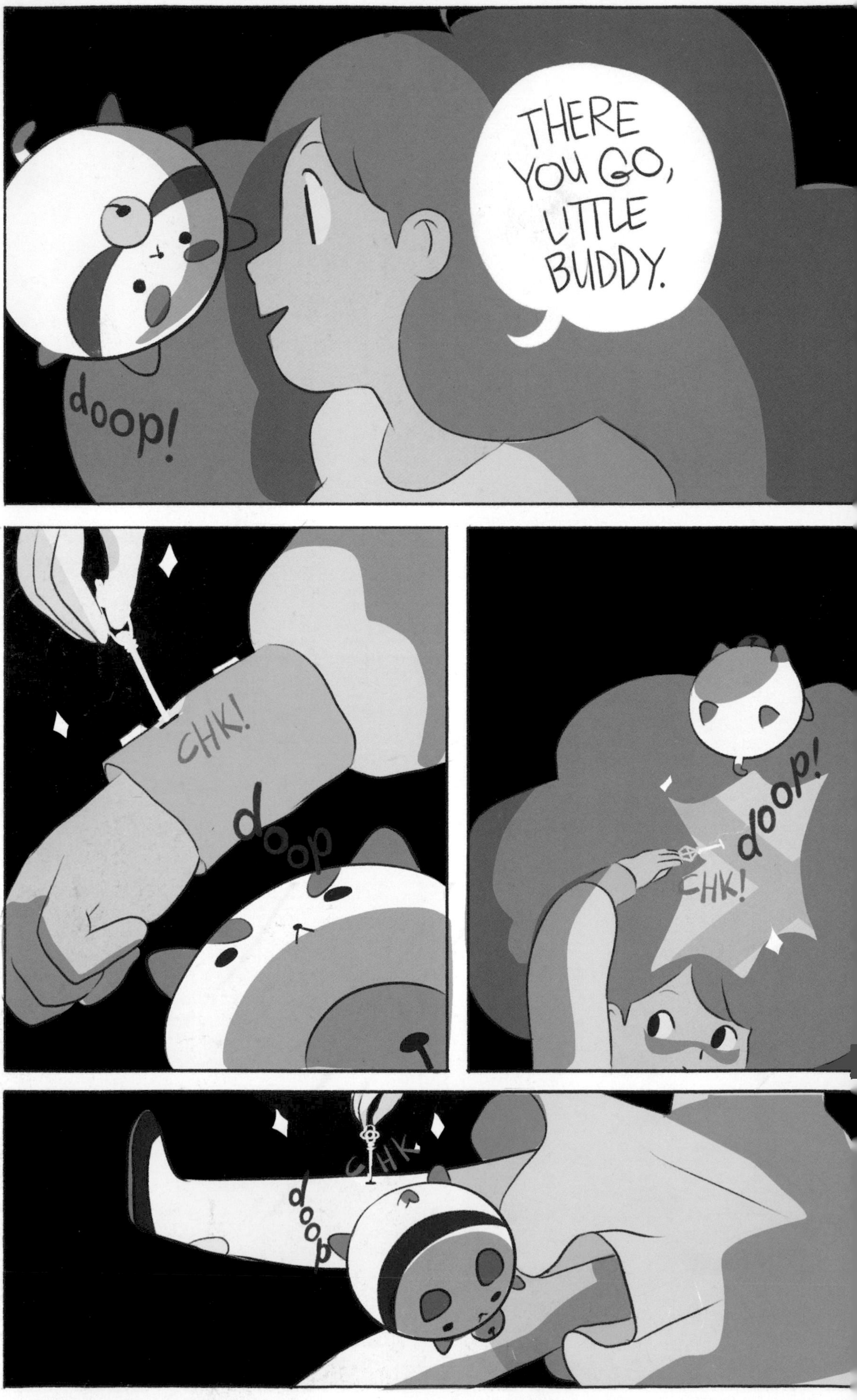

THERE YOU GO, LITTLE BUDDY.
doop!
CHK!
doop
doop!
CHK!
CHK
doop

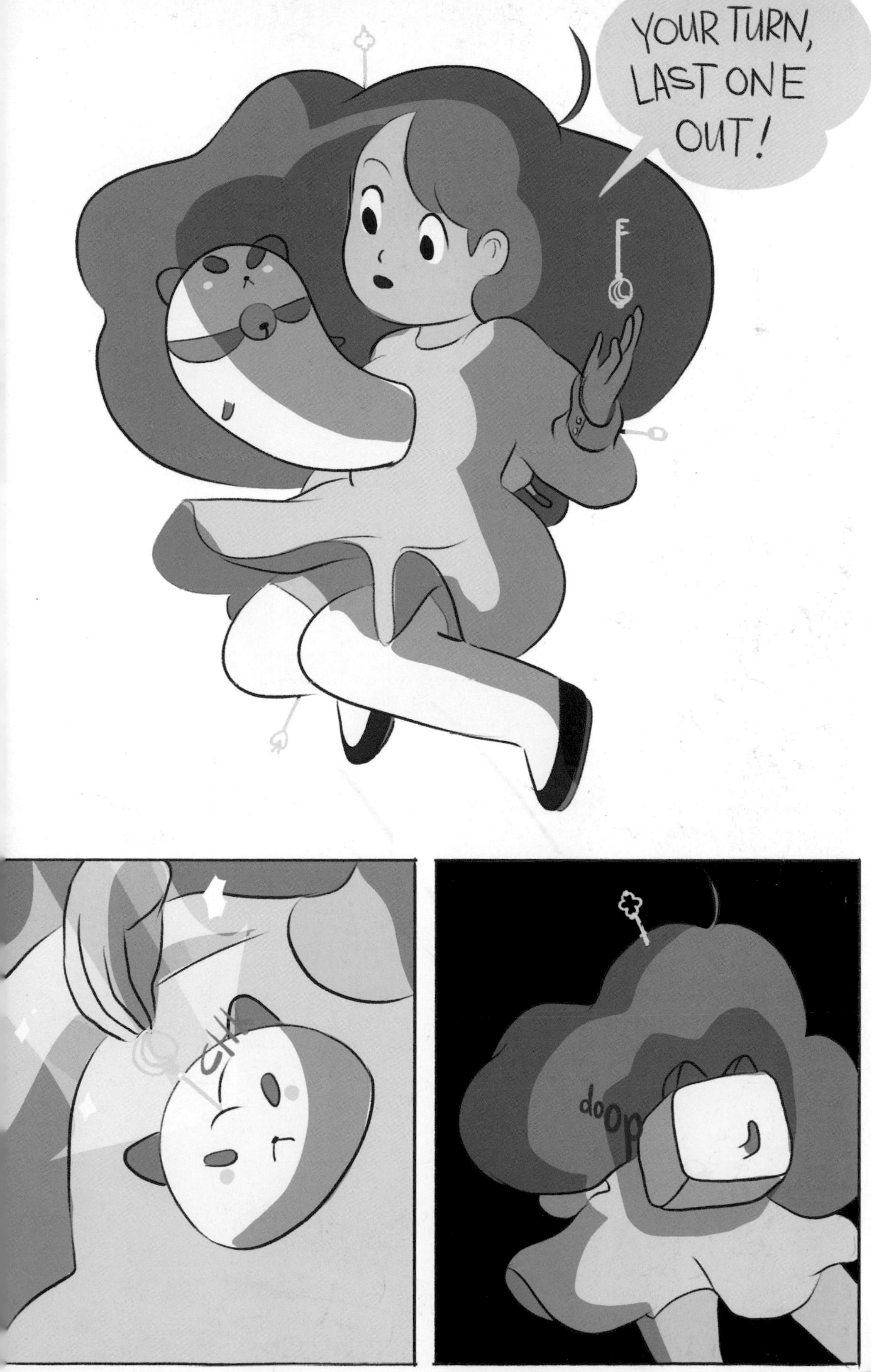
YOUR TURN, LAST ONE OUT!
doop

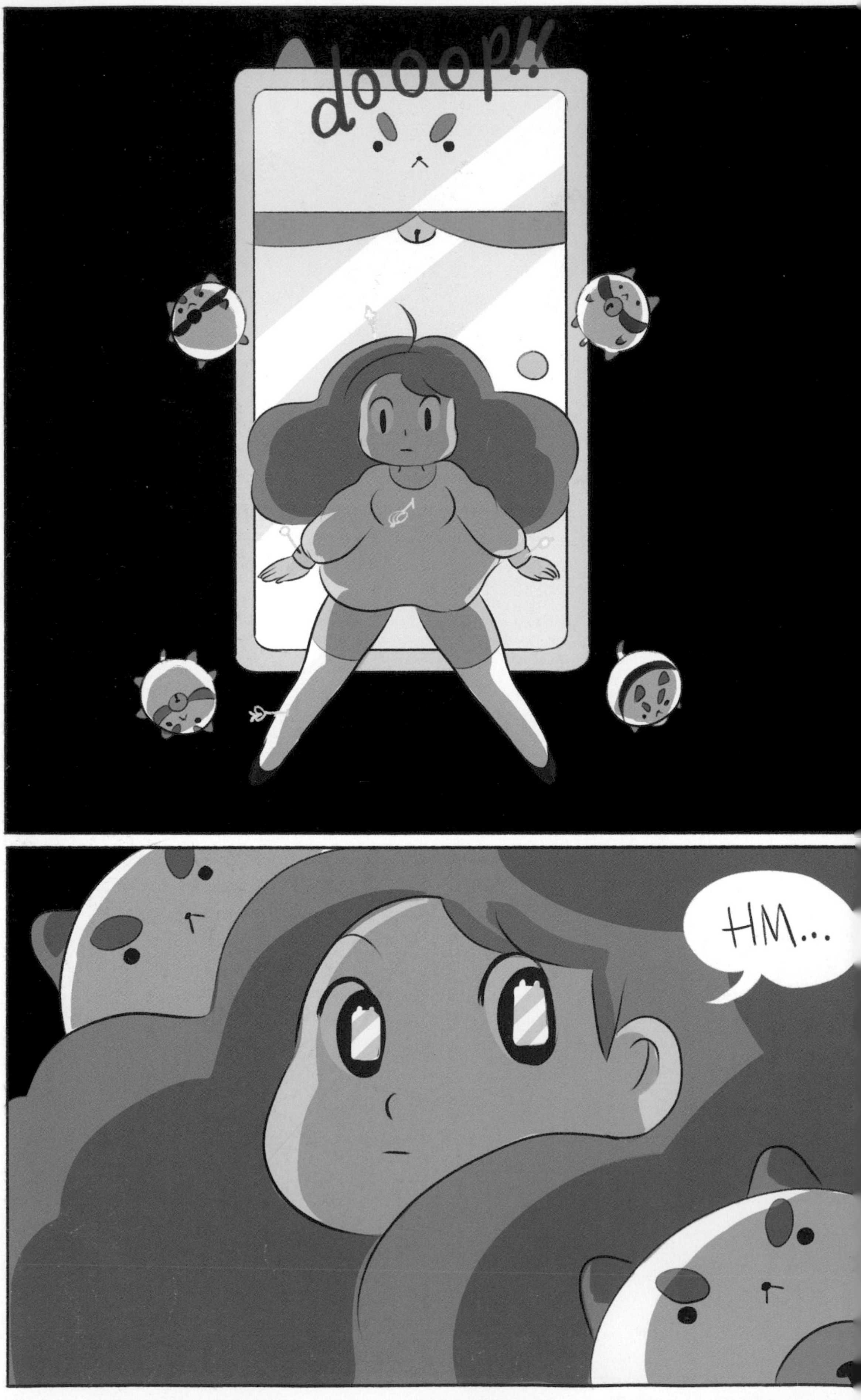
dooop!!
HM...

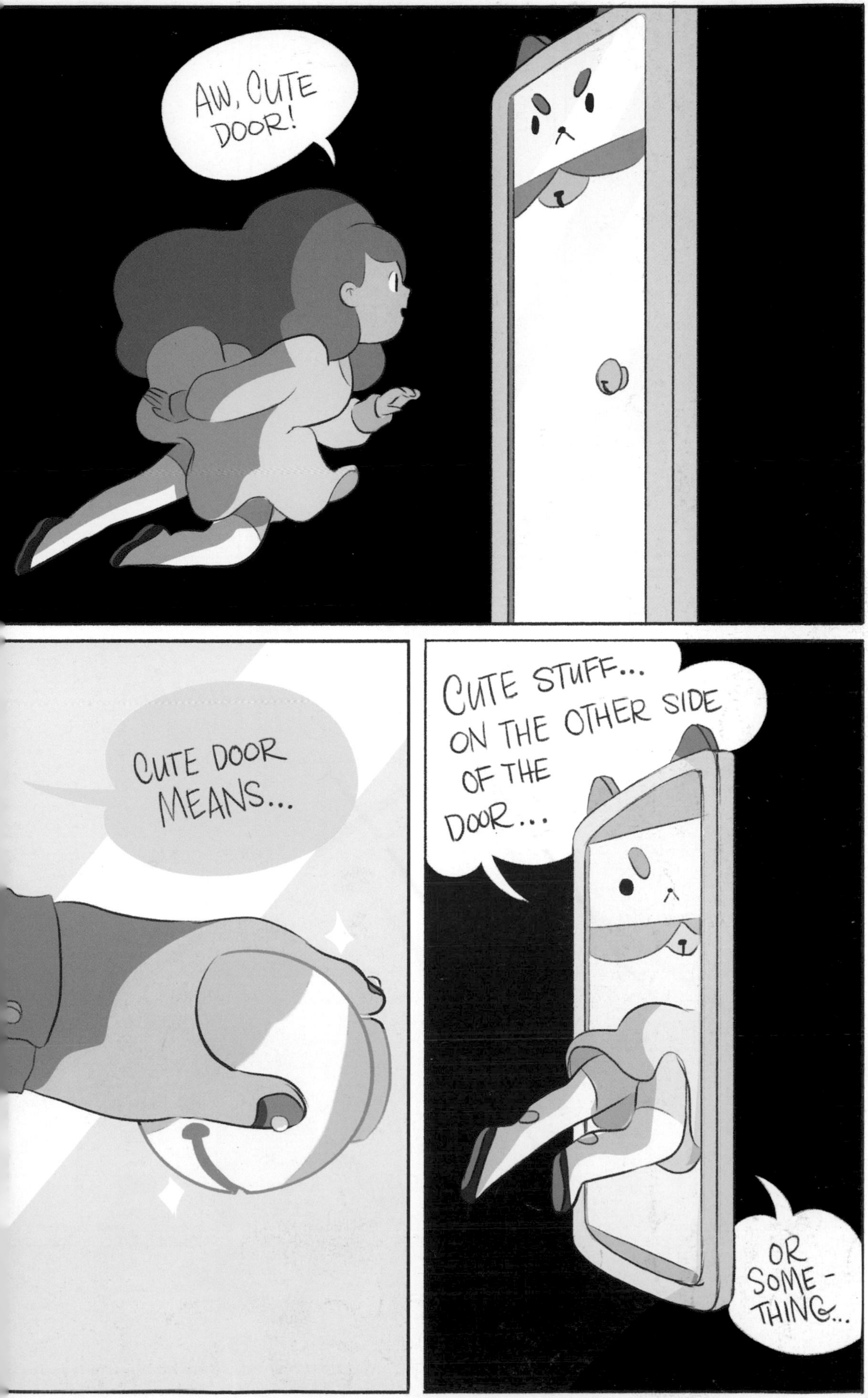
AW, CUTE DOOR!
CUTE DOOR MEANS...
CUTE STUFF... ON THE OTHER SIDE OF THE DOOR...
OR SOME-THING...

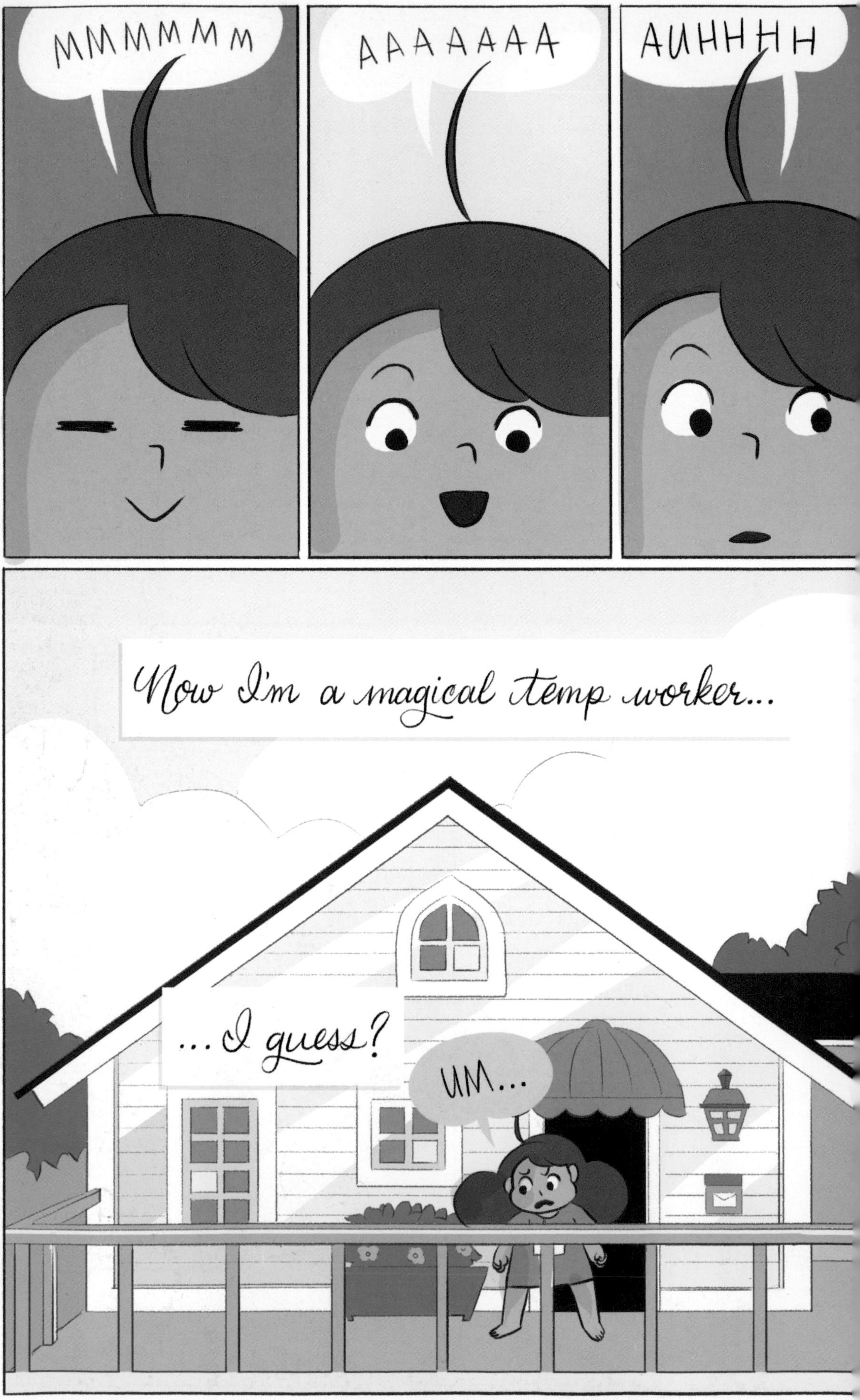
MMMMMM
AAAAAAA
AUHHHH
Now I'm a magical temp worker...
...I guess?
UM...

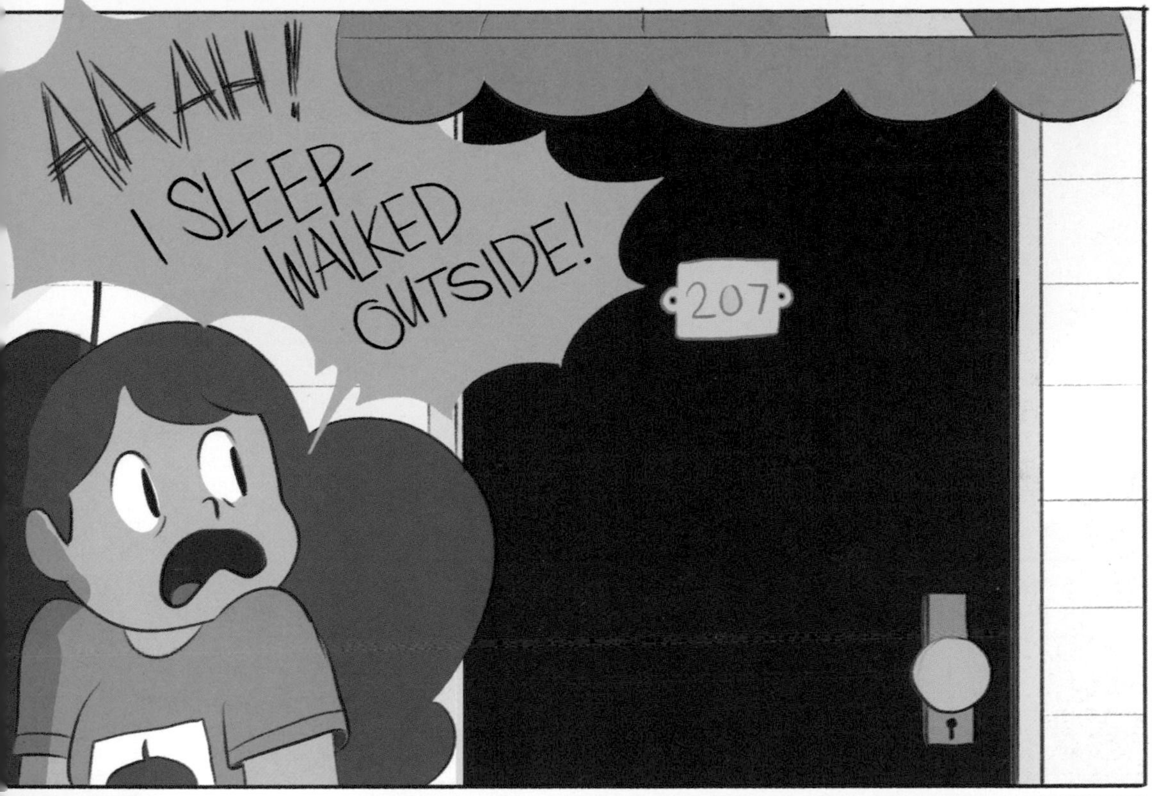
AAAH! I SLEEP-WALKED OUTSIDE!
207

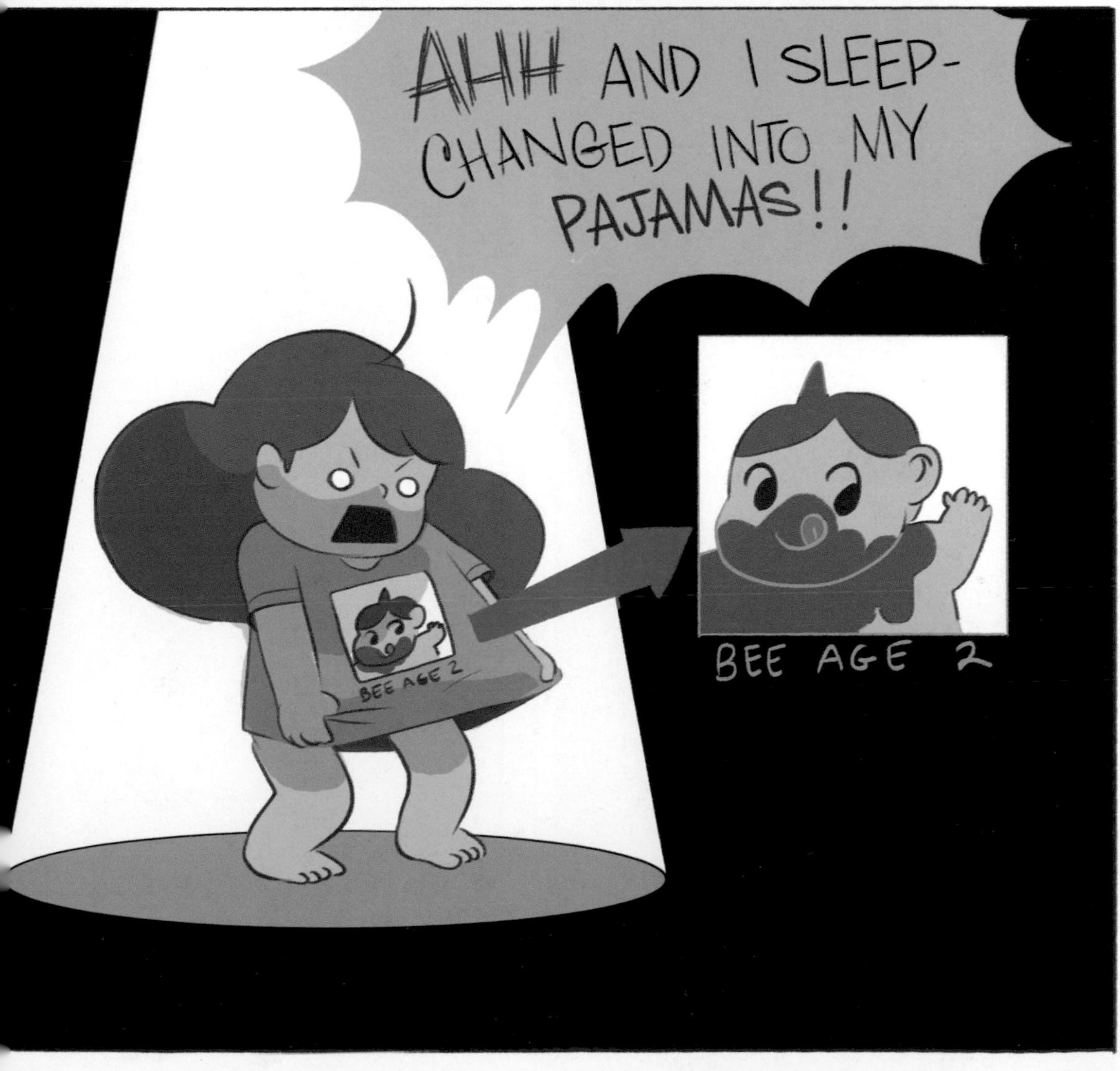
AHH AND I SLEEP-CHANGED INTO MY PAJAMAS!!
BEE AGE 2
BEE AGE 2

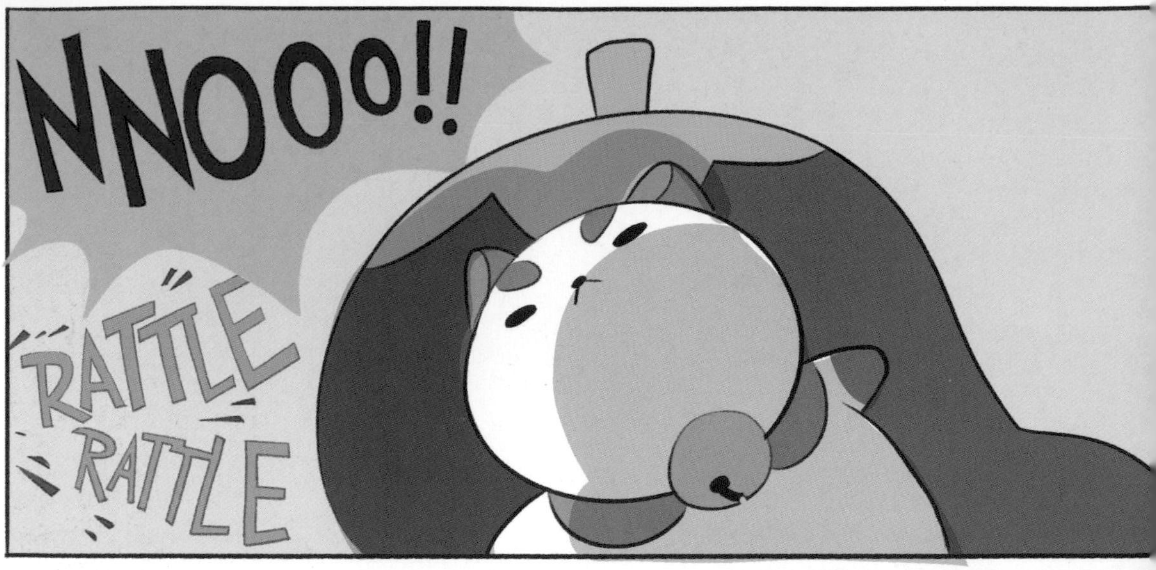
NNOOO!!
RATTLE
RATTLE

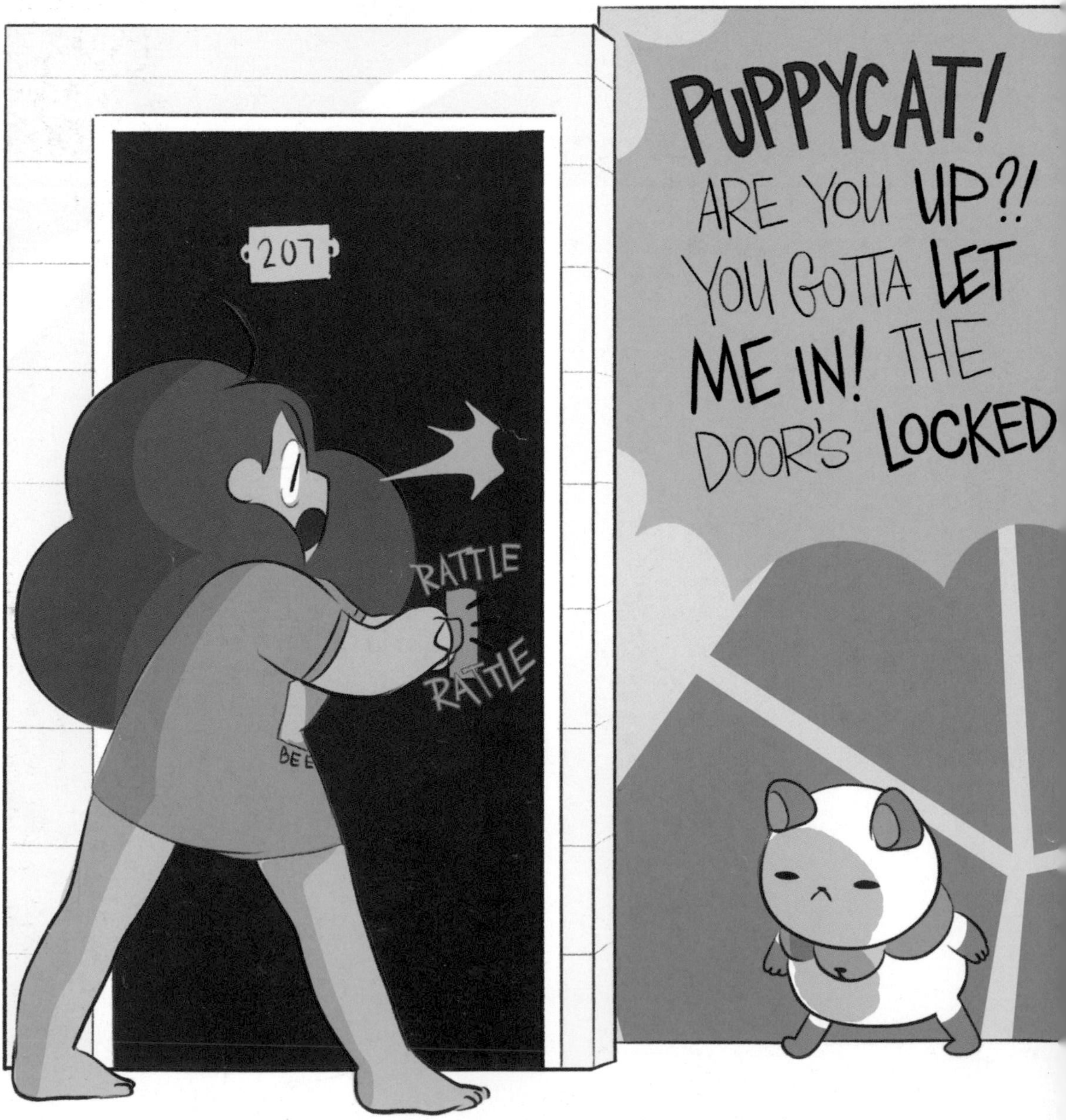
207
RATTLE
RATTLE
PUPPYCAT! ARE YOU UP?! YOU GOTTA LET ME IN! THE DOOR'S LOCKED

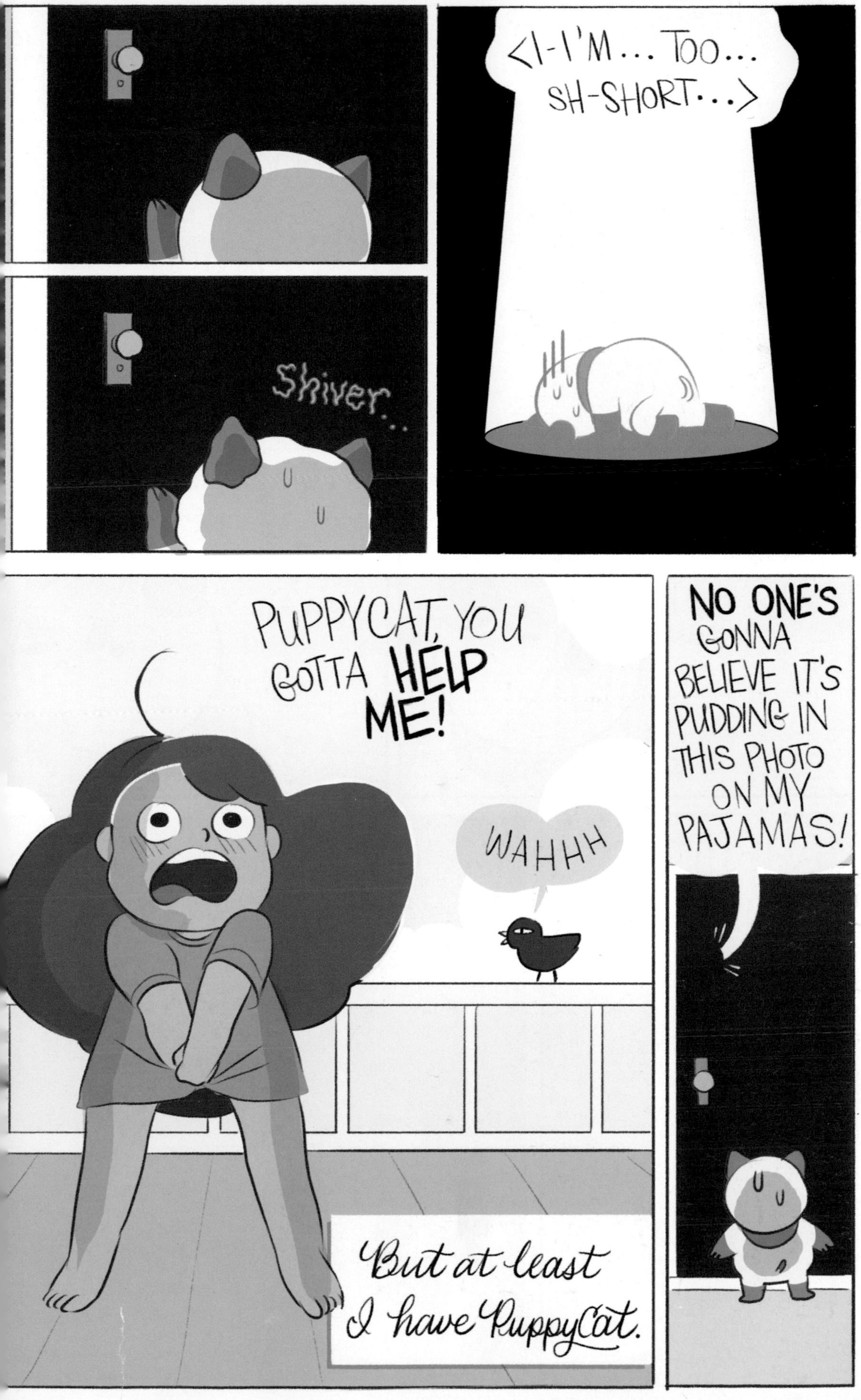
<I-I'M... TOO...
SH-SHORT...>
Shiver...
PUPPYCAT, YOU GOTTA HELP ME!
WAHHH
NO ONE'S GONNA BELIEVE IT'S PUDDING IN THIS PHOTO ON MY PAJAMAS!
But at least I have PuppyCat.

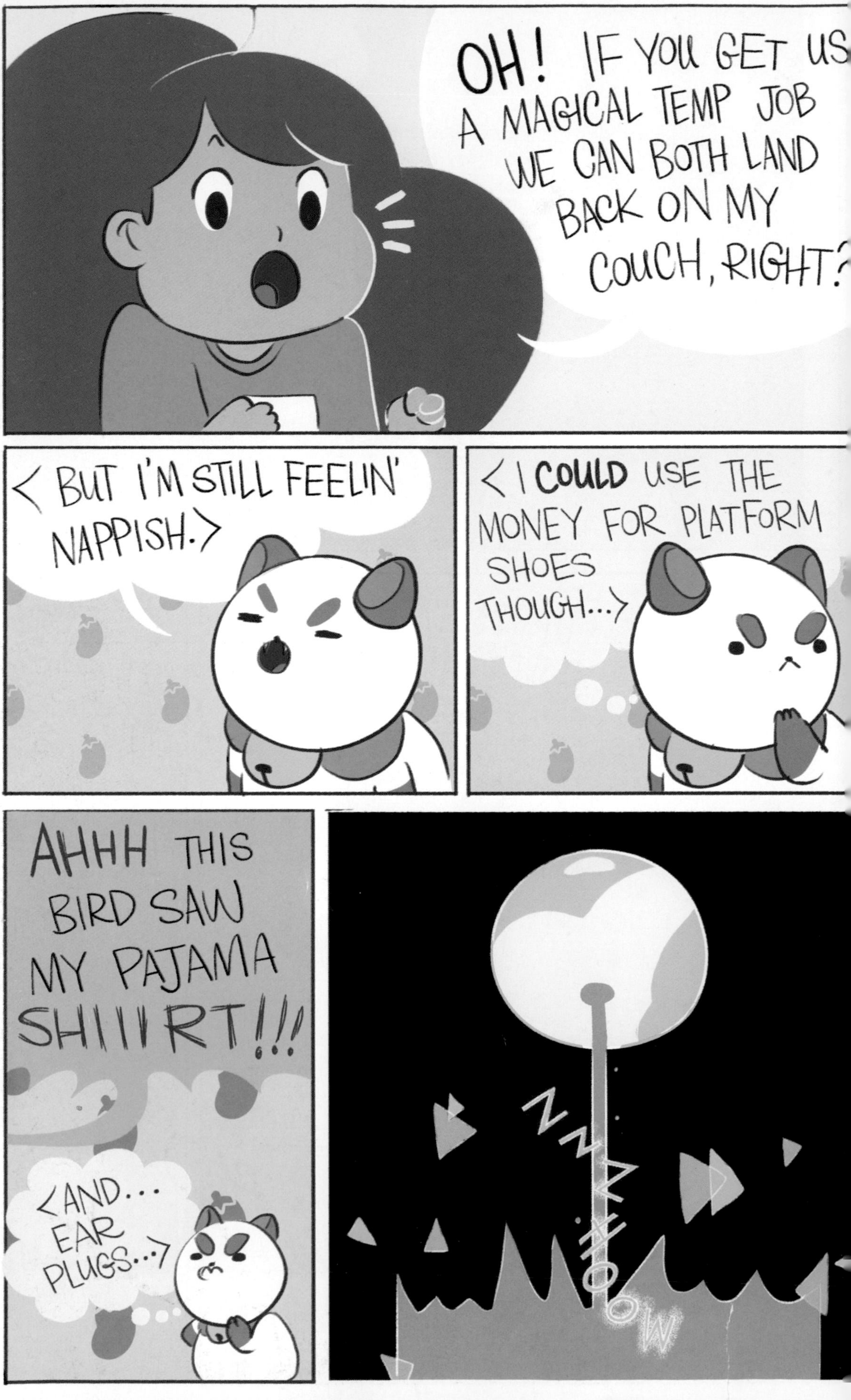
OH! IF YOU GET US A MAGICAL TEMP JOB WE CAN BOTH LAND BACK ON MY COUCH, RIGHT?
< BUT I'M STILL FEELIN' NAPPISH.>
<I COULD USE THE MONEY FOR PLATFORM SHOES THOUGH...>
AHHH THIS BIRD SAW MY PAJAMA SHIIIRT!!!
<AND... EAR PLUGS...>
NNNZZOOOW

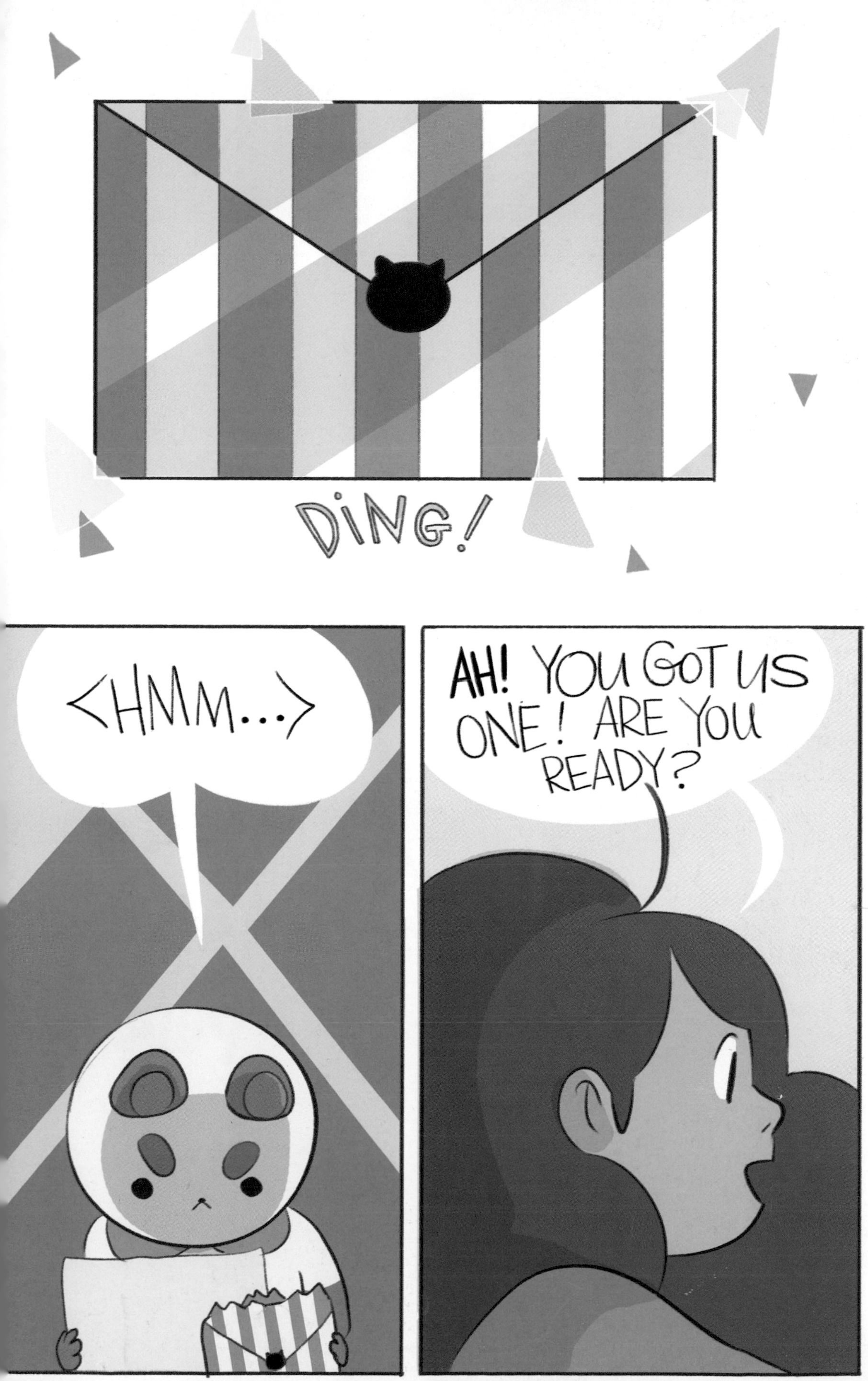
DING!
<HMM...>
AH! YOU GOT US ONE! ARE YOU READY?

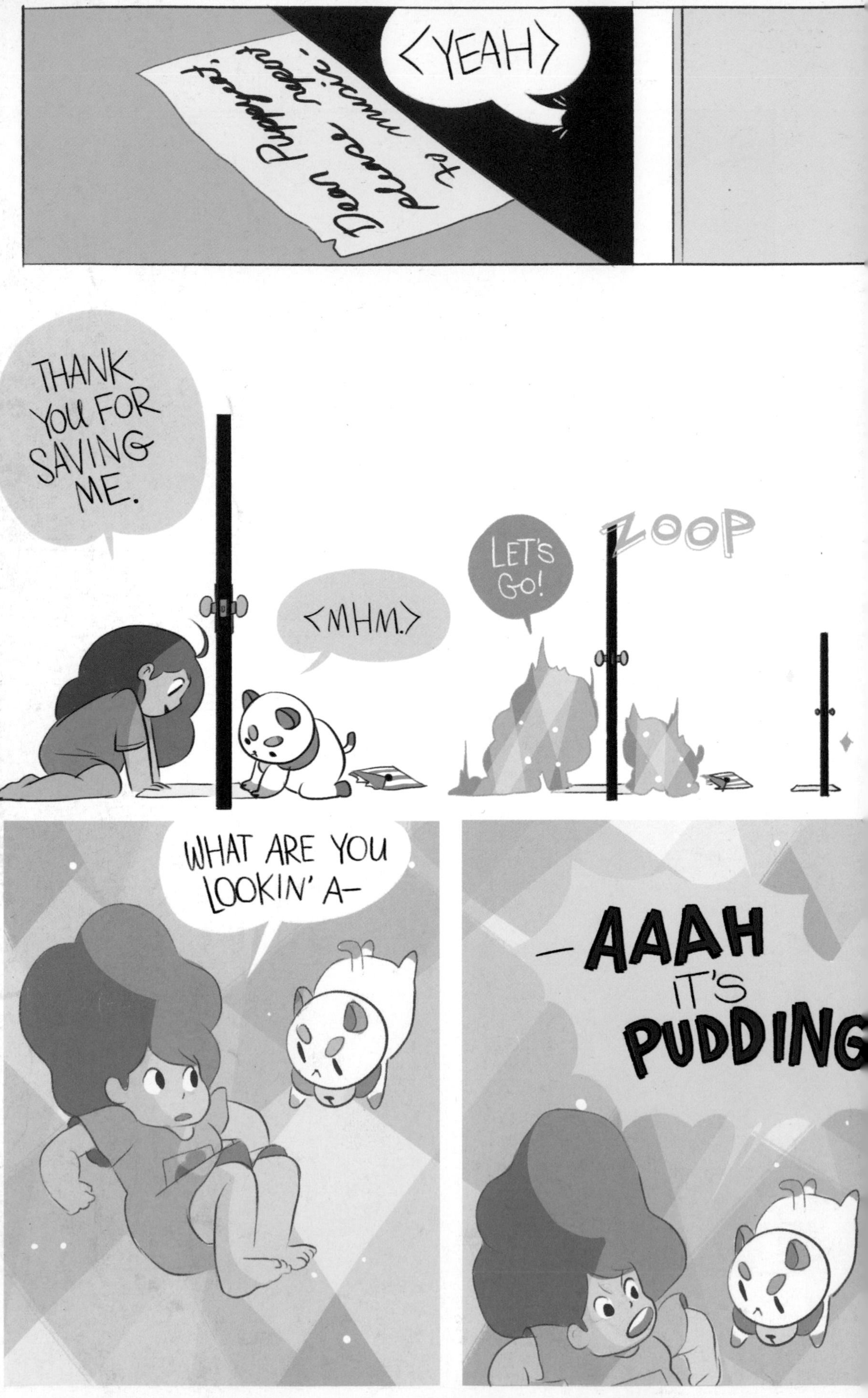

Dear Puppycat!
please repeat
to music:
<YEAH>
THANK YOU FOR SAVING ME.
<MHM.>
LET'S GO!
ZOOP
WHAT ARE YOU LOOKIN' A-
-AAAH IT'S PUDDING

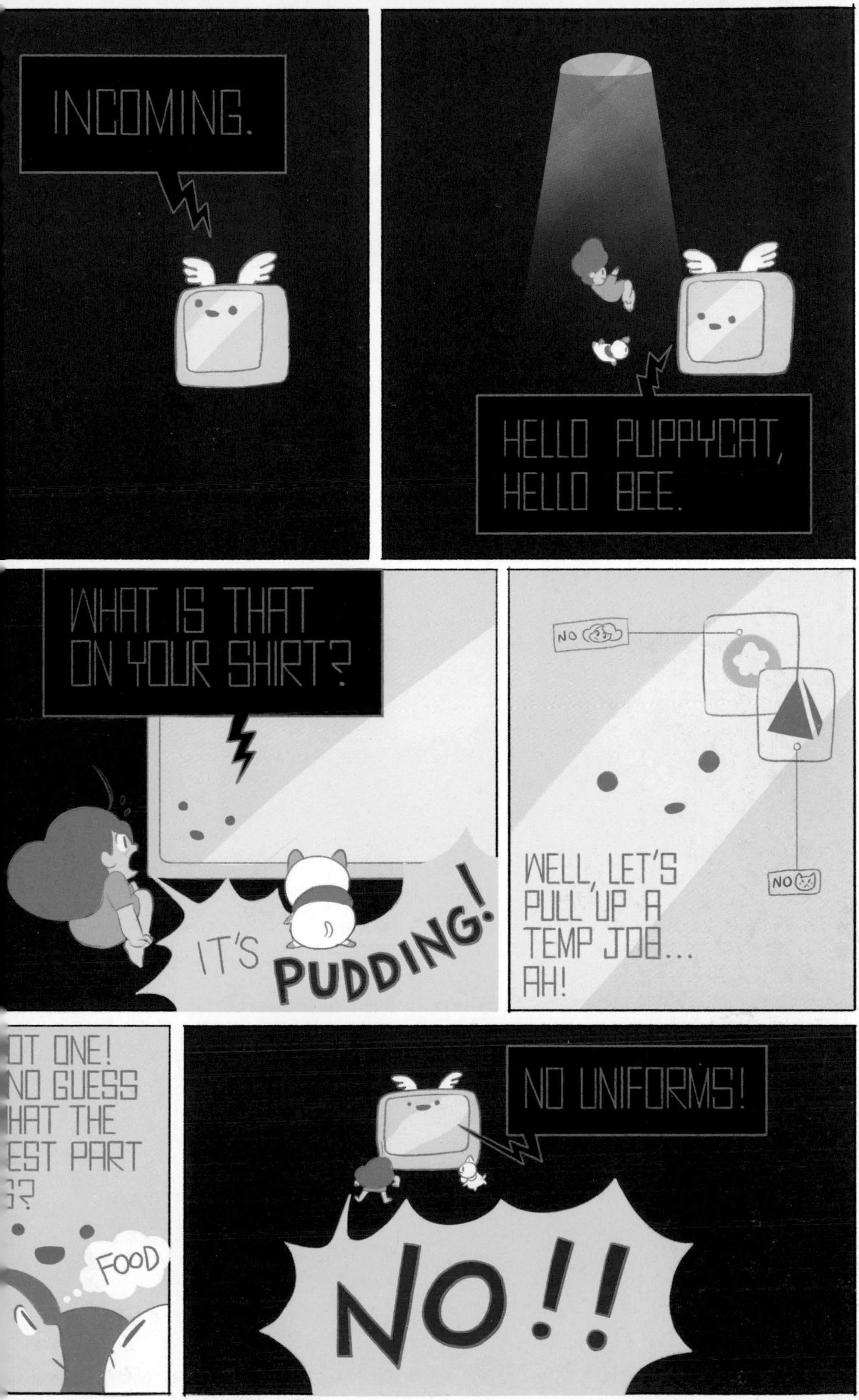
INCOMING.
HELLO PUPPYCAT, HELLO BEE.
WHAT IS THAT ON YOUR SHIRT?
IT'S PUDDING!
NO
NO
WELL, LET'S PULL UP A TEMP JOB... AH!
OT ONE! NO GUESS HAT THE EST PART G?
FOOD
NO UNIFORMS!
NO!!

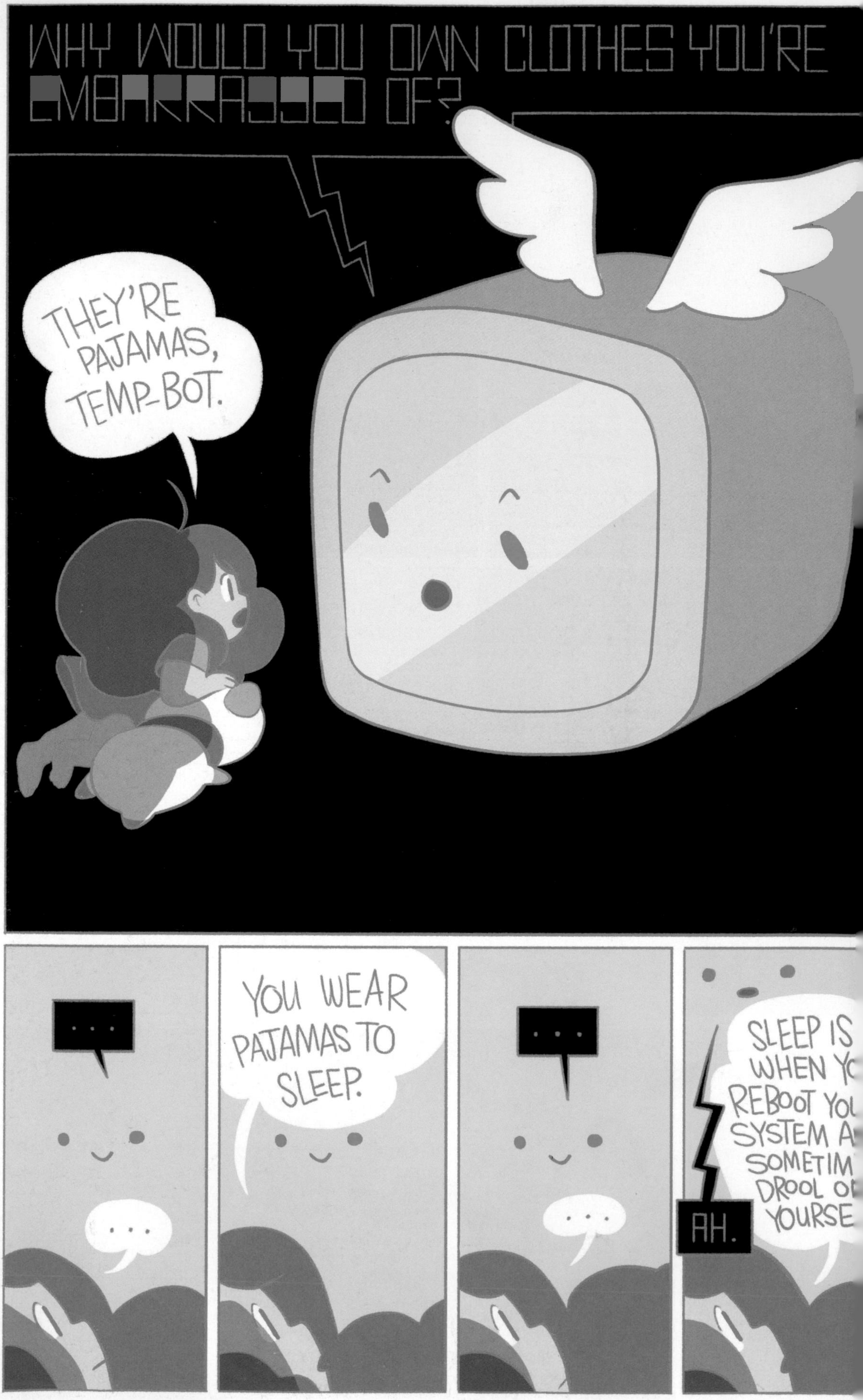

WHY WOULD YOU OWN CLOTHES YOU'RE EMBARRASSED OF?
THEY'RE PAJAMAS, TEMP-BOT.
...
...
YOU WEAR PAJAMAS TO SLEEP.
...
...
AH.
SLEEP IS WHEN YO REBOOT YOU SYSTEM A SOMETIM DROOL O YOURSE

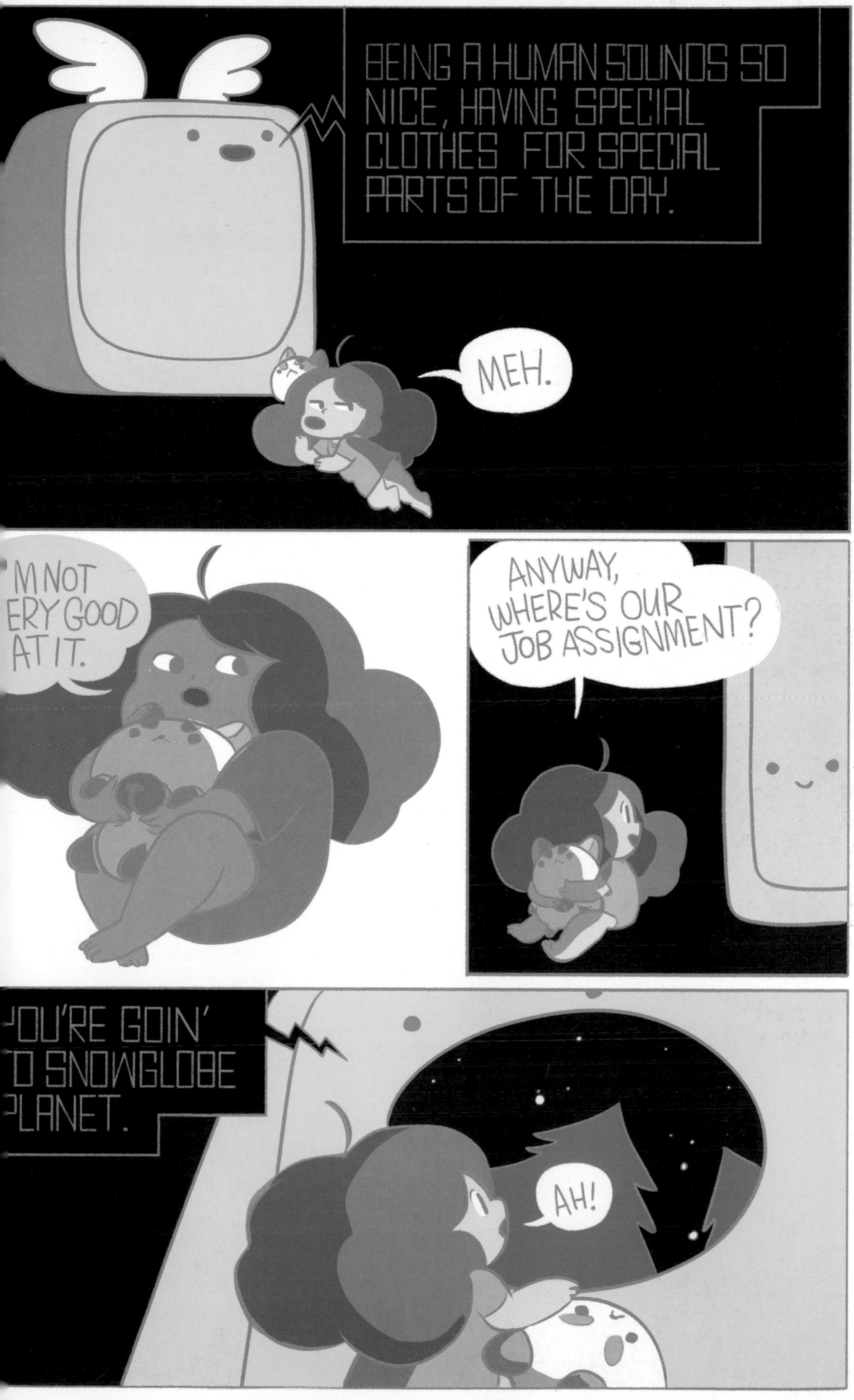
BEING A HUMAN SOUNDS SO NICE, HAVING SPECIAL CLOTHES FOR SPECIAL PARTS OF THE DAY.
MEH.
M NOT ERY GOOD AT IT.
ANYWAY, WHERE'S OUR JOB ASSIGNMENT?
OU'RE GOIN' O SNOWGLOBE LANET.
AH!

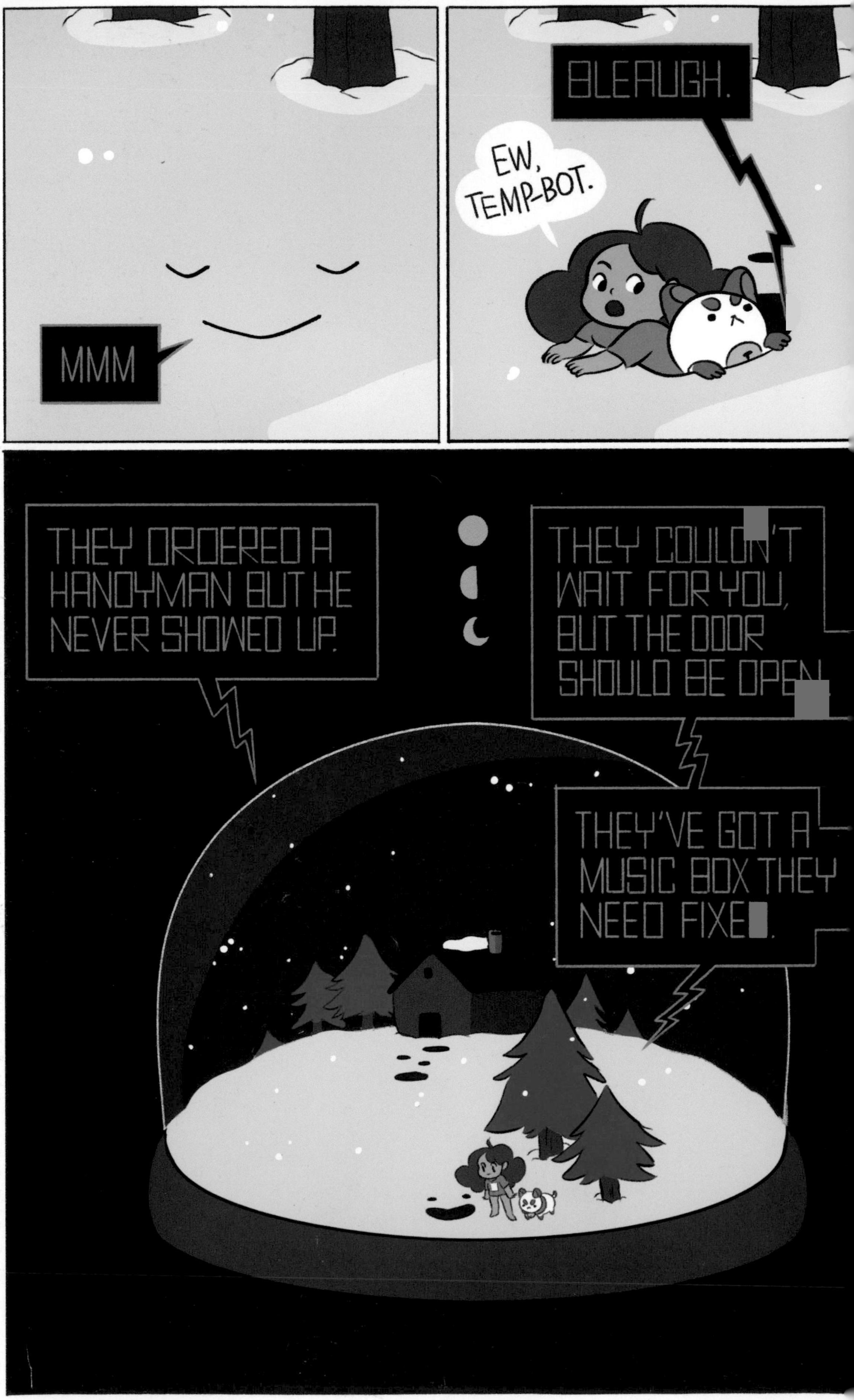
MMM
BLEAUGH.
EW, TEMP-BOT.
THEY ORDERED A HANDYMAN BUT HE NEVER SHOWED UP.
THEY COULDN'T WAIT FOR YOU, BUT THE DOOR SHOULD BE OPEN.
THEY'VE GOT A MUSIC BOX THEY NEED FIXE.

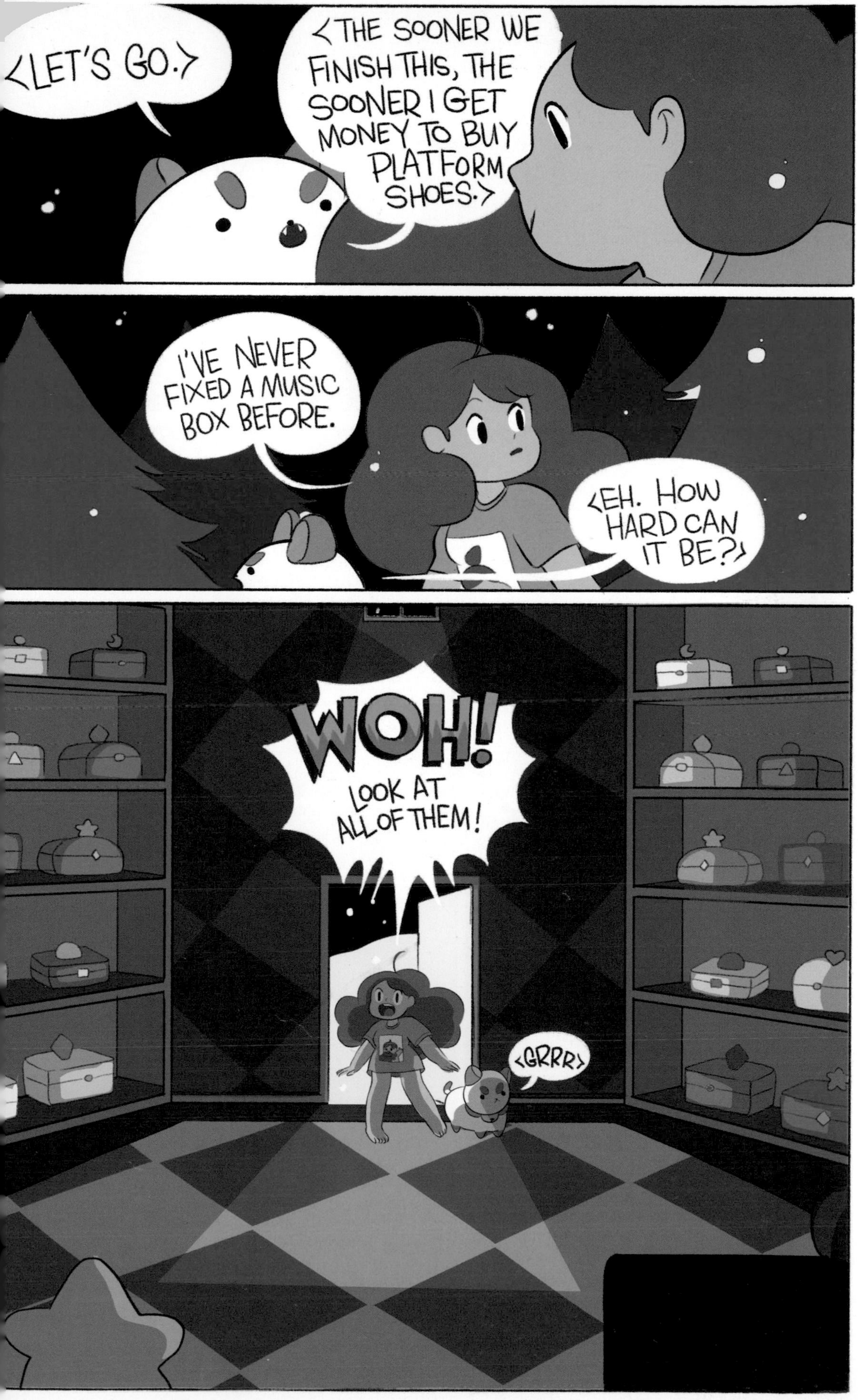
<LET'S GO.>
<THE SOONER WE FINISH THIS, THE SOONER I GET MONEY TO BUY PLATFORM SHOES.>
I'VE NEVER FIXED A MUSIC BOX BEFORE.
<EH. HOW HARD CAN IT BE?>
WOH!
LOOK AT ALL OF THEM!
<GRRR>

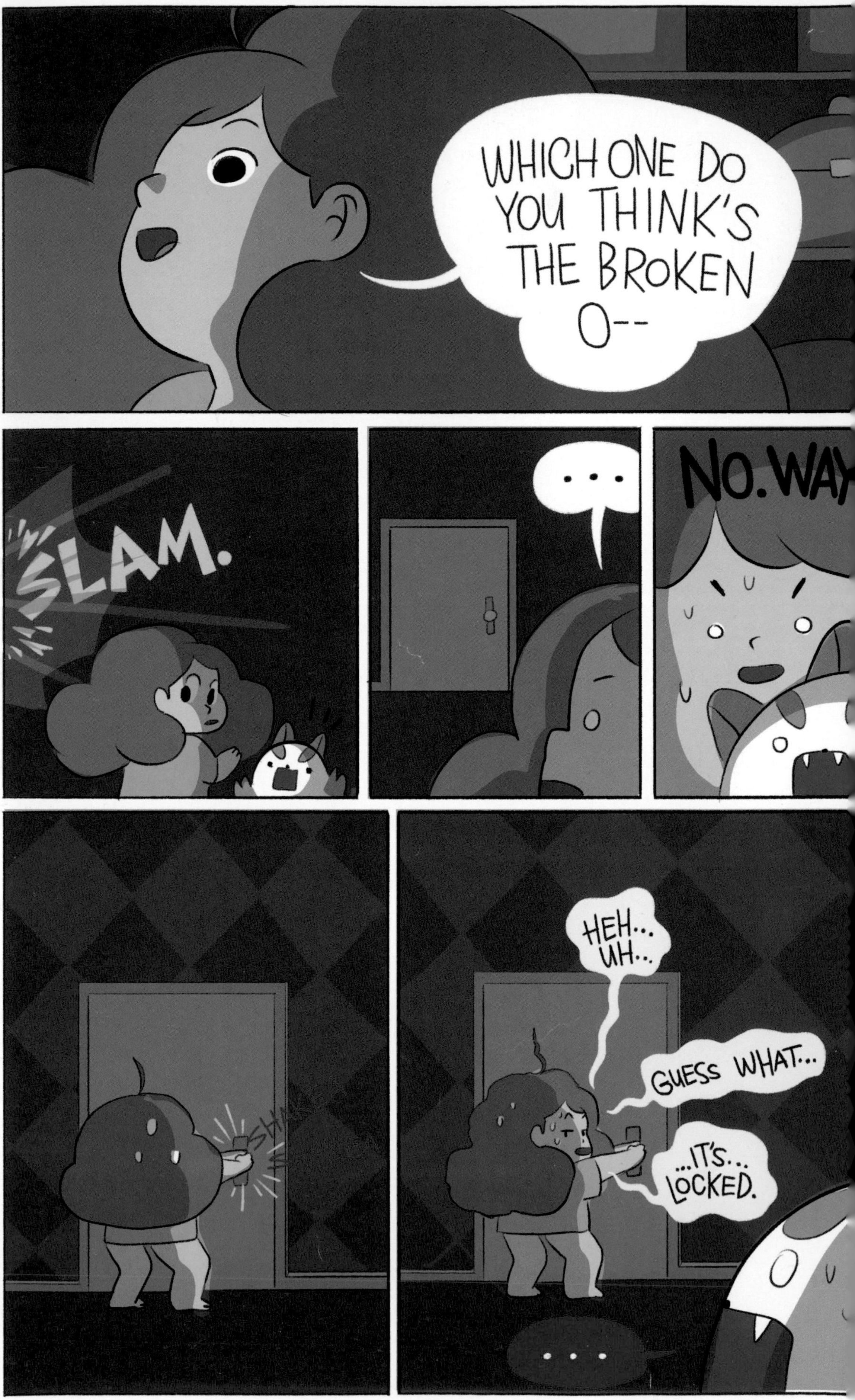
WHICH ONE DO YOU THINK'S THE BROKEN O--
SLAM.
...
NO. WAY
HEH... UH...
GUESS WHAT...
...IT'S... LOCKED.
...

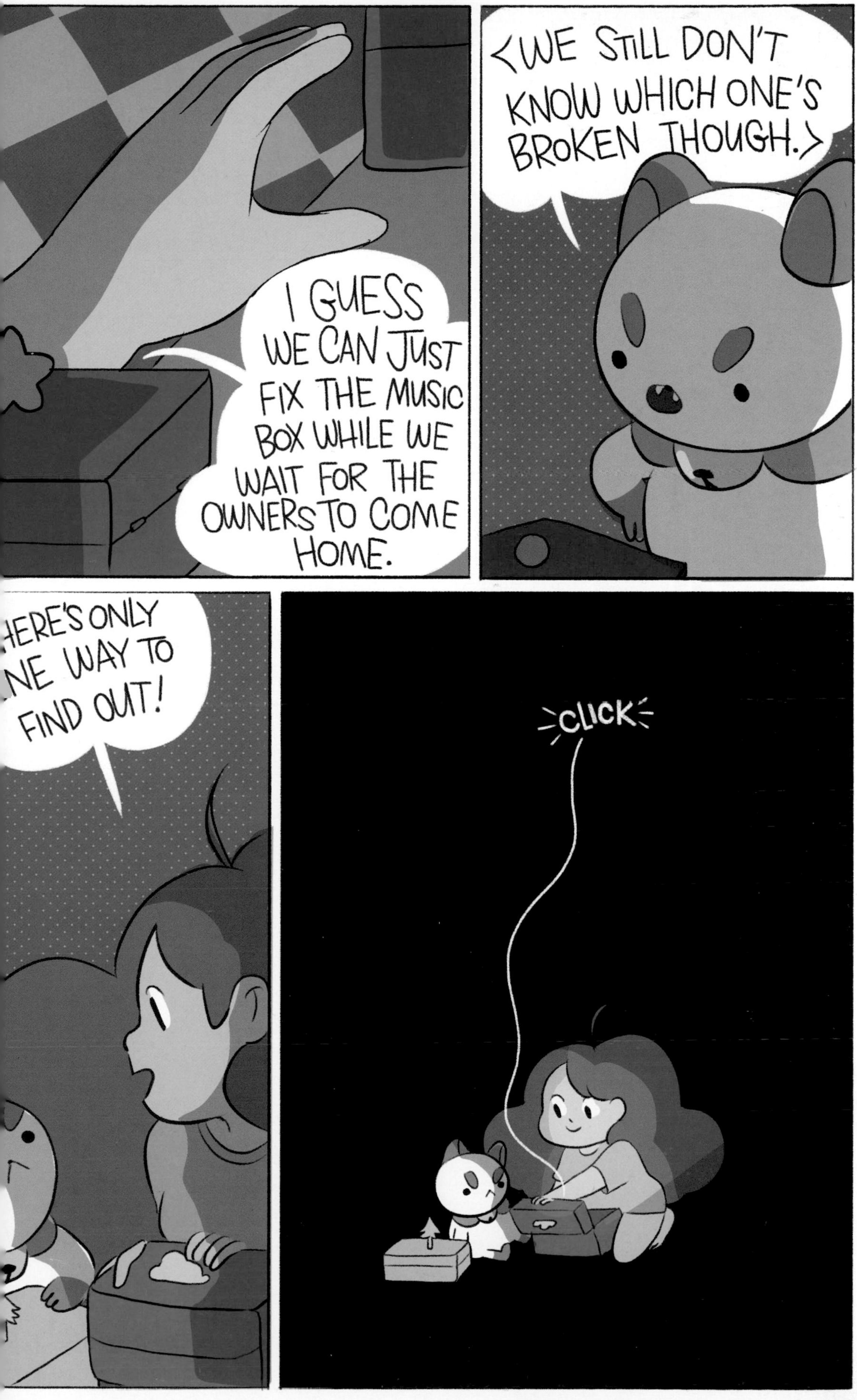

I GUESS WE CAN JUST FIX THE MUSIC BOX WHILE WE WAIT FOR THE OWNERS TO COME HOME.
<WE STILL DON'T KNOW WHICH ONE'S BROKEN THOUGH.>
ERE'S ONLY NE WAY TO FIND OUT!
CLICK

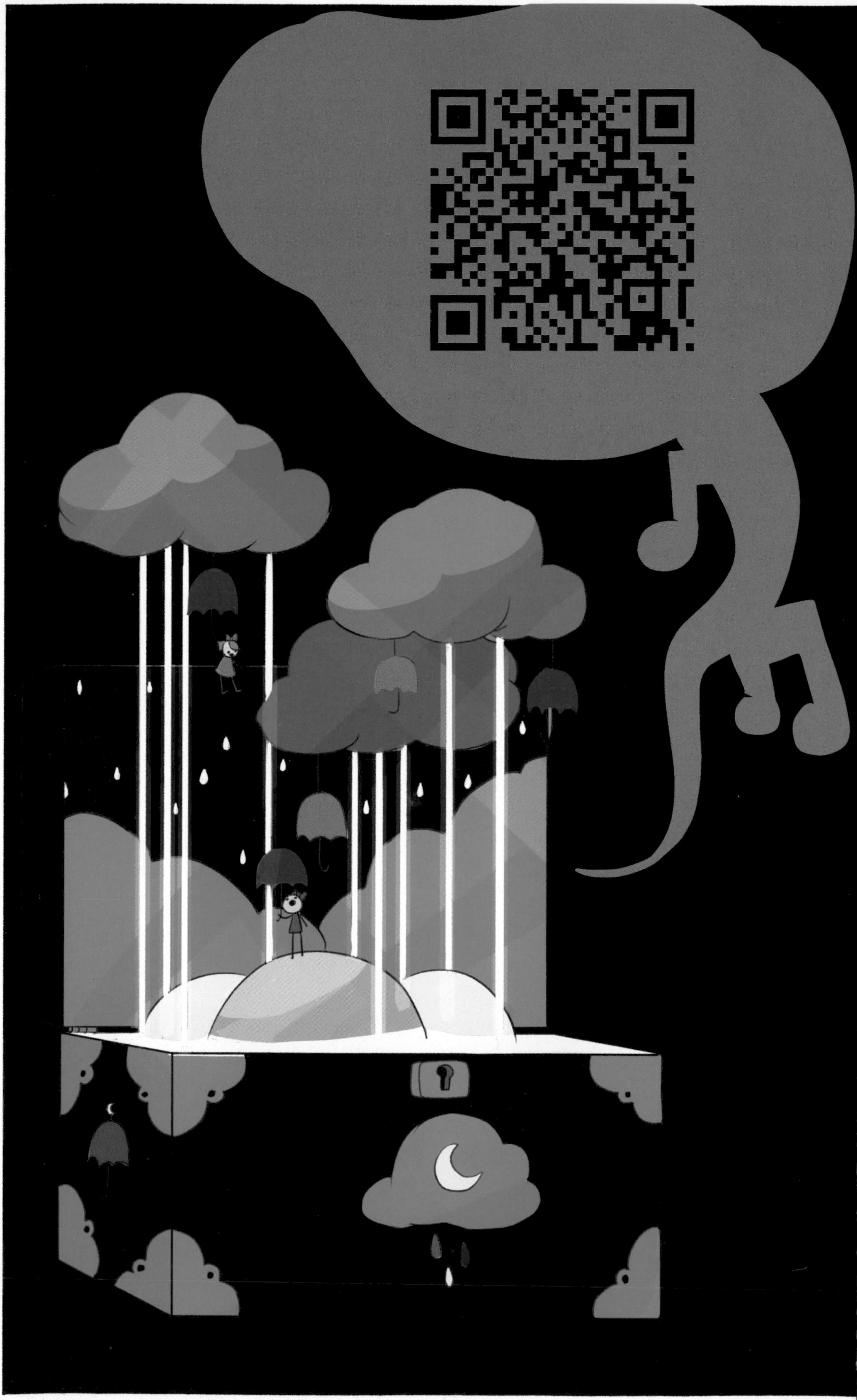

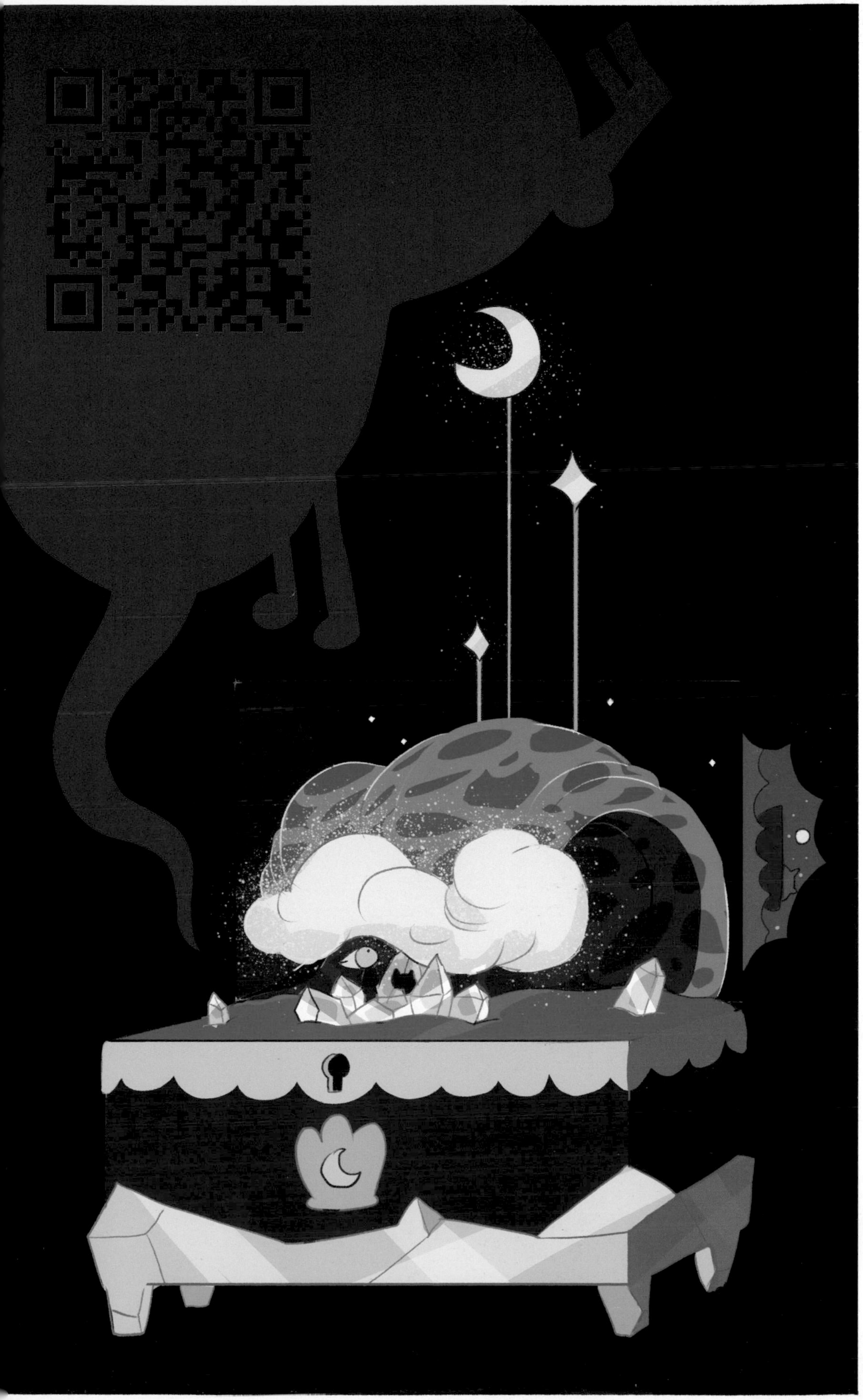

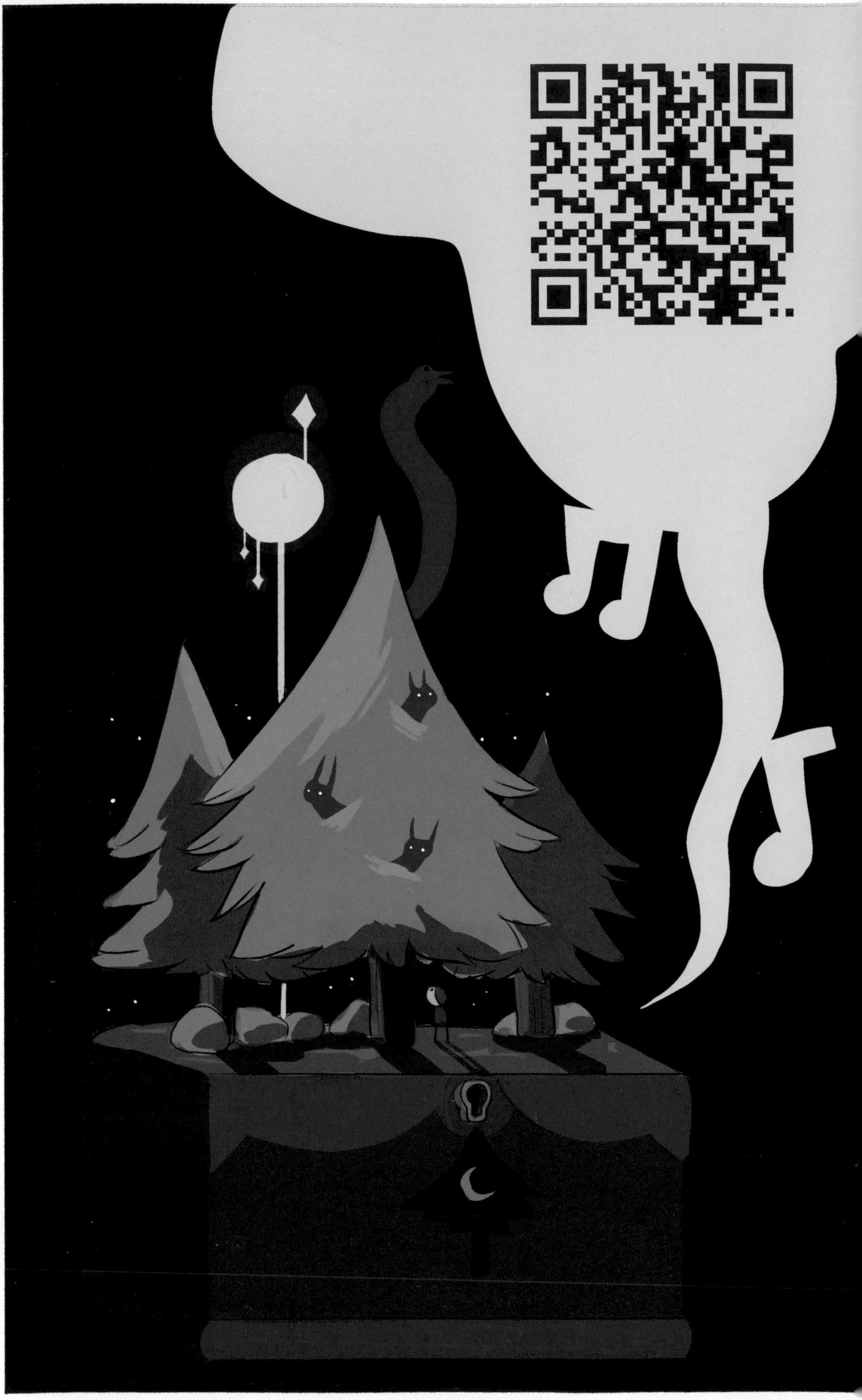

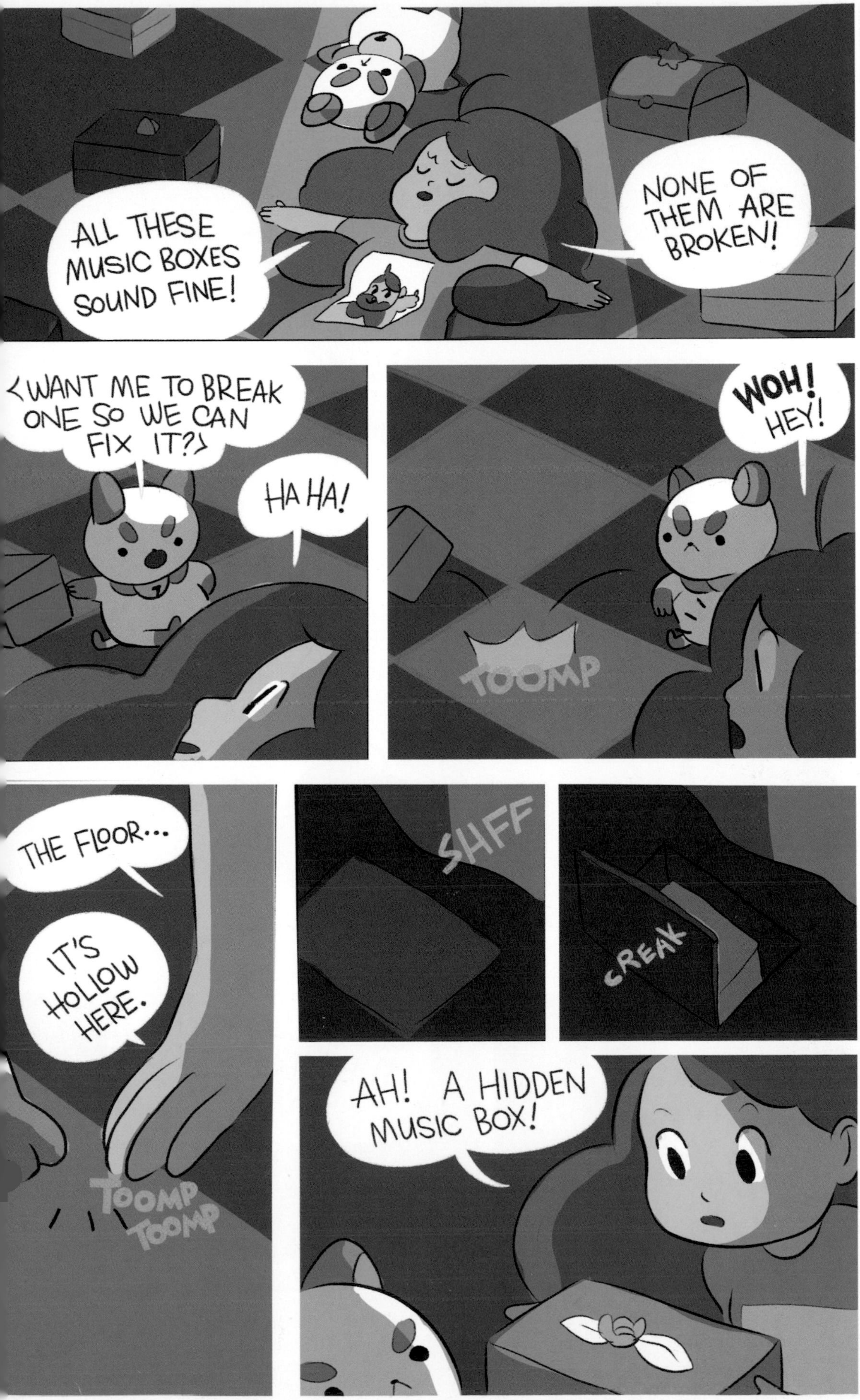
ALL THESE MUSIC BOXES SOUND FINE!
NONE OF THEM ARE BROKEN!
<WANT ME TO BREAK ONE SO WE CAN FIX IT?>
HA HA!
WOH! HEY!
TOOMP
THE FLOOR...
IT'S HOLLOW HERE.
TOOMP TOOMP
SHFF
CREAK
AH! A HIDDEN MUSIC BOX!

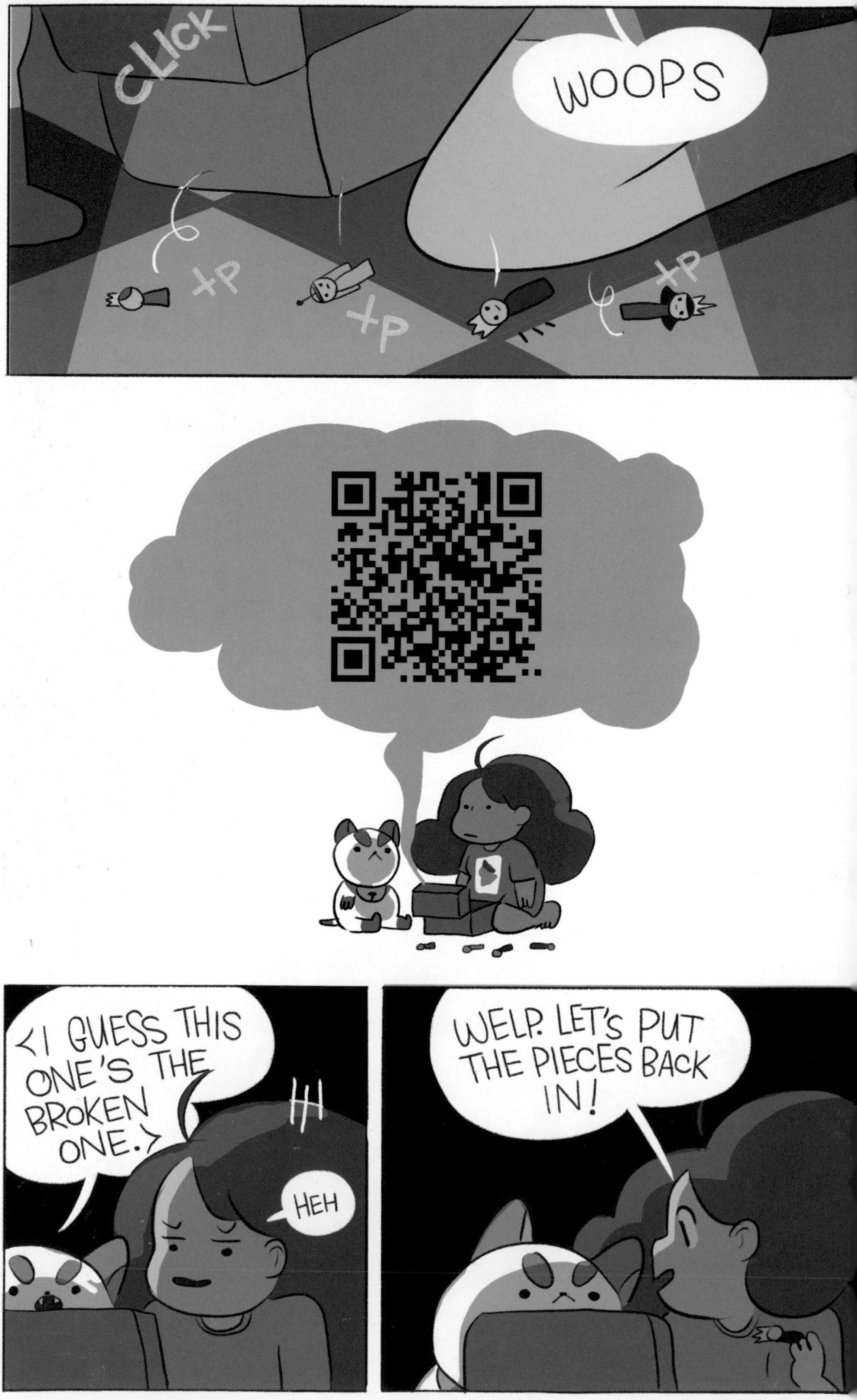
CLICK
WOOPS
+P
+P
+P
+P
<I GUESS THIS ONE'S THE BROKEN ONE.>
HEH
WELP. LET'S PUT THE PIECES BACK IN!

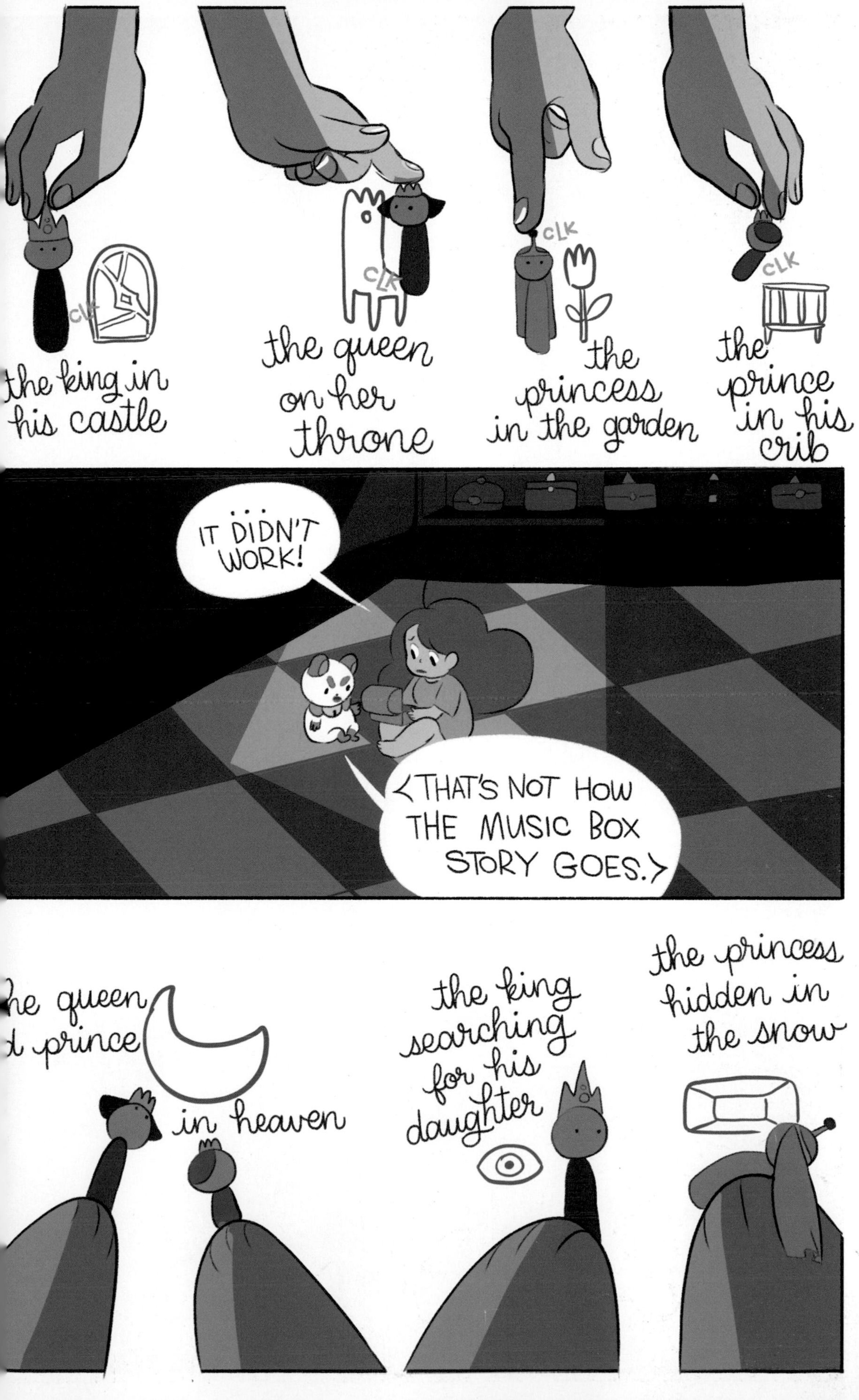
CLK
the king in his castle
CLK
the queen on her throne
CLK
the princess in the garden
CLK
the prince in his crib
... IT DIDN'T WORK!
<THAT'S NOT HOW THE MUSIC BOX STORY GOES.>
he queen
d prince
in heaven
the king searching for his daughter
the princess hidden in the snow

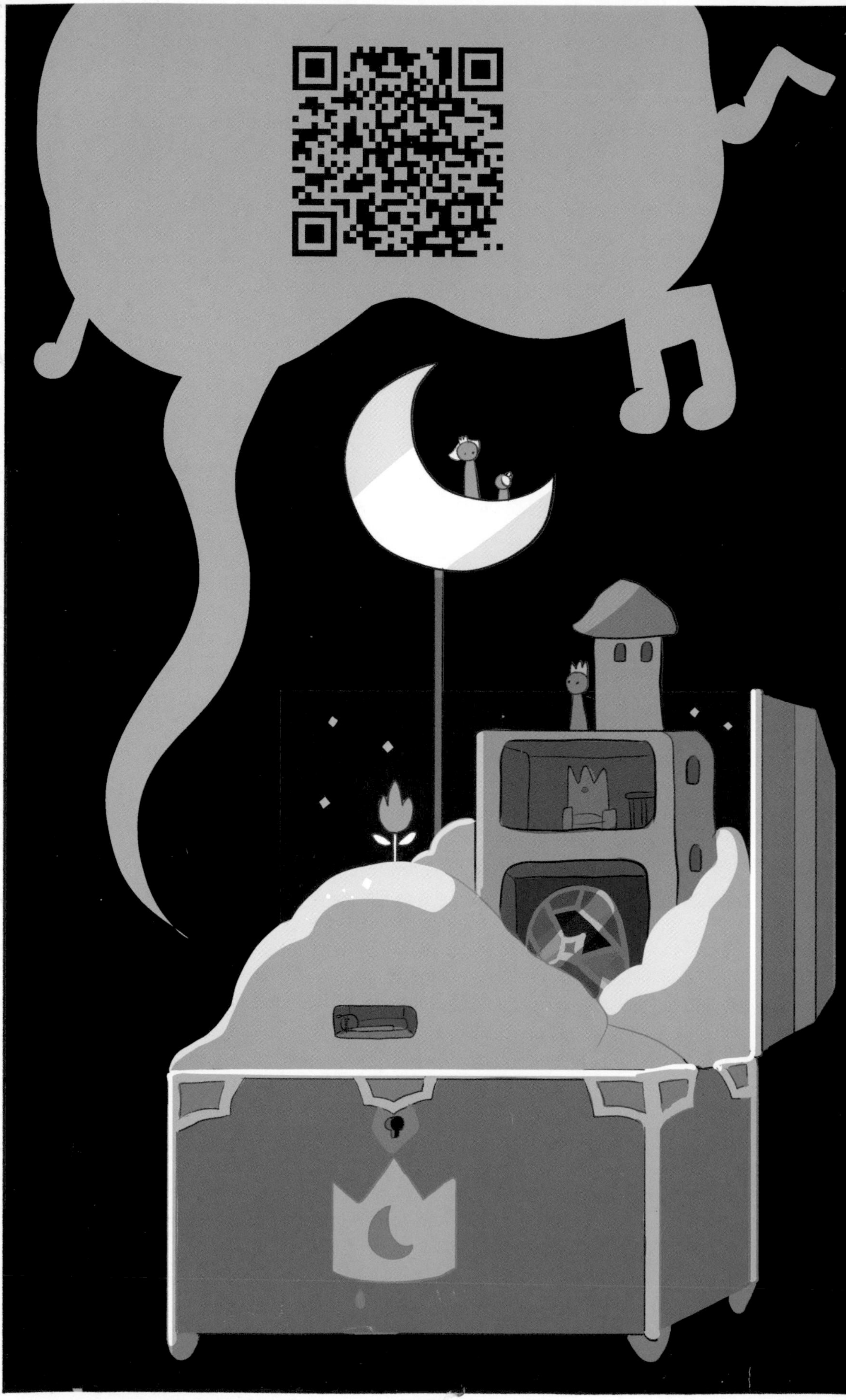

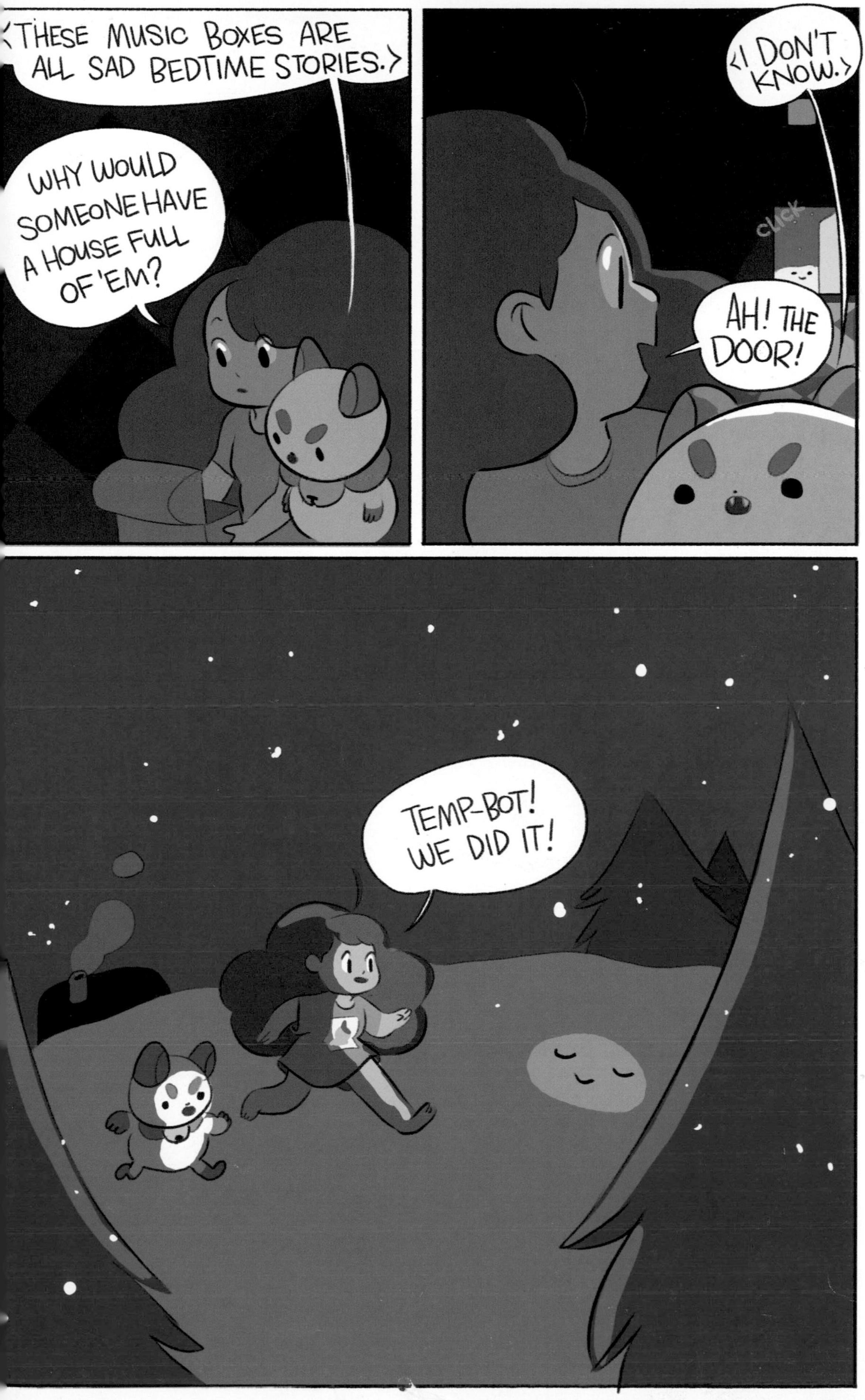
<THESE MUSIC BOXES ARE ALL SAD BEDTIME STORIES.>
WHY WOULD SOMEONE HAVE A HOUSE FULL OF 'EM?
<I DON'T KNOW.>
CLICK
AH! THE DOOR!
TEMP-BOT! WE DID IT!

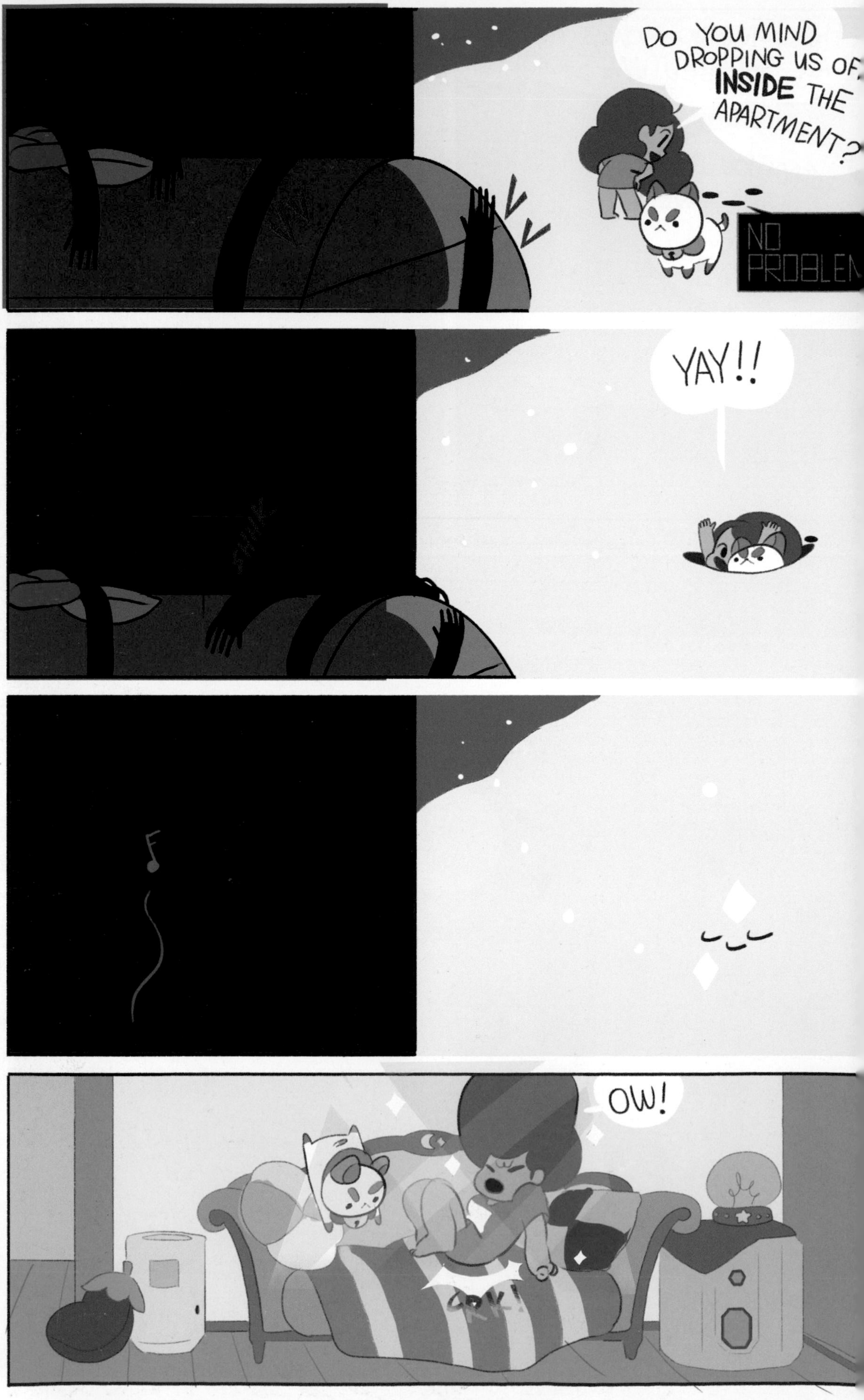
DO YOU MIND DROPPING US OF INSIDE THE APARTMENT?
NO PROBLE
YAY!!
OW!
GRK!

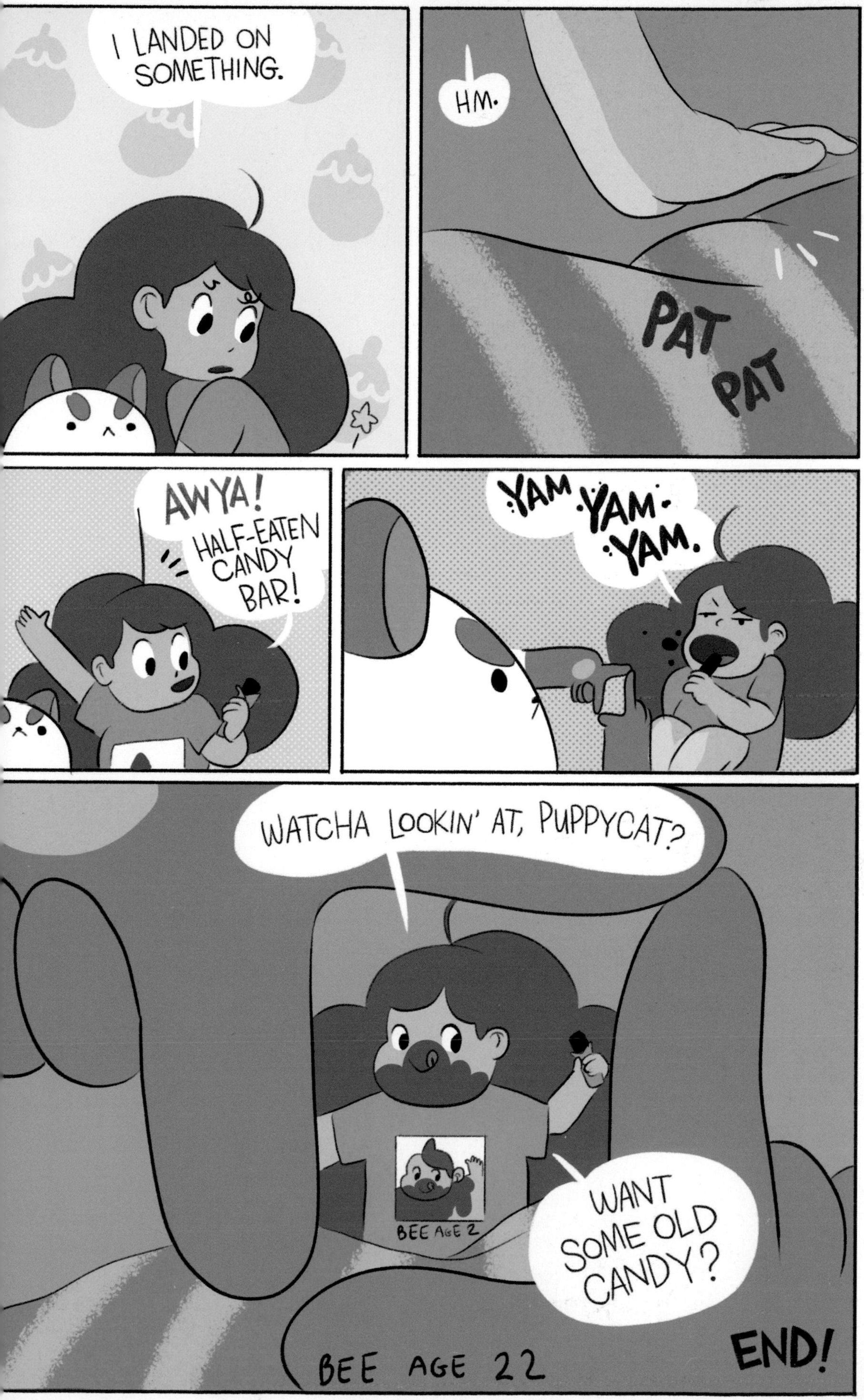
I LANDED ON SOMETHING.
HM.
PAT
PAT
AWYA!
HALF-EATEN CANDY BAR!
YAM YAM YAM.
WATCHA LOOKIN' AT, PUPPYCAT?
BEE AGE 2
WANT SOME OLD CANDY?
BEE AGE 22
END!

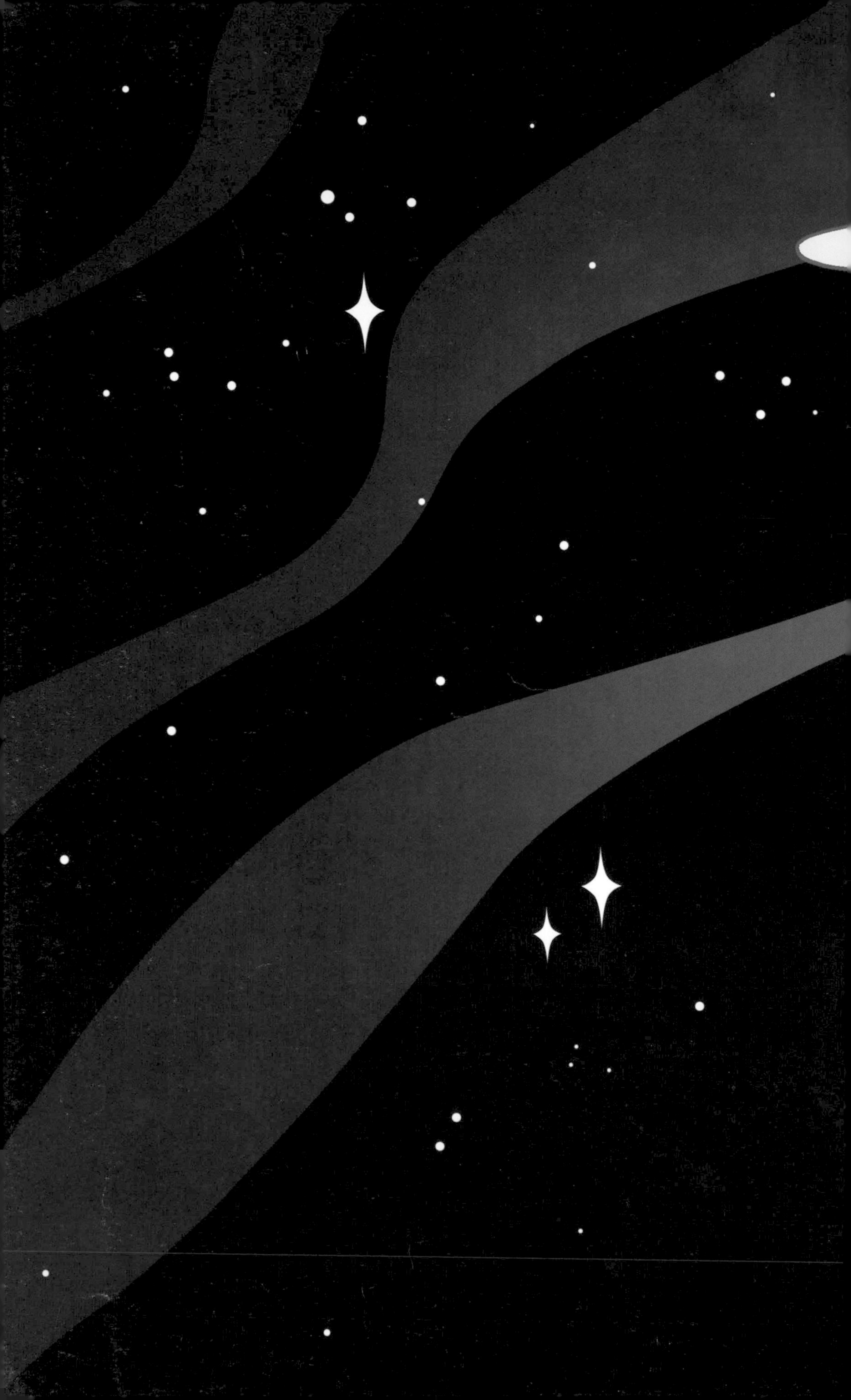

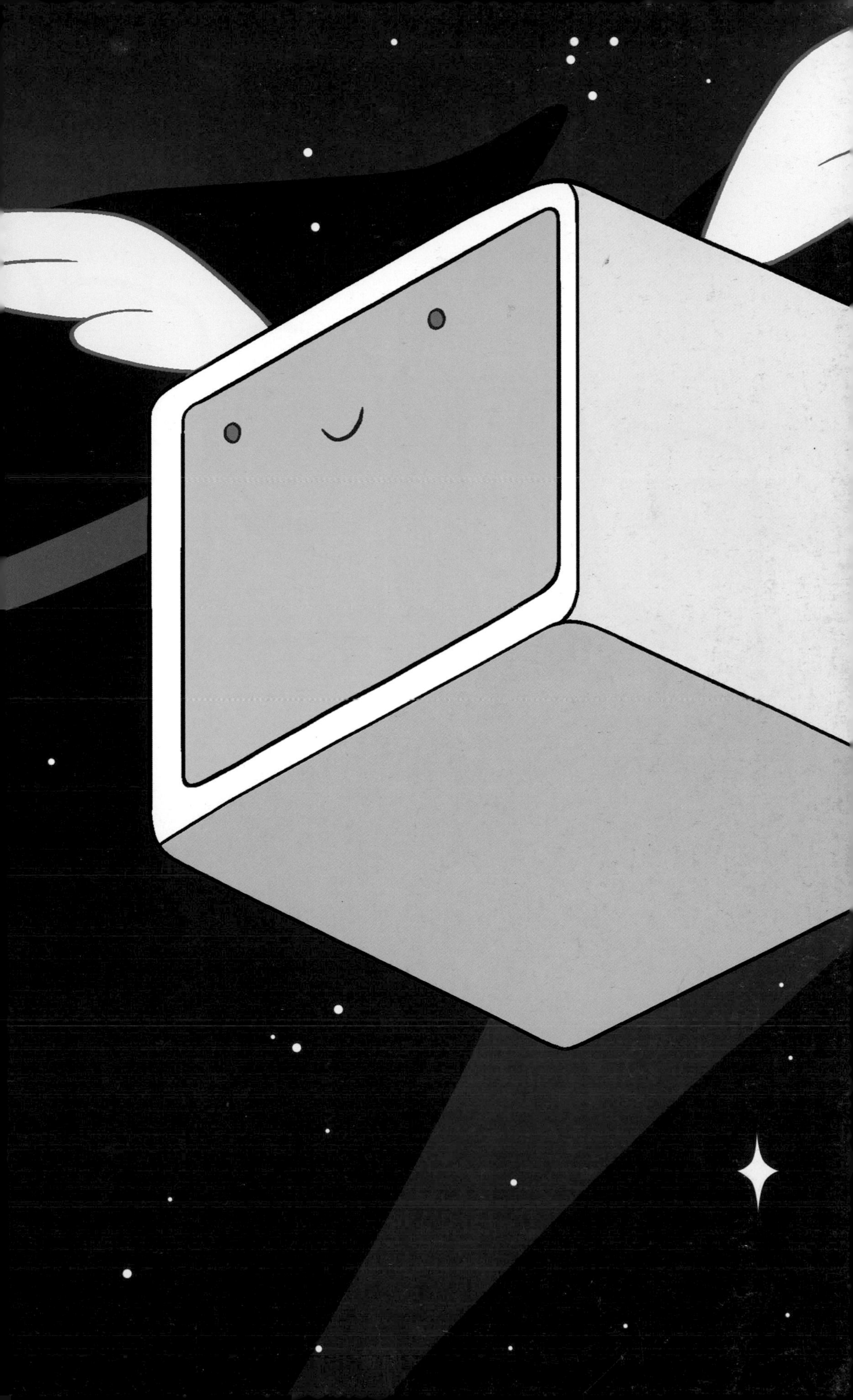

PUPP

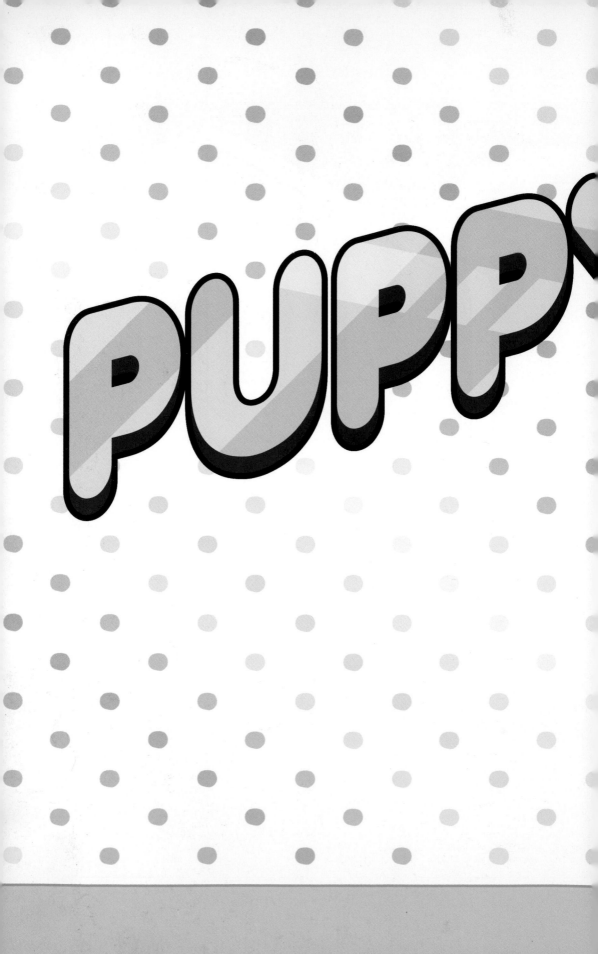

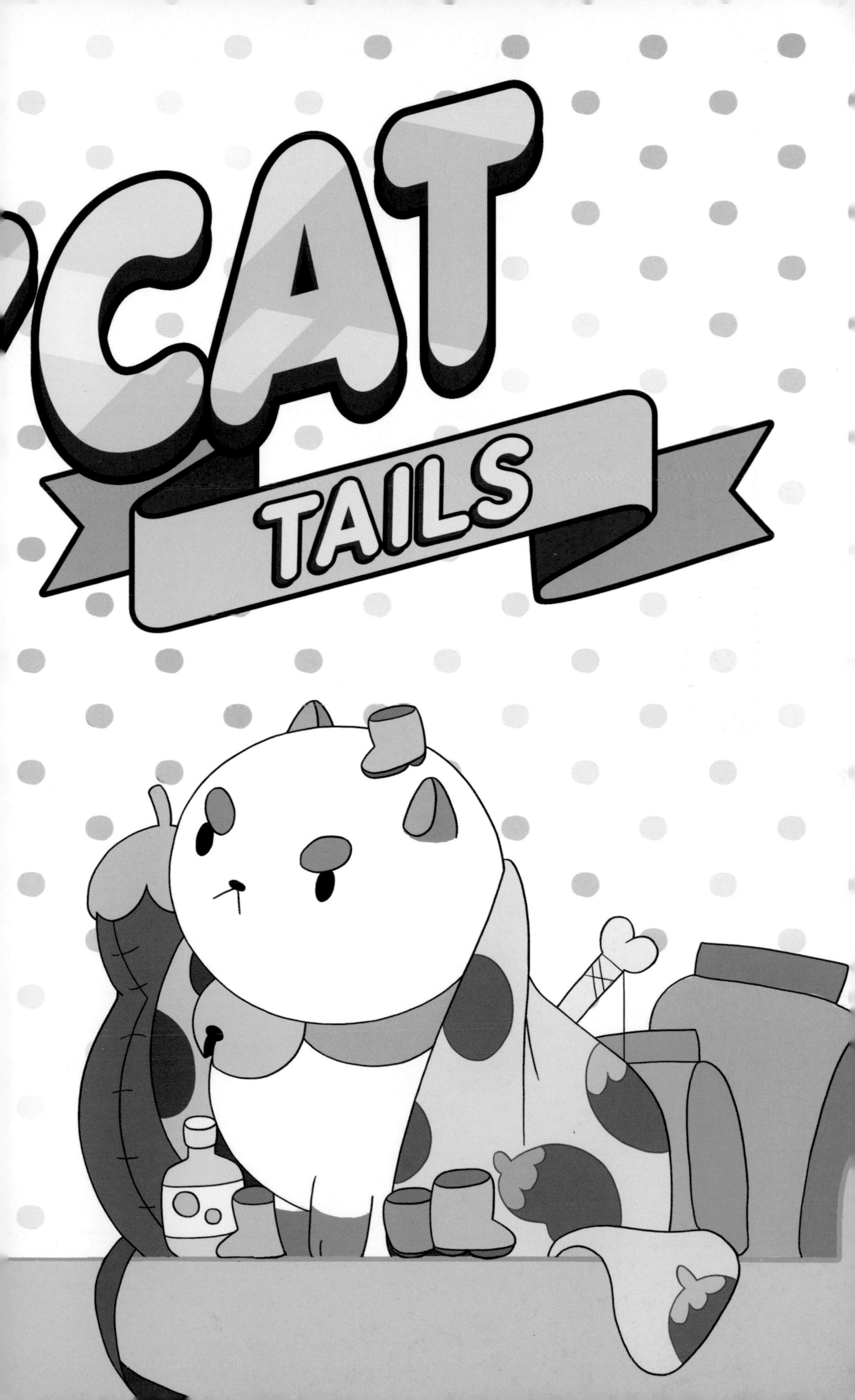
CAT
TAILS

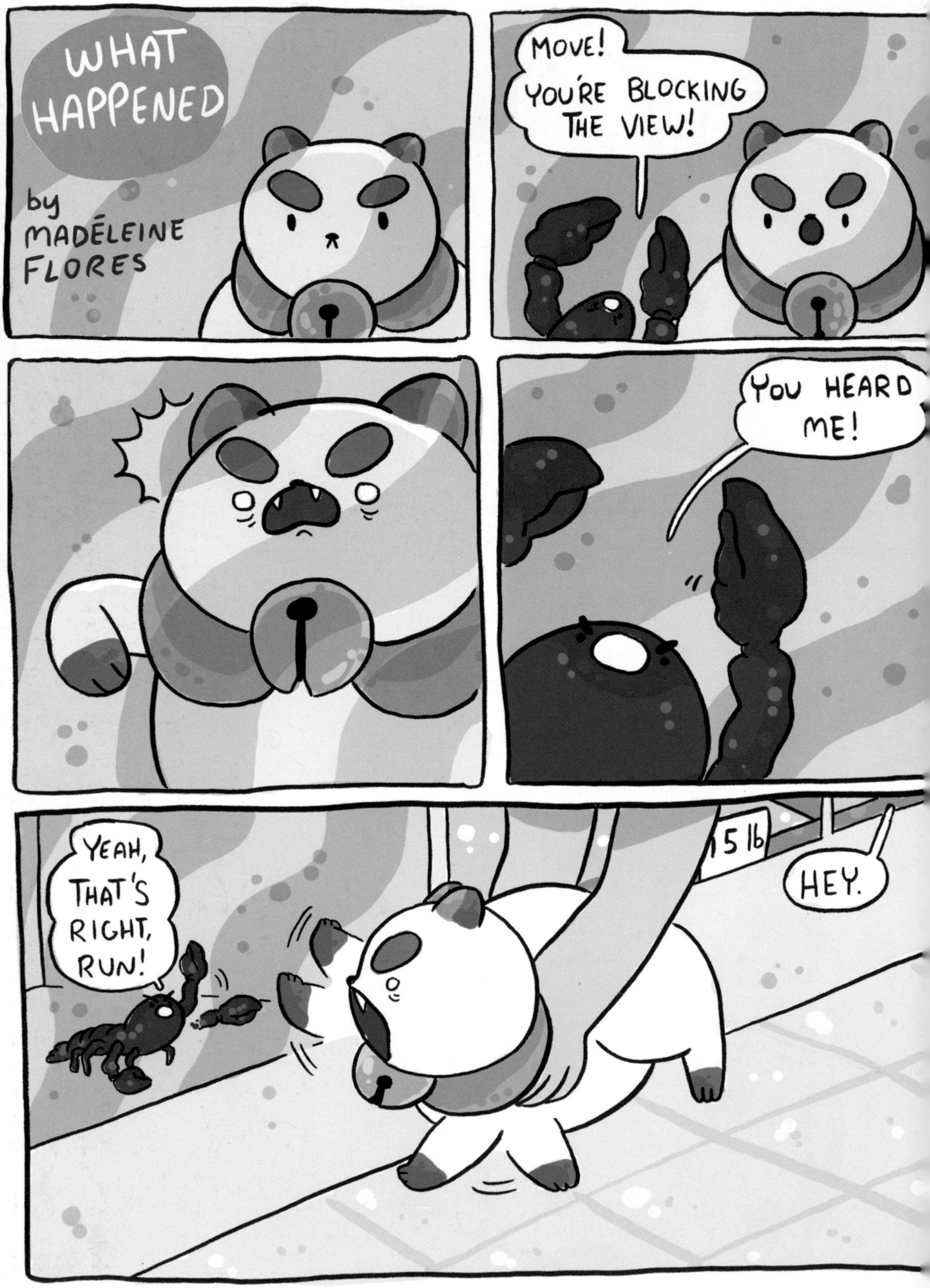
WHAT HAPPENED
by MADÉLEINE FLORES
MOVE!
YOU'RE BLOCKING THE VIEW!
YOU HEARD ME!
YEAH, THAT'S RIGHT, RUN!
15 lb
HEY.

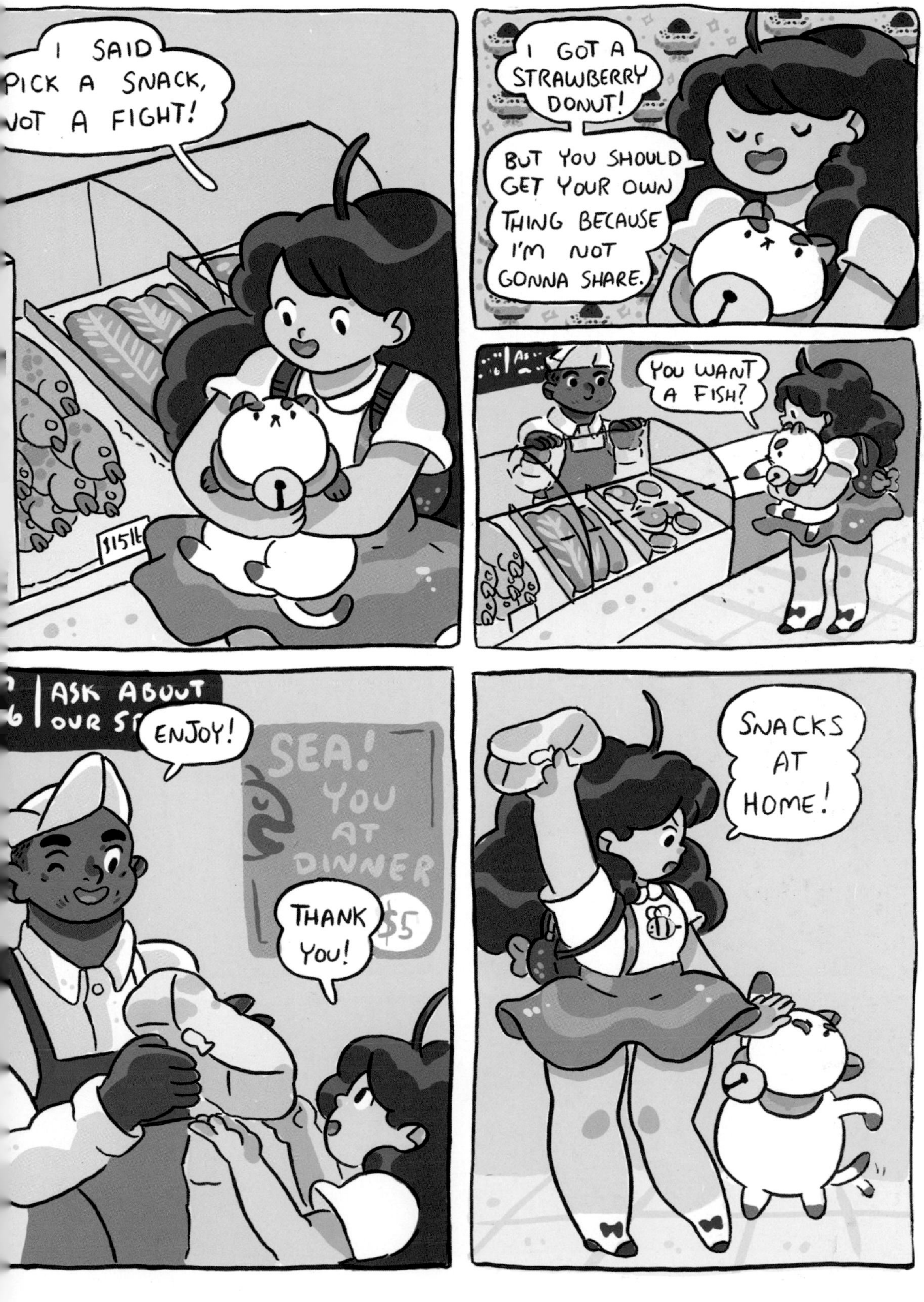
I SAID PICK A SNACK, NOT A FIGHT!
$1516
I GOT A STRAWBERRY DONUT!
BUT YOU SHOULD GET YOUR OWN THING BECAUSE I'M NOT GONNA SHARE.
YOU WANT A FISH?
ASK ABOUT OUR ST
ENJOY!
SEA! YOU AT DINNER
$5
THANK YOU!
SNACKS AT HOME!

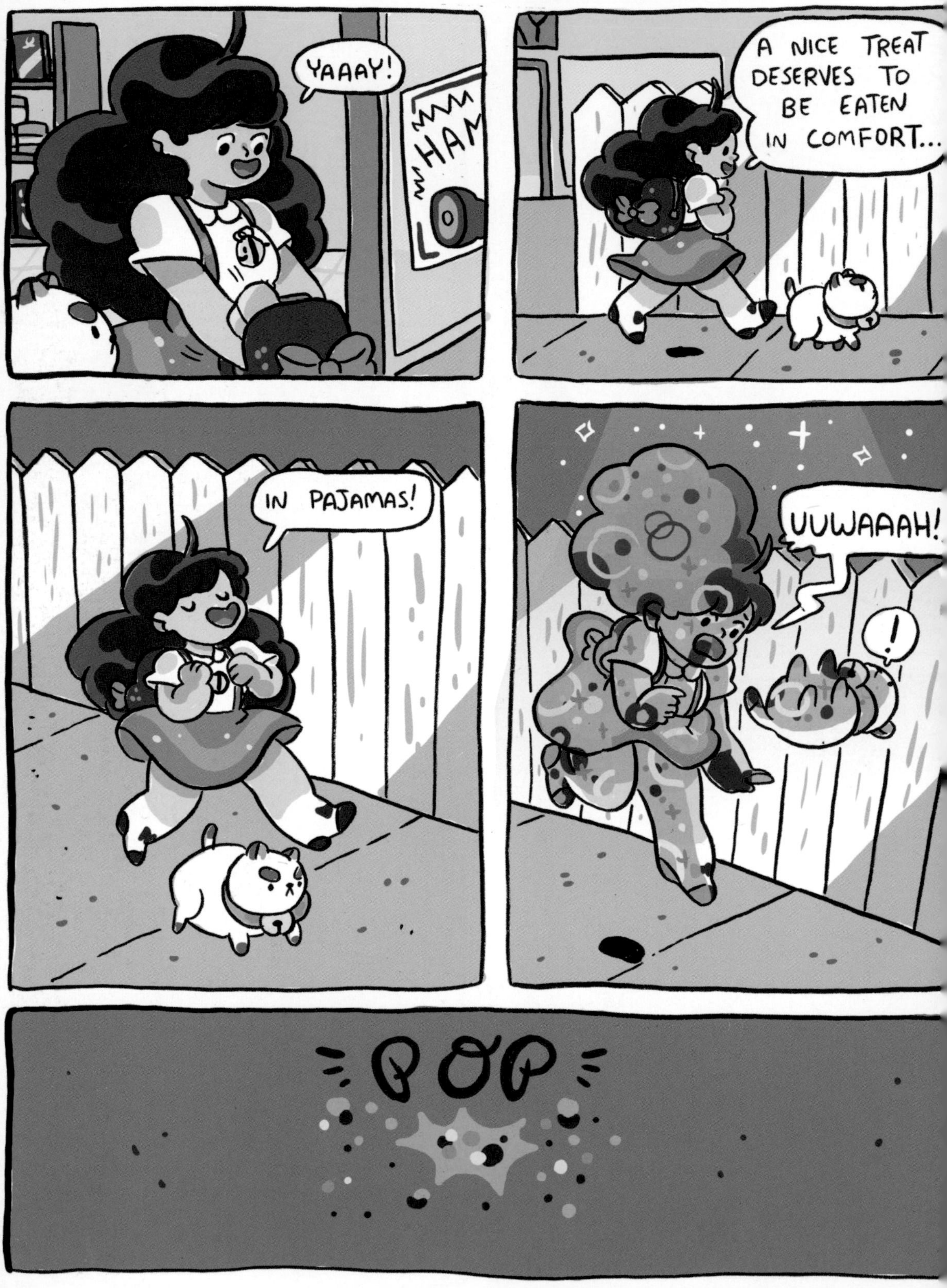
YAAAY!
A NICE TREAT DESERVES TO BE EATEN IN COMFORT...
IN PAJAMAS!
UUWAAAH!
!
POP

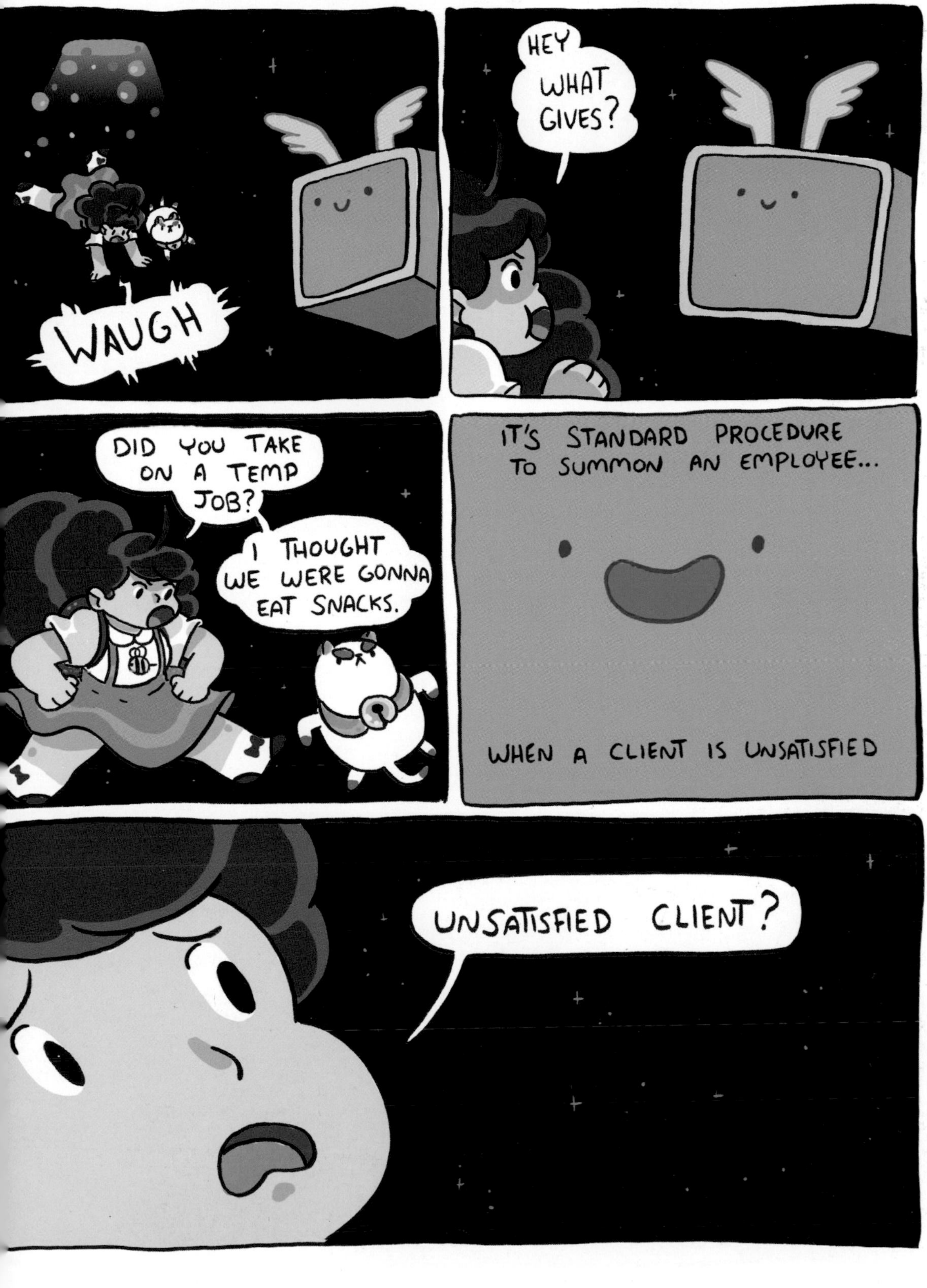
WAUGH
HEY WHAT GIVES?
DID YOU TAKE ON A TEMP JOB?
I THOUGHT WE WERE GONNA EAT SNACKS.
IT'S STANDARD PROCEDURE TO SUMMON AN EMPLOYEE...
WHEN A CLIENT IS UNSATISFIED
UNSATISFIED CLIENT?

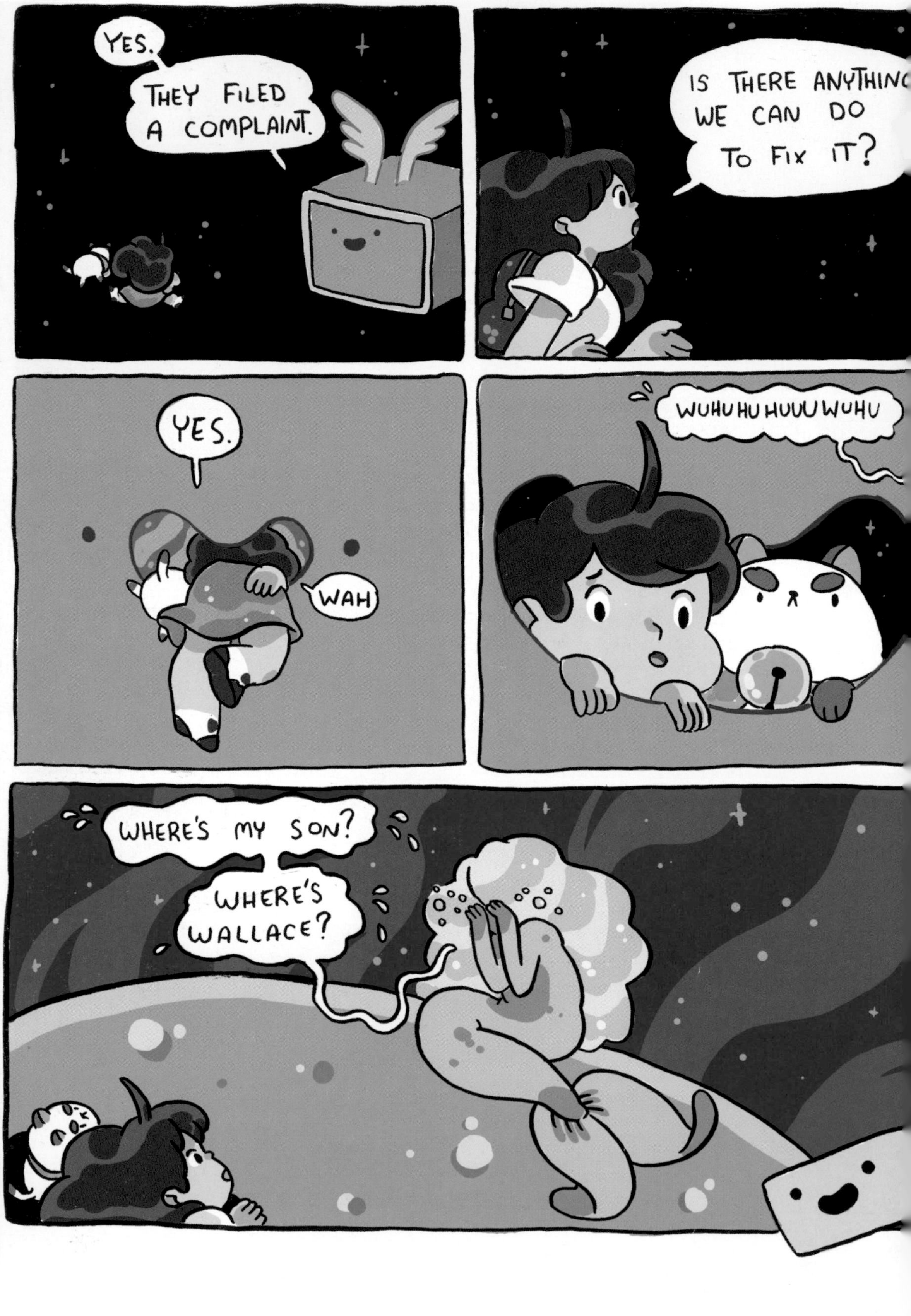
YES.
THEY FILED A COMPLAINT.
IS THERE ANYTHING WE CAN DO TO FIX IT?
YES.
WAH
WUHU HU HUUU WUHU
WHERE'S MY SON?
WHERE'S WALLACE?

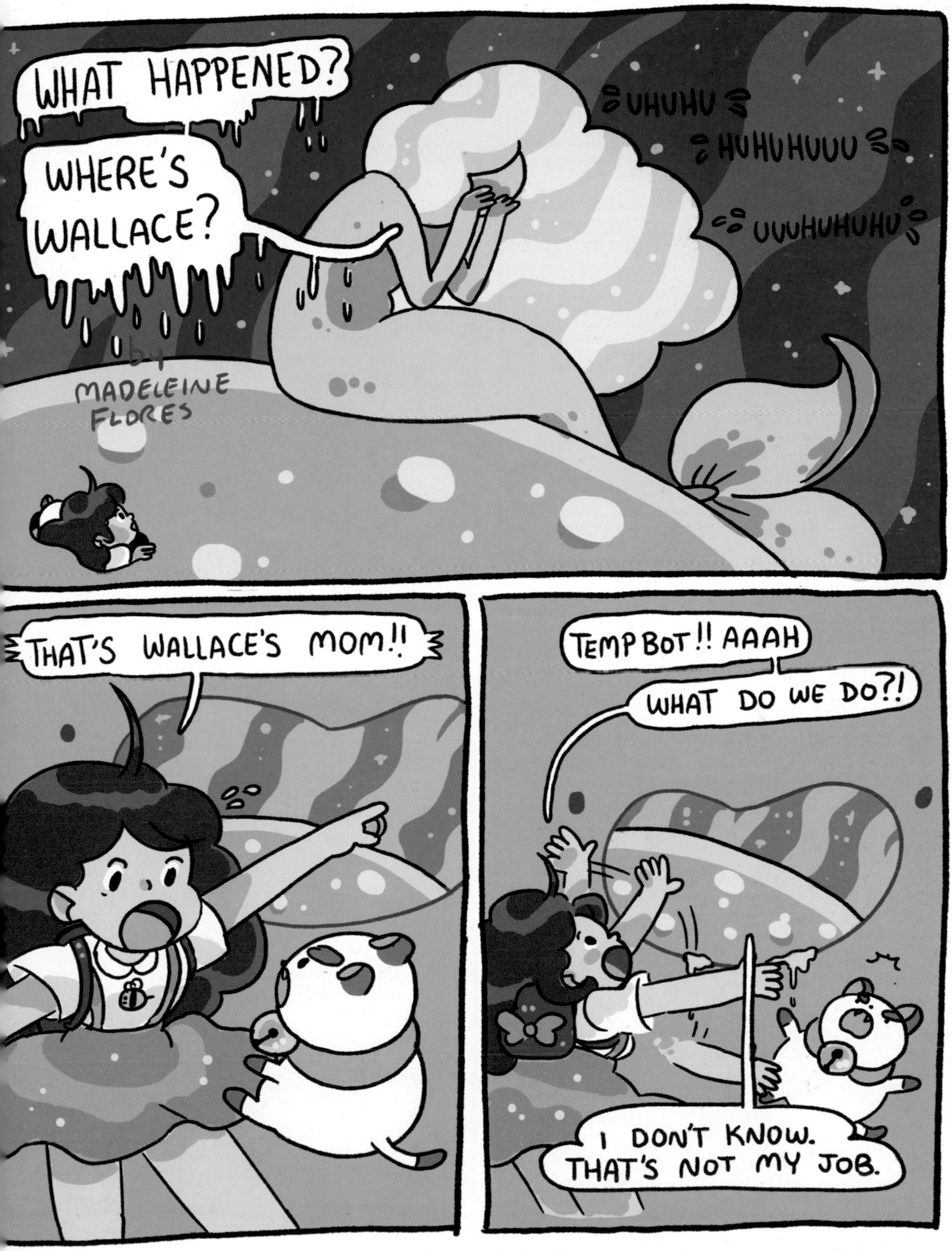
WHAT HAPPENED?
WHERE'S WALLACE?
UHUHU
HUHUHUUU
UUUHUHUHU
by MADELEINE FLORES
THAT'S WALLACE'S MOM!!
TEMPBOT!! AAAH
WHAT DO WE DO?!
I DON'T KNOW. THAT'S NOT MY JOB.

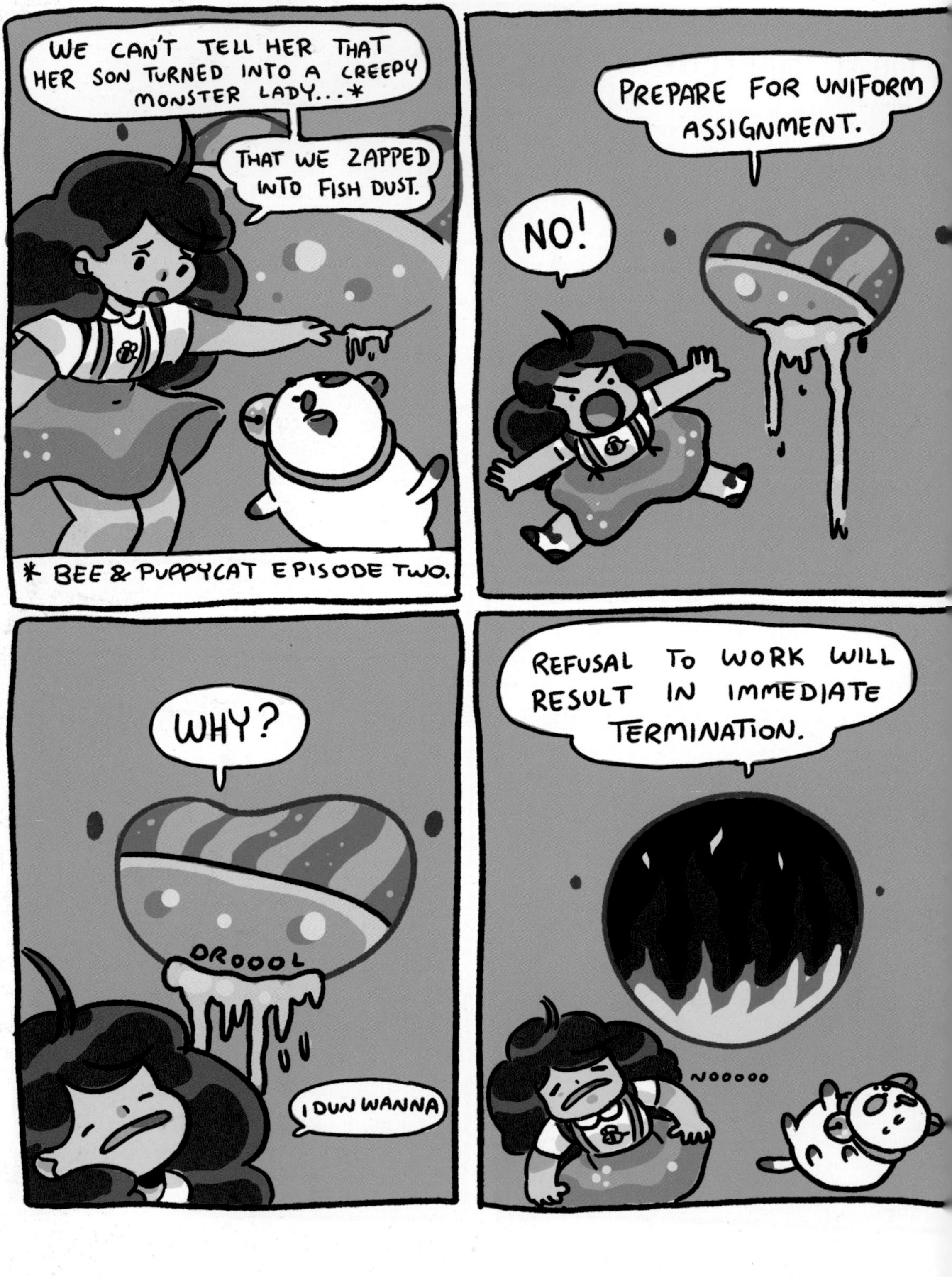
WE CAN'T TELL HER THAT HER SON TURNED INTO A CREEPY MONSTER LADY...*
THAT WE ZAPPED INTO FISH DUST.
* BEE & PUPPYCAT EPISODE TWO.
PREPARE FOR UNIFORM ASSIGNMENT.
NO!
WHY?
DROOOL
I DUN WANNA
REFUSAL TO WORK WILL RESULT IN IMMEDIATE TERMINATION.
NOOOOO

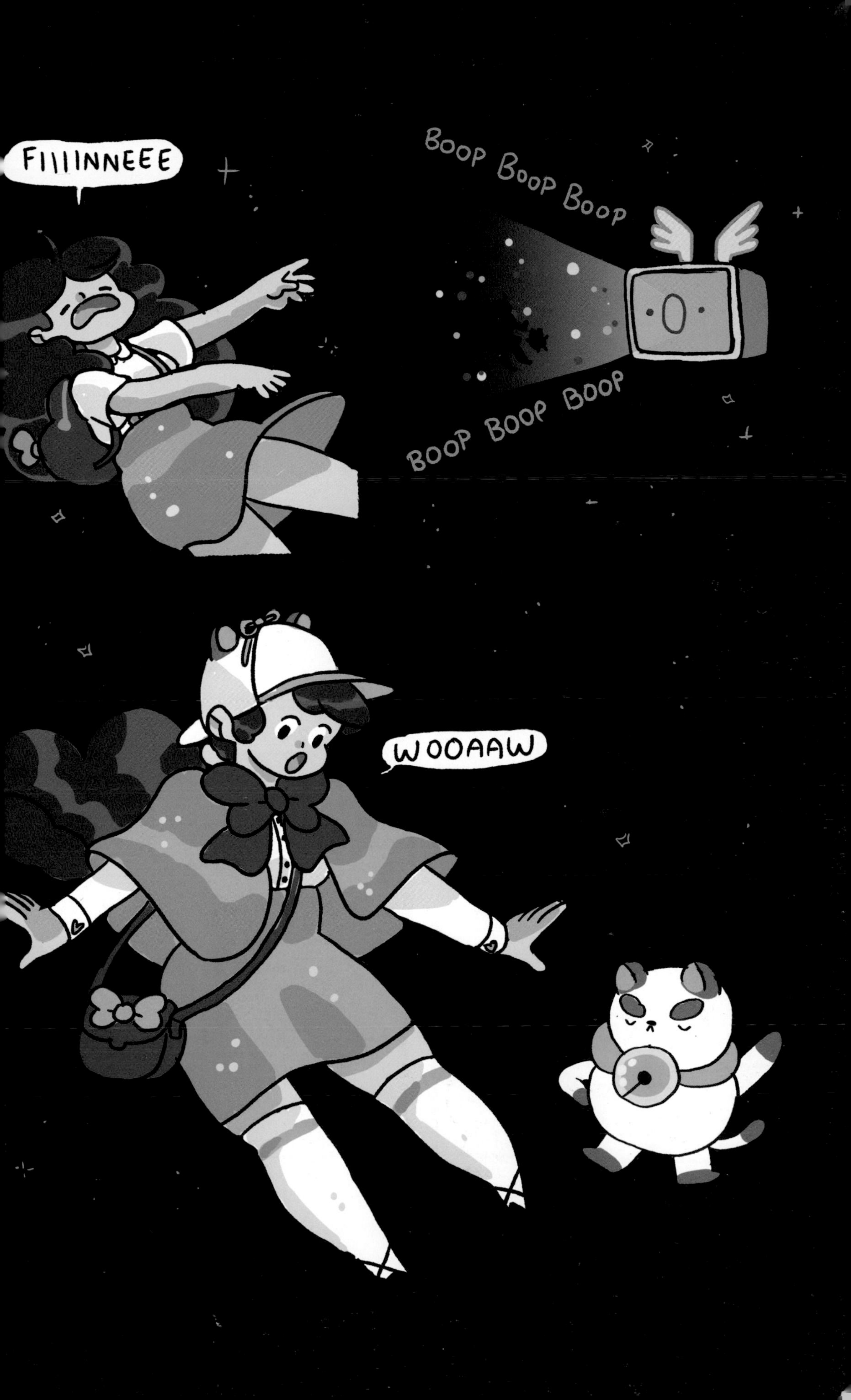
FIIIINNEEE
BOOP BOOP BOOP
BOOP BOOP BOOP
WOOAAW

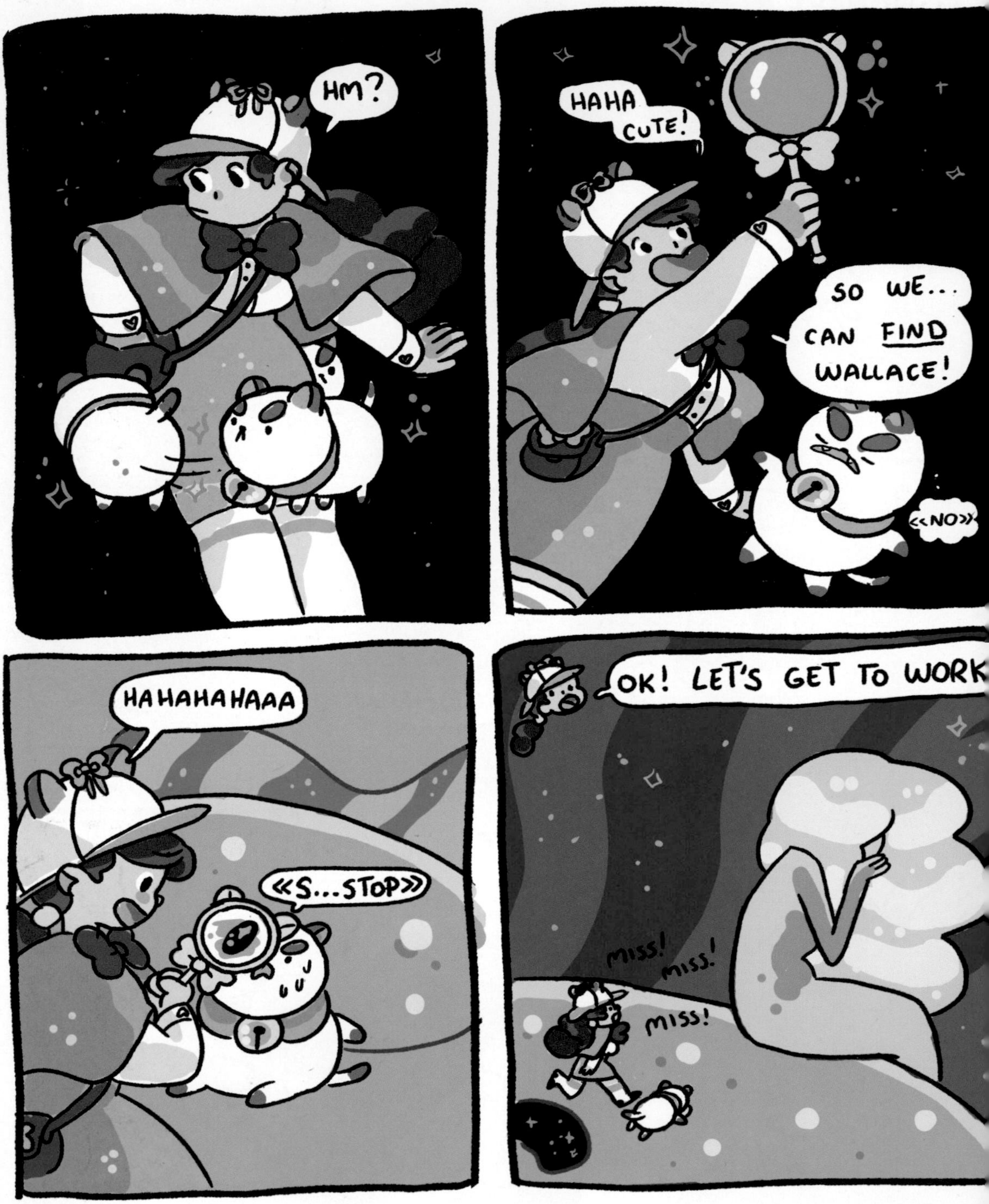
HM?
HAHA CUTE!
SO WE... CAN FIND WALLACE!
«NO»
HAHAHAHAAA
«S...STOP»
OK! LET'S GET TO WORK
MISS!
MISS!
MISS!

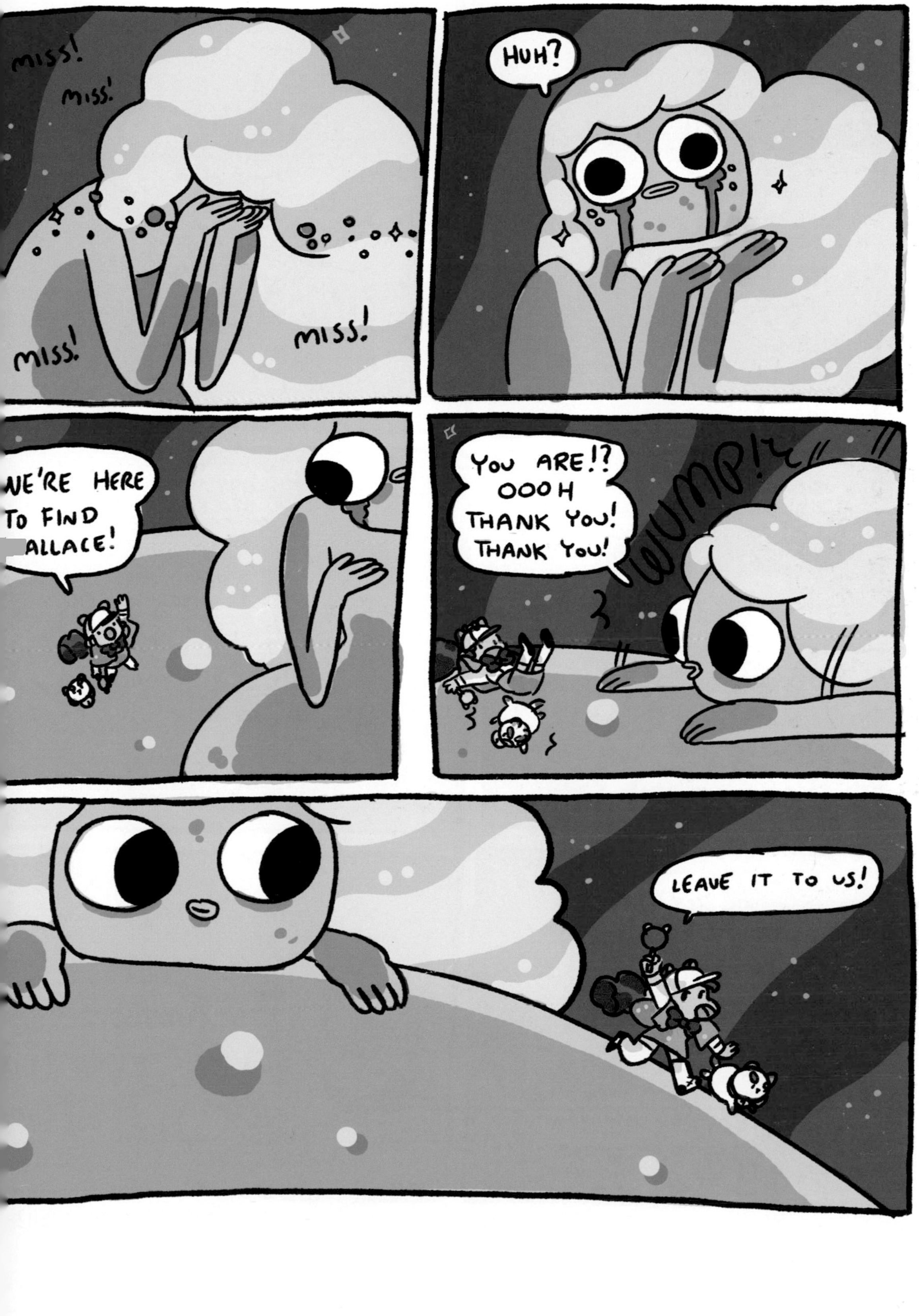
MISS!
MISS!
MISS!
MISS!
HUH?
E'RE HERE TO FIND ALLACE!
YOU ARE!? OOOH THANK YOU! THANK YOU!
WUMP!
LEAVE IT TO US!

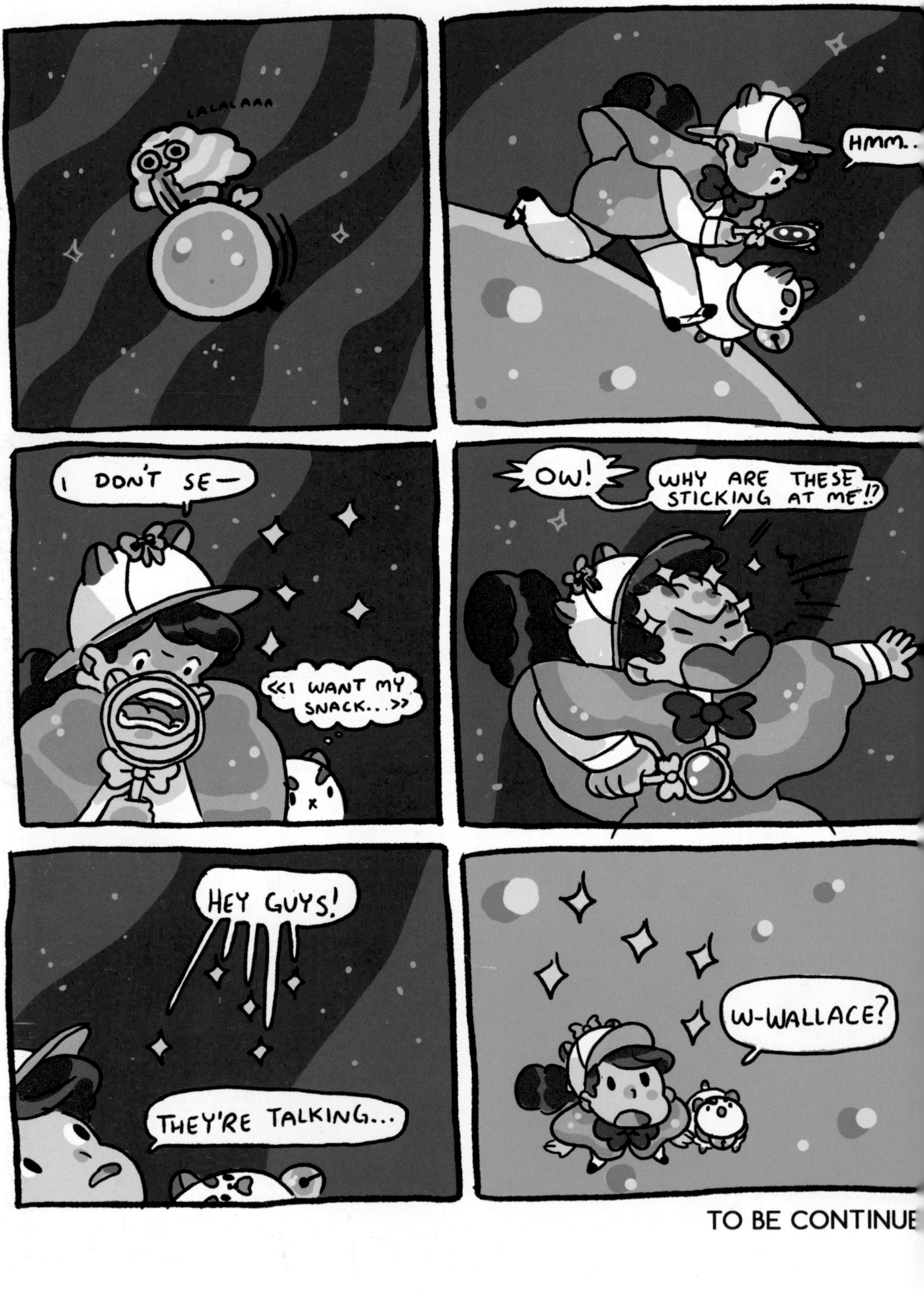
LALALAAA
HMM..
I DON'T SE—
<<I WANT MY SNACK...>>
OW!
WHY ARE THESE STICKING AT ME!?
HEY GUYS!
THEY'RE TALKING...
W-WALLACE?

TO BE CONTINUE

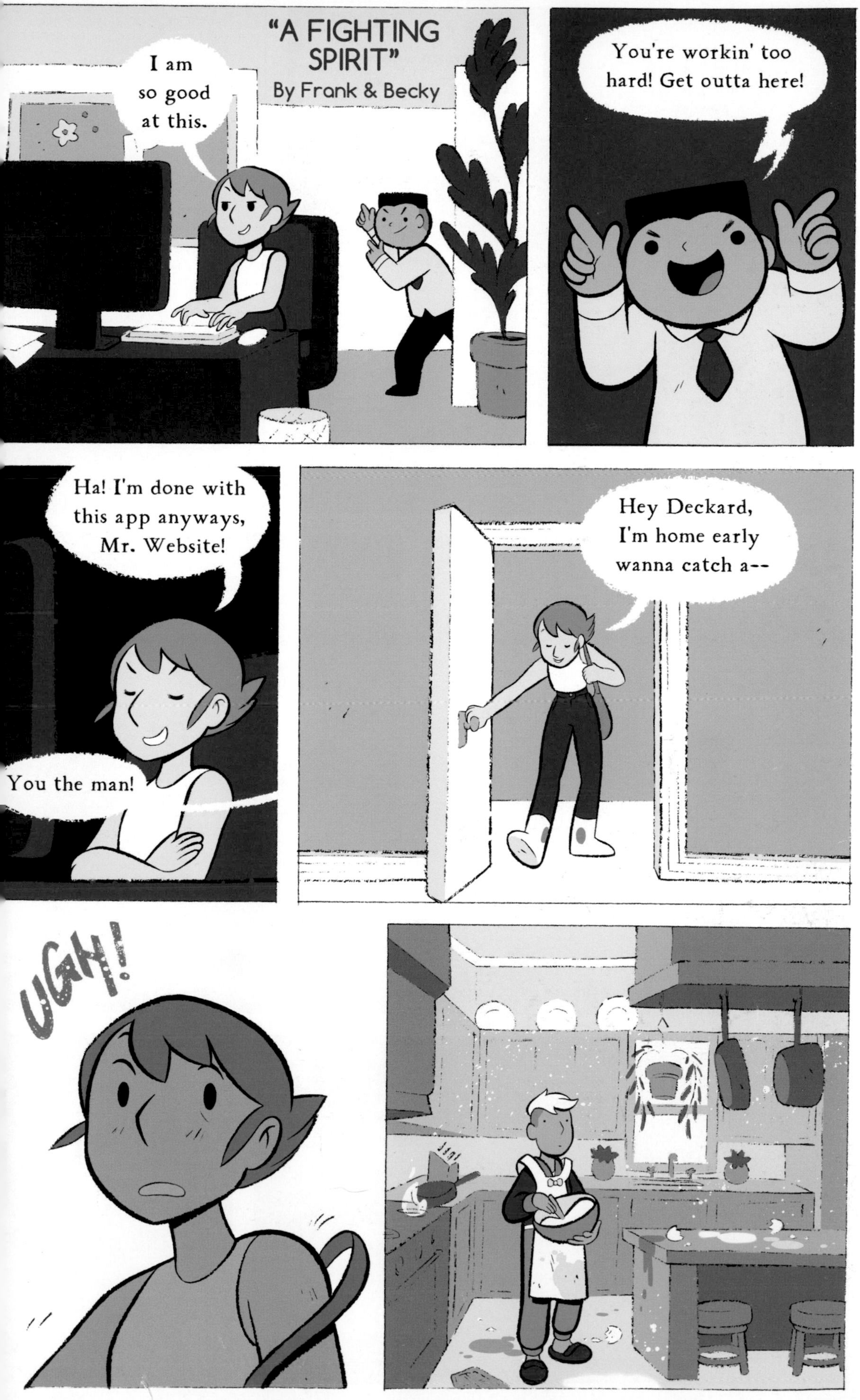
"A FIGHTING SPIRIT"
By Frank & Becky
I am so good at this.
You're workin' too hard! Get outta here!
Ha! I'm done with this app anyways, Mr. Website!
You the man!
Hey Deckard, I'm home early wanna catch a--
UGH!

I uh, worked out how to turn eggs into a powder.

I'm gonna go to my room and when I come back, this is going to be clean, like magic.

Can do!

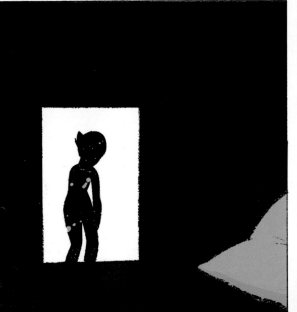

FLOP

SIGH

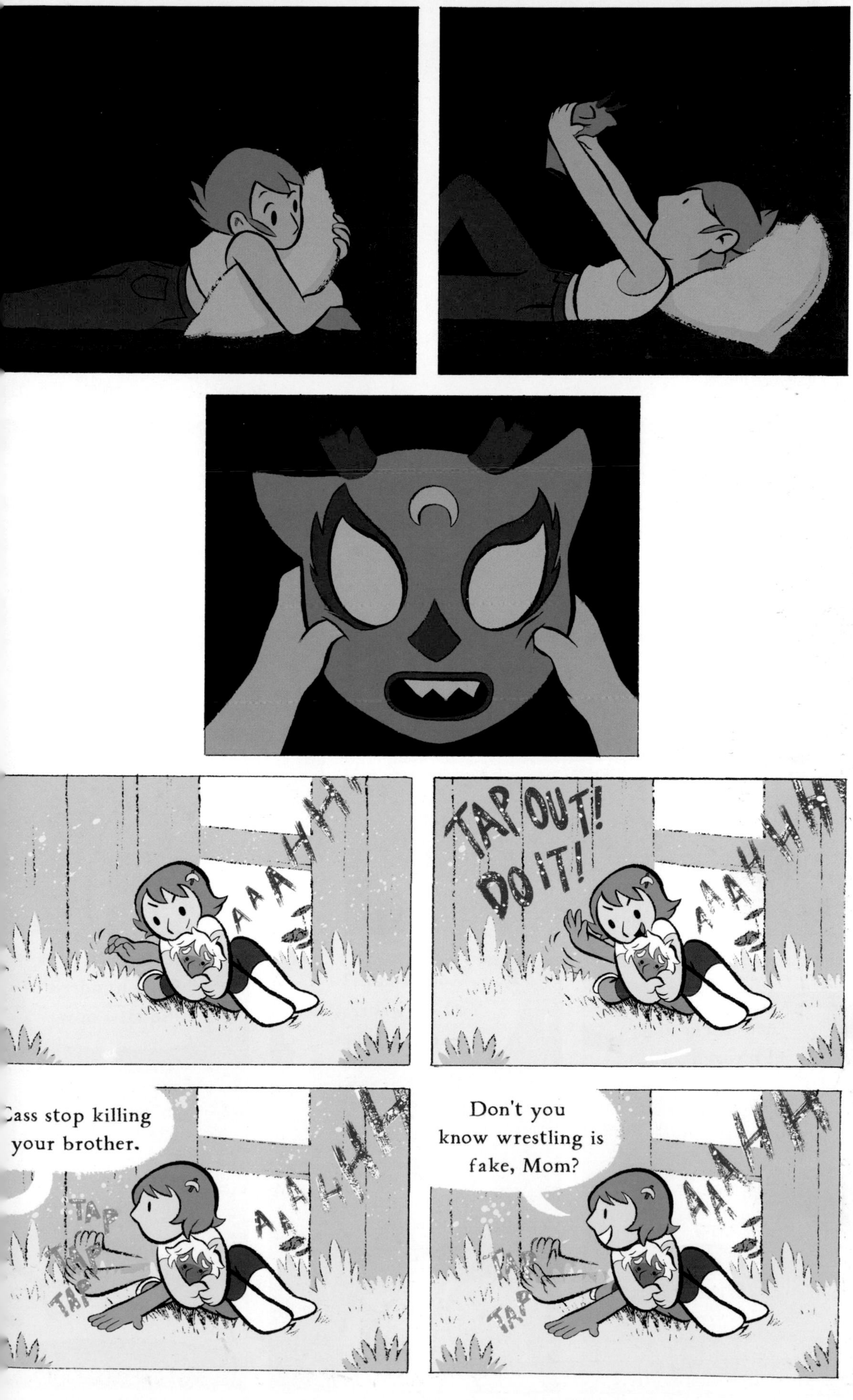
AAAHHH
TAP OUT!
DO IT!
AAAHHH
Cass stop killing your brother.
TAP
TAP
TAP
AAHHH
Don't you know wrestling is fake, Mom?
TAP
TAP
AAAHHH

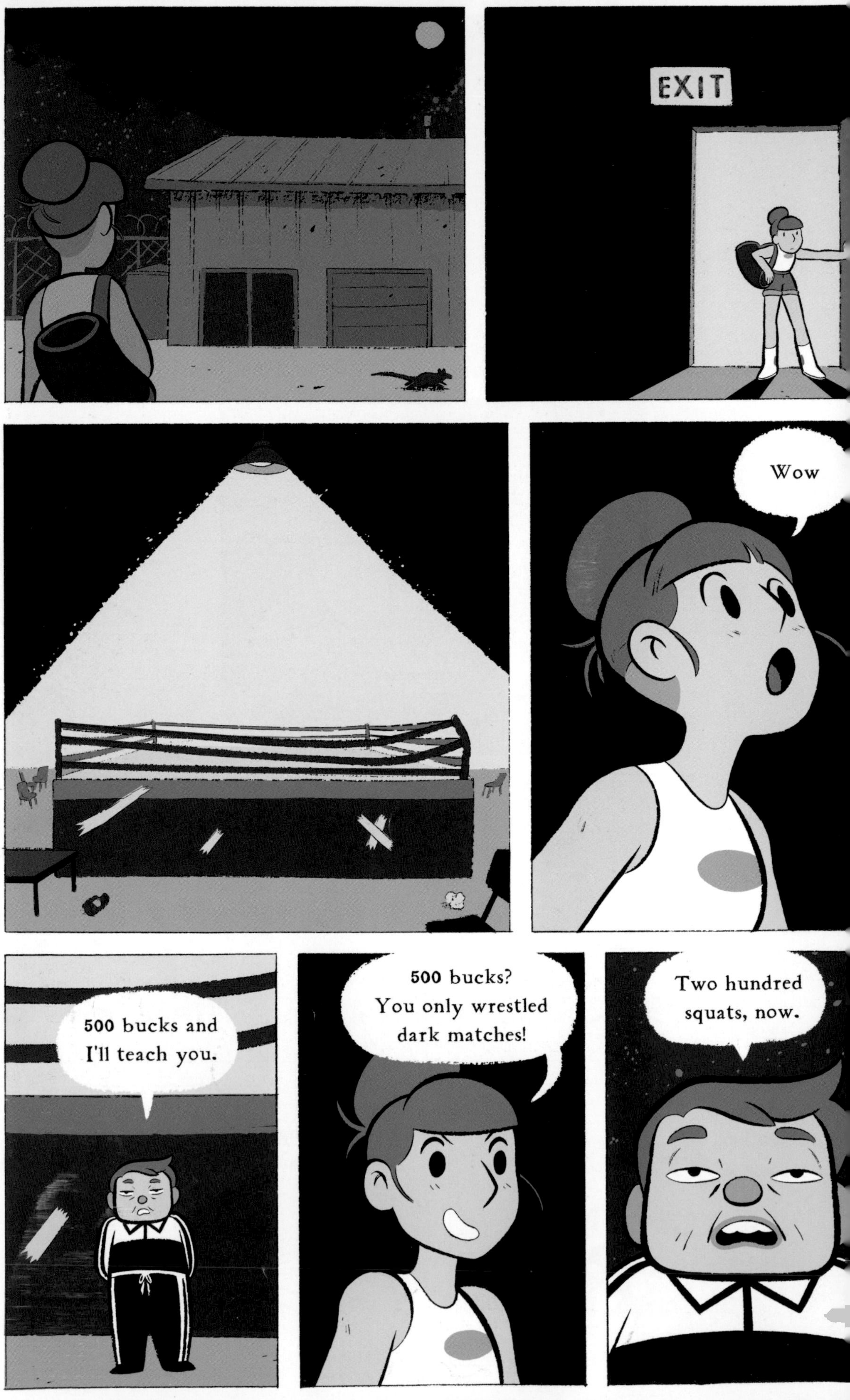
EXIT
Wow
500 bucks and I'll teach you.
500 bucks? You only wrestled dark matches!
Two hundred squats, now.

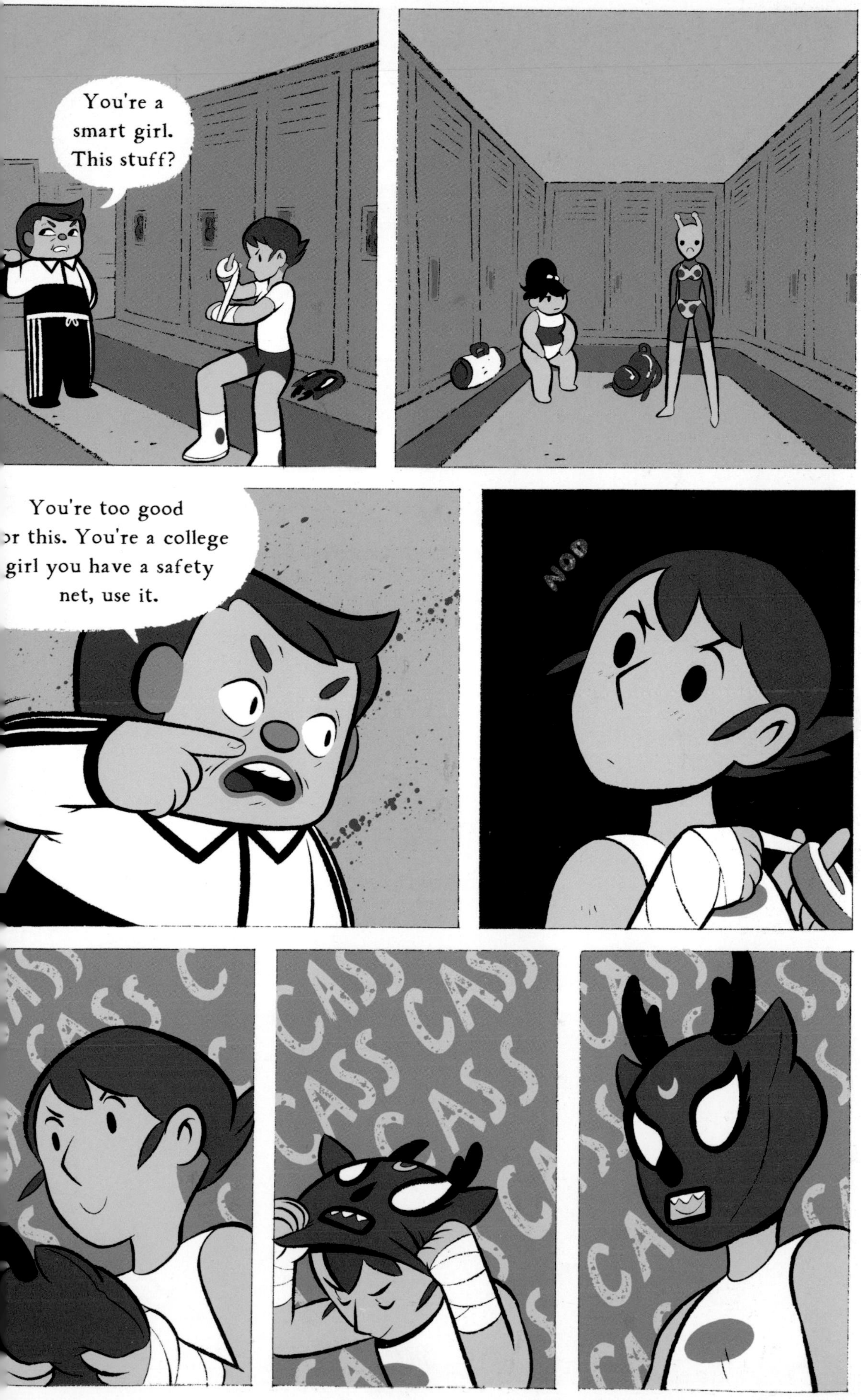

You're a smart girl. This stuff?
You're too good or this. You're a college girl you have a safety net, use it.
NOD

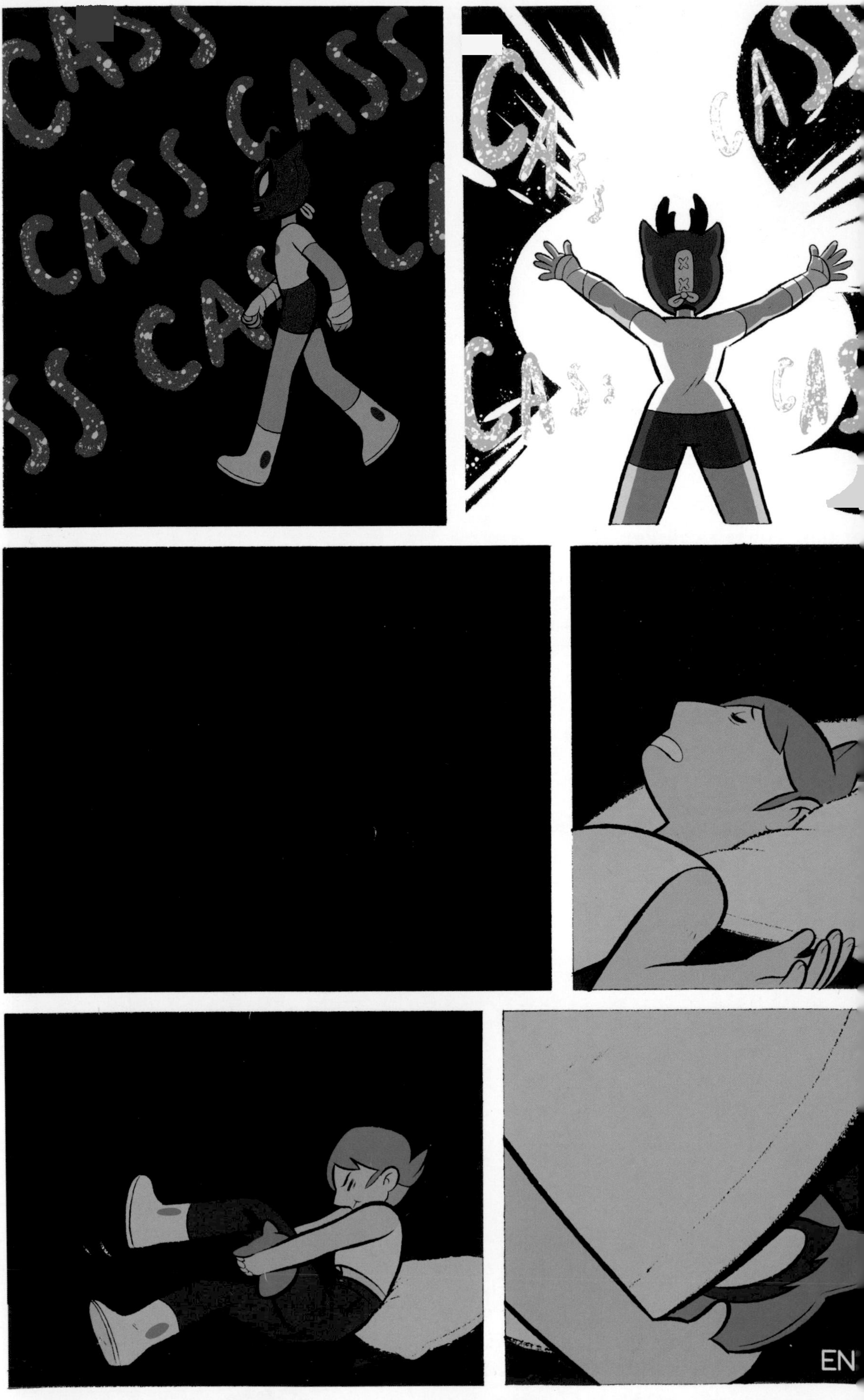
CASS
CASS
CASS
CASS
CASS
CASS
CASS
CASS
EN

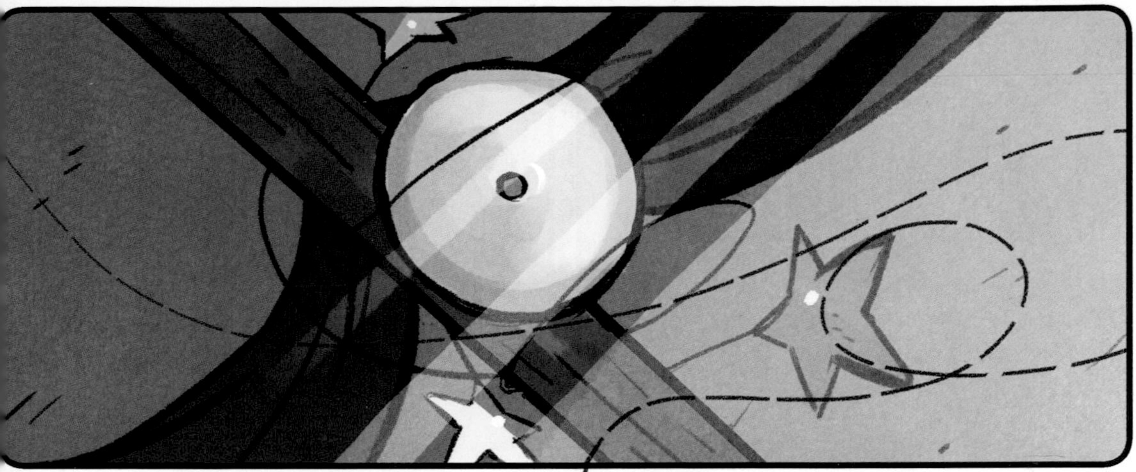

A Nice Day Off

BY: ANISSA ESPINOSA

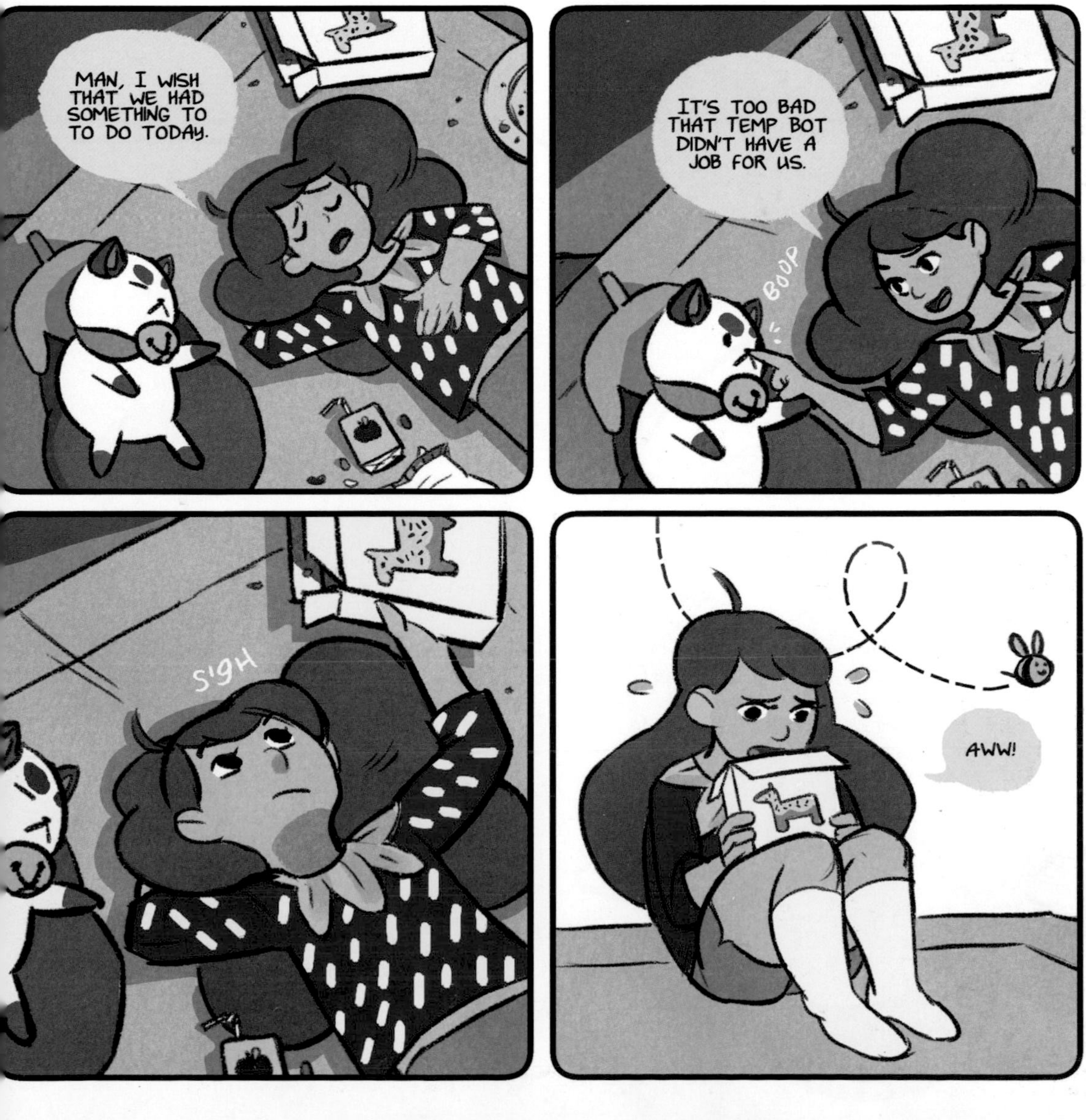
MAN, I WISH THAT WE HAD SOMETHING TO TO DO TODAY.
IT'S TOO BAD THAT TEMP BOT DIDN'T HAVE A JOB FOR US.
BOOP
SIGH
AWW!

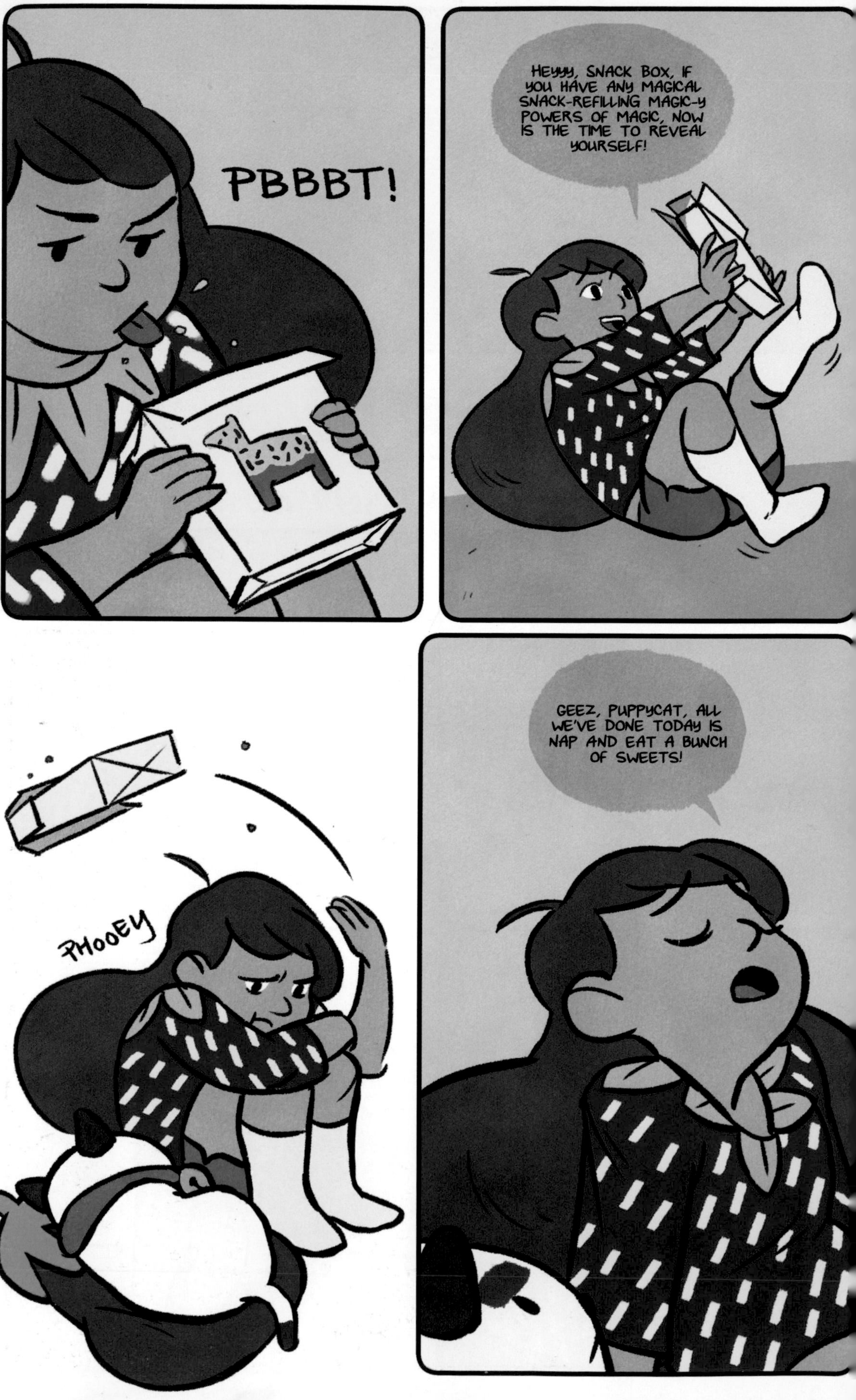
PBBBT!
HEYYY, SNACK BOX, IF YOU HAVE ANY MAGICAL SNACK-REFILLING MAGIC-Y POWERS OF MAGIC, NOW IS THE TIME TO REVEAL YOURSELF!
PHOOEY
GEEZ, PUPPYCAT, ALL WE'VE DONE TODAY IS NAP AND EAT A BUNCH OF SWEETS!

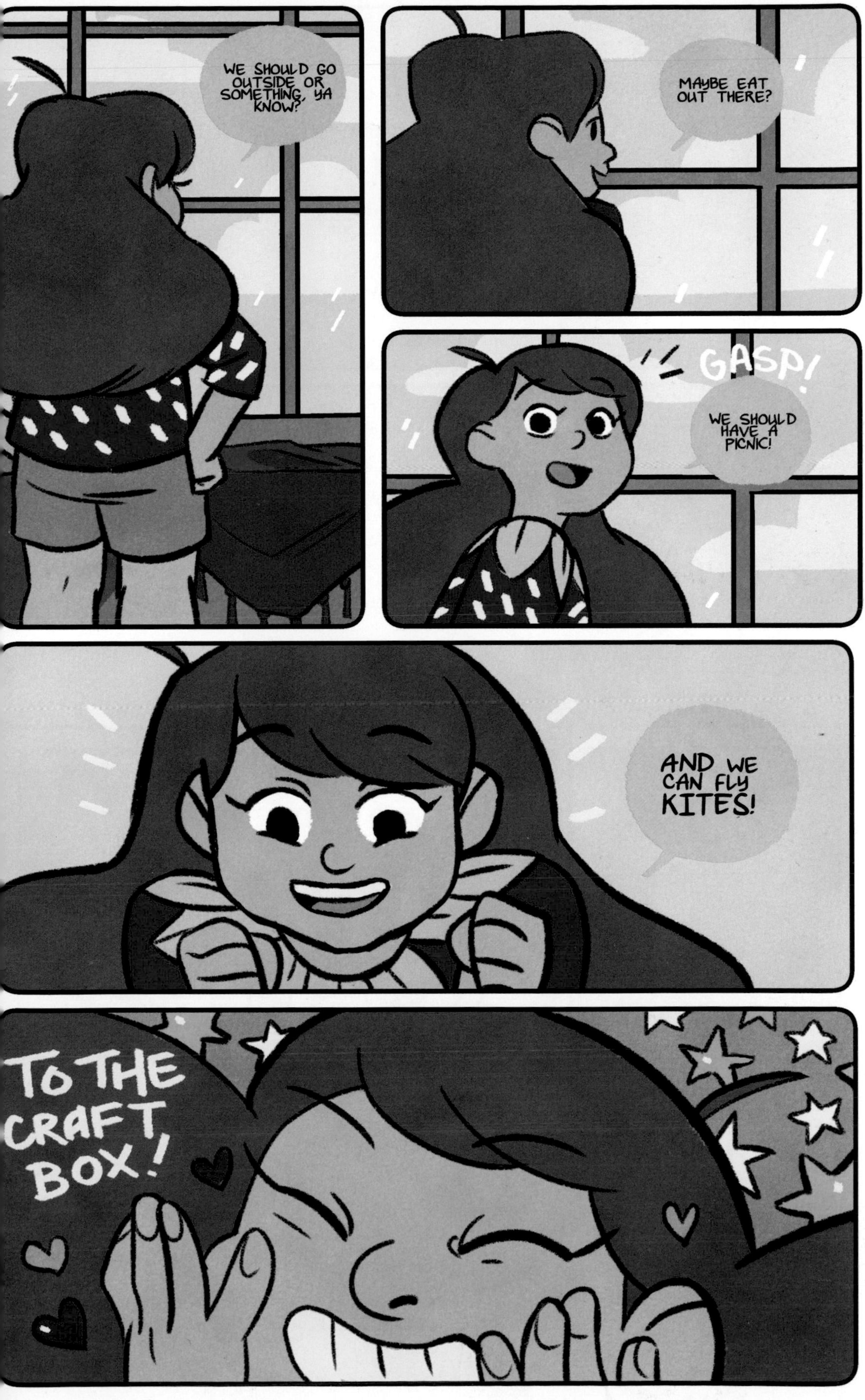
WE SHOULD GO OUTSIDE OR SOMETHING, YA KNOW?
MAYBE EAT OUT THERE?
GASP!
WE SHOULD HAVE A PICNIC!
AND WE CAN FLY KITES!
TO THE CRAFT BOX!

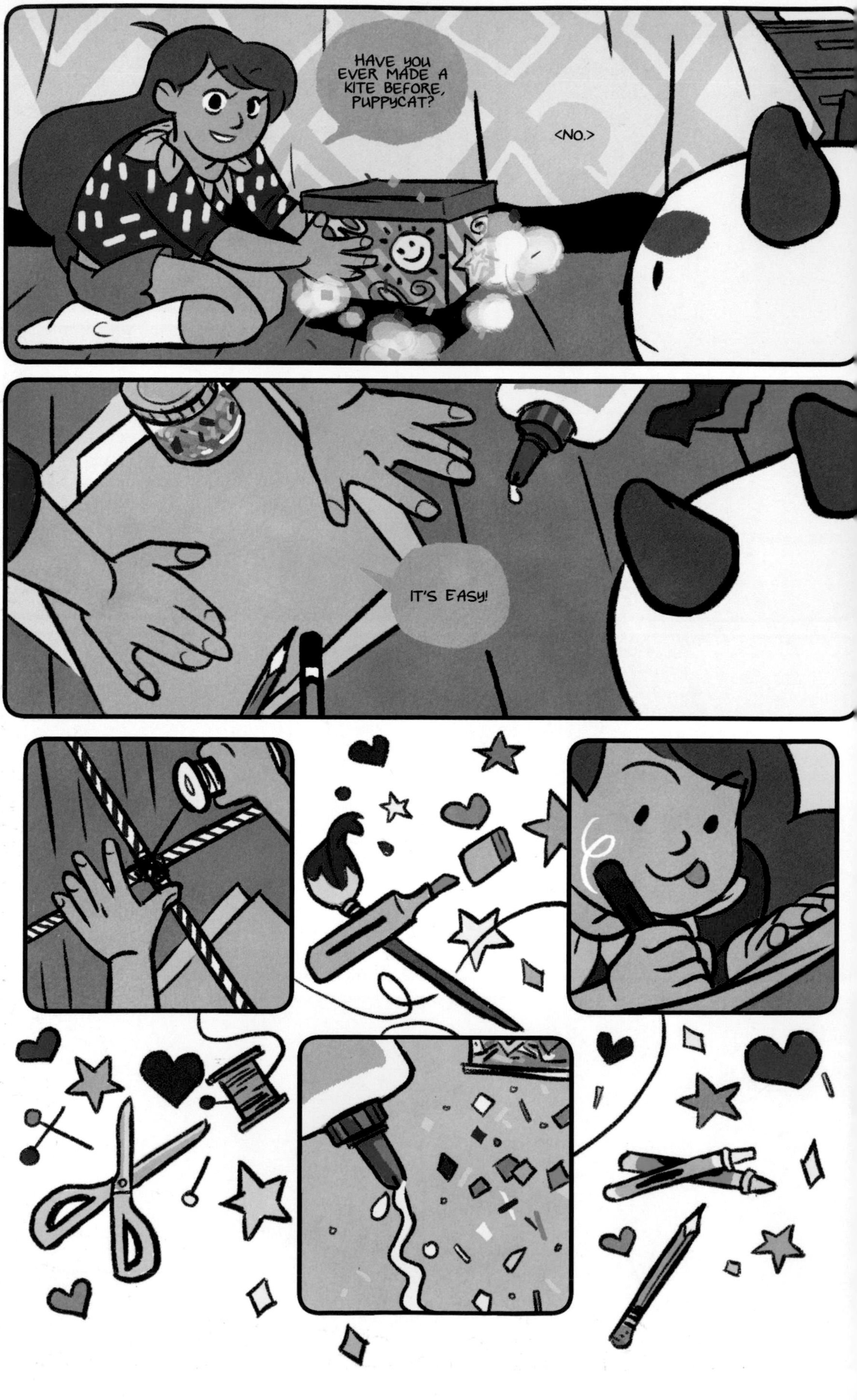
HAVE YOU EVER MADE A KITE BEFORE, PUPPYCAT?
<NO.>
IT'S EASY!

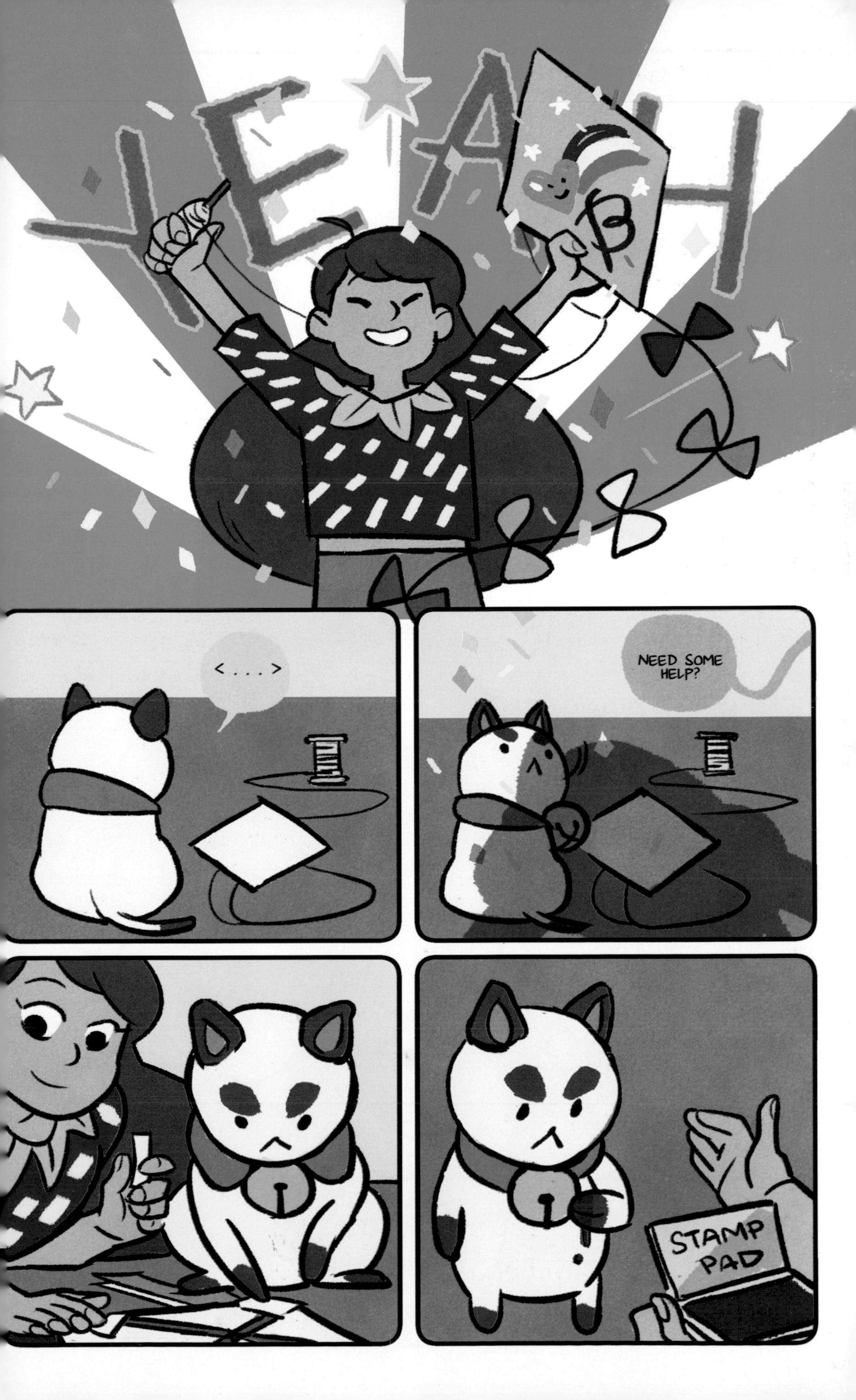
YEAH
< . . . >
NEED SOME HELP?
STAMP PAD

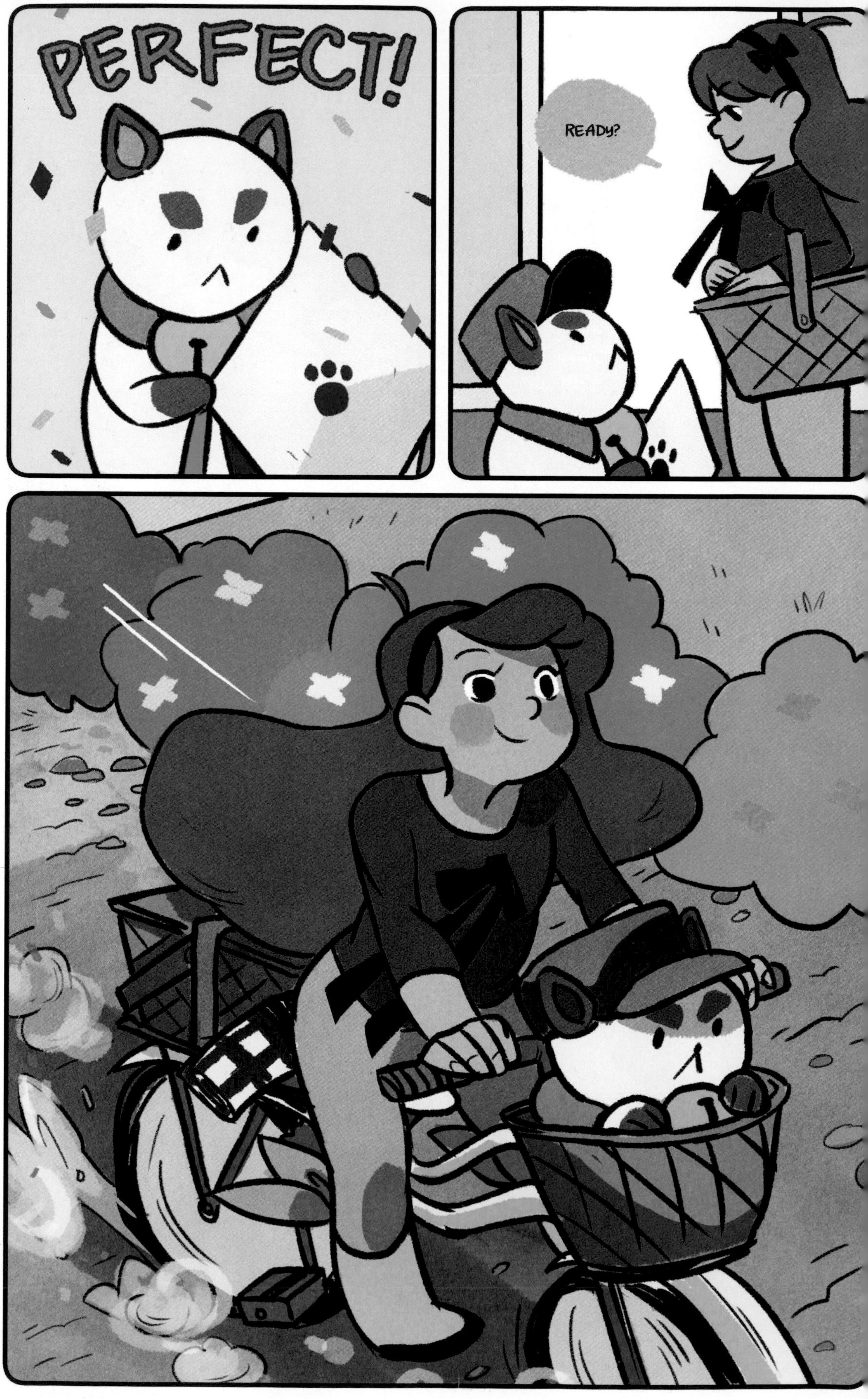
PERFECT!
READY?

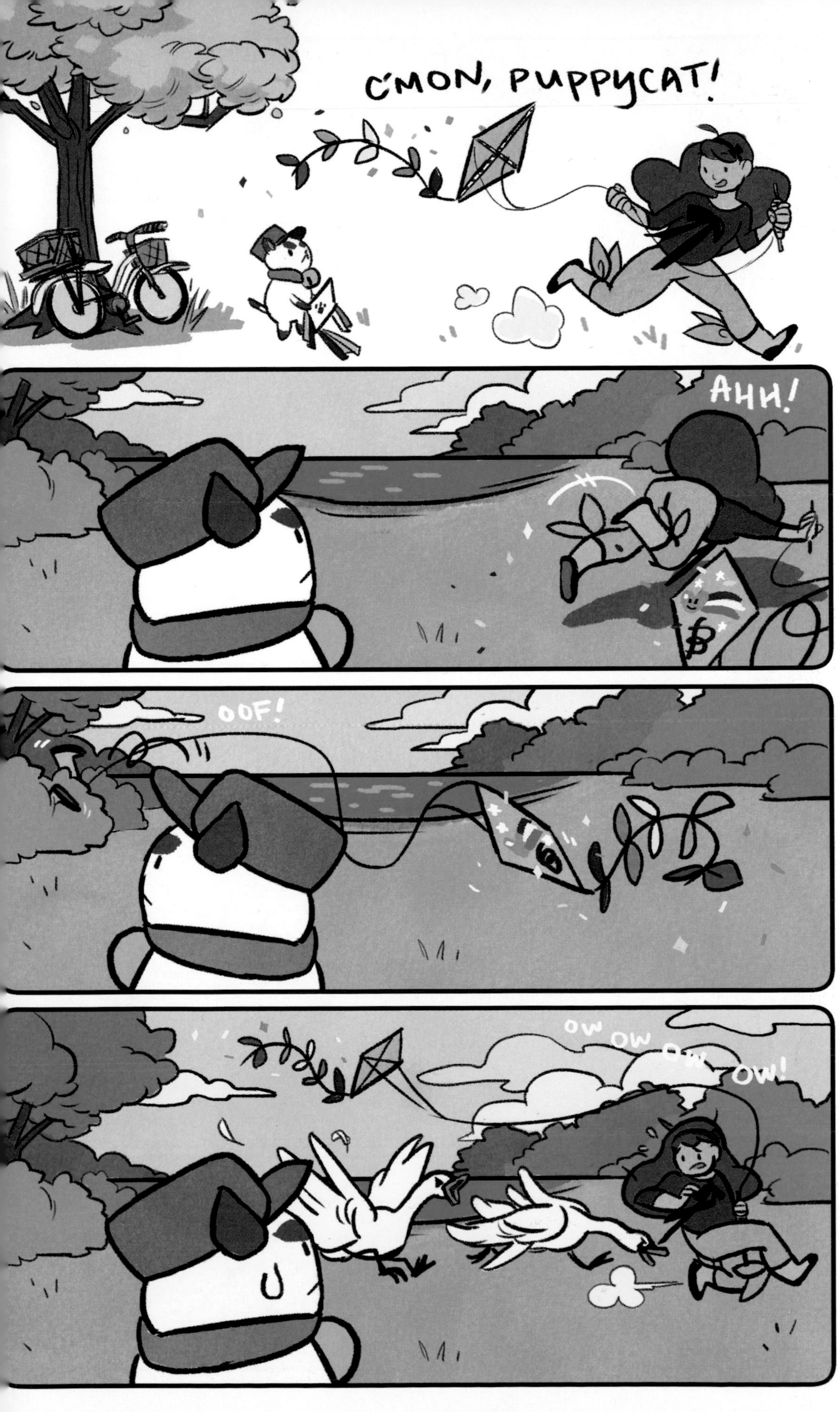
C'MON, PUPPYCAT!
AHH!
OOF!
OW OW OW OW!

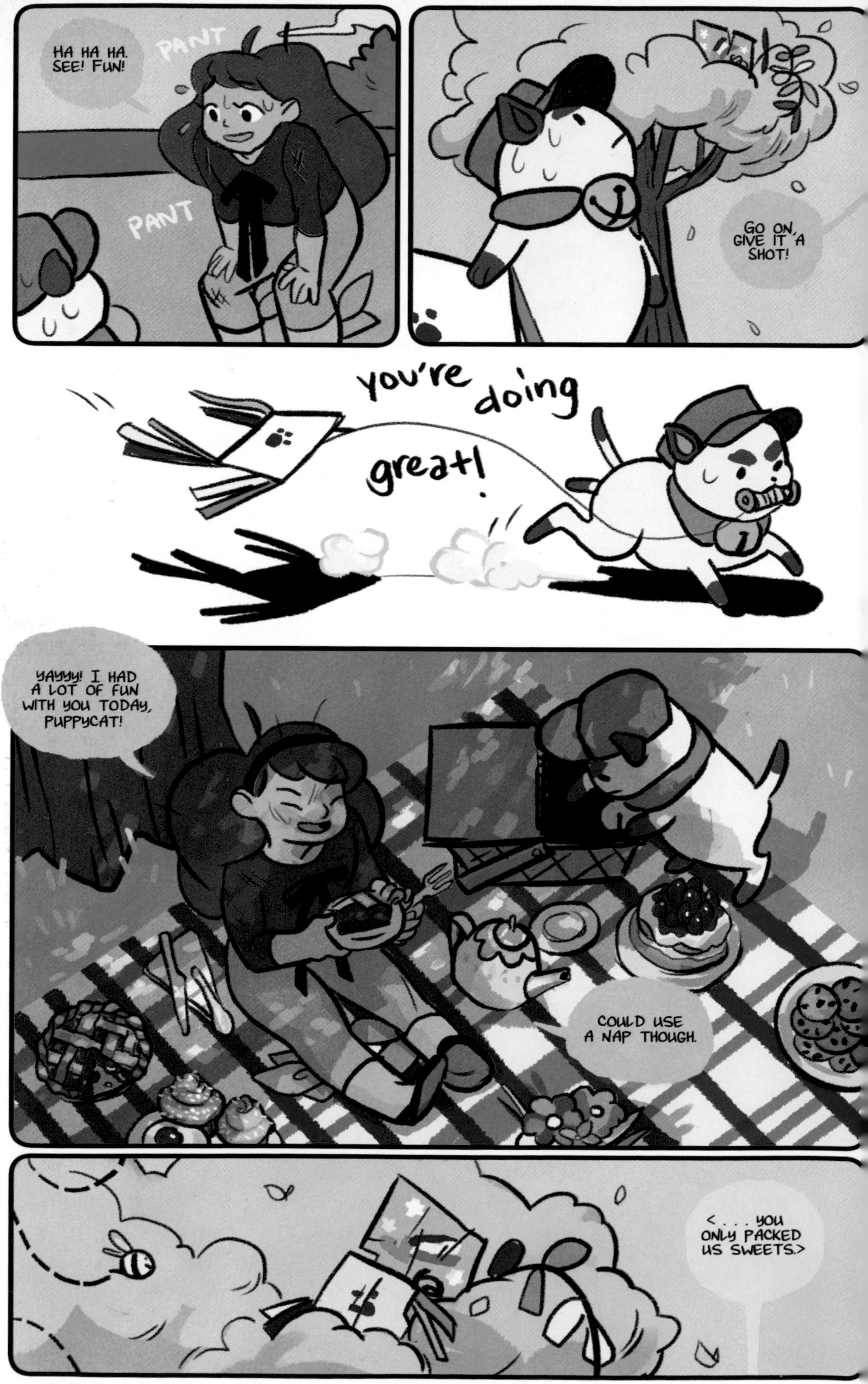
HA HA HA. SEE! FUN!
PANT
PANT
GO ON, GIVE IT A SHOT!
you're doing great!
YAYYY! I HAD A LOT OF FUN WITH YOU TODAY, PUPPYCAT!
COULD USE A NAP THOUGH.
<. . . YOU ONLY PACKED US SWEETS.>

EN

Clean Up

Written & Illustrated by
Tait Howard
Letters by
Aubrey Aiese

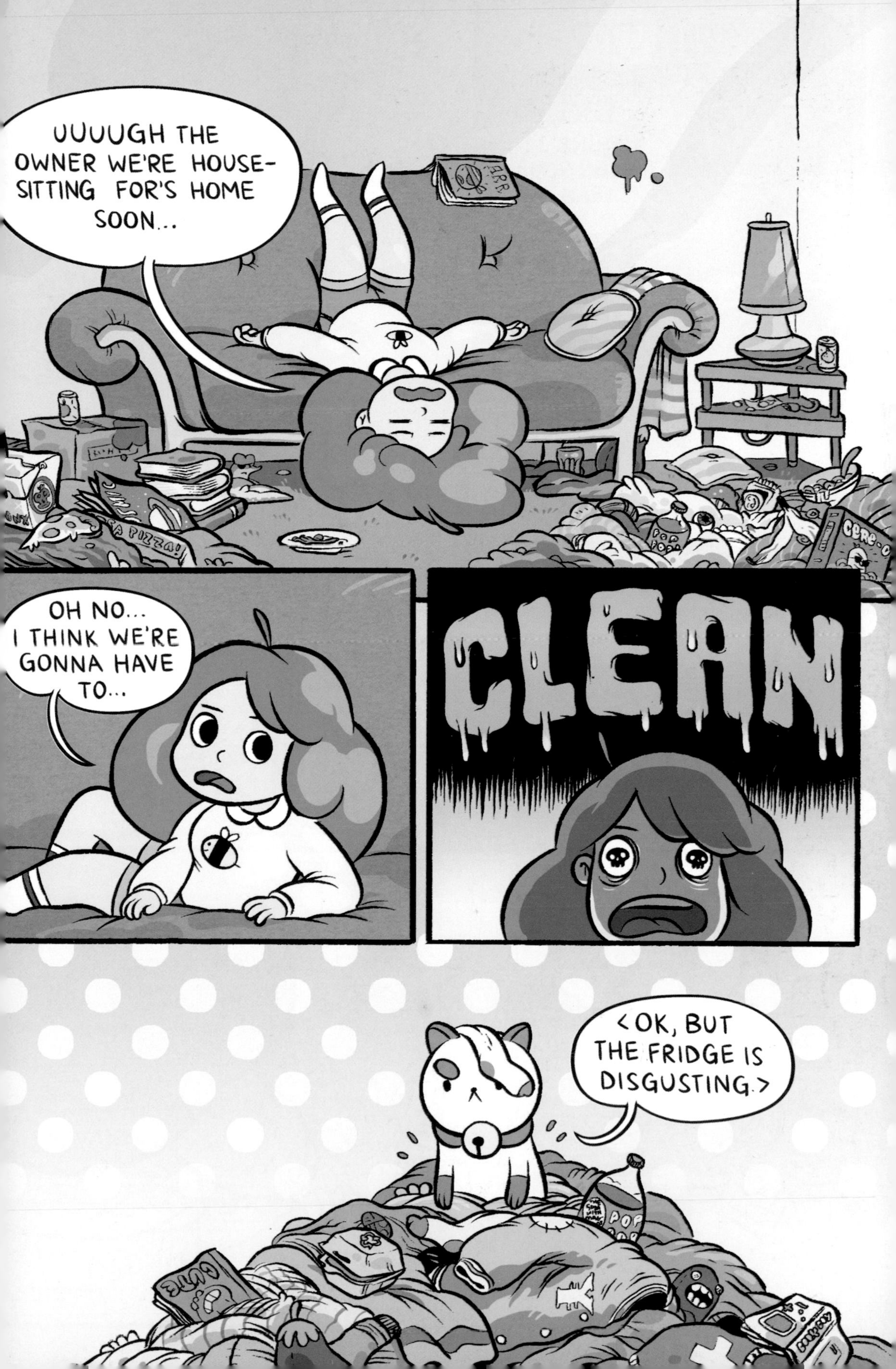
UUUUGH THE OWNER WE'RE HOUSE-SITTING FOR'S HOME SOON...
OH NO... I THINK WE'RE GONNA HAVE TO...
CLEAN
<OK, BUT THE FRIDGE IS DISGUSTING.>

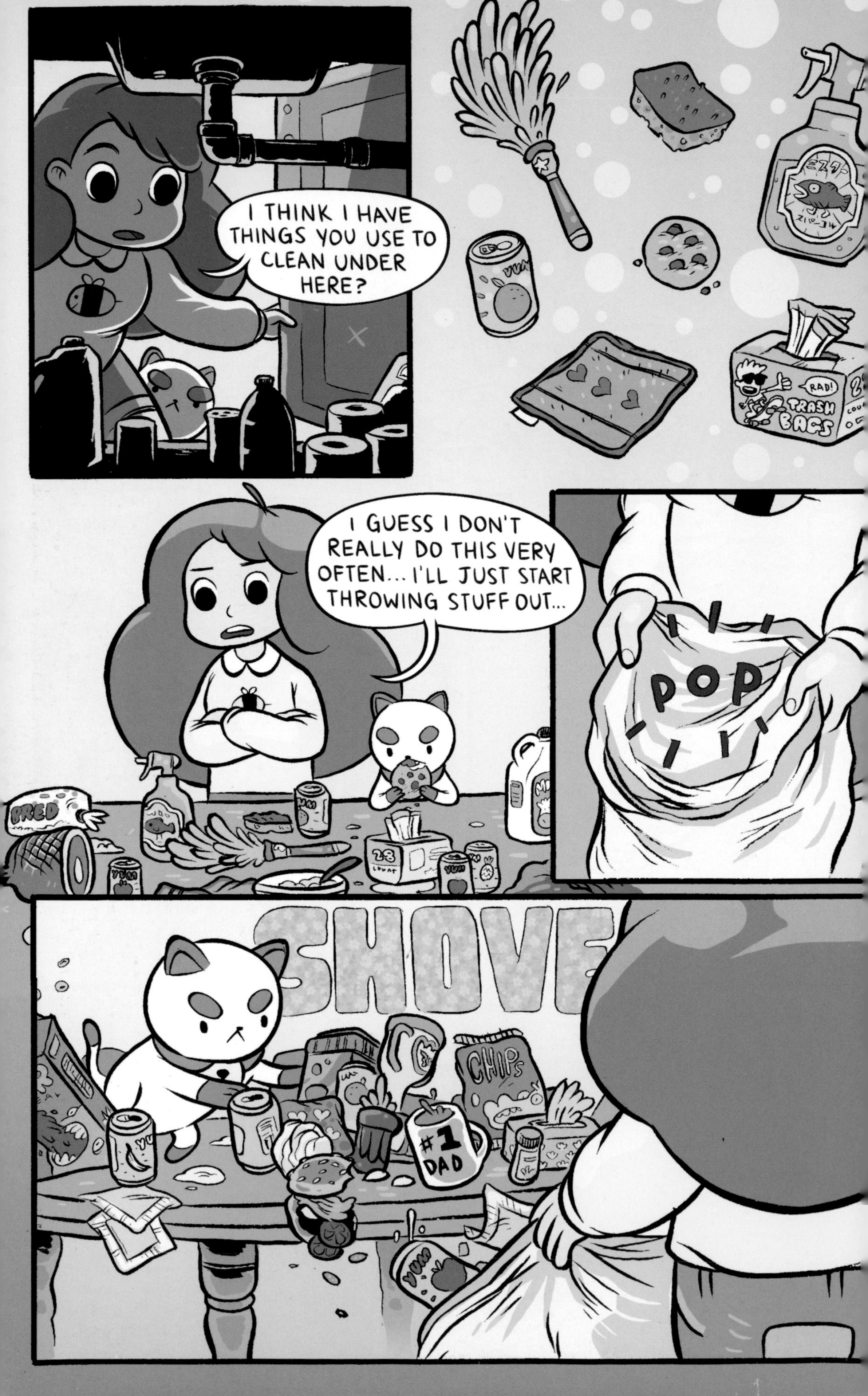

I THINK I HAVE THINGS YOU USE TO CLEAN UNDER HERE?
RAD!
TRASH BAGS
I GUESS I DON'T REALLY DO THIS VERY OFTEN... I'LL JUST START THROWING STUFF OUT...
POP
SHOVE
CHIPS
#1 DAD

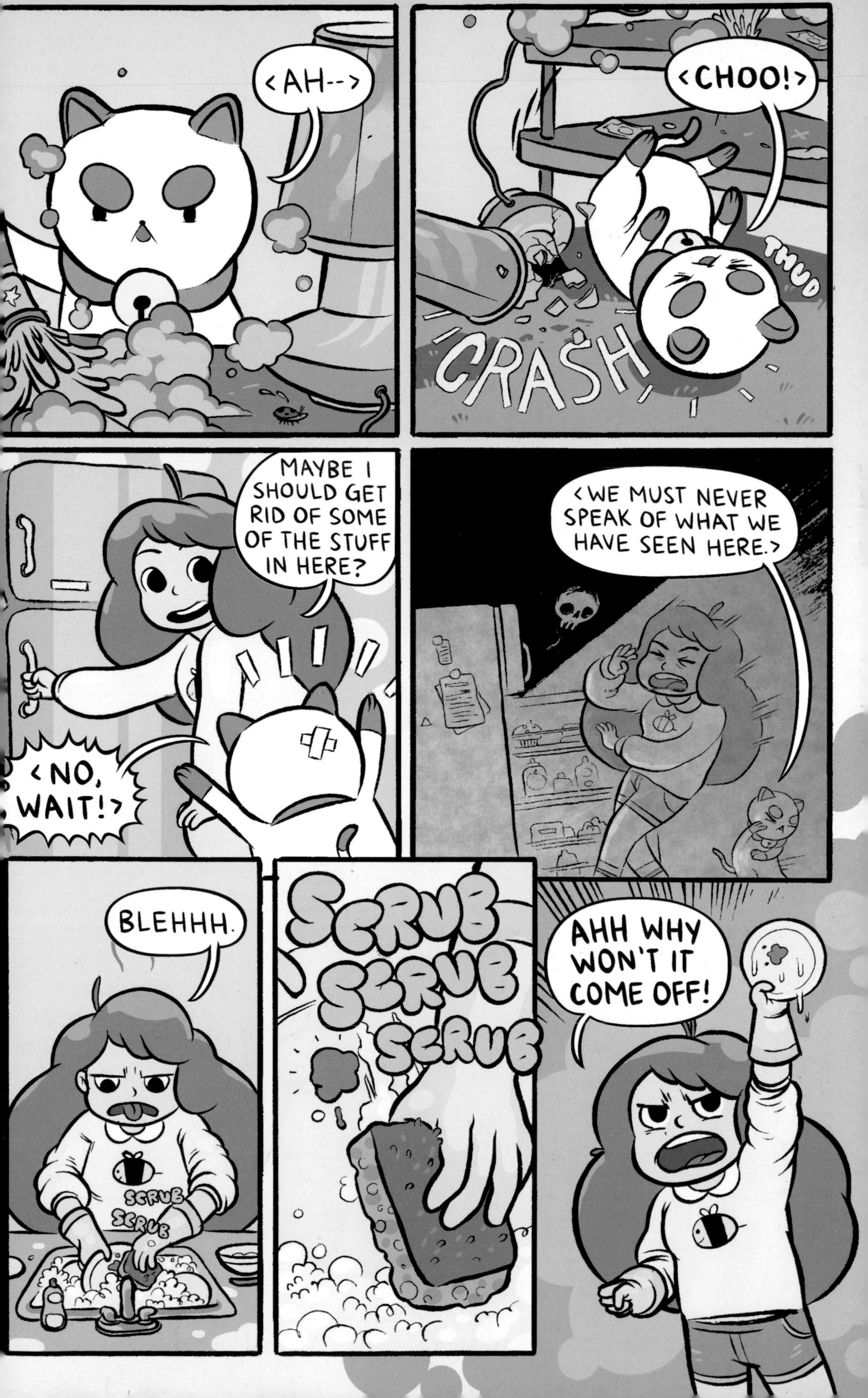

<AH-->
<CHOO!>
THUD
CRASH
MAYBE I SHOULD GET RID OF SOME OF THE STUFF IN HERE?
<NO, WAIT!>
<WE MUST NEVER SPEAK OF WHAT WE HAVE SEEN HERE.>
BLEHHH.
SCRUB
SCRUB
SCRUB SCRUB SCRUB
AHH WHY WON'T IT COME OFF!

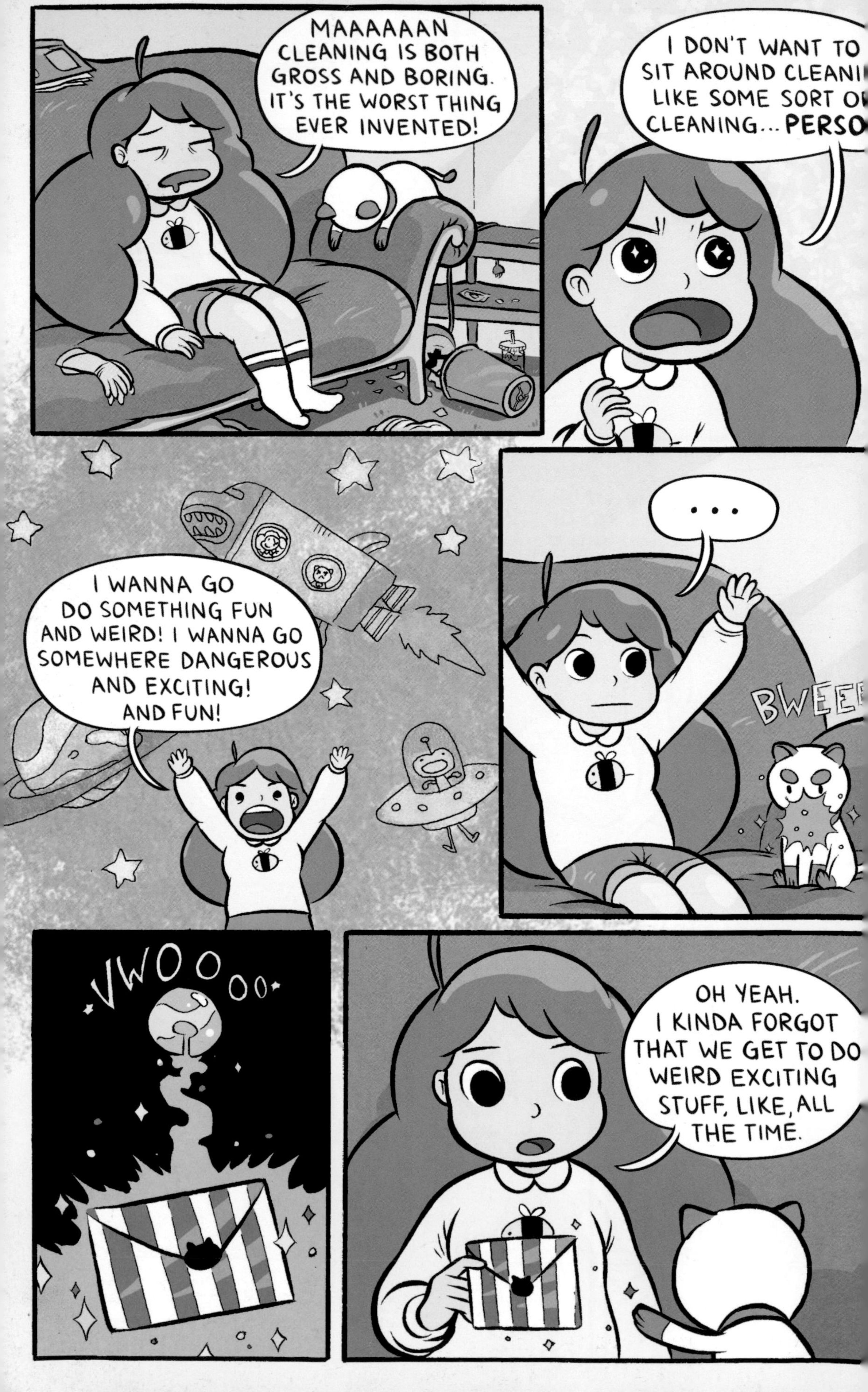
MAAAAAAN CLEANING IS BOTH GROSS AND BORING. IT'S THE WORST THING EVER INVENTED!
I DON'T WANT TO SIT AROUND CLEANI LIKE SOME SORT O CLEANING... PERSO
I WANNA GO DO SOMETHING FUN AND WEIRD! I WANNA GO SOMEWHERE DANGEROUS AND EXCITING! AND FUN!
...
BWEE
VWOOOOO
OH YEAH. I KINDA FORGOT THAT WE GET TO DO WEIRD EXCITING STUFF, LIKE, ALL THE TIME.

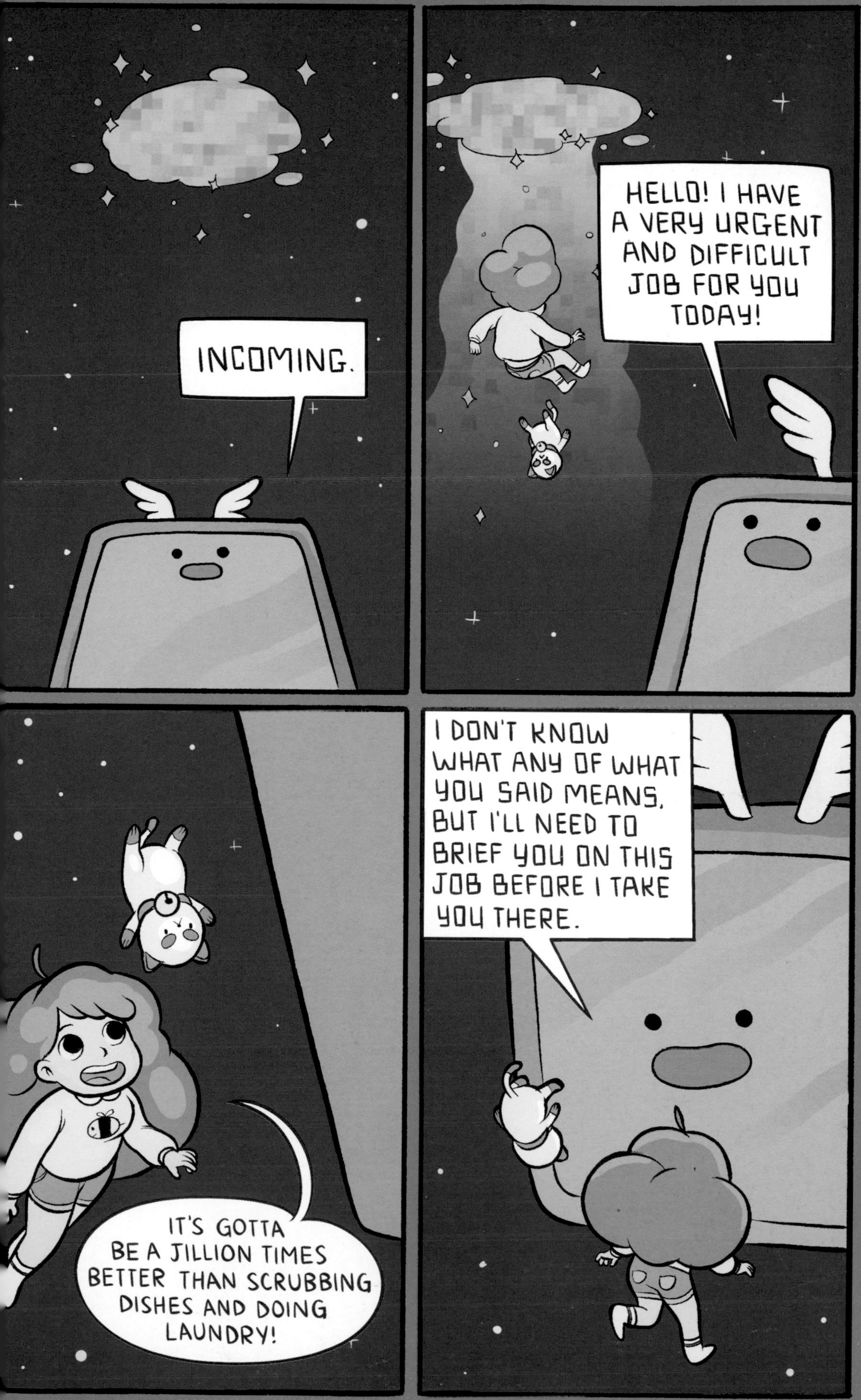
INCOMING.
HELLO! I HAVE A VERY URGENT AND DIFFICULT JOB FOR YOU TODAY!
IT'S GOTTA BE A JILLION TIMES BETTER THAN SCRUBBING DISHES AND DOING LAUNDRY!
I DON'T KNOW WHAT ANY OF WHAT YOU SAID MEANS, BUT I'LL NEED TO BRIEF YOU ON THIS JOB BEFORE I TAKE YOU THERE.

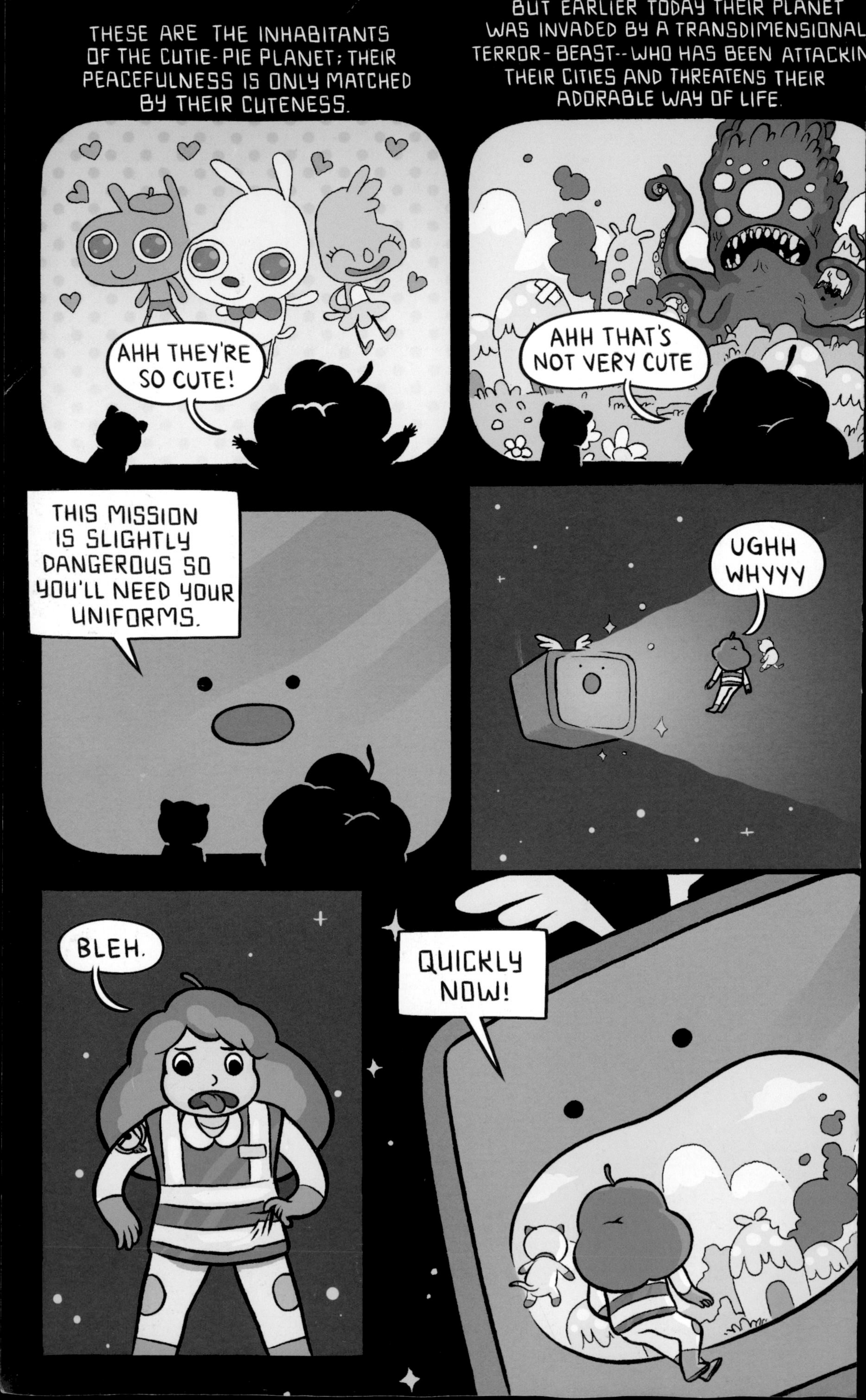
THESE ARE THE INHABITANTS OF THE CUTIE-PIE PLANET; THEIR PEACEFULNESS IS ONLY MATCHED BY THEIR CUTENESS.
AHH THEY'RE SO CUTE!
BUT EARLIER TODAY THEIR PLANET WAS INVADED BY A TRANSDIMENSIONAL TERROR-BEAST--WHO HAS BEEN ATTACKIN
THEIR CITIES AND THREATENS THEIR ADORABLE WAY OF LIFE.
AHH THAT'S NOT VERY CUTE
THIS MISSION IS SLIGHTLY DANGEROUS SO YOU'LL NEED YOUR UNIFORMS.
UGHH WHYYY
BLEH.
QUICKLY NOW!

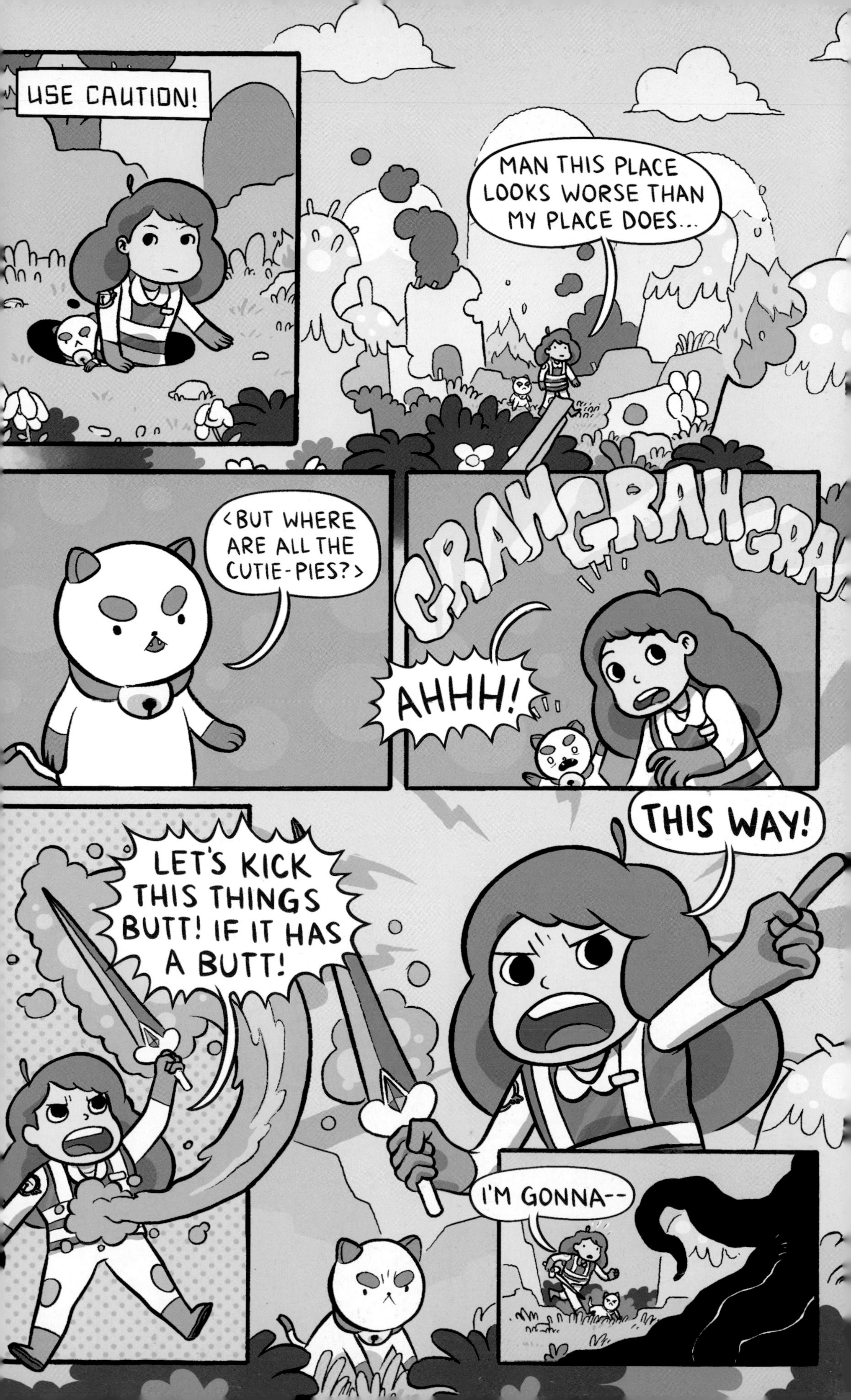
USE CAUTION!
MAN THIS PLACE LOOKS WORSE THAN MY PLACE DOES...
<BUT WHERE ARE ALL THE CUTIE-PIES?>
GRAHGRAHGRAHGRA
AHHH!
THIS WAY!
LET'S KICK THIS THINGS BUTT! IF IT HAS A BUTT!
I'M GONNA--

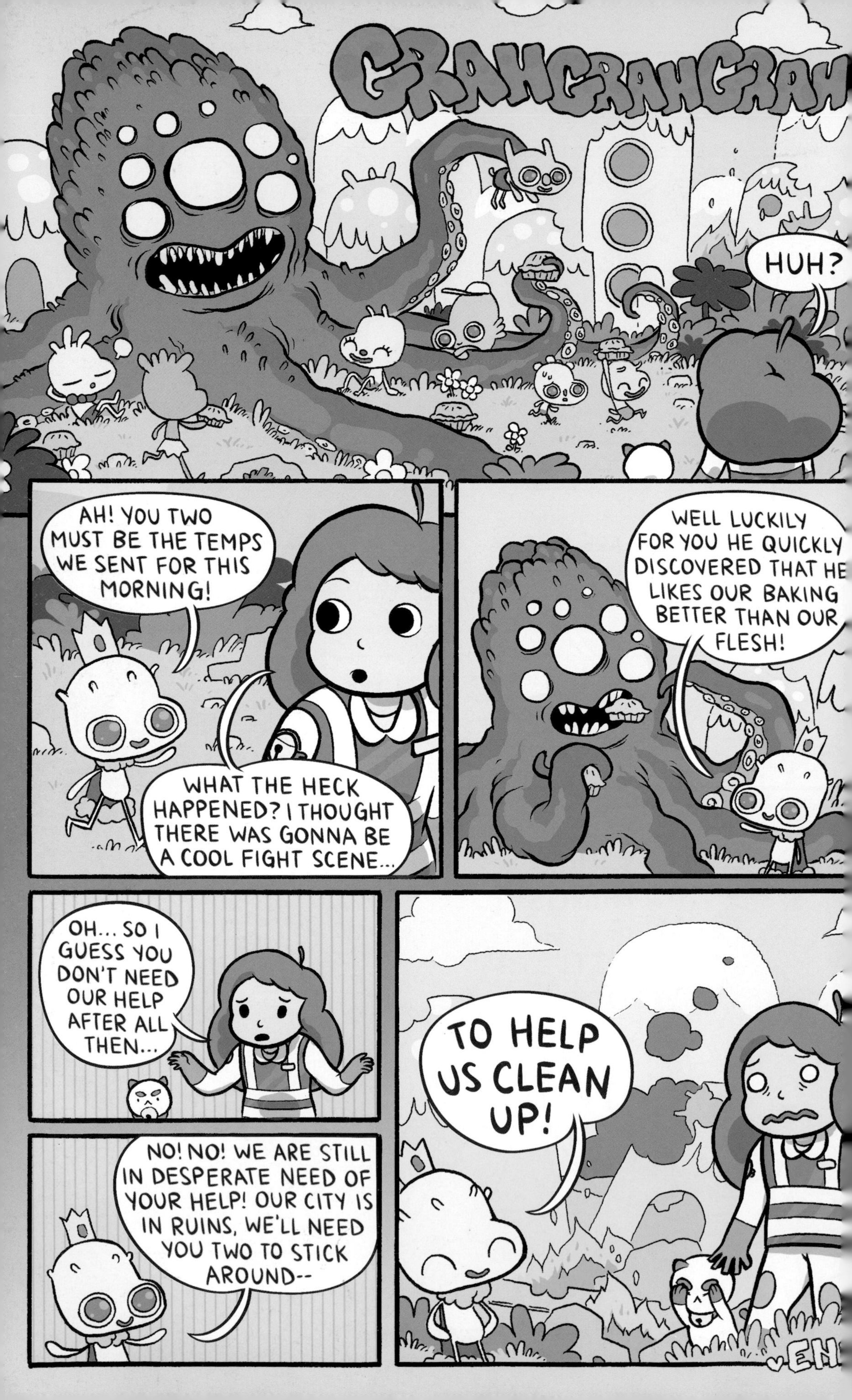
GRAHGRAHGRAH
HUH?
AH! YOU TWO MUST BE THE TEMPS WE SENT FOR THIS MORNING!
WHAT THE HECK HAPPENED? I THOUGHT THERE WAS GONNA BE A COOL FIGHT SCENE...
WELL LUCKILY FOR YOU HE QUICKLY DISCOVERED THAT HE LIKES OUR BAKING BETTER THAN OUR FLESH!
OH... SO I GUESS YOU DON'T NEED OUR HELP AFTER ALL THEN...
NO! NO! WE ARE STILL IN DESPERATE NEED OF YOUR HELP! OUR CITY IS IN RUINS, WE'LL NEED YOU TWO TO STICK AROUND--
TO HELP US CLEAN UP!
EH

DUMGUY

Written & Illustrated by Ian McGinty
Colors by Fred Stresing

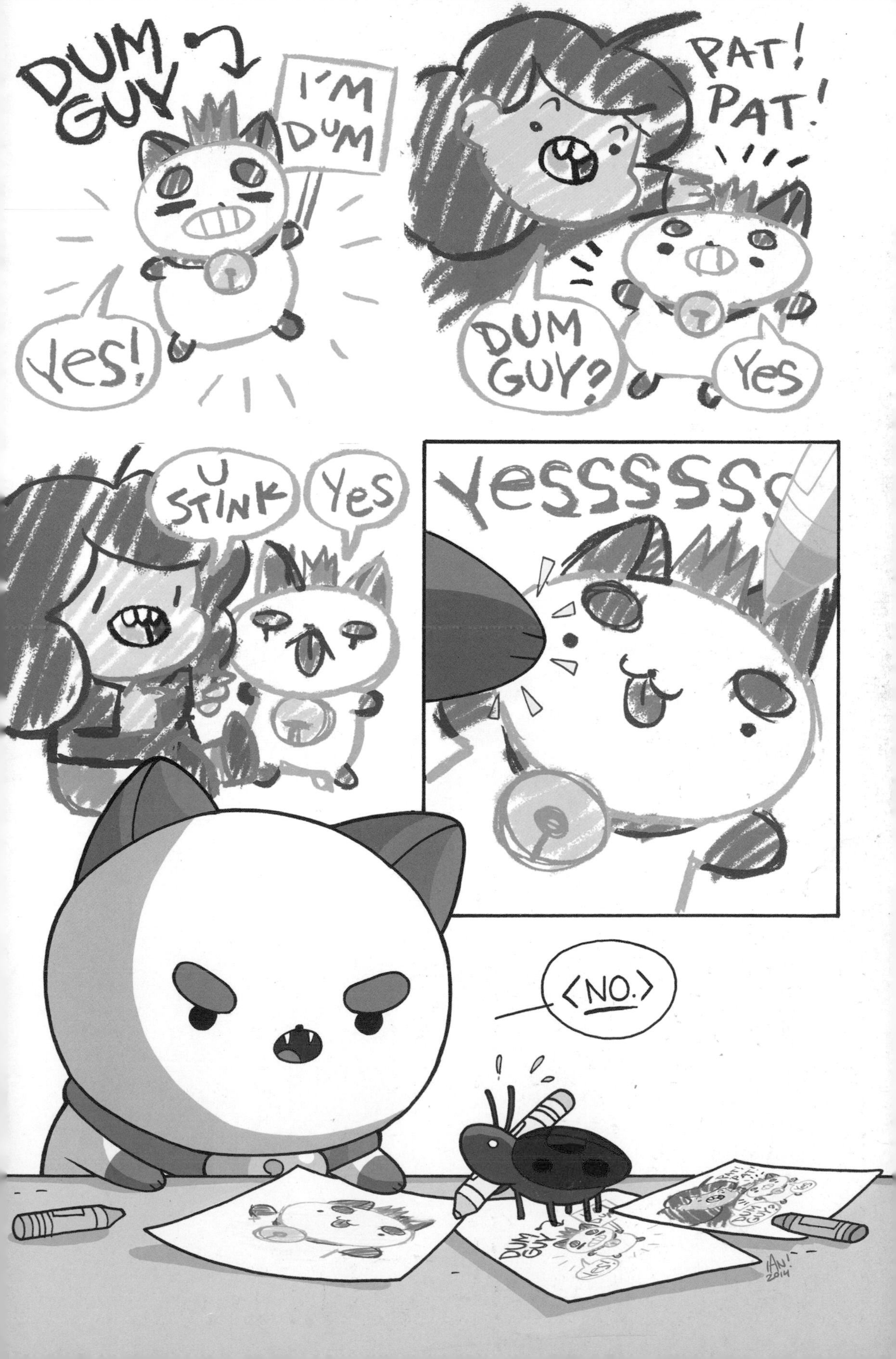
DUM GUY
I'M DUM
Yes!
PAT! PAT!
DUM GUY?
Yes
U STINK
Yes
Yesssss
<NO.>
IAN! 2014

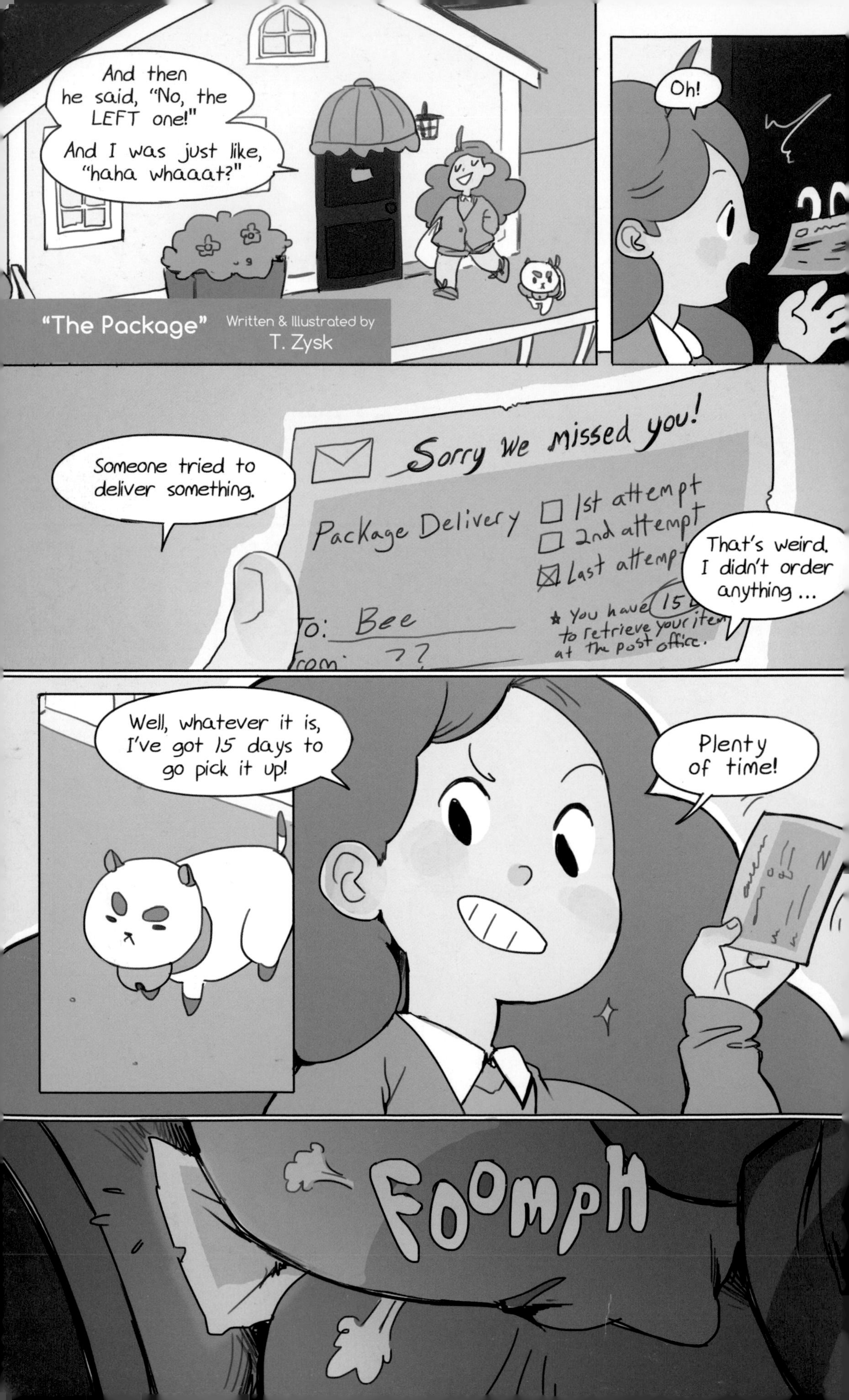
And then he said, "No, the LEFT one!"
And I was just like, "haha whaaat?"
"The Package" Written & Illustrated by T. Zysk
Oh!
Someone tried to deliver something.
Sorry we missed you!
Package Delivery
1st attempt
2nd attempt
Last attempt
To: Bee
From: ??
at the post office.
That's weird. I didn't order anything ...
Well, whatever it is, I've got 15 days to go pick it up!
Plenty of time!
FOOMPH

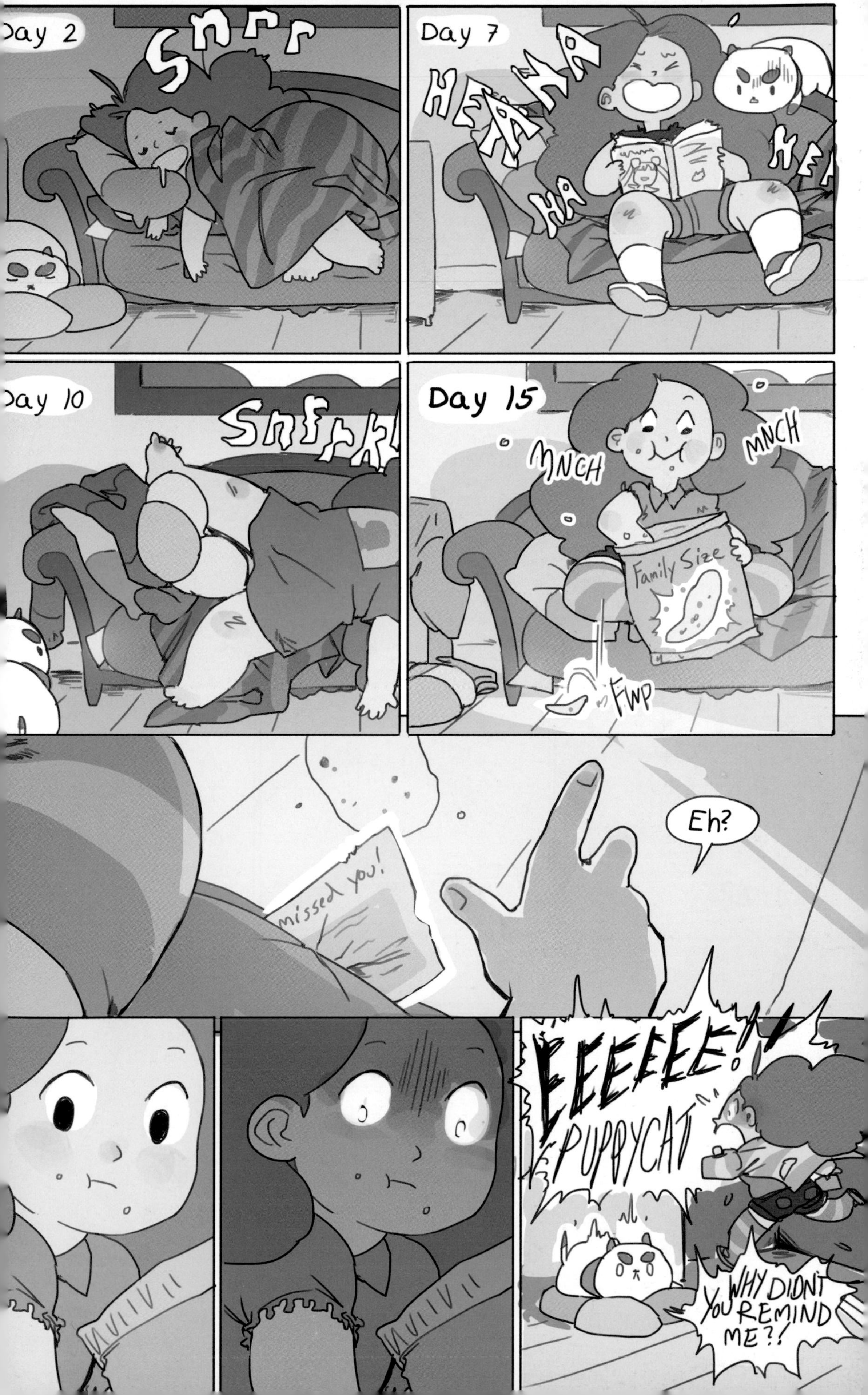
Day 2
SNRR
Day 7
HEHAHA
HA
HEH
Day 10
SNFRKL
Day 15
MNCH
MNCH
Family Size
FWP
missed you!
Eh?
EEEEE!
PUPPYCAT
WHY DIDN'T YOU REMIND ME?!

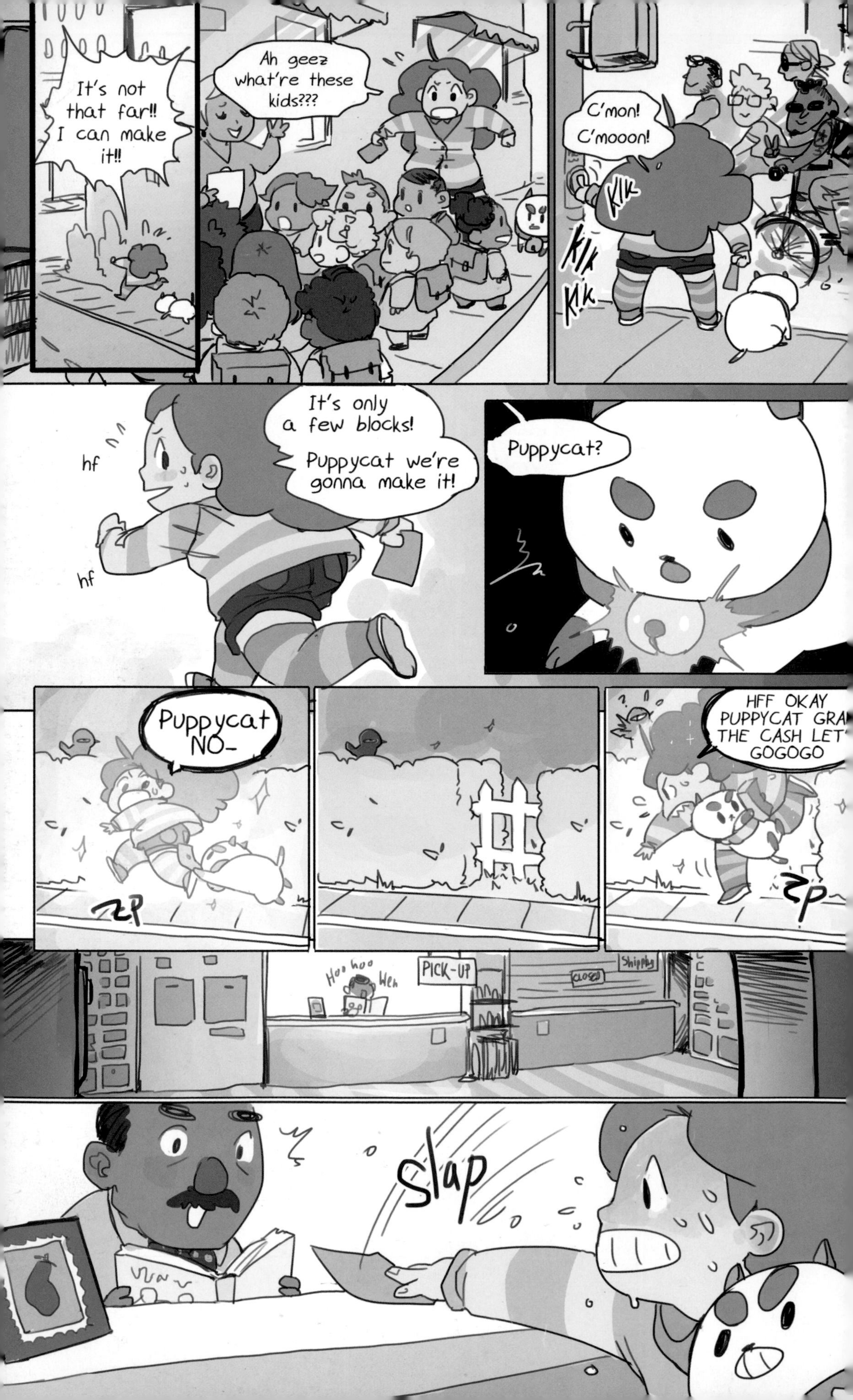

It's not that far!! I can make it!!
Ah geez what're these kids???
C'mon! C'mooon!
KIK
KIK
KIK
hf
It's only a few blocks!
Puppycat we're gonna make it!
hf
Puppycat?
Puppycat NO-
ZP
HFF OKAY PUPPYCAT GRA THE CASH LET GOGOGO
ZP
PICK-UP
CLOSED
Slap

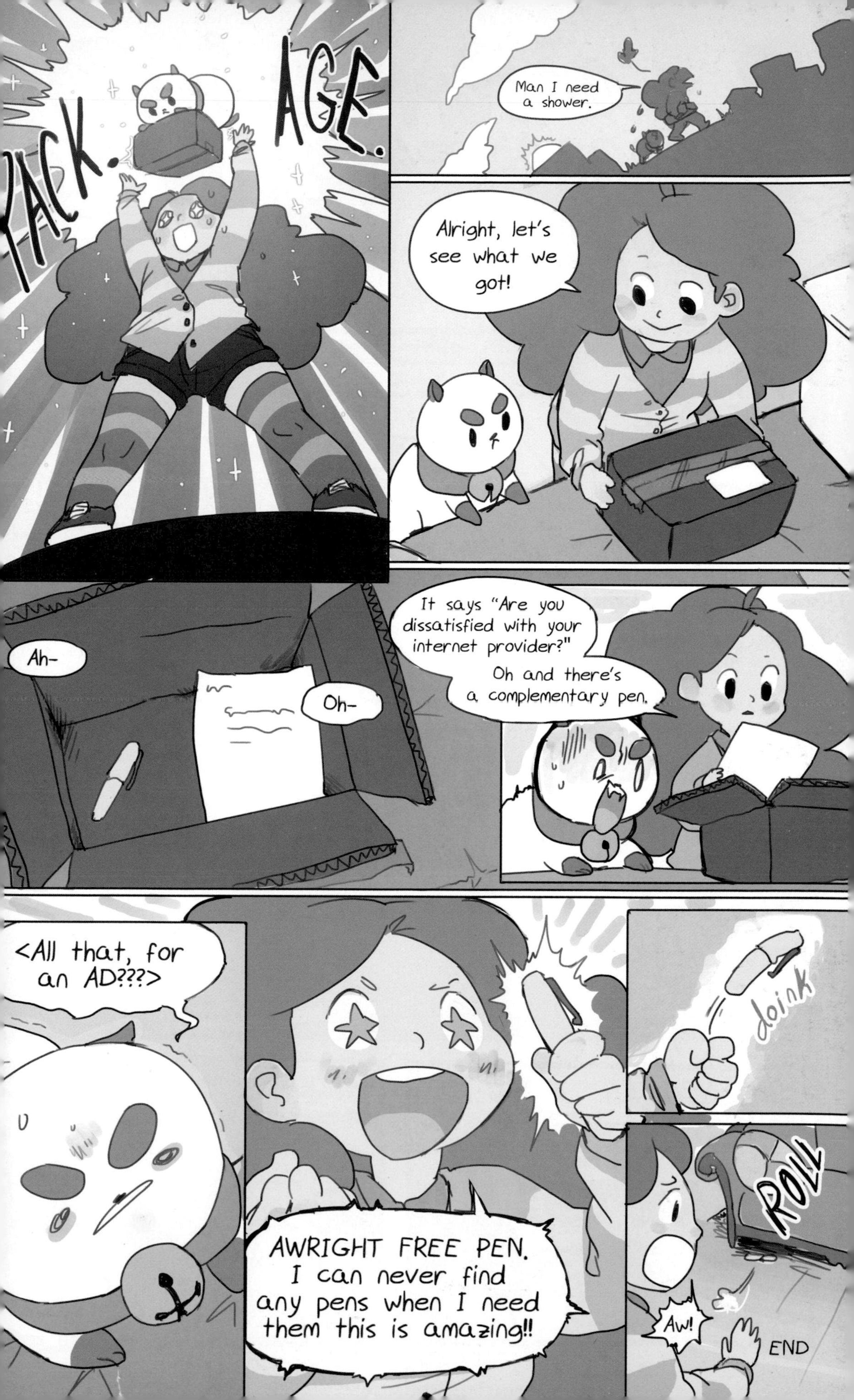
YACK. AGE.
Man I need a shower.
Alright, let's see what we got!
Ah-
Oh-
It says "Are you dissatisfied with your internet provider?"
Oh and there's a complementary pen.
<All that, for an AD???>
AWRIGHT FREE PEN. I can never find any pens when I need them this is amazing!!
doink
ROLL
Aw!
END

Bee n' Puppycat in PLANTSAPALOOZA

~ BY MAD RUPERT ~ COLORS BY WHITNEY COGAR

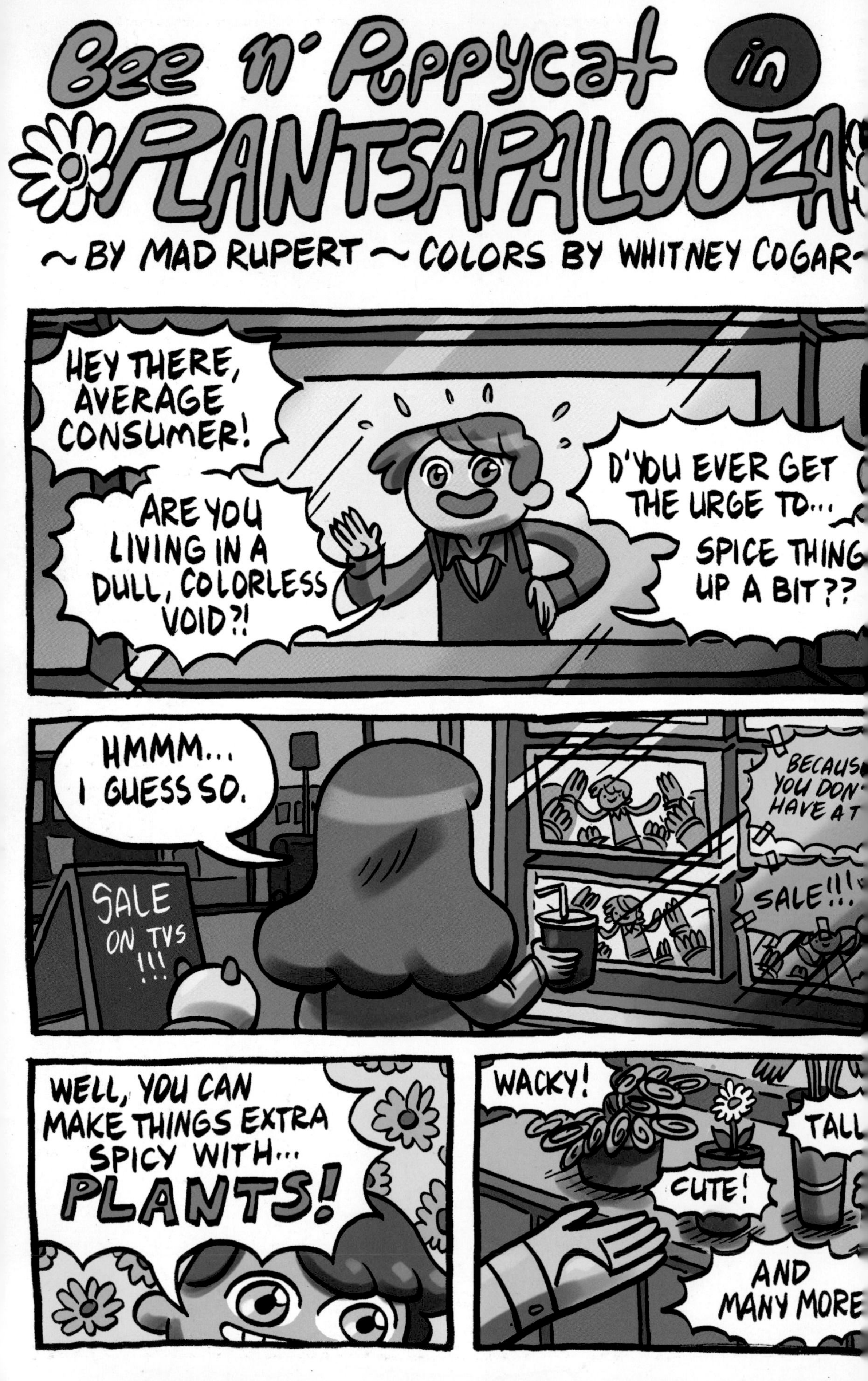

HEY THERE, AVERAGE CONSUMER!
ARE YOU LIVING IN A DULL, COLORLESS VOID?!
D'YOU EVER GET THE URGE TO...
SPICE THING UP A BIT??
HMMM... I GUESS SO.
SALE ON TVS !!!
BECAUS YOU DON HAVE A T
SALE!!!
WELL, YOU CAN MAKE THINGS EXTRA SPICY WITH... PLANTS!
WACKY!
CUTE!
TALL
AND MANY MORE

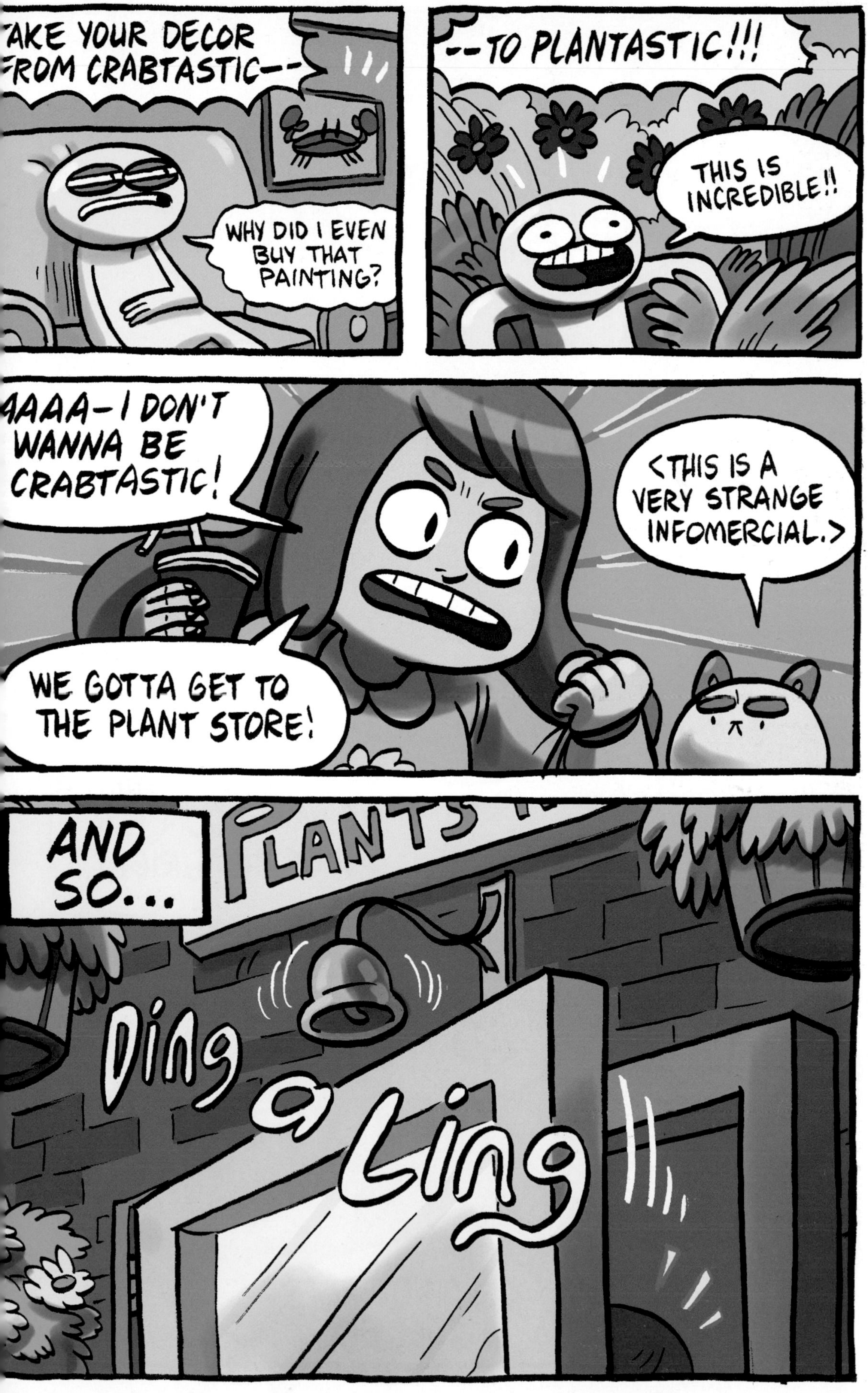
AKE YOUR DECOR FROM CRABTASTIC--
WHY DID I EVEN BUY THAT PAINTING?
--TO PLANTASTIC!!!
THIS IS INCREDIBLE!!
AAAA-I DON'T WANNA BE CRABTASTIC!
<THIS IS A VERY STRANGE INFOMERCIAL.>
WE GOTTA GET TO THE PLANT STORE!
AND SO...
PLANTS
Ding a Ling

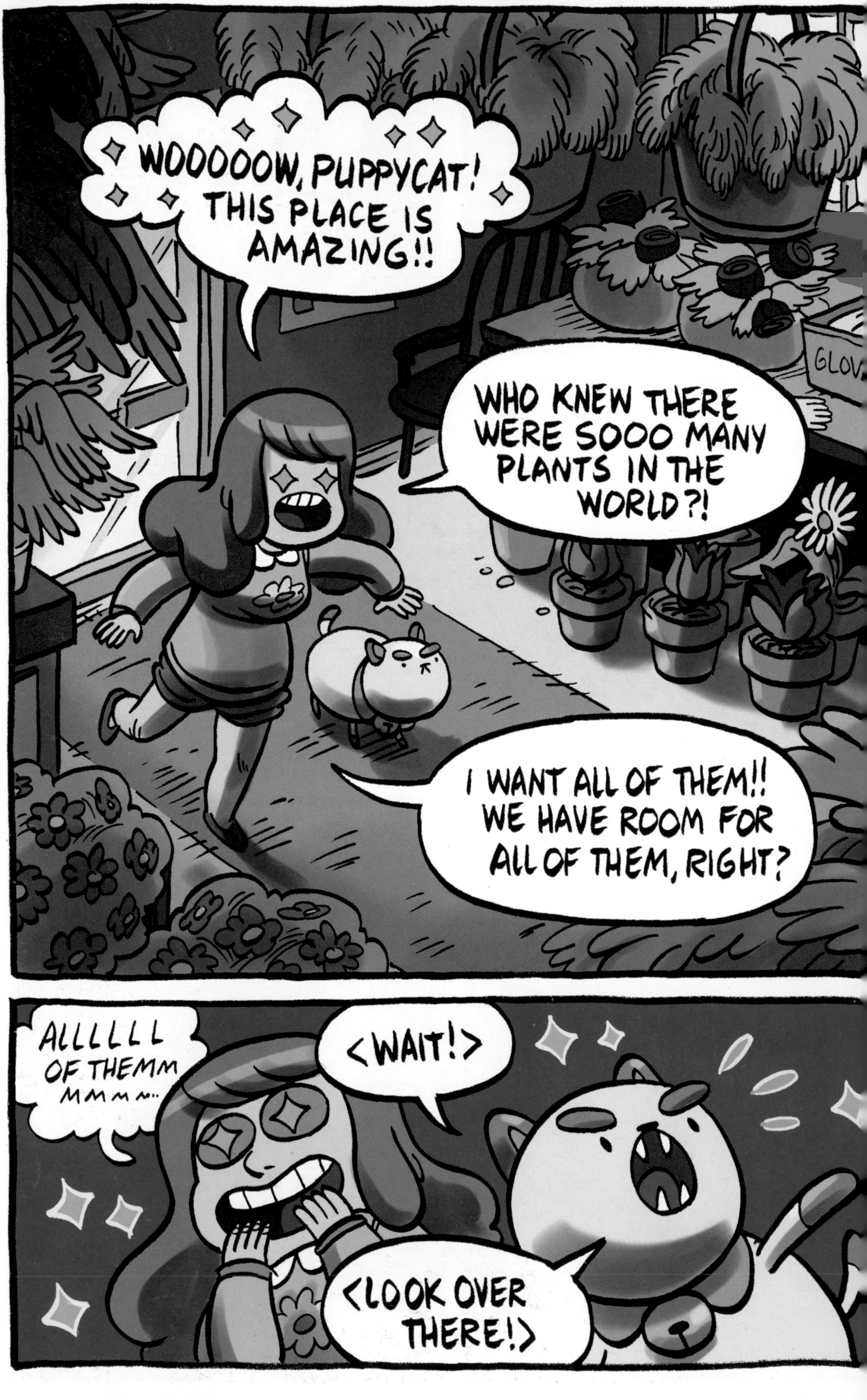
WOOOOOW, PUPPYCAT! THIS PLACE IS AMAZING!!
WHO KNEW THERE WERE SOOO MANY PLANTS IN THE WORLD?!
I WANT ALL OF THEM!! WE HAVE ROOM FOR ALL OF THEM, RIGHT?
ALLLLLL OF THEMM MMMM...
<WAIT!>
<LOOK OVER THERE!>

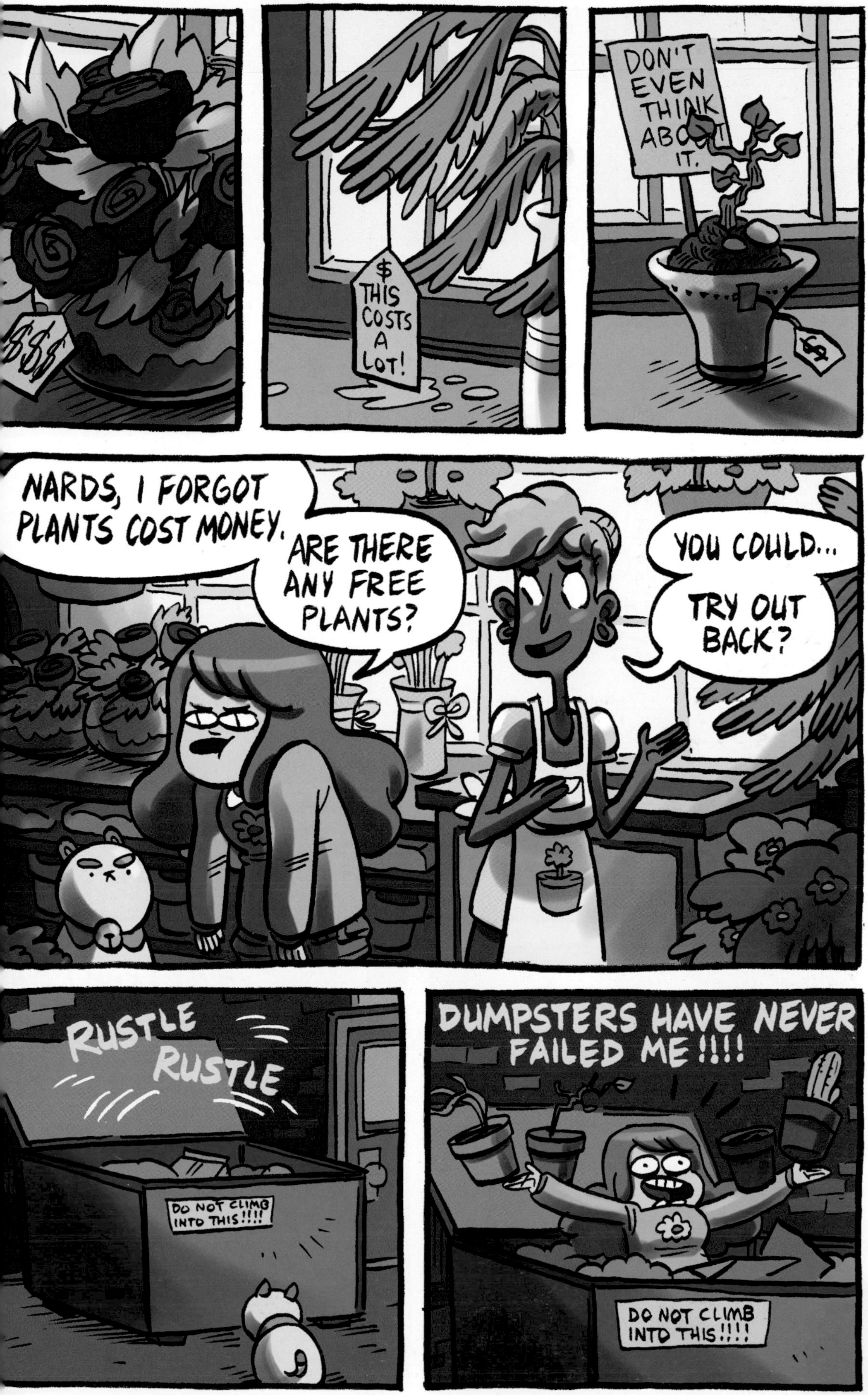

$$$
$
THIS
COSTS
A
LOT!
DON'T
EVEN
THINK
ABOUT
IT.
$
NARDS, I FORGOT PLANTS COST MONEY.
ARE THERE ANY FREE PLANTS?
YOU COULD...
TRY OUT BACK?
RUSTLE
RUSTLE
DO NOT CLIMB INTO THIS!!!!
DUMPSTERS HAVE NEVER FAILED ME!!!!
DO NOT CLIMB INTO THIS!!!!

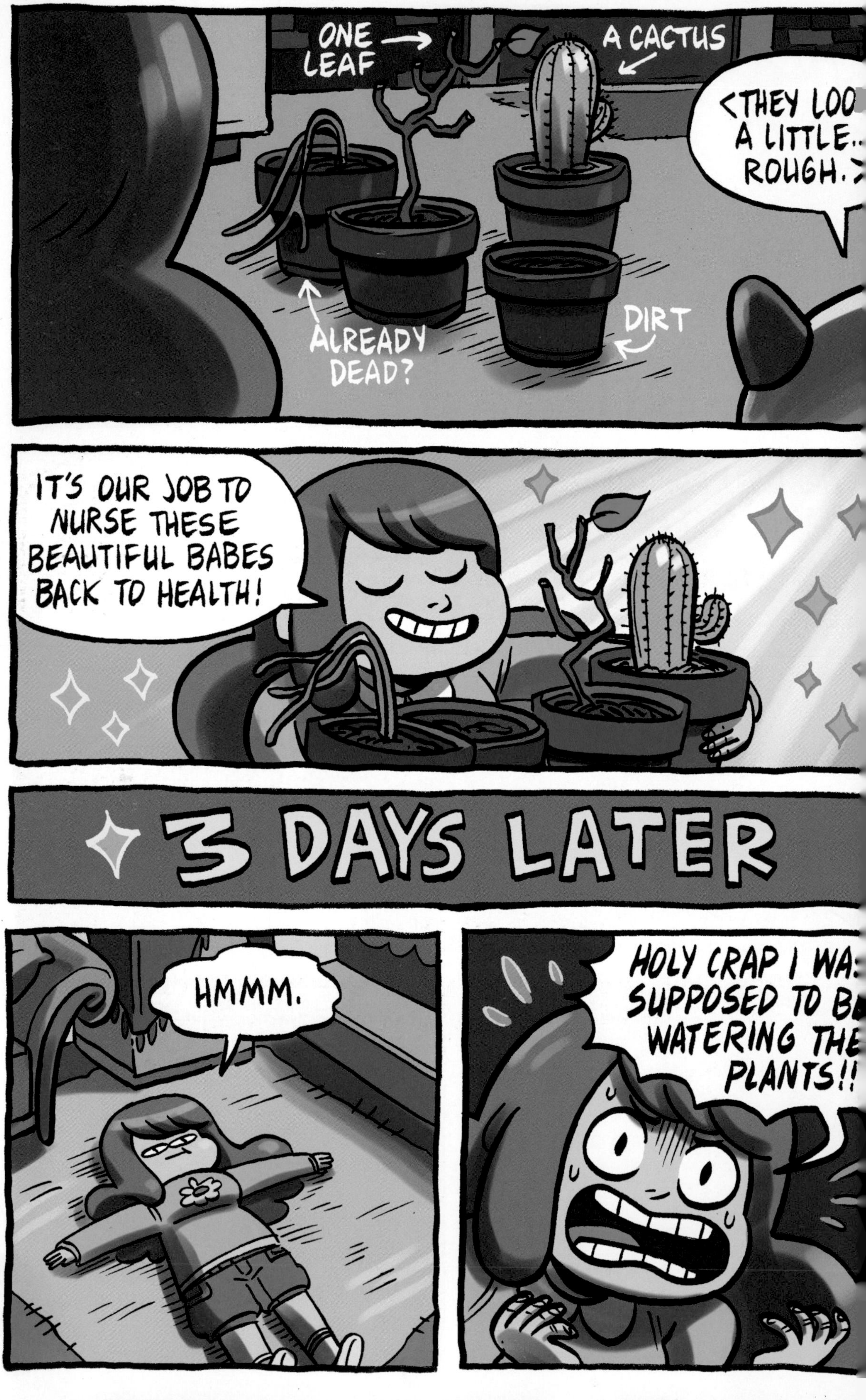
ONE LEAF
A CACTUS
<THEY LOO A LITTLE.. ROUGH.>
ALREADY DEAD?
DIRT
IT'S OUR JOB TO NURSE THESE BEAUTIFUL BABES BACK TO HEALTH!
3 DAYS LATER
HMMM.
HOLY CRAP I WA SUPPOSED TO B WATERING THE PLANTS!!

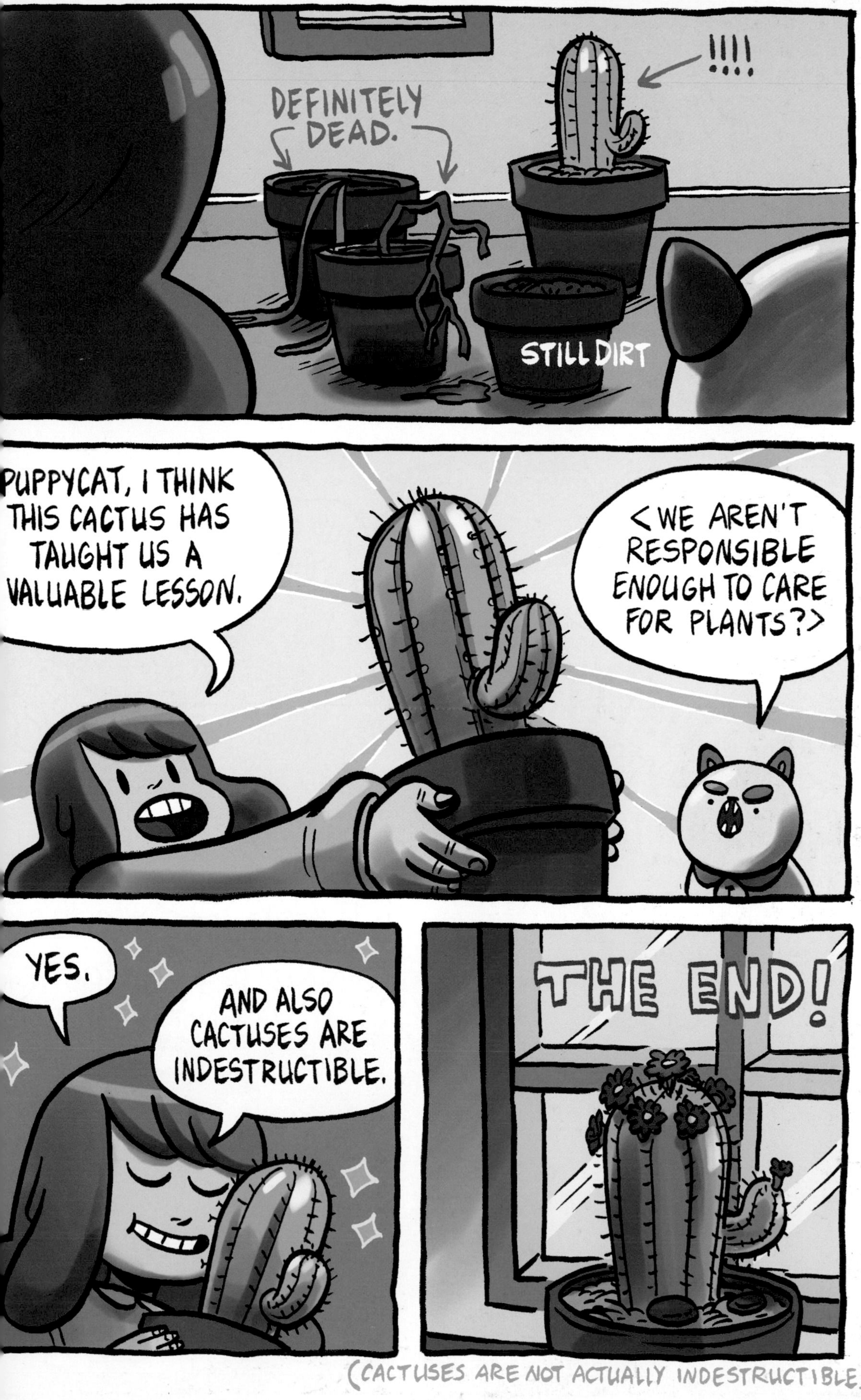
DEFINITELY DEAD.
!!!!
STILL DIRT
PUPPYCAT, I THINK THIS CACTUS HAS TAUGHT US A VALUABLE LESSON.
<WE AREN'T RESPONSIBLE ENOUGH TO CARE FOR PLANTS?>
YES.
AND ALSO CACTUSES ARE INDESTRUCTIBLE.
THE END!

(CACTUSES ARE NOT ACTUALLY INDESTRUCTIBLE)

"Play The Game!" *Written & Illustrated by* Coleman Engle

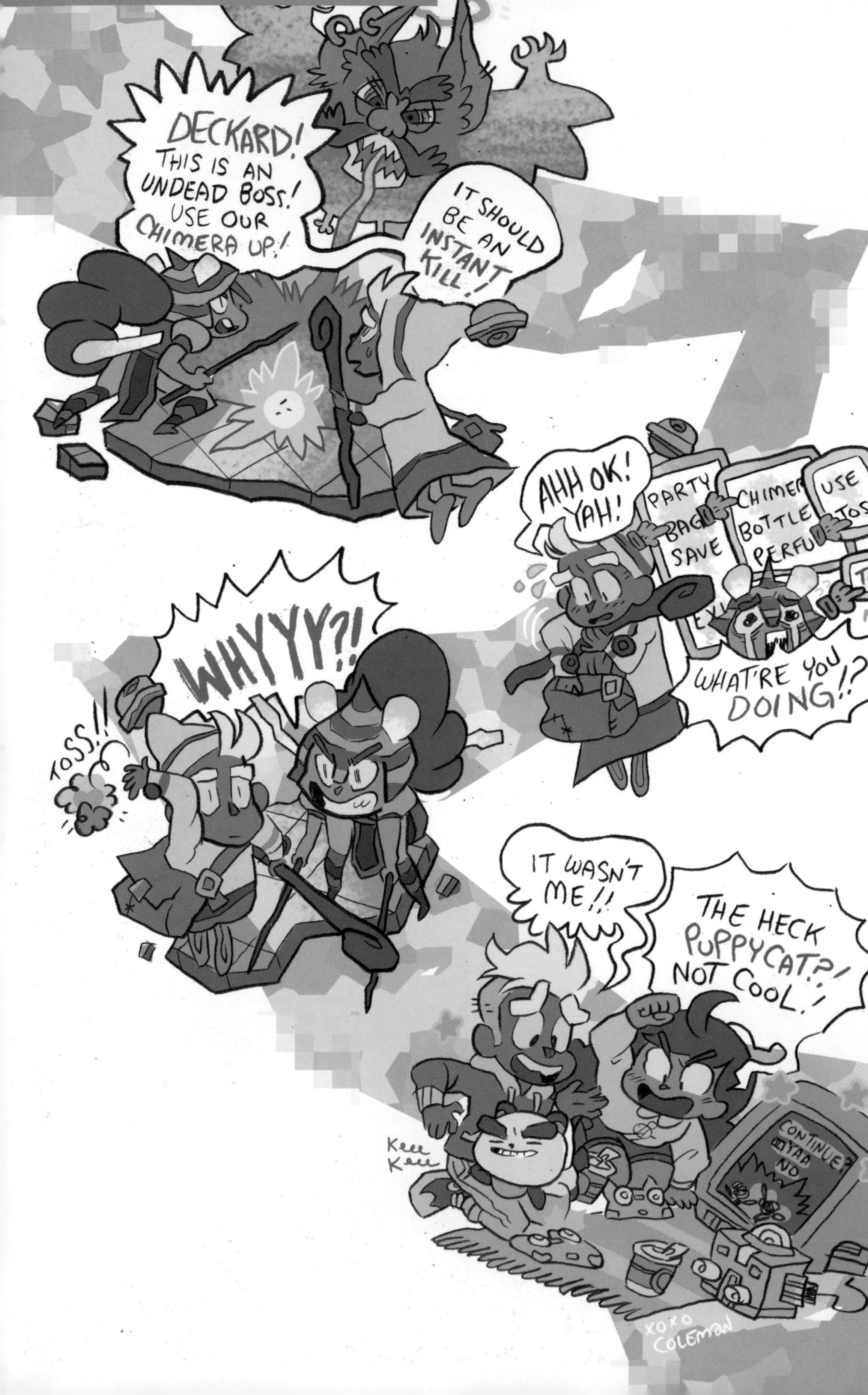

DECKARD! THIS IS AN UNDEAD BOSS! USE OUR CHIMERA UP!
IT SHOULD BE AN INSTANT KILL!
AHH OK! YAH!
PARTY
BAG
SAVE
CHIMER
BOTTLE
PERFU
USE
TOSS
TOS
WHAT'RE YOU DOING!?
WHYYY?!
TOSS!!
IT WASN'T ME!!
THE HECK PUPPYCAT?! NOT COOL!
Keee Keee
CONTINUE?
YAA
NO
XOXO COLEMAN

E

"The Perfect Sandwich"

Written & Illustrated by
Aimee Fleck

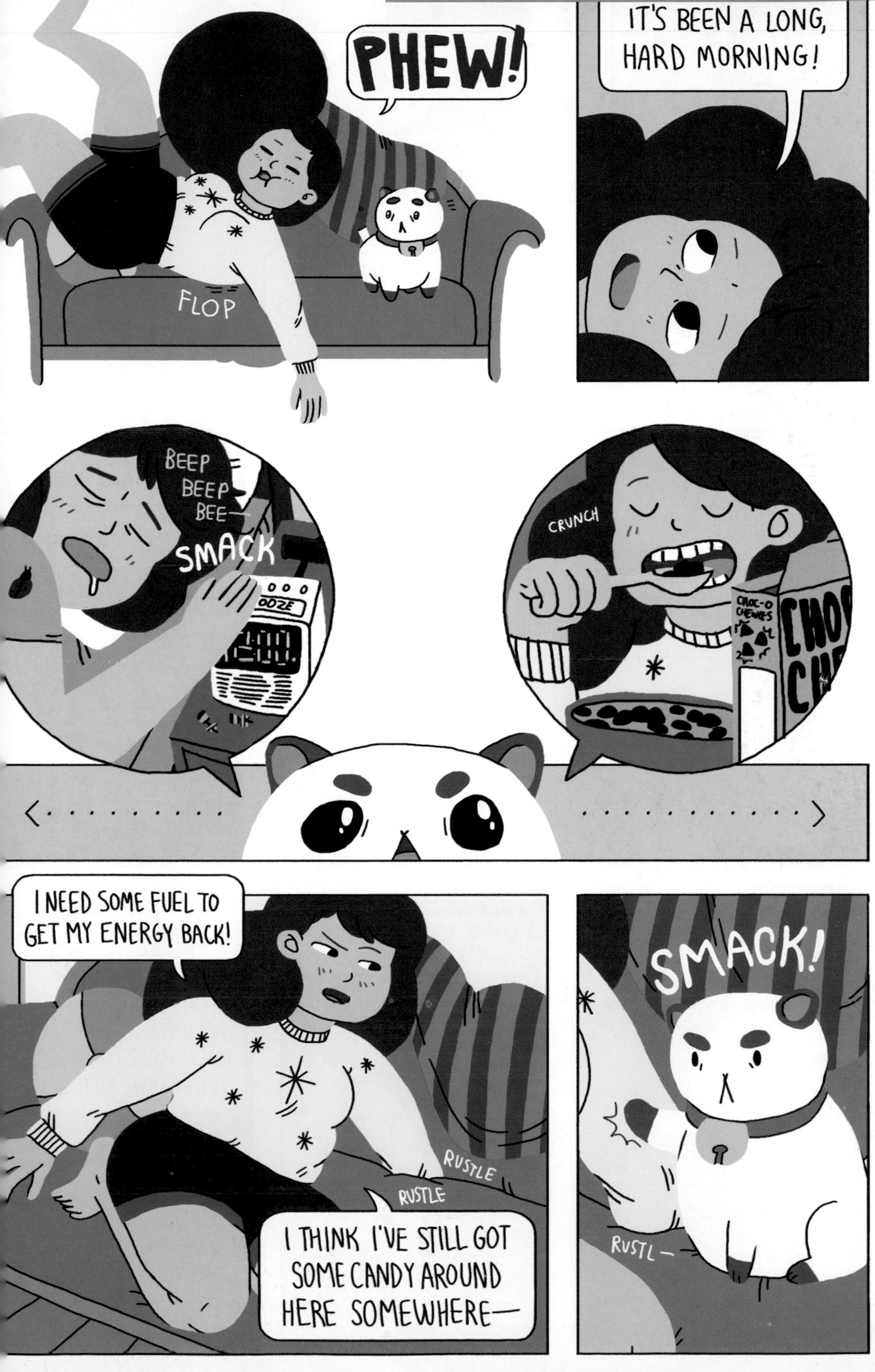
PHEW!
FLOP
IT'S BEEN A LONG, HARD MORNING!
BEEP
BEEP
BEE—
SMACK
CRUNCH
I NEED SOME FUEL TO GET MY ENERGY BACK!
RUSTLE
RUSTLE
I THINK I'VE STILL GOT SOME CANDY AROUND HERE SOMEWHERE—
SMACK!
RUSTL—

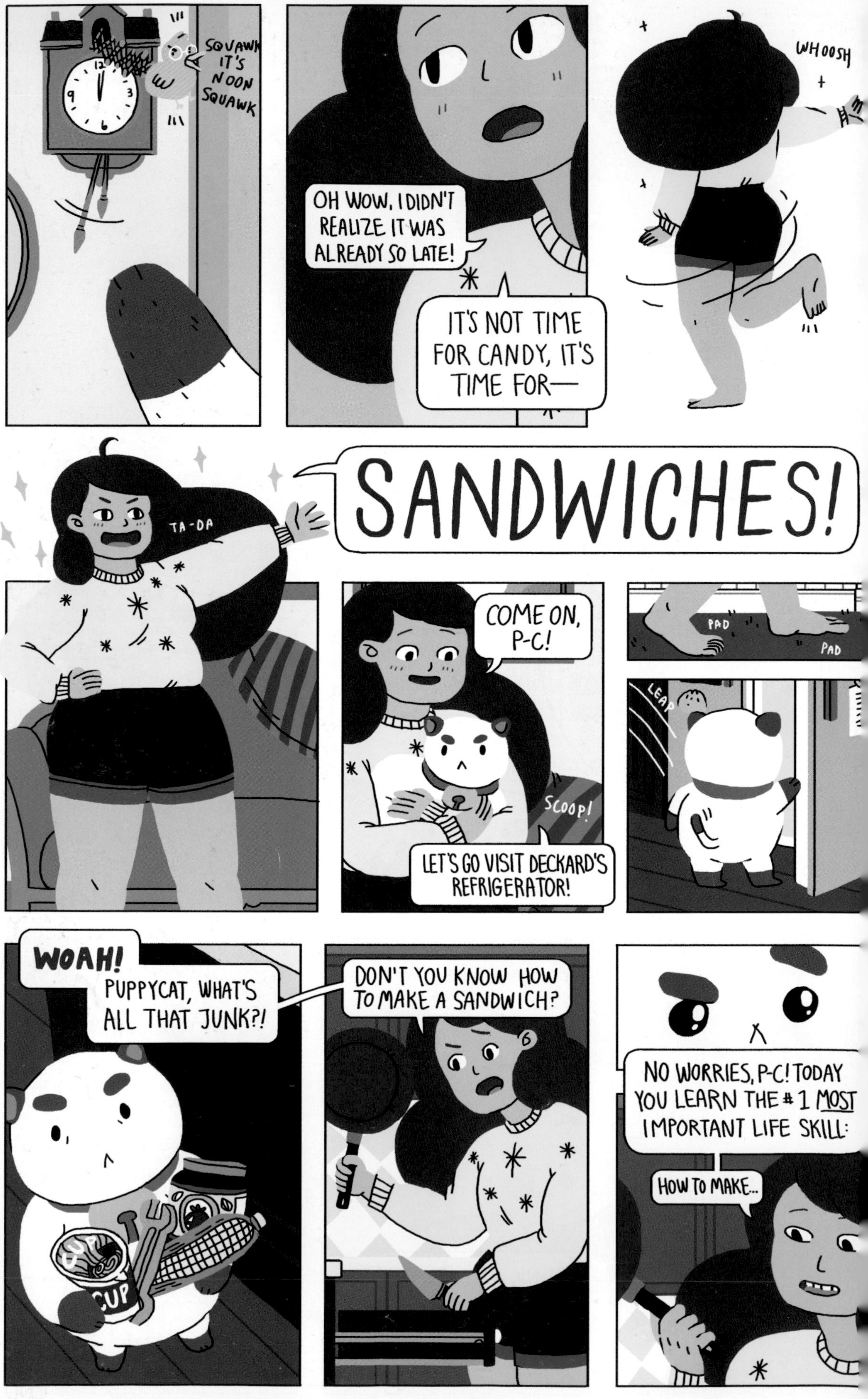
SQUAWK IT'S NOON SQUAWK
OH WOW, I DIDN'T REALIZE IT WAS ALREADY SO LATE!
IT'S NOT TIME FOR CANDY, IT'S TIME FOR—
WHOOSH
TA-DA
SANDWICHES!
COME ON, P-C!
SCOOP!
LET'S GO VISIT DECKARD'S REFRIGERATOR!
PAD
PAD
LEAP
WOAH!
PUPPYCAT, WHAT'S ALL THAT JUNK?!
CUP
DON'T YOU KNOW HOW TO MAKE A SANDWICH?
NO WORRIES, P-C! TODAY YOU LEARN THE # 1 MOST IMPORTANT LIFE SKILL:
HOW TO MAKE...

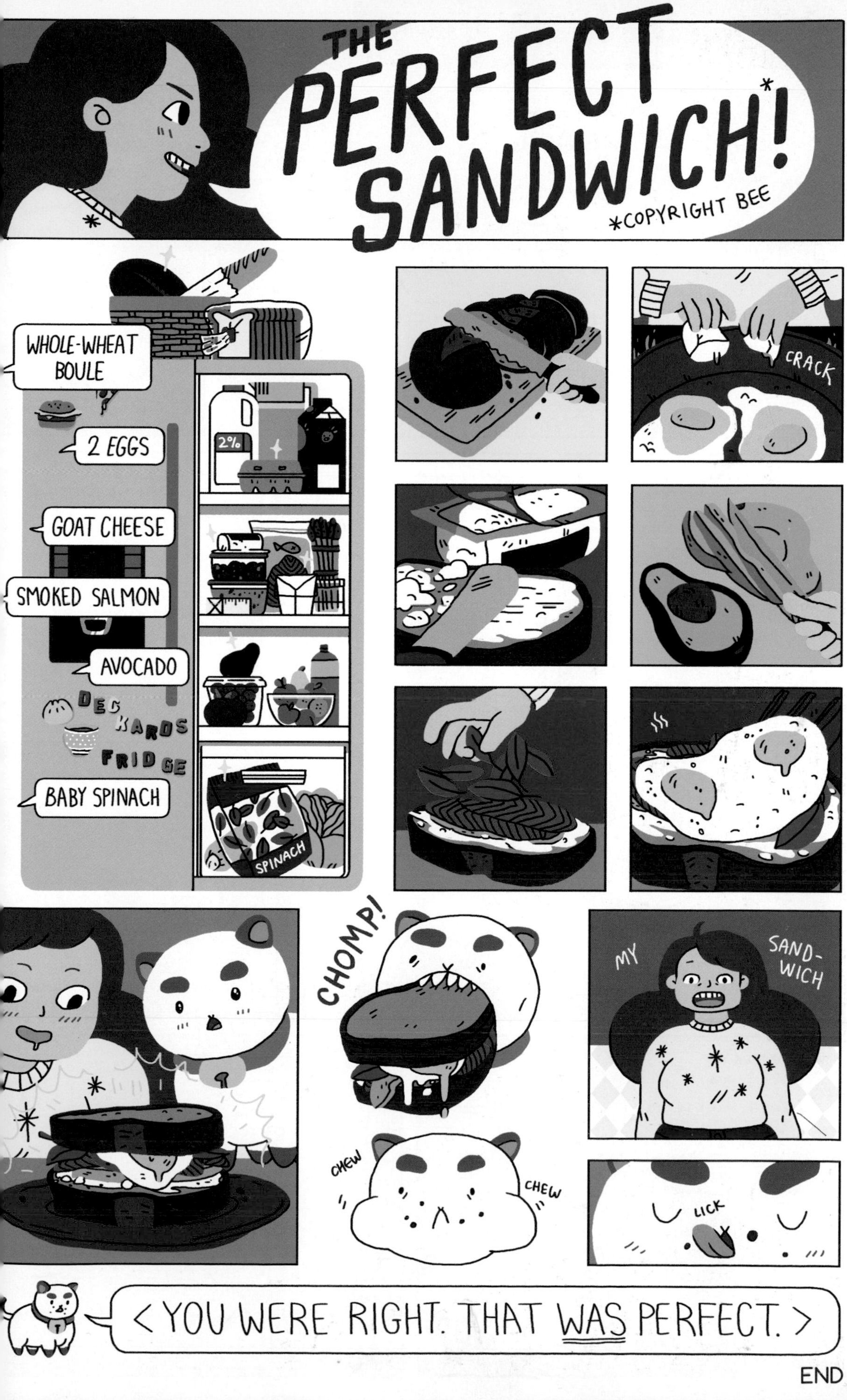
THE PERFECT SANDWICH!*
*COPYRIGHT BEE
WHOLE-WHEAT BOULE
2 EGGS
GOAT CHEESE
SMOKED SALMON
AVOCADO
DECKARDS FRIDGE
BABY SPINACH
2%
SPINACH
CRACK
CHOMP!
MY SANDWICH
CHEW
CHEW
LICK
< YOU WERE RIGHT. THAT WAS PERFECT. >
END

"Hungry"

Written & Illustrated by Pranas Naujokaitis
Colors by Whitney Cogar

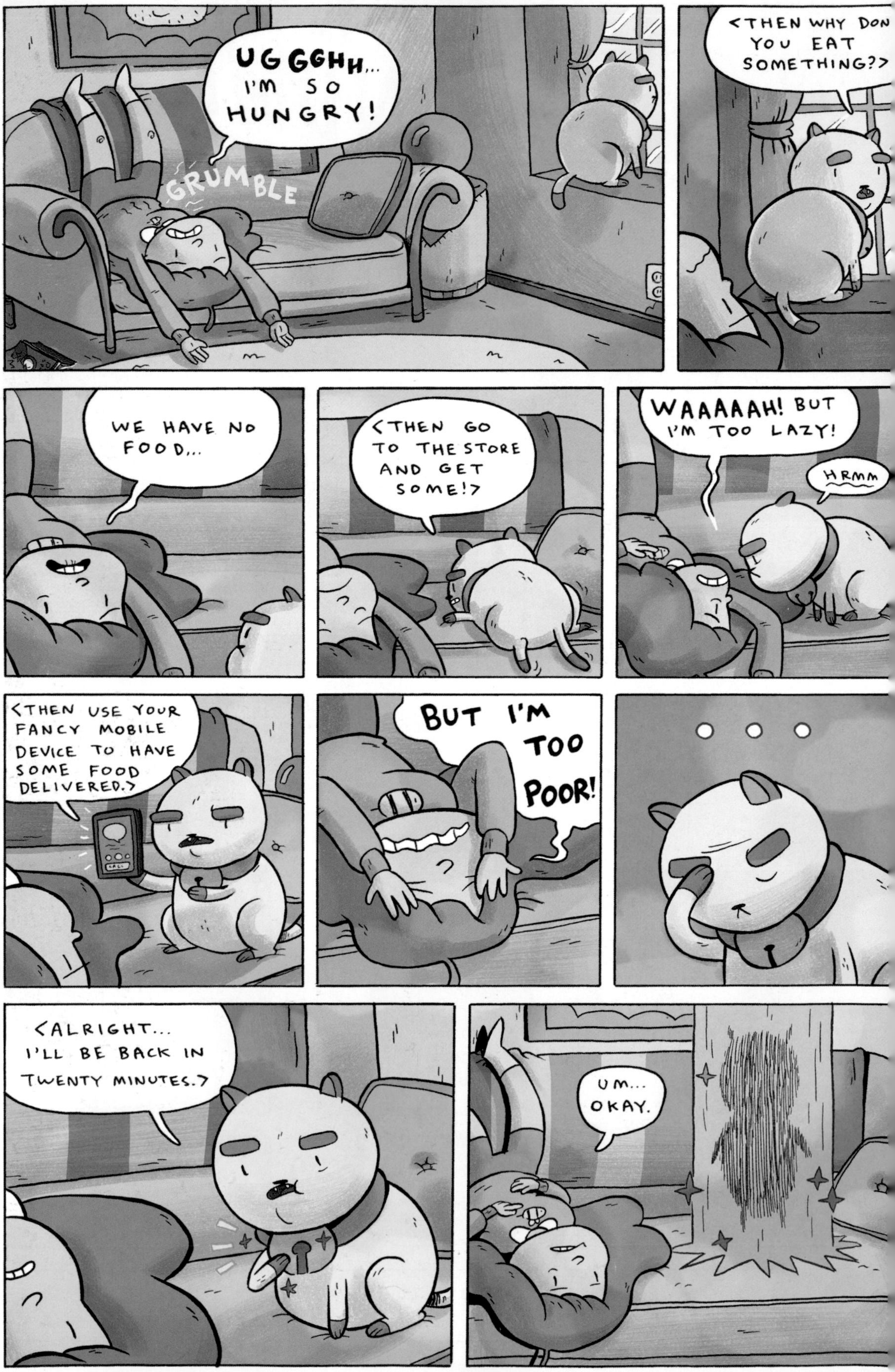
UGGGHH... I'M SO HUNGRY!
GRUMBLE
<THEN WHY DON YOU EAT SOMETHING?>
WE HAVE NO FOOD...
<THEN GO TO THE STORE AND GET SOME!>
WAAAAAH! BUT I'M TOO LAZY!
HRMM
<THEN USE YOUR FANCY MOBILE DEVICE TO HAVE SOME FOOD DELIVERED.>
BUT I'M TOO POOR!
<ALRIGHT... I'LL BE BACK IN TWENTY MINUTES.>
UM... OKAY.

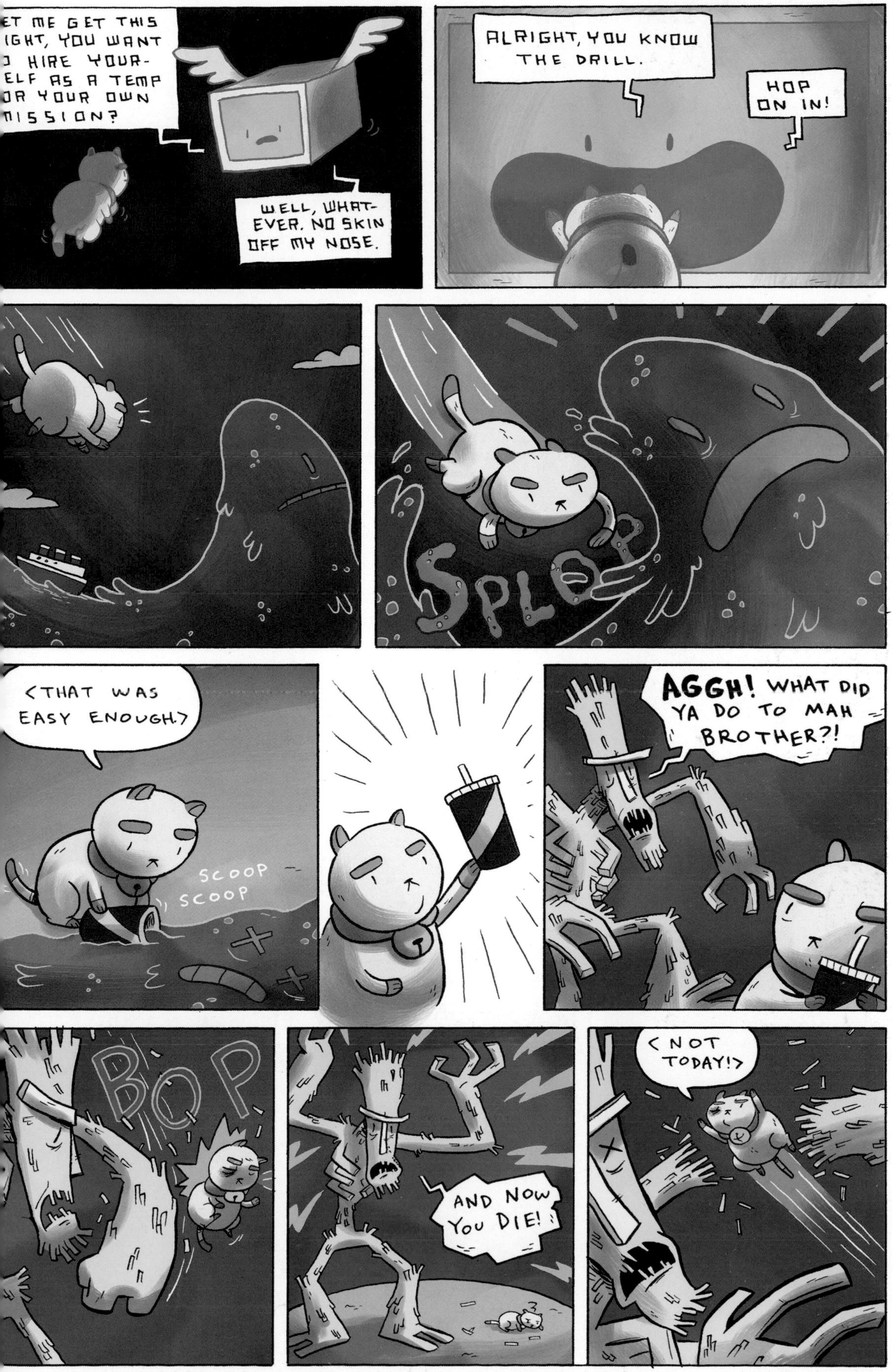
ET ME GET THIS IGHT, YOU WANT D HIRE YOUR-ELF AS A TEMP OR YOUR OWN MISSION?
WELL, WHAT-EVER. NO SKIN OFF MY NOSE.
ALRIGHT, YOU KNOW THE DRILL.
HOP ON IN!
SPLOP
<THAT WAS EASY ENOUGH.>
SCOOP SCOOP
AGGH! WHAT DID YA DO TO MAH BROTHER?!
BOP
AND NOW YOU DIE!
<NOT TODAY!>

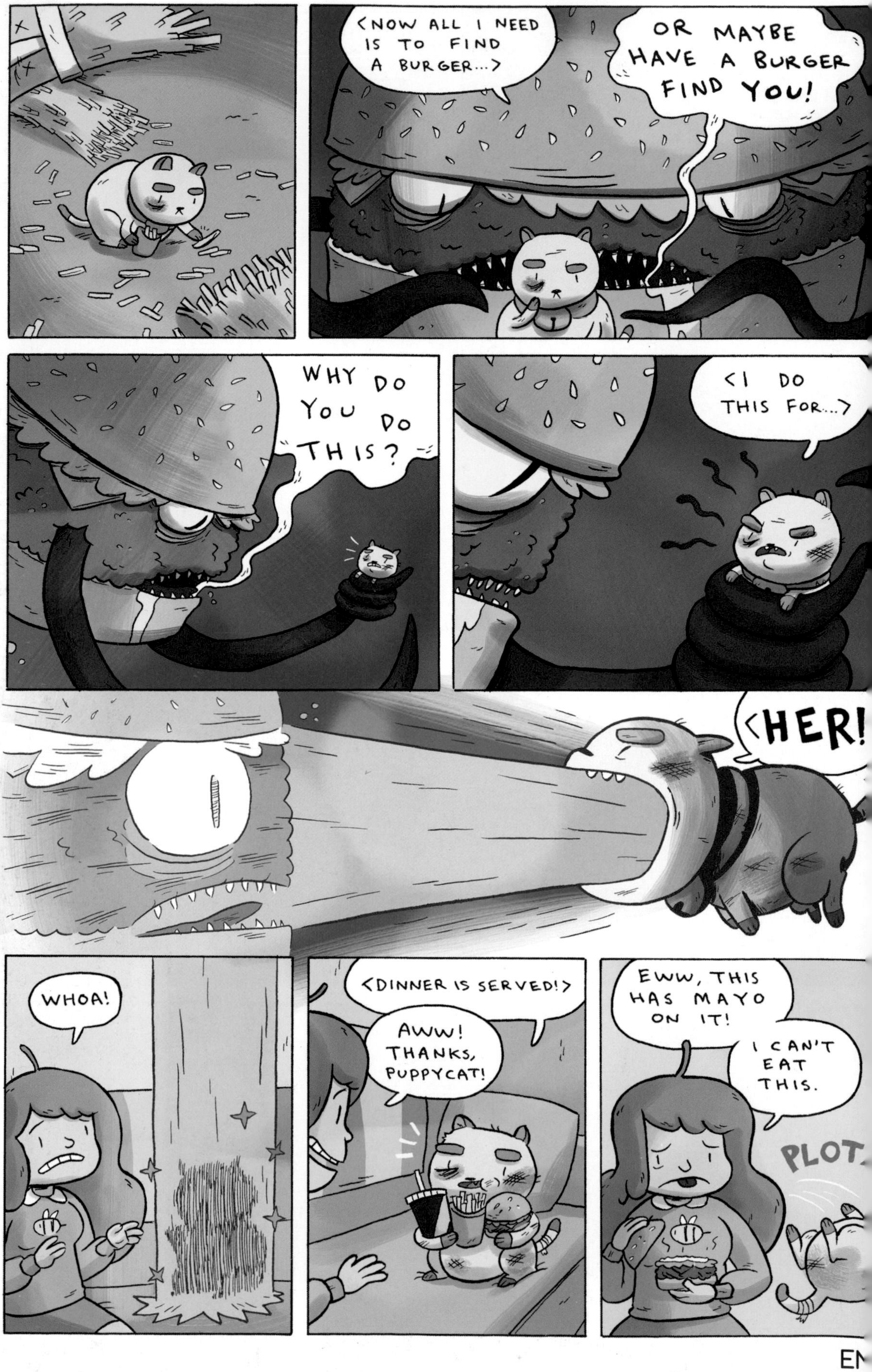
<NOW ALL I NEED IS TO FIND A BURGER...>
OR MAYBE HAVE A BURGER FIND YOU!
WHY DO YOU DO THIS?
<I DO THIS FOR...>
<HER!
WHOA!
<DINNER IS SERVED!>
AWW! THANKS, PUPPYCAT!
EWW, THIS HAS MAYO ON IT!
I CAN'T EAT THIS.
PLOT

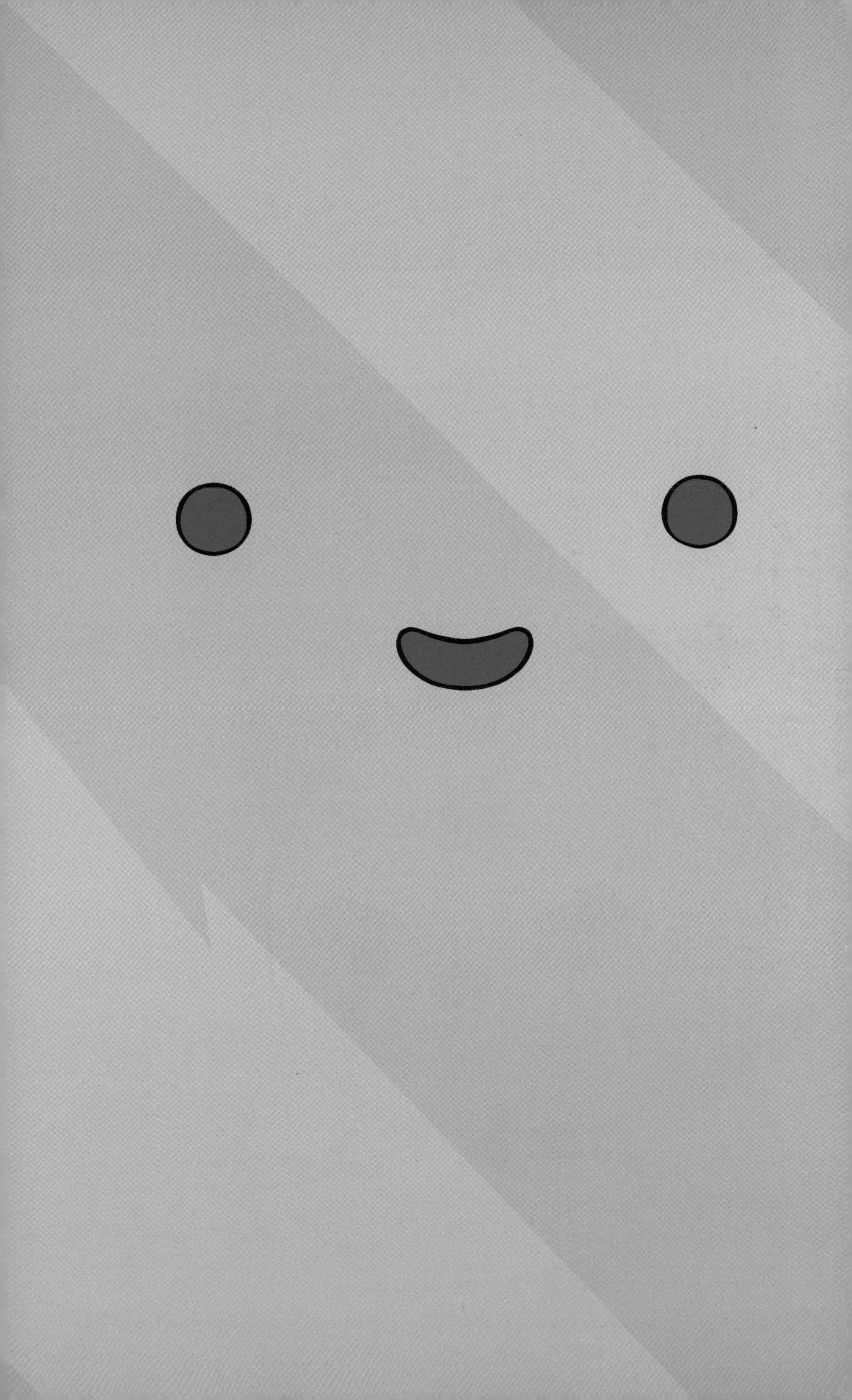

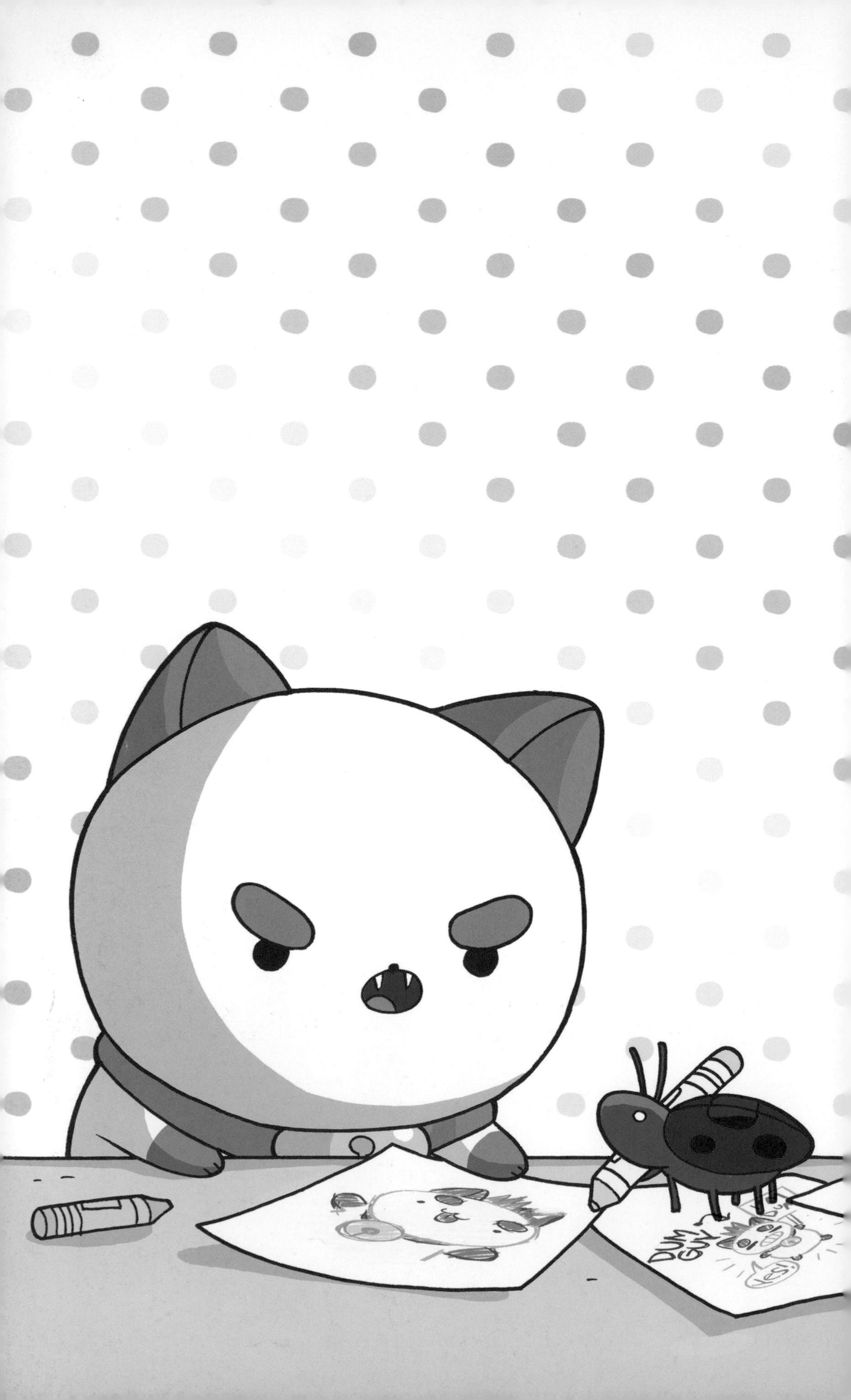
DUM GUY
Yes!

cover gallery

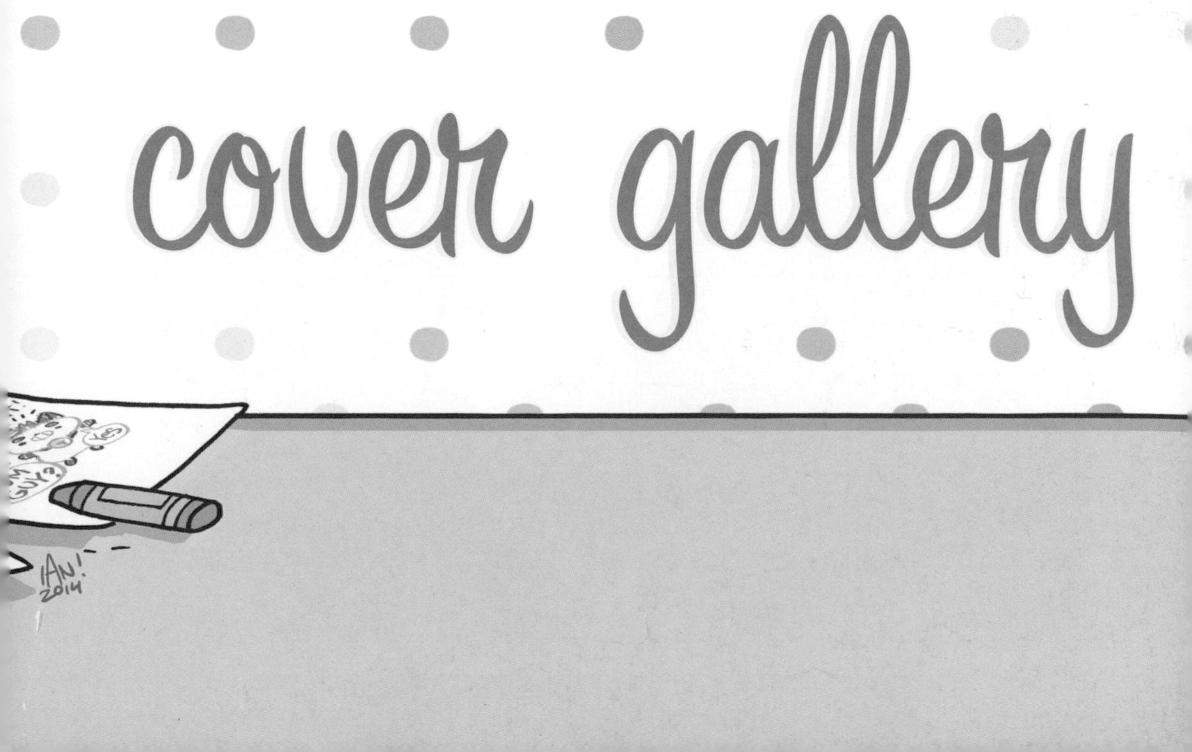
IAN!
2014

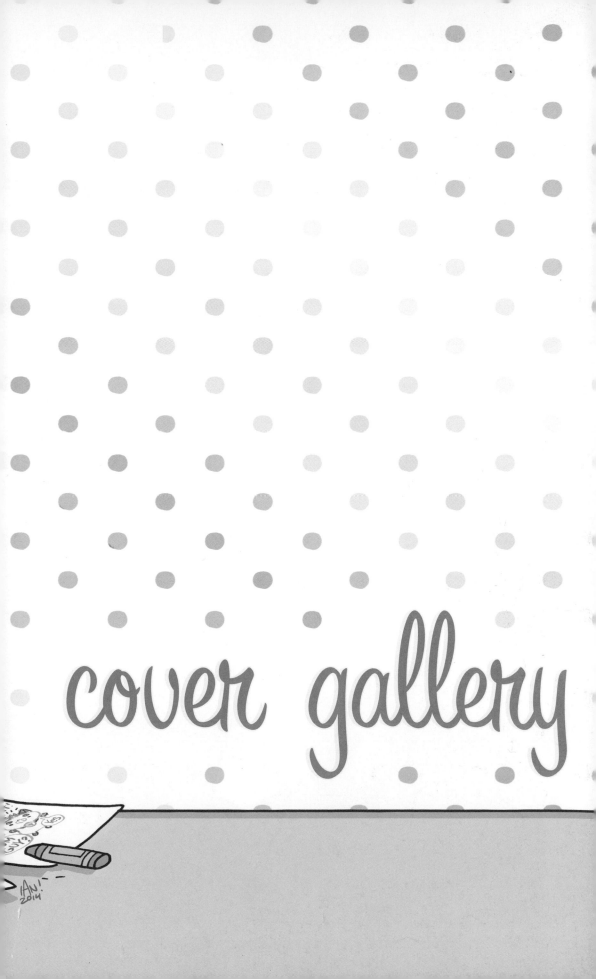

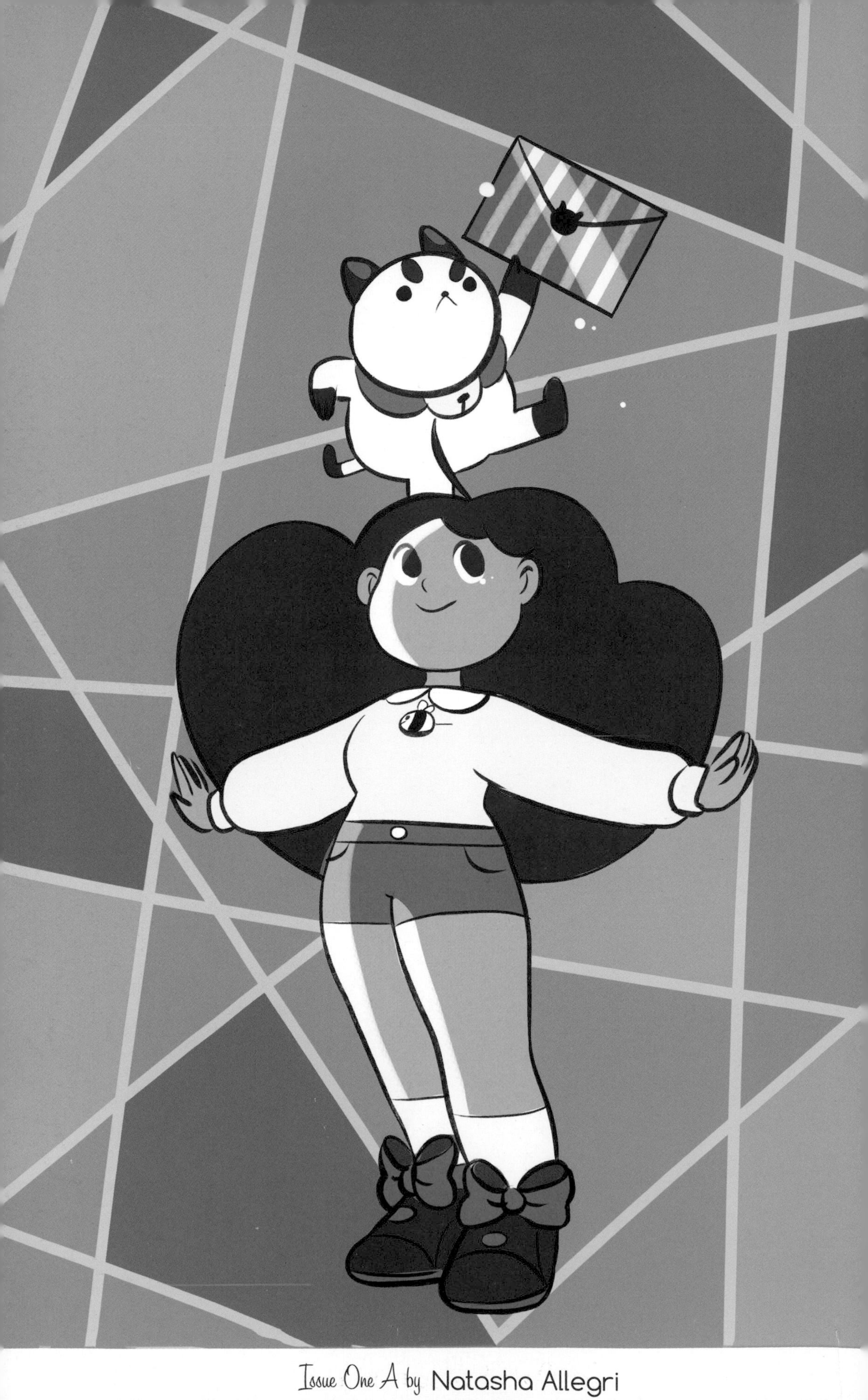

Issue One A by Natasha Allegri

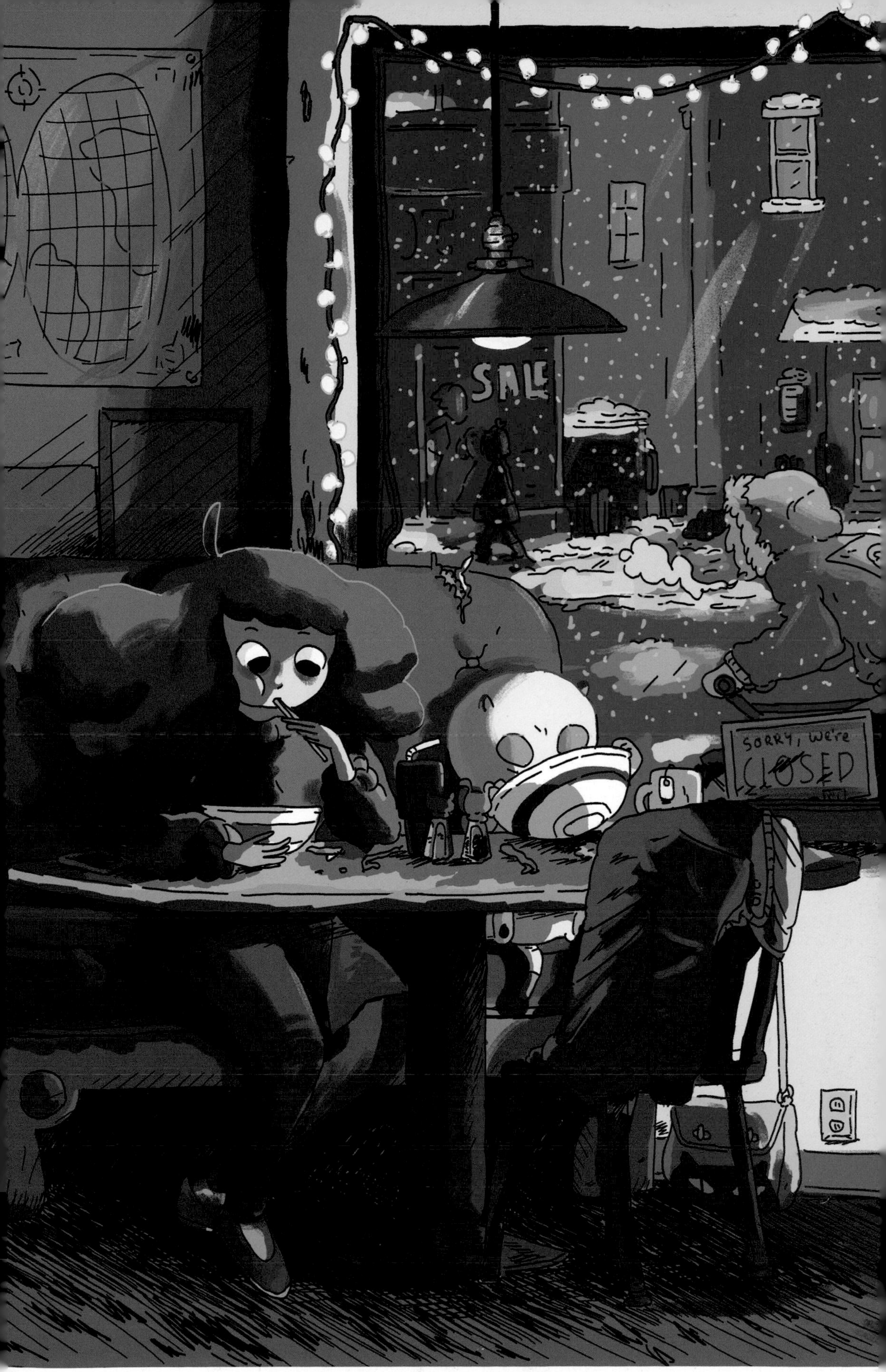
SALE
SORRY, We're
CLOSED

Issue One B by Zac Gorman

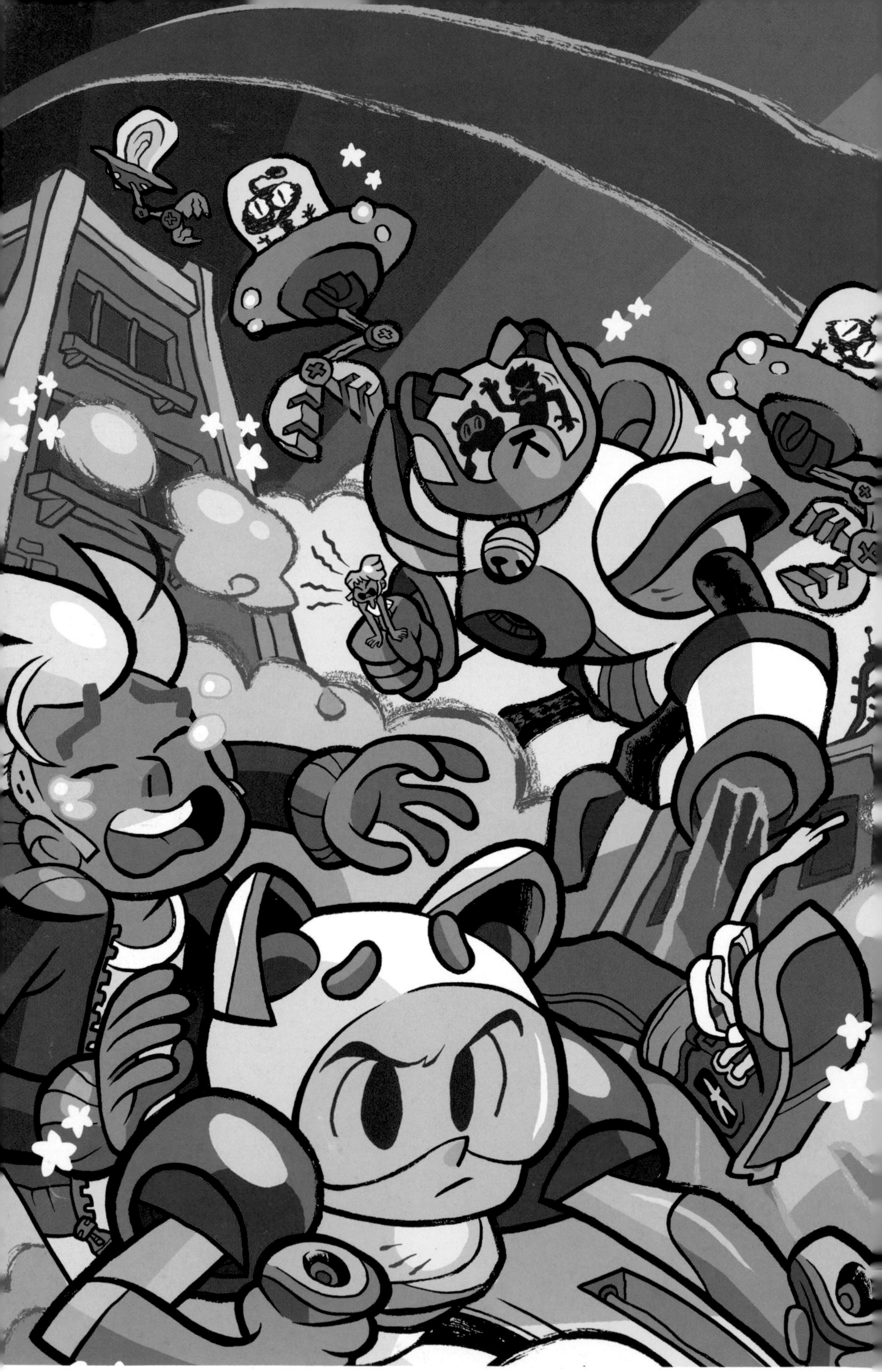

Issue One C by Coleman Engle

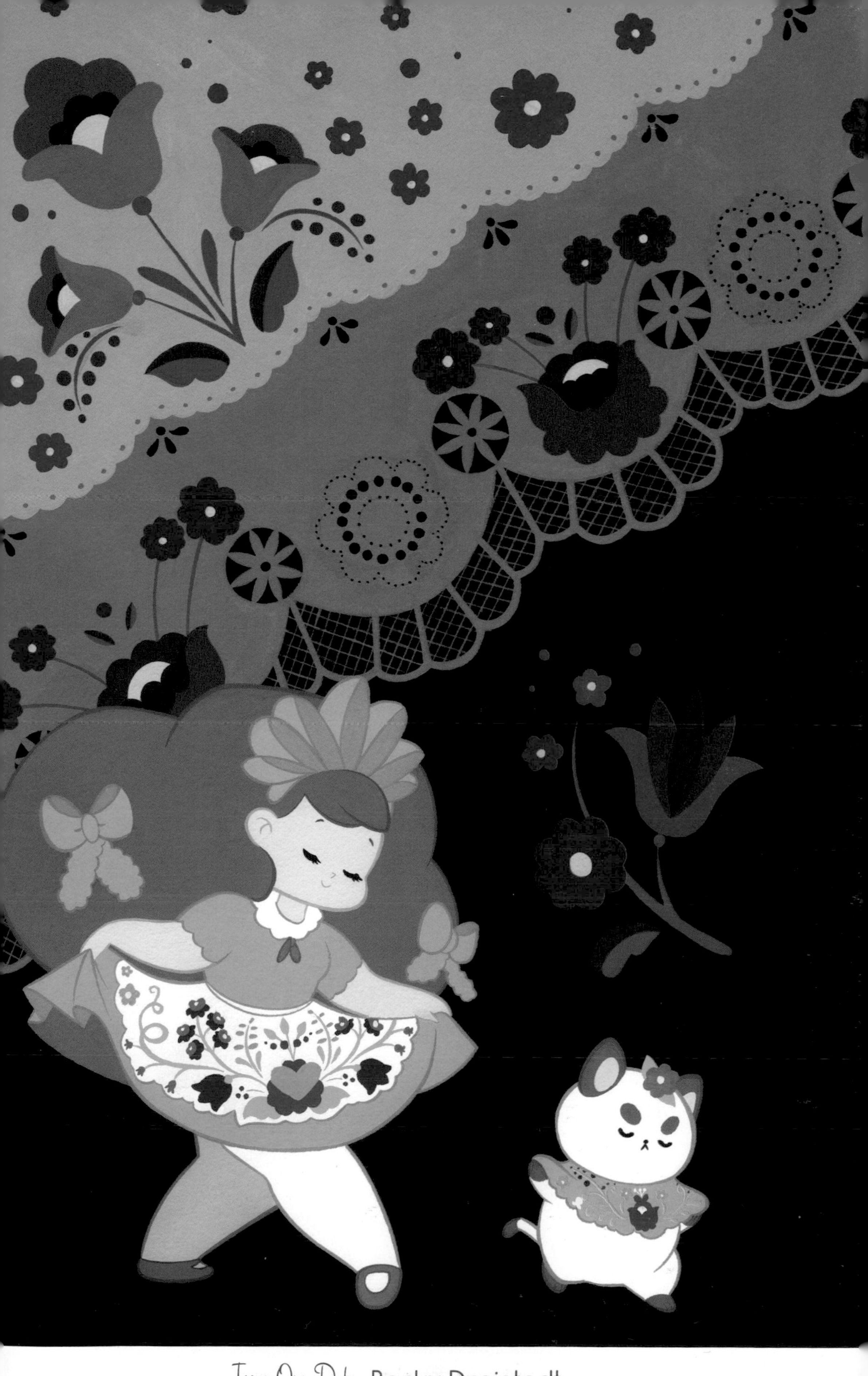

Issue One D by Becky Dreistadt

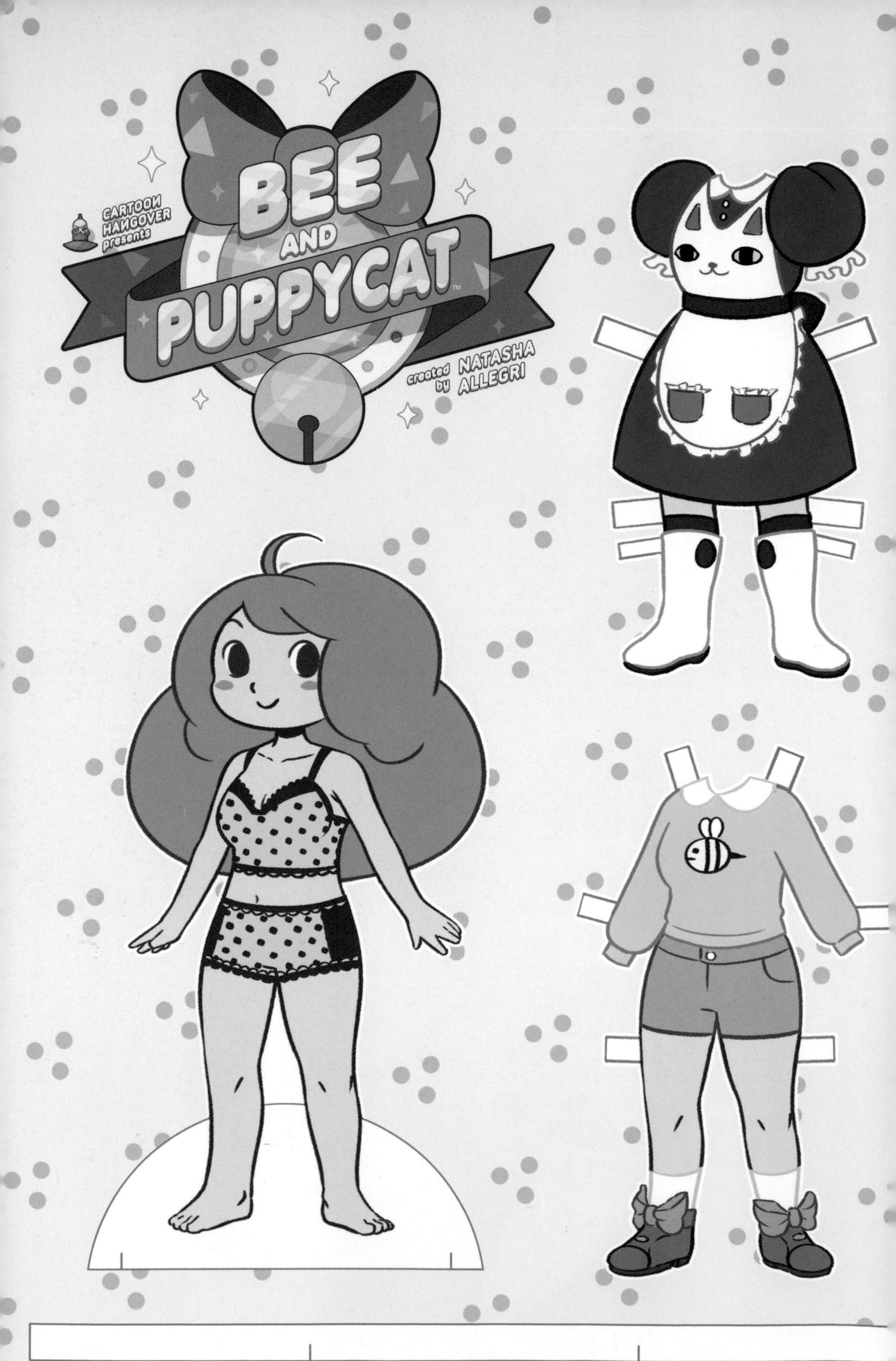
CARTOON HANGOVER presents
BEE AND PUPPYCAT
created by NATASHA ALLEGRI

Issue One Boom! Studios Exclusive by Stephanie Gonzaga

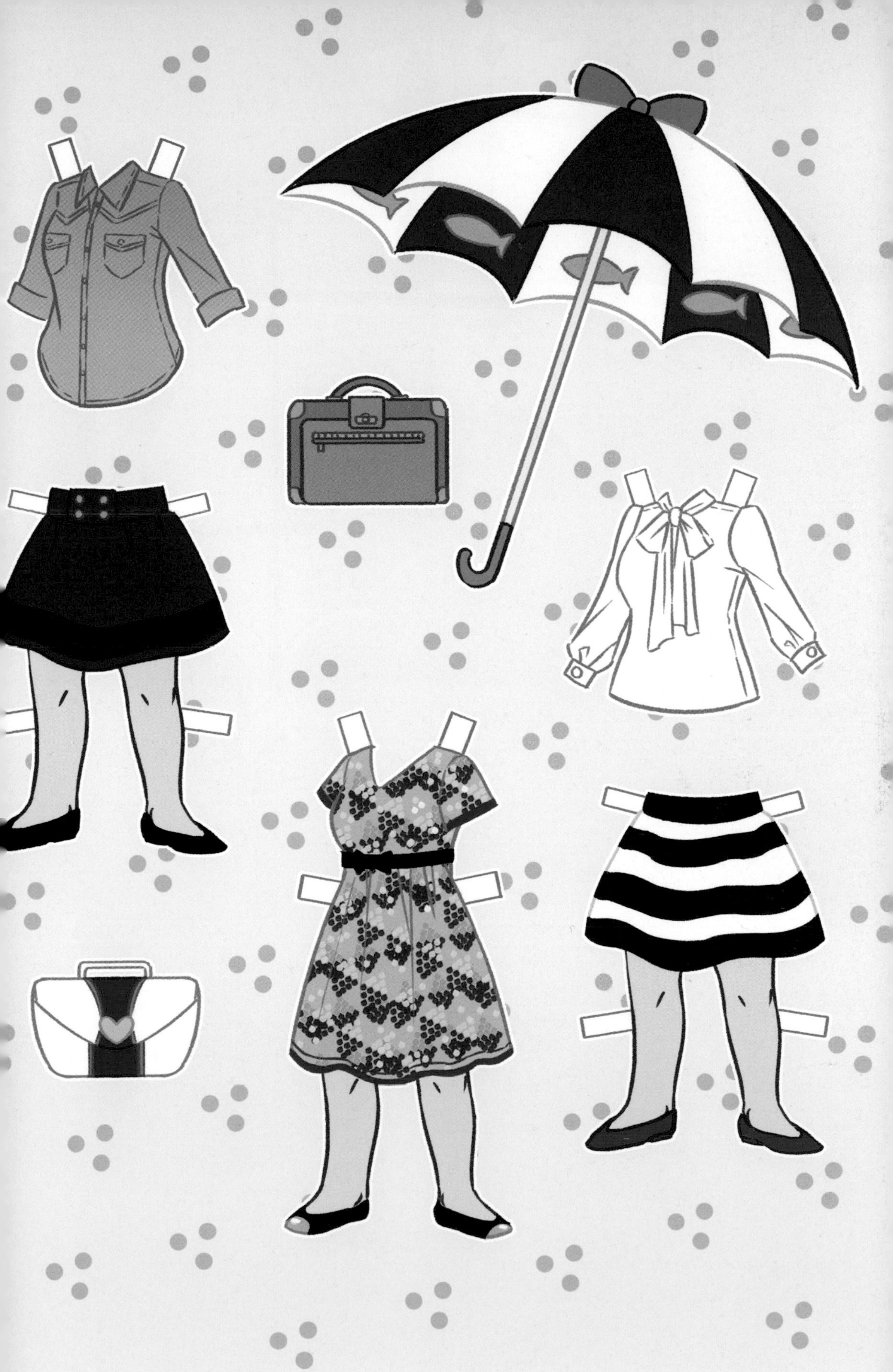

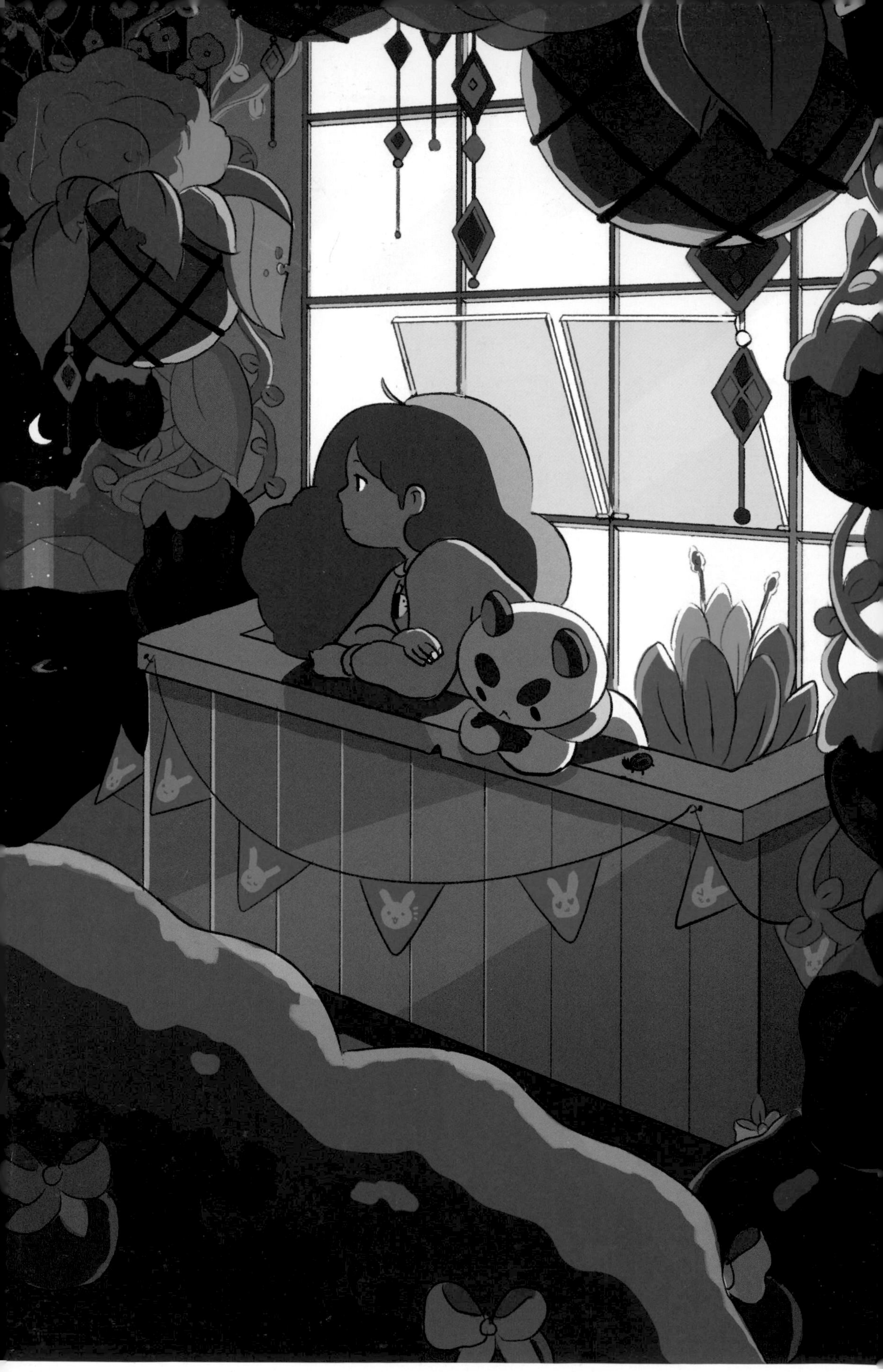

Issue One Kickstarter Exclusive by Natasha Allegri

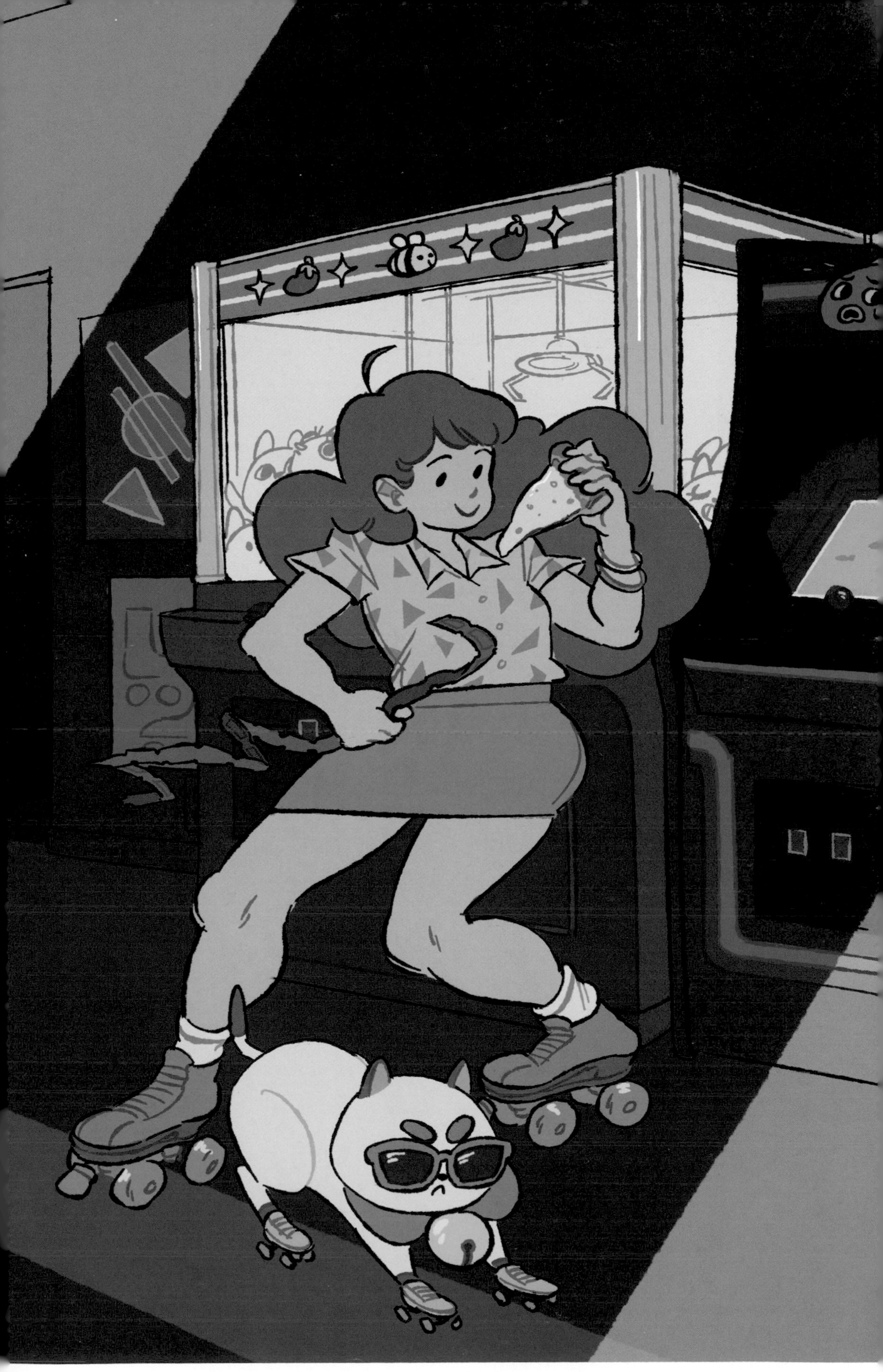

Issue One Challengers Exclusive by Trillian Gunn

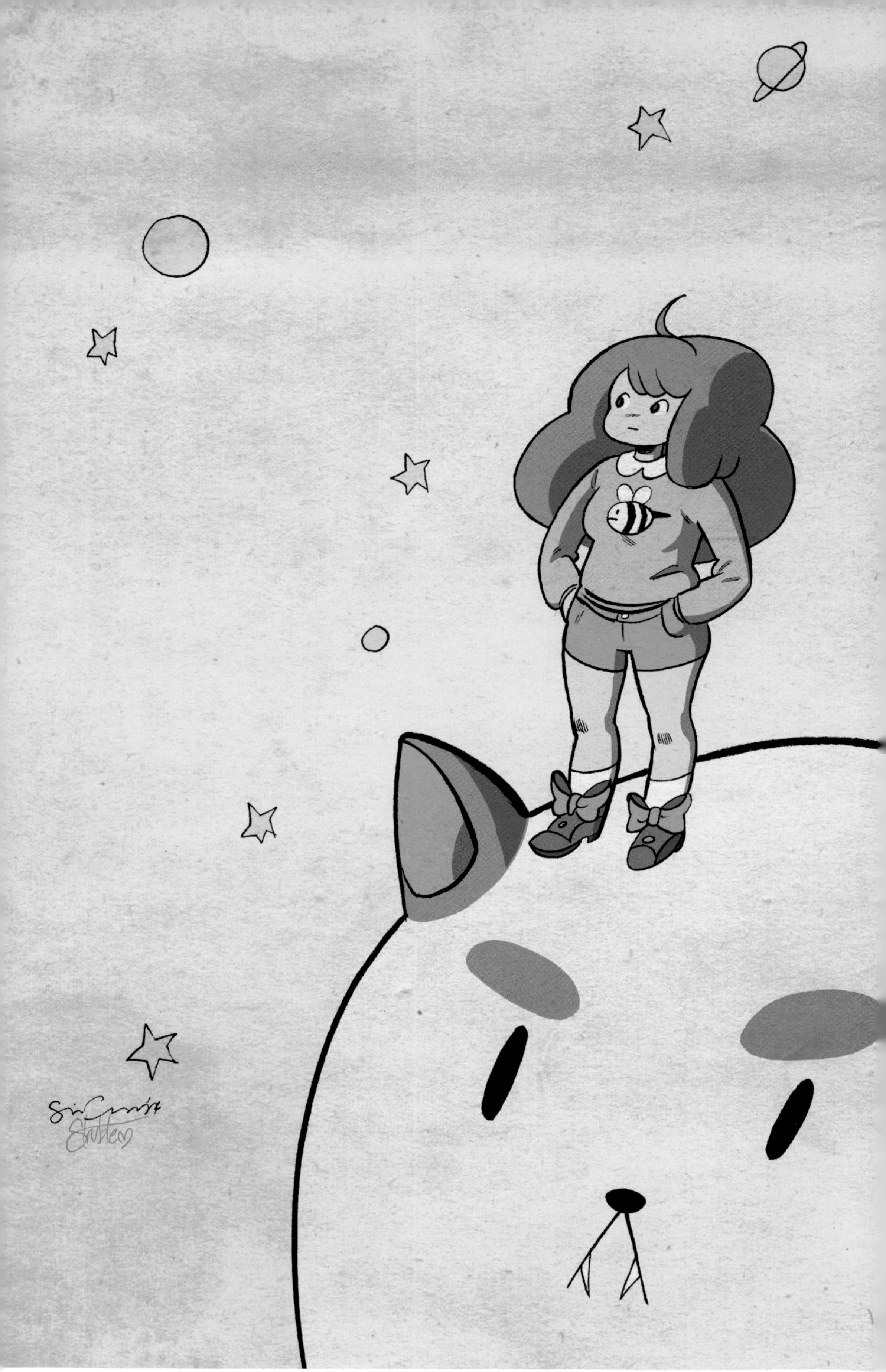

Issue One Hastings Exclusive by Sina Grace with colors by Shaun Steven Struble

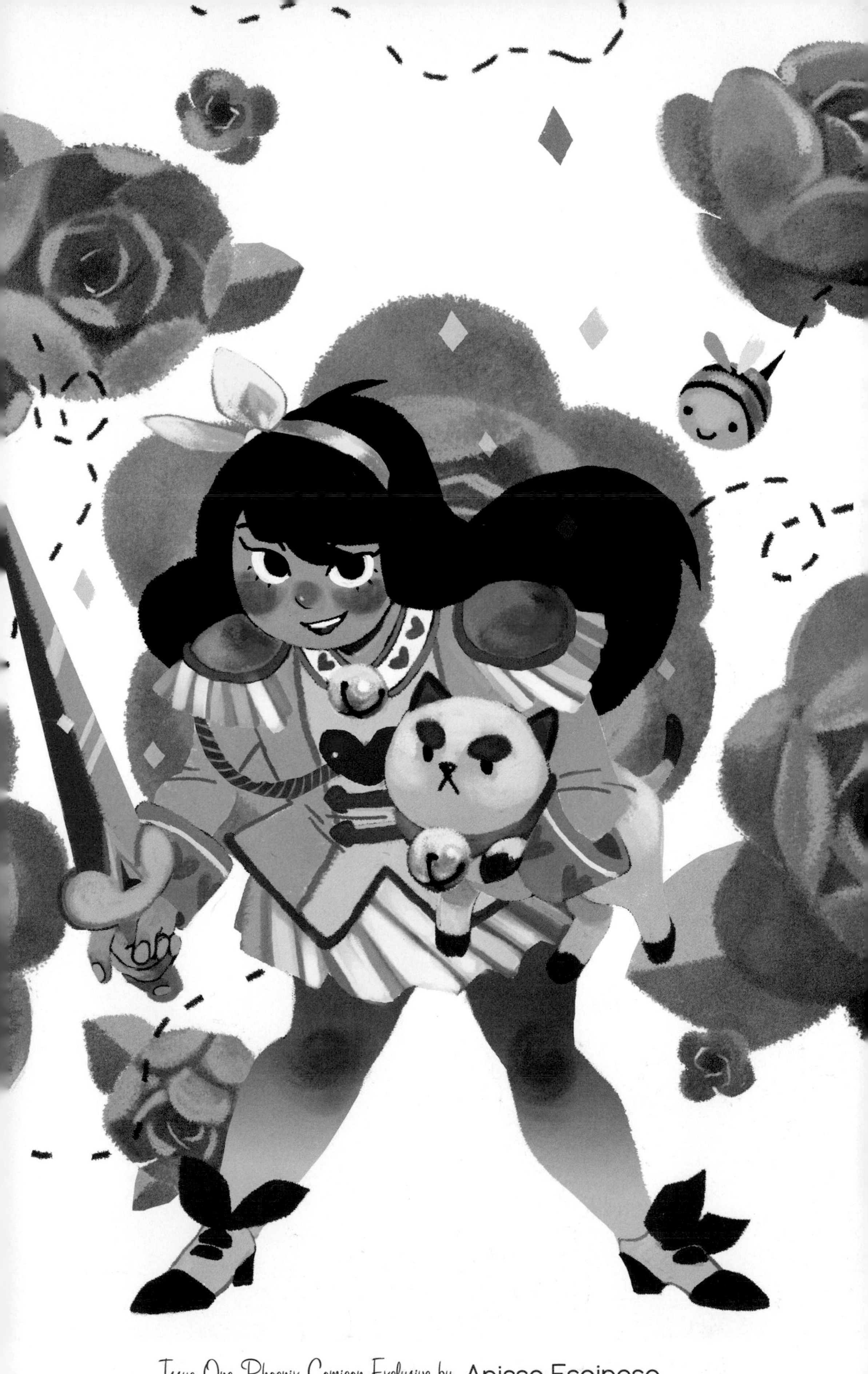

Issue One Phoenix Comicon Exclusive by Anissa Espinosa

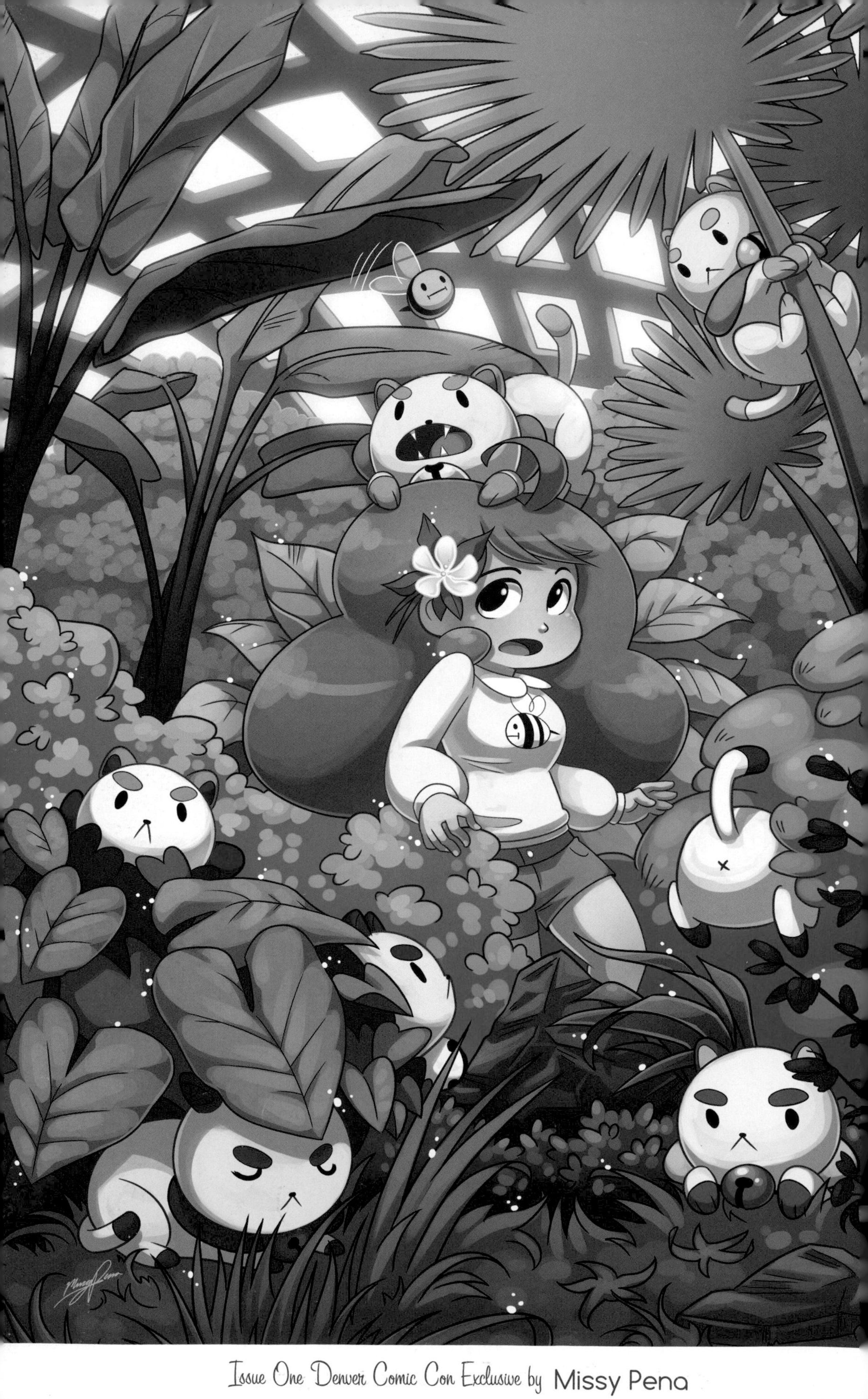

Issue One Denver Comic Con Exclusive by Missy Pena

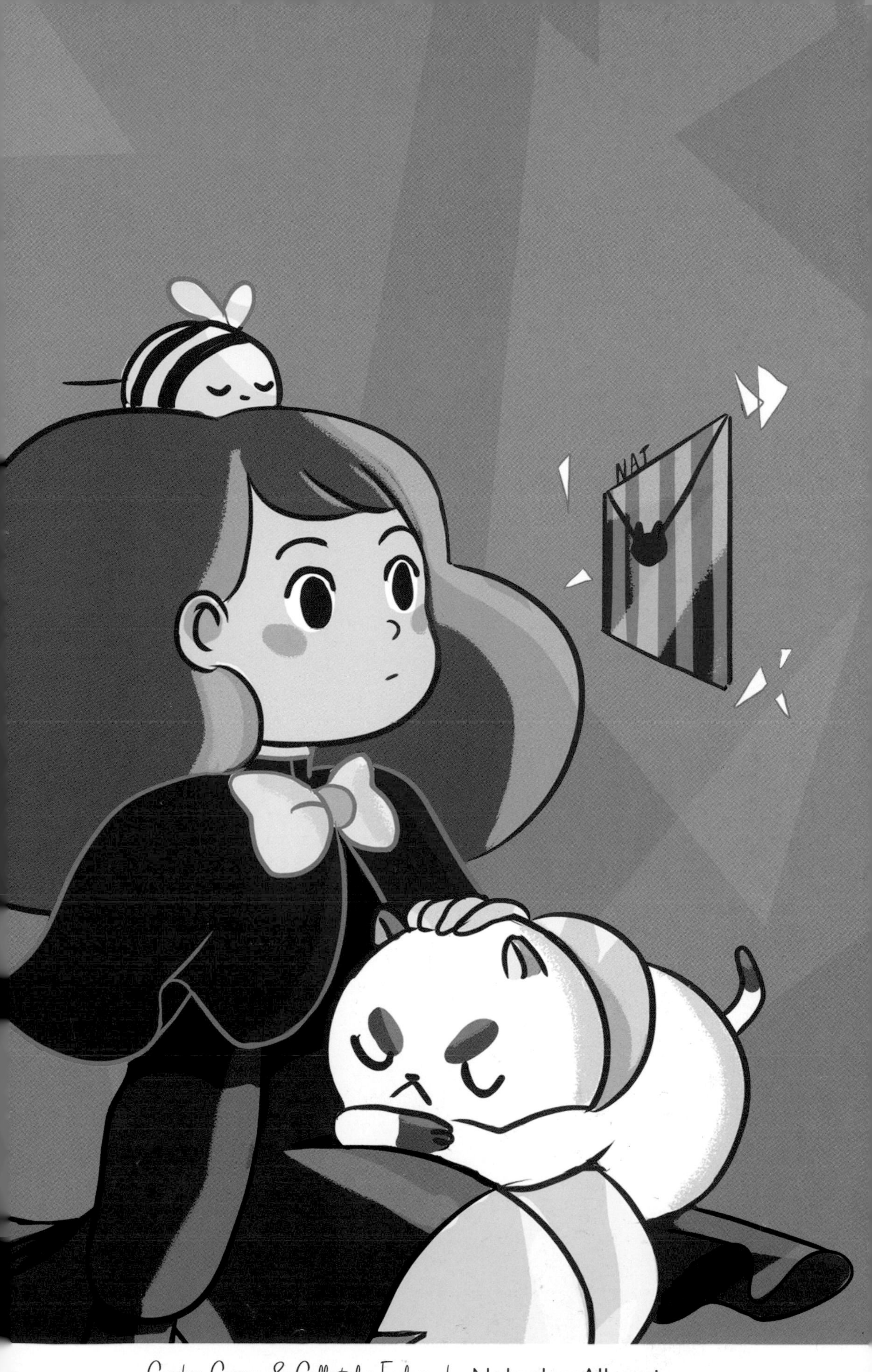
NAT

Cardsm Comics, & Collectinles Exclusive by Natasha Allegri

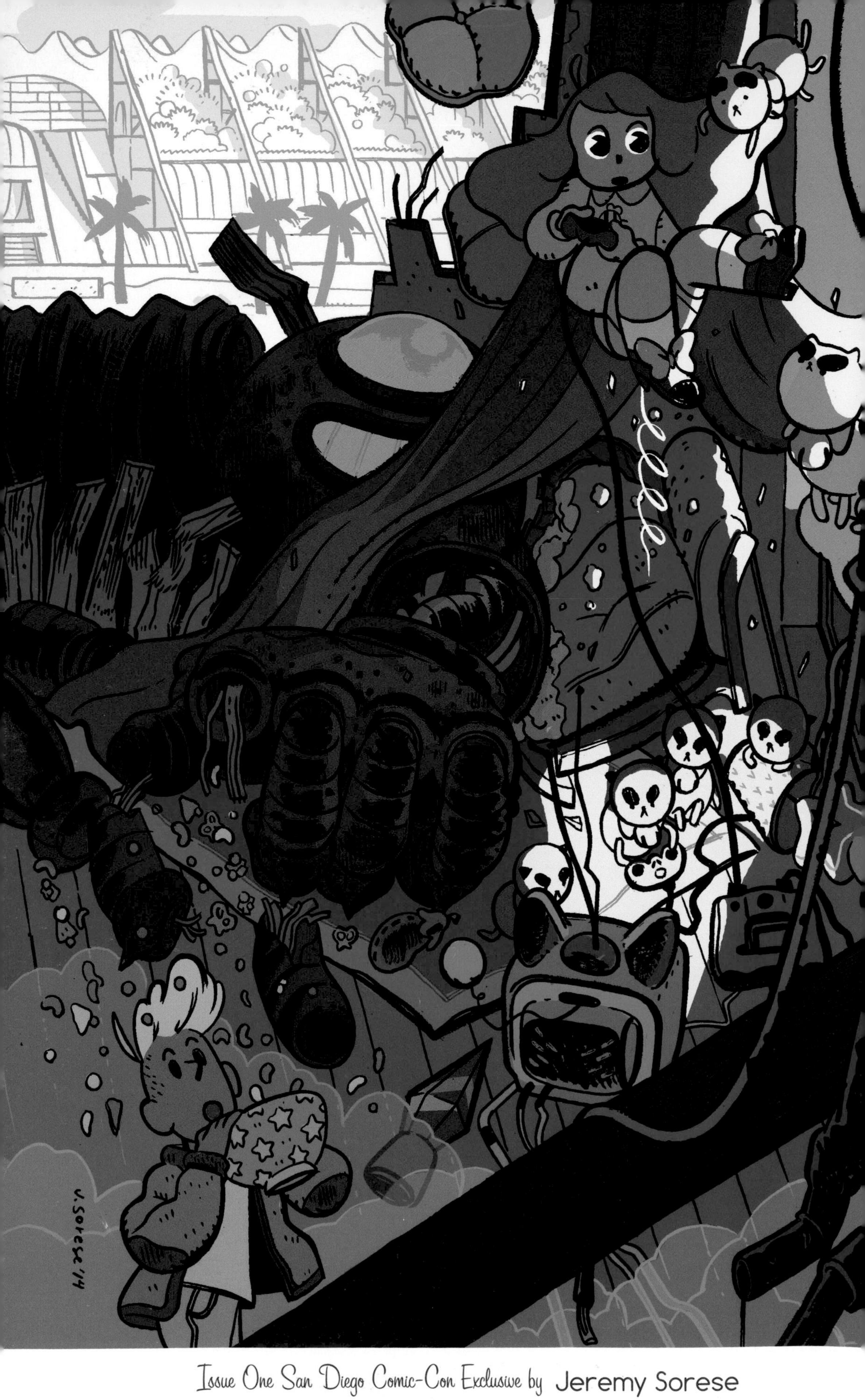
J.Sorese '14

Issue One San Diego Comic-Con Exclusive by Jeremy Sorese

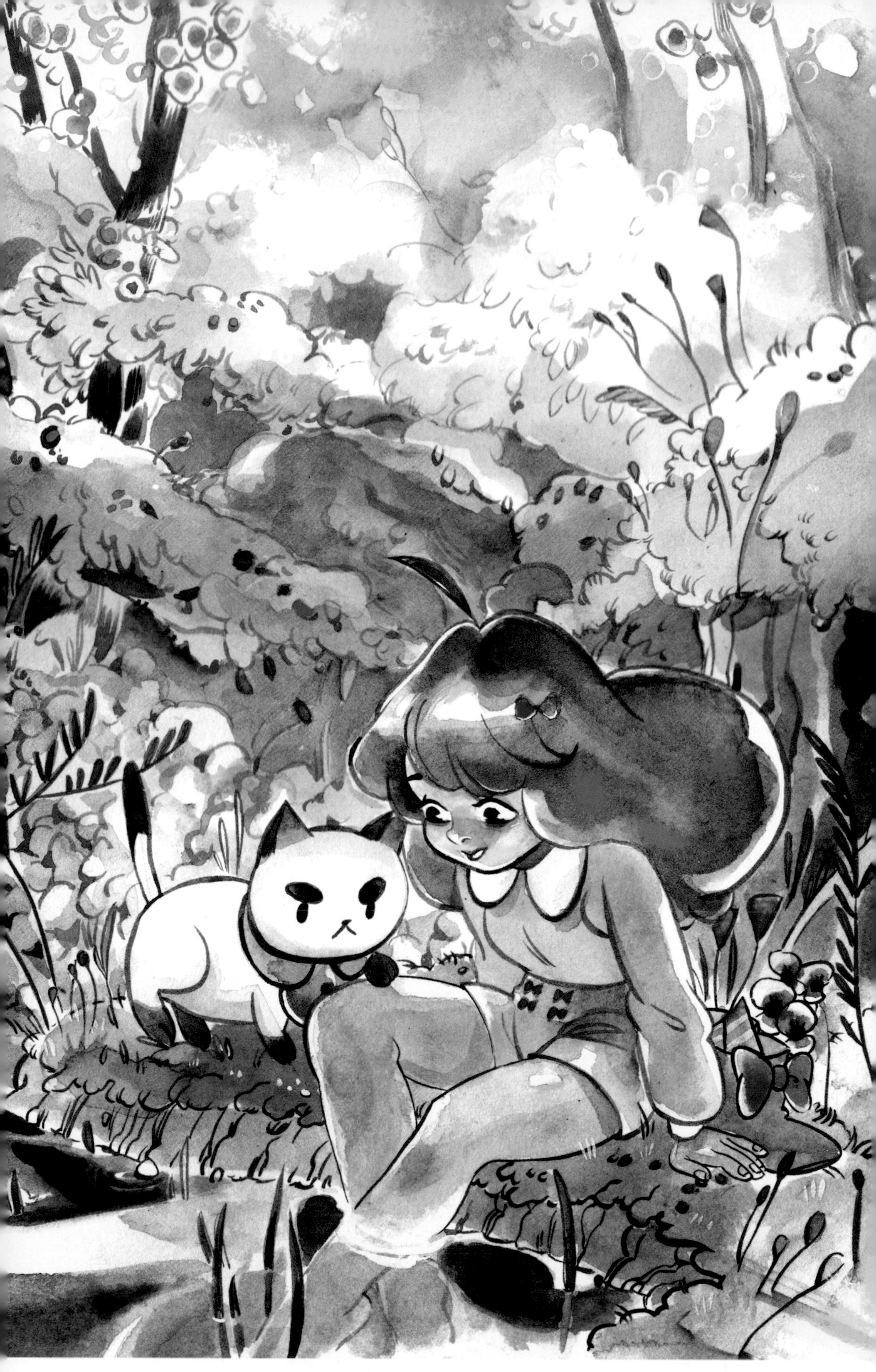

Issue One Second Print by Leslie Hung

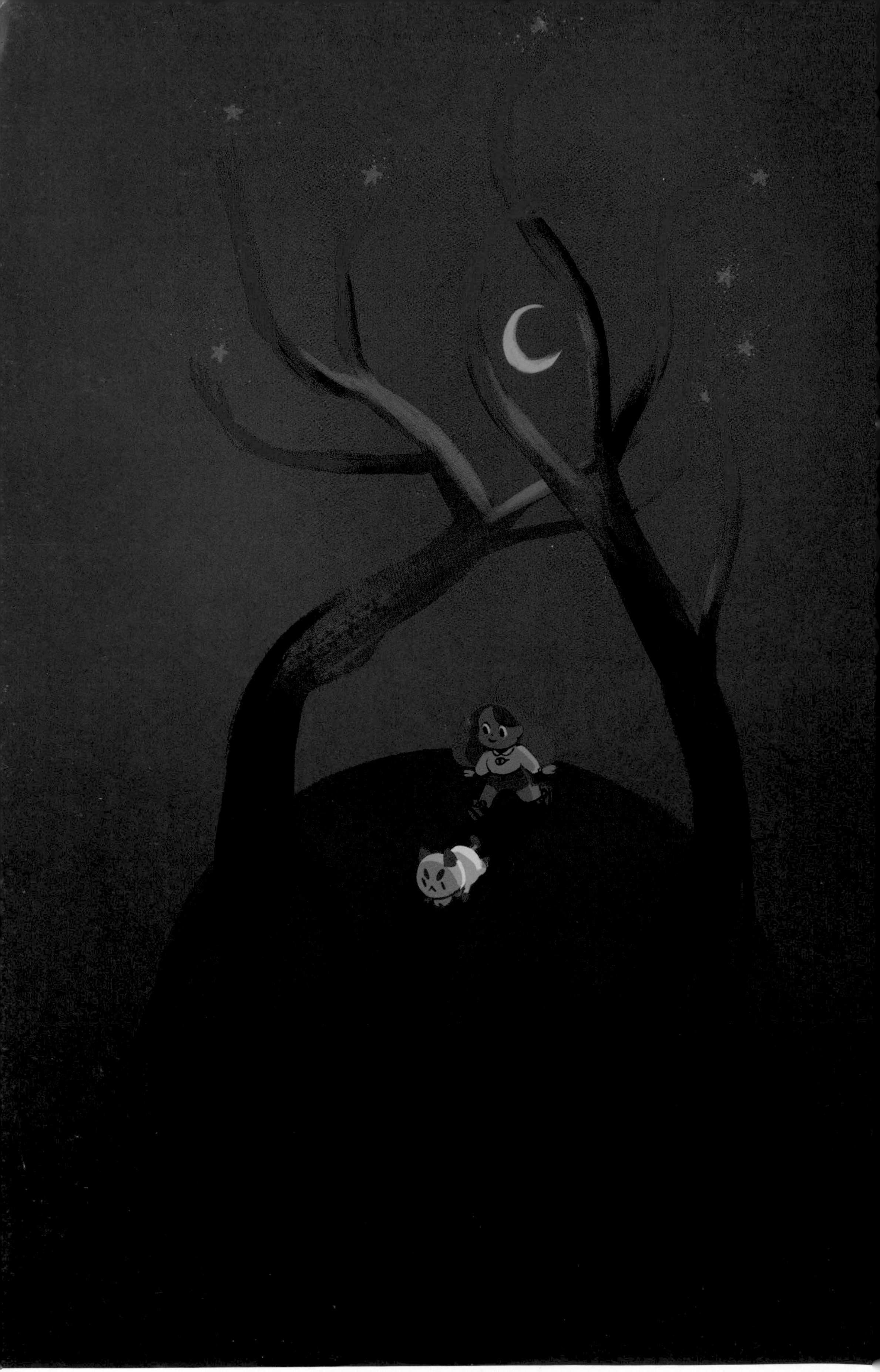

Issue Two A by Natasha Allegri

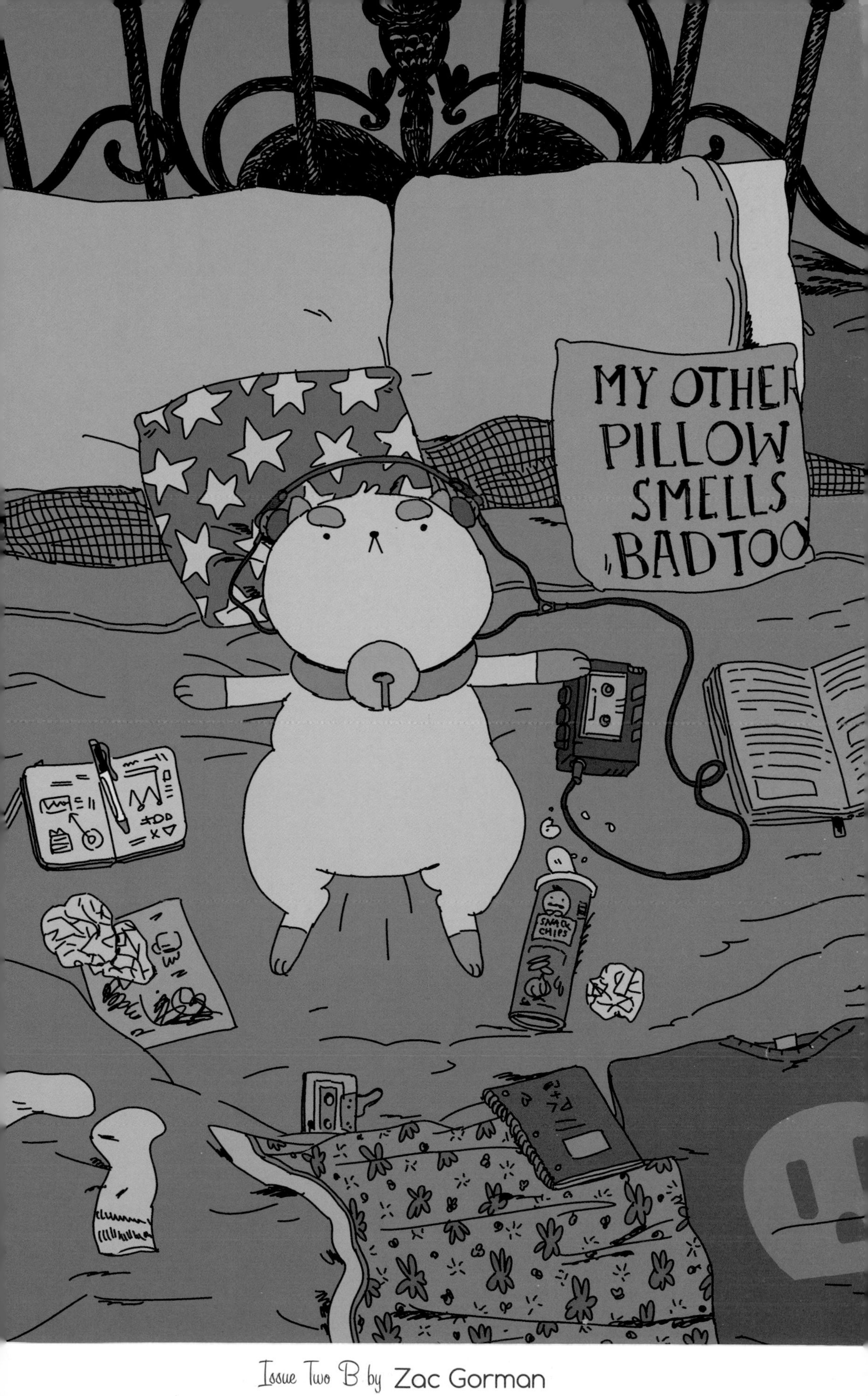
MY OTHER
PILLOW
SMELLS
BAD TOO
SNACK CHIPS

Issue Two B by Zac Gorman

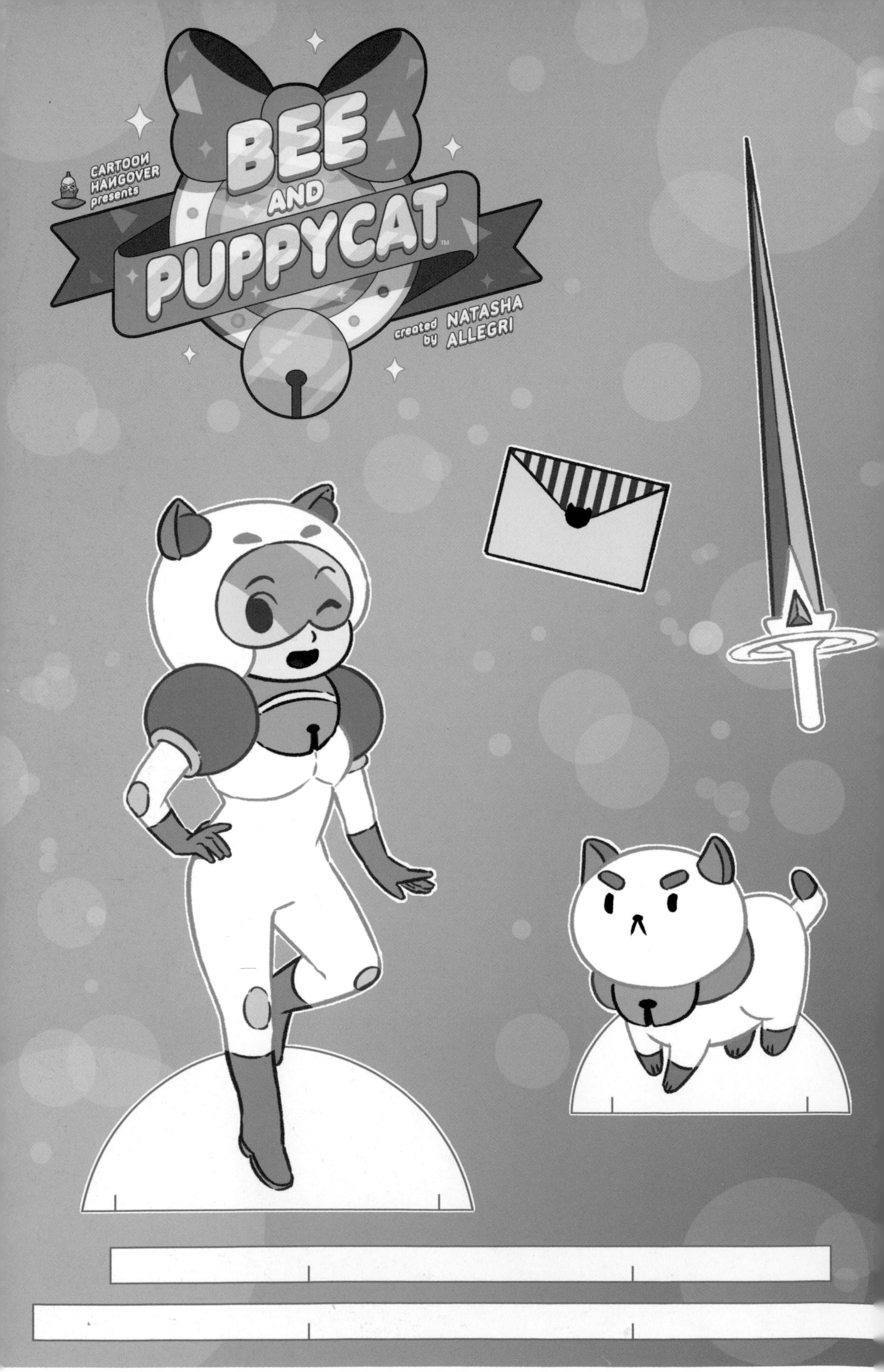
CARTOON HANGOVER presents
BEE AND PUPPYCAT™
created by NATASHA ALLEGRI

Issue Two Boom! Studios Exclusive by Stephanie Gonzaga

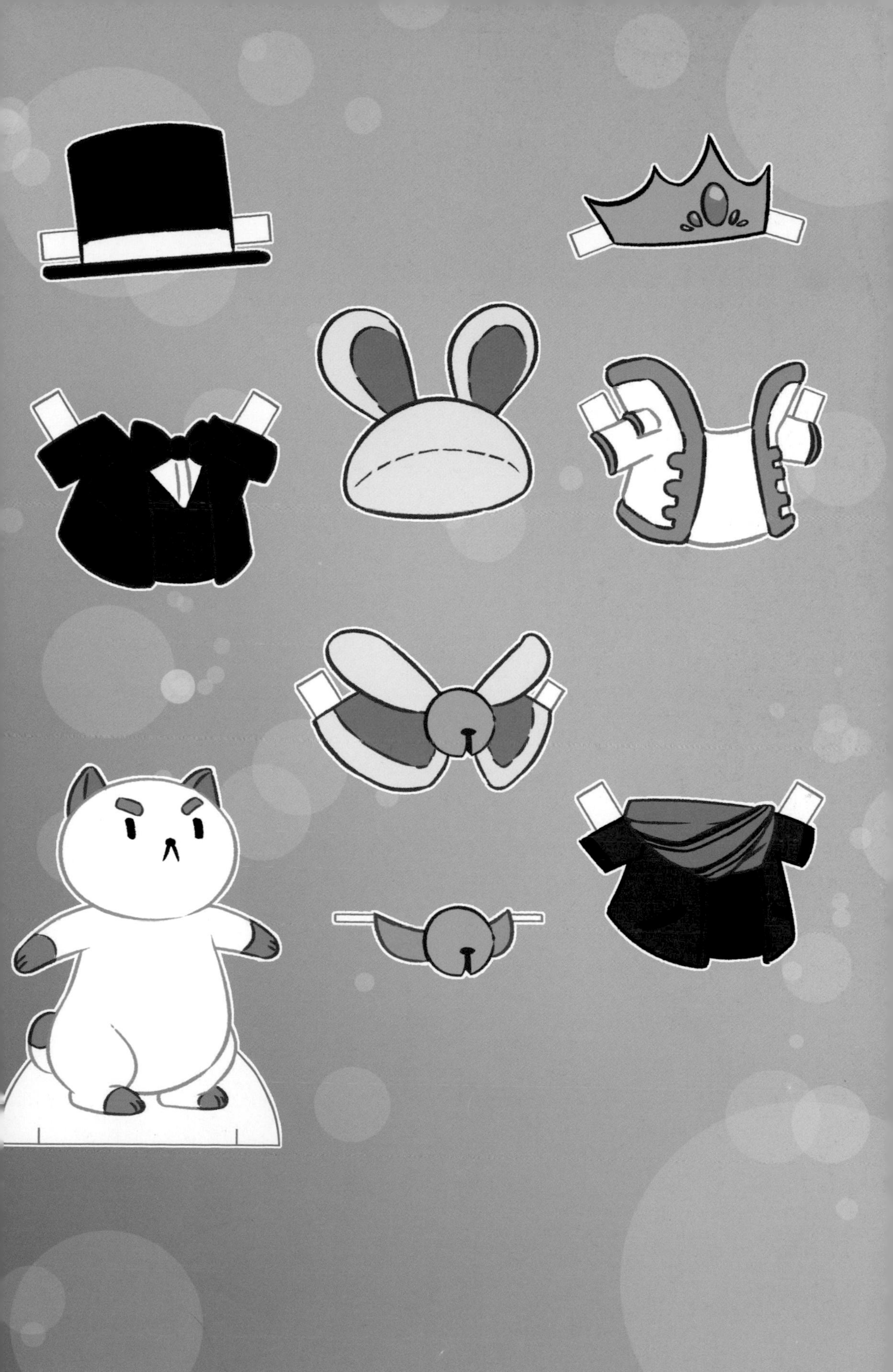

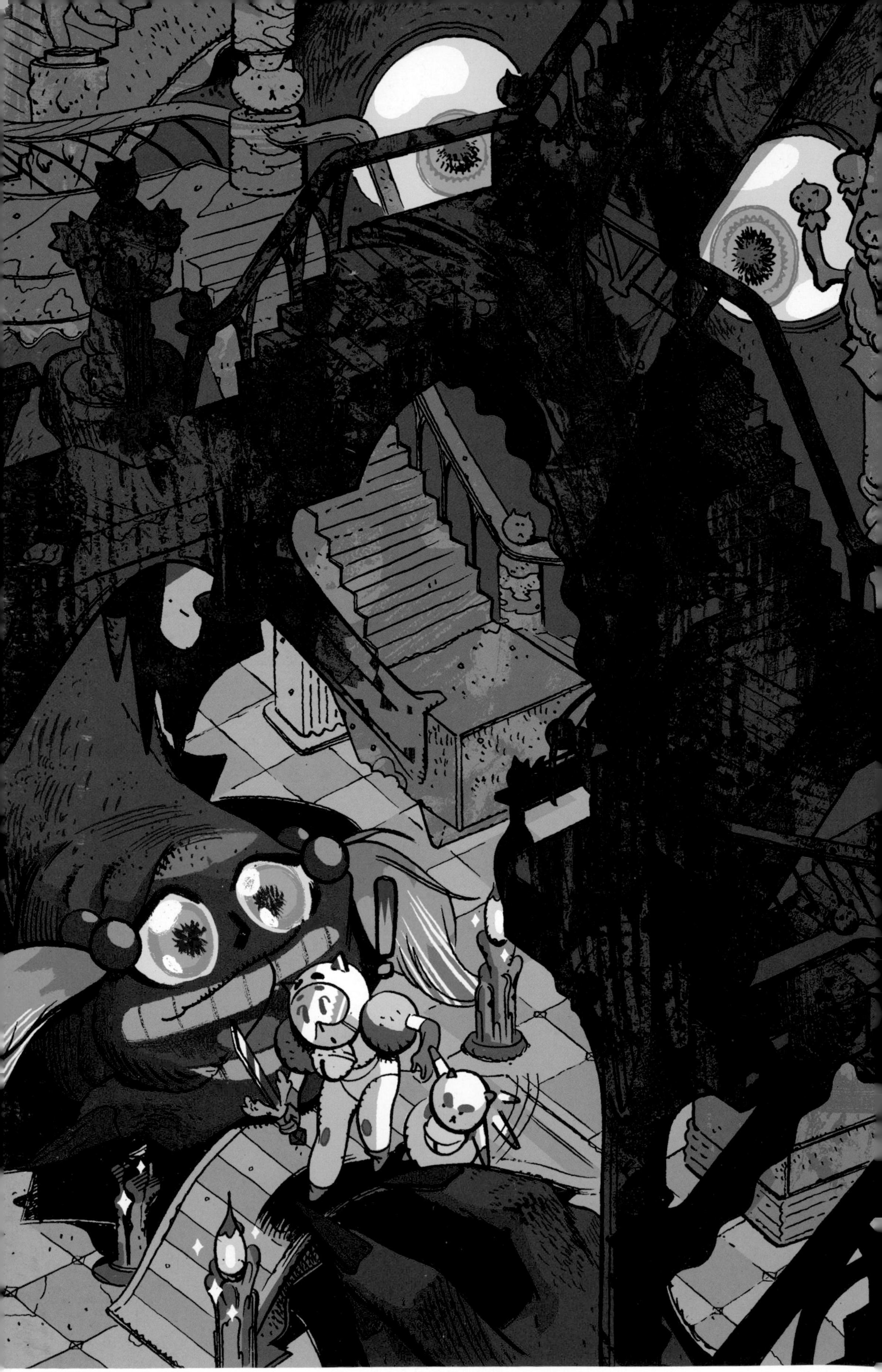

Issue Two C by Jeremy Sorese

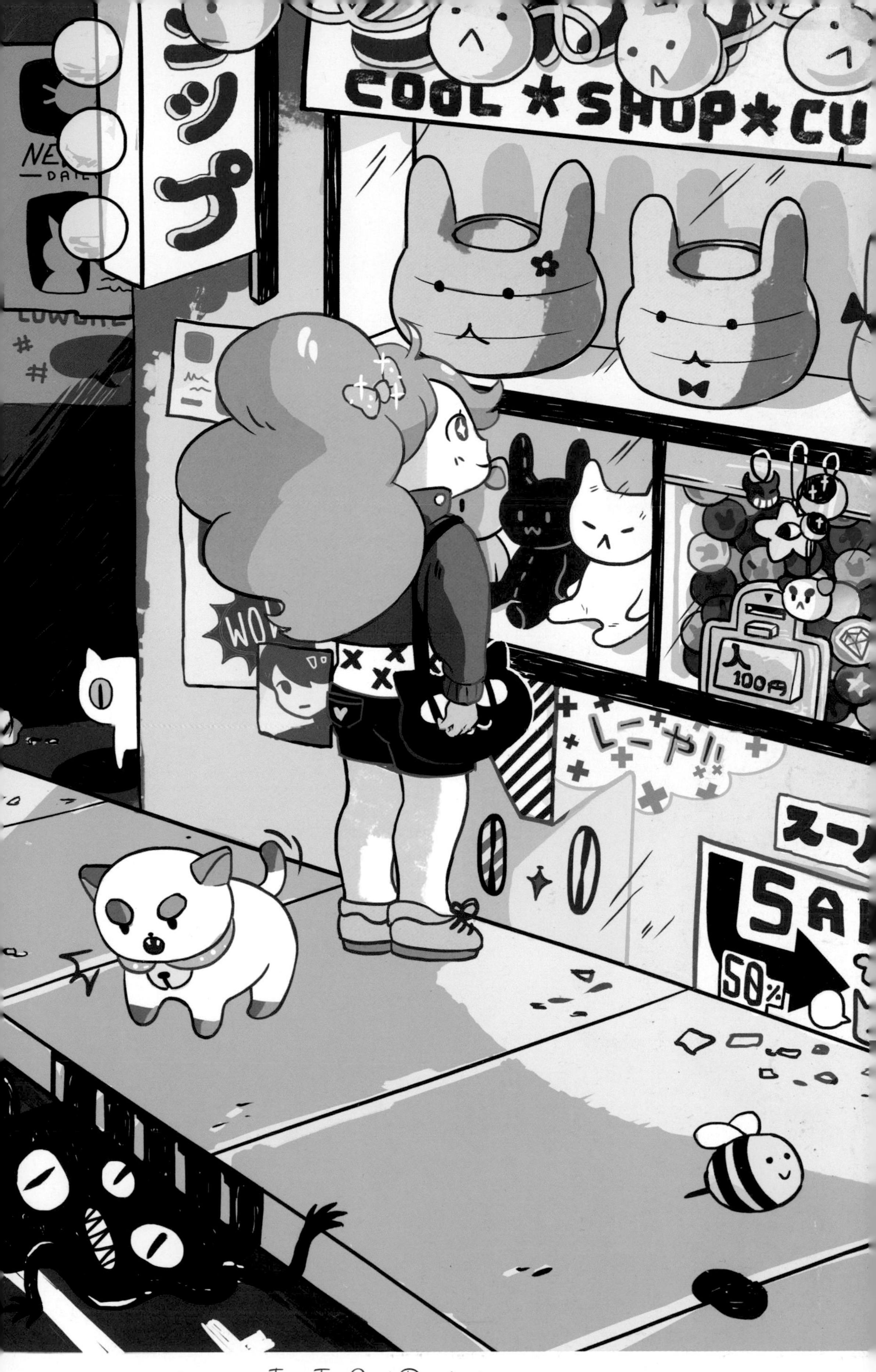
COOL ★ SHOP ★ CU
人
100円
SA
50%

Issue Two Secod Print by Buntoo

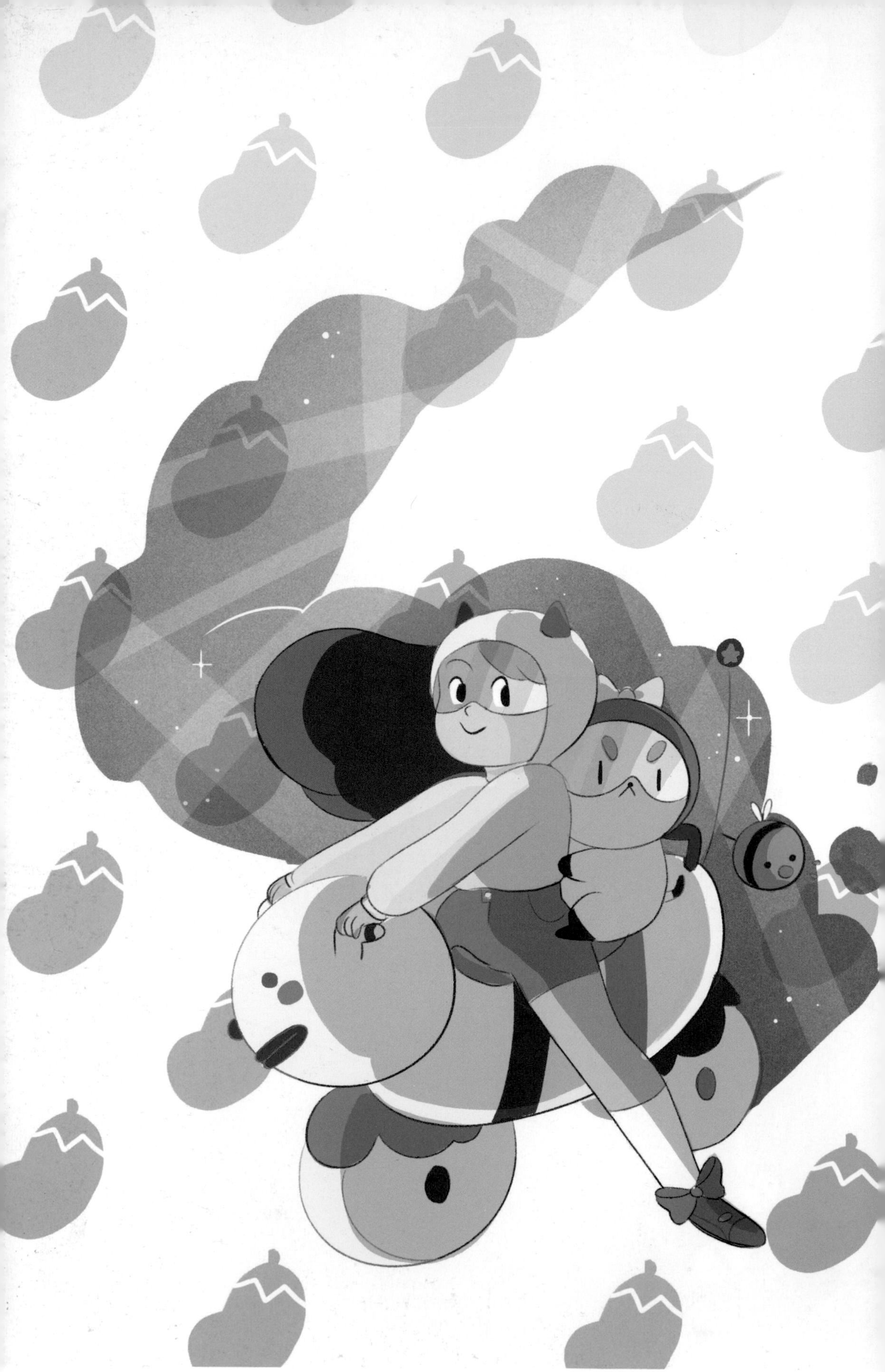

Issue Three A by Natasha Allegri

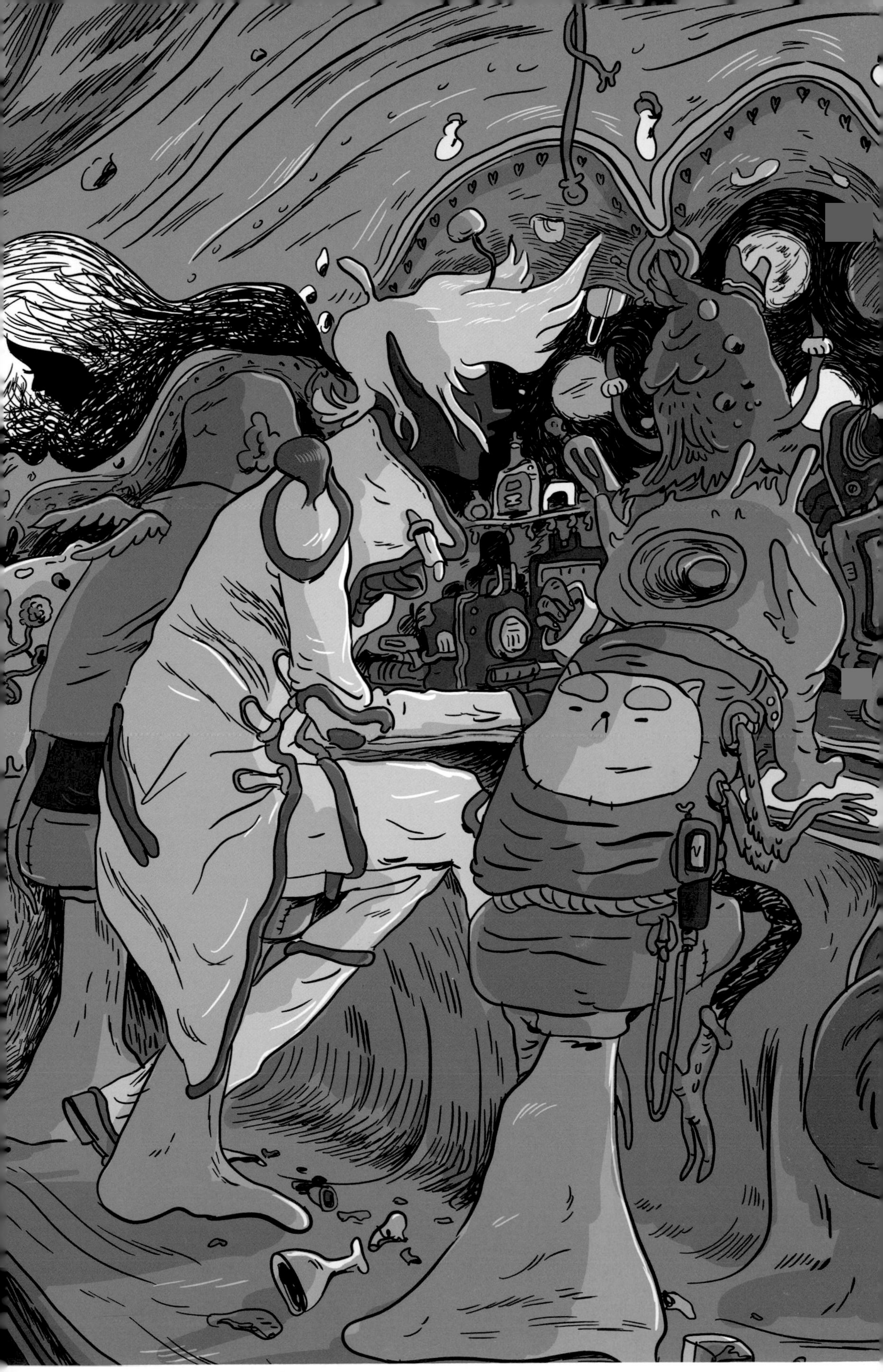

Issue Three B by Zac Gorman

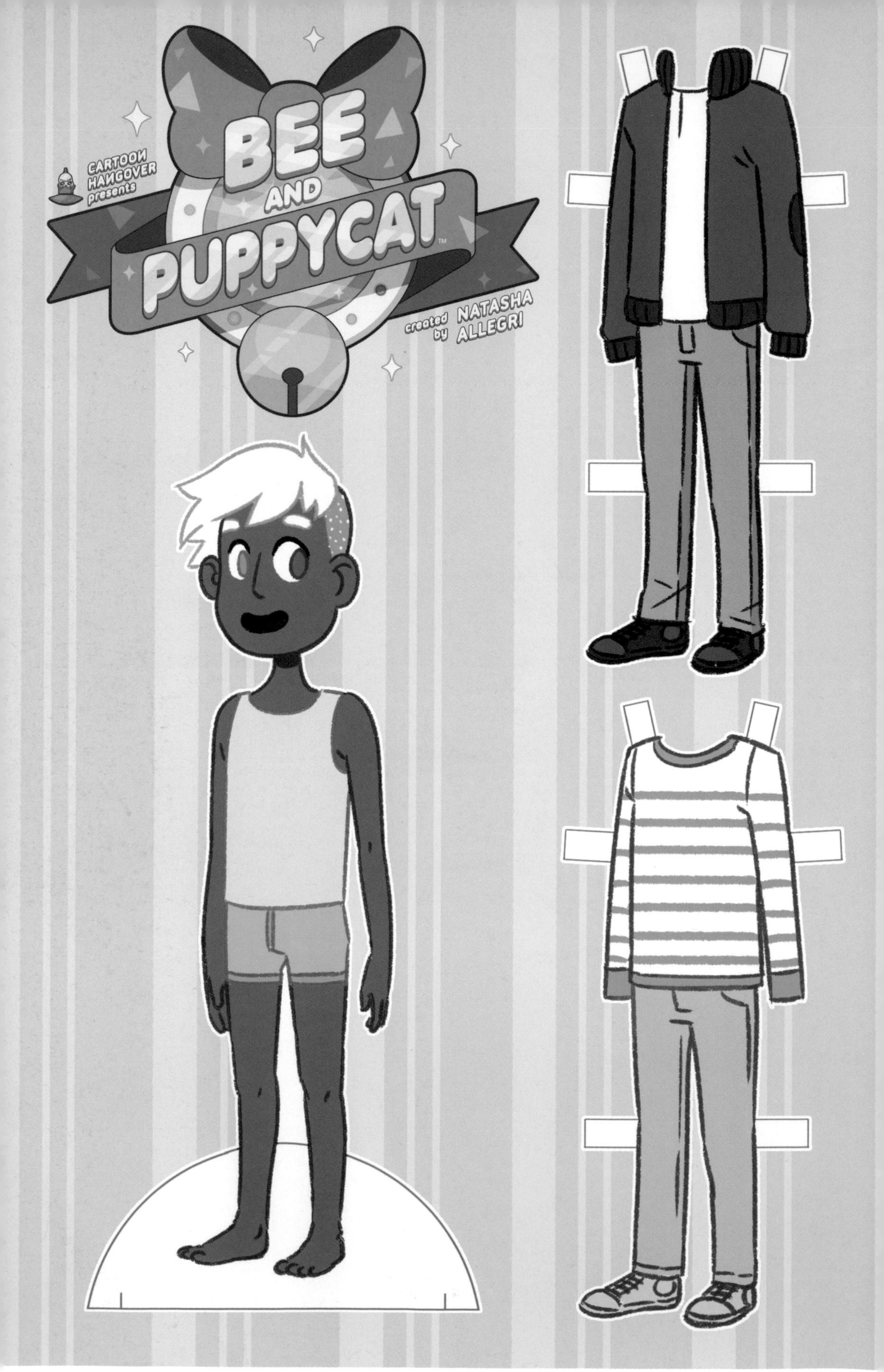
CARTOON HANGOVER presents
BEE AND PUPPYCAT™
created by NATASHA ALLEGRI

Issue Three Boom! Exclusive by Stephanie Gonzaga

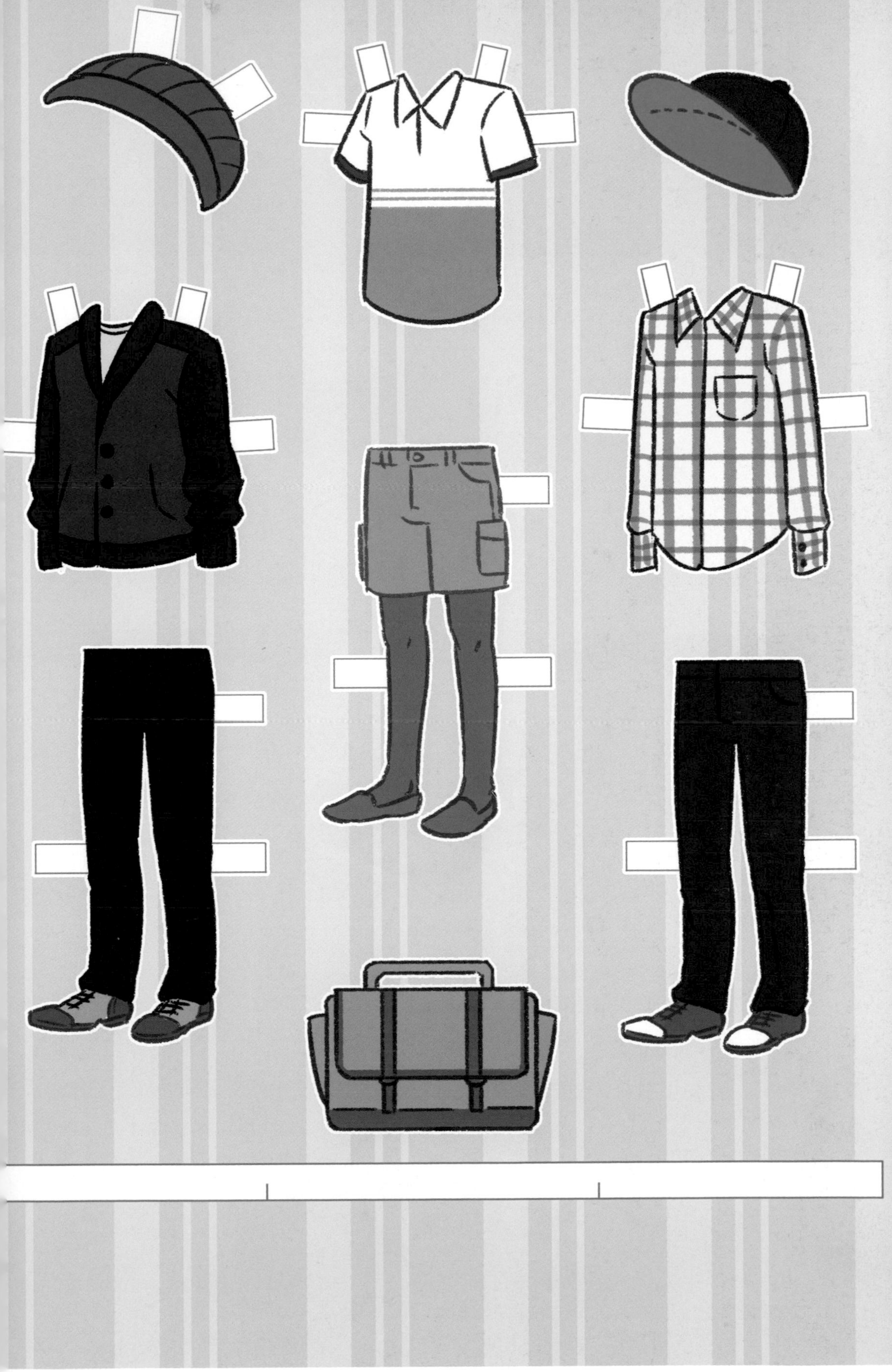

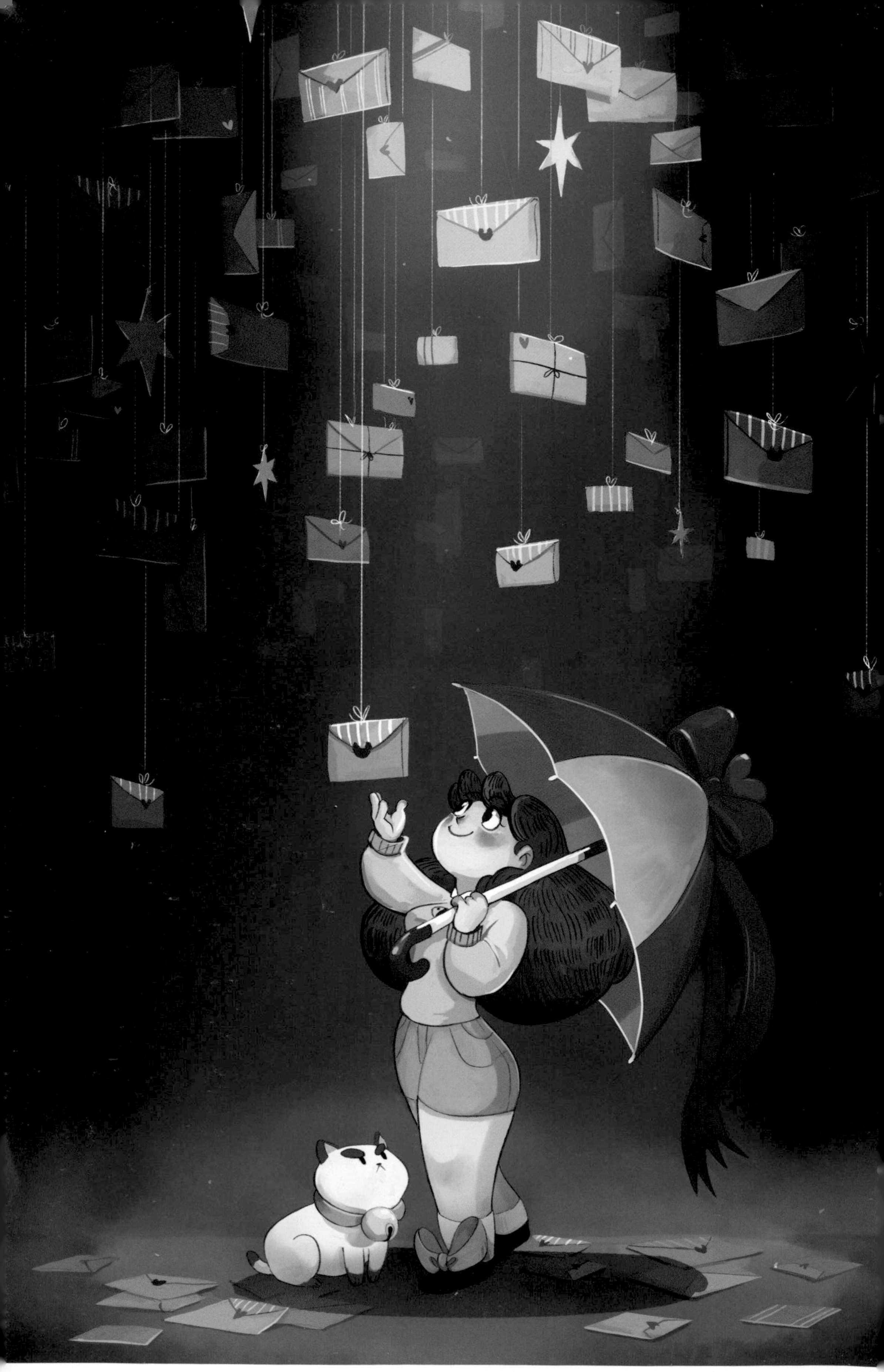

Issue Three C by Chrystin Garland

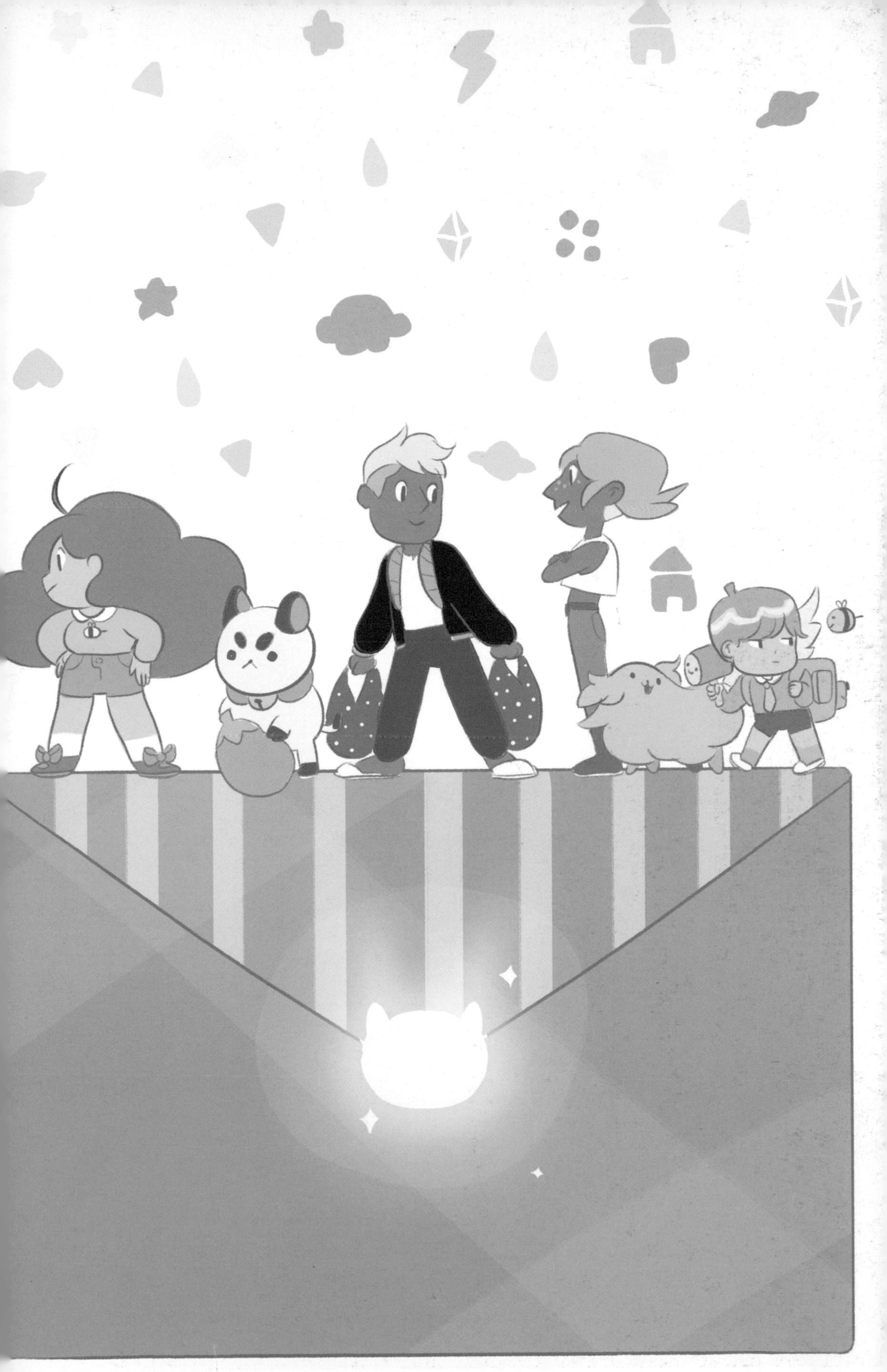

Issue Four A by Natasha Allegri

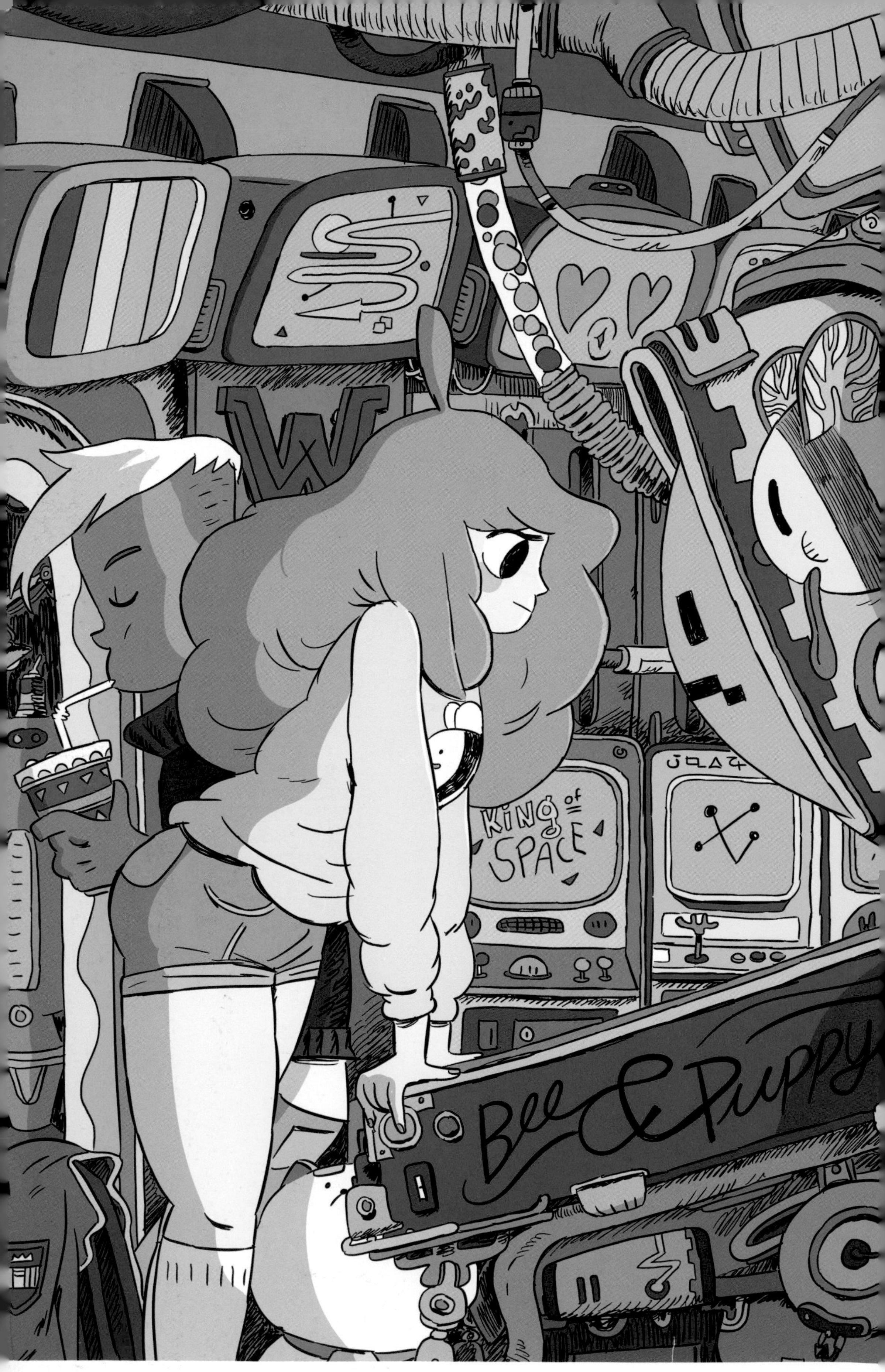
W
KING of SPACE
Bee & Puppy

Issue Four B by Zac Gorman

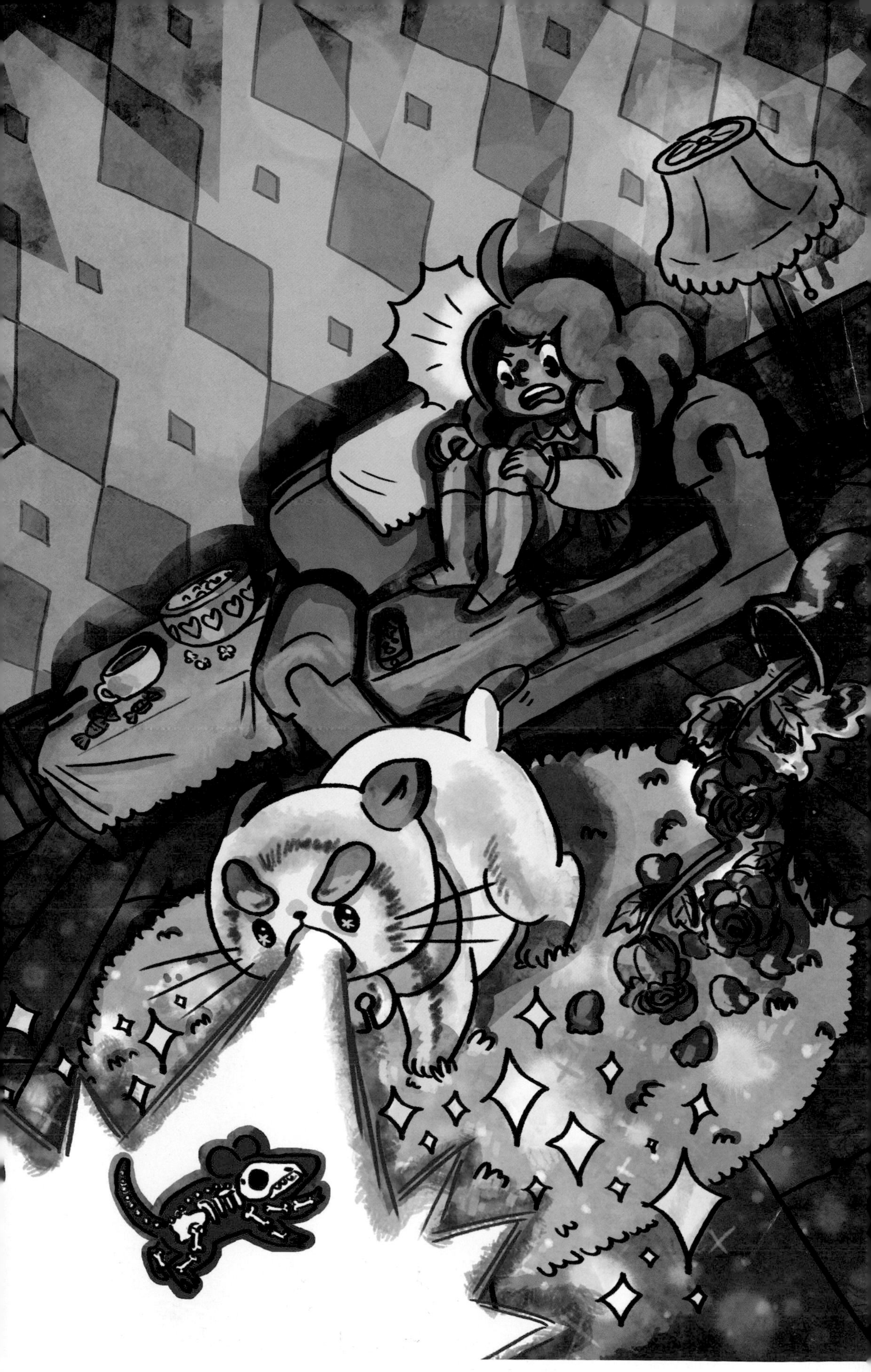

Issue Four C by Megan Brennan

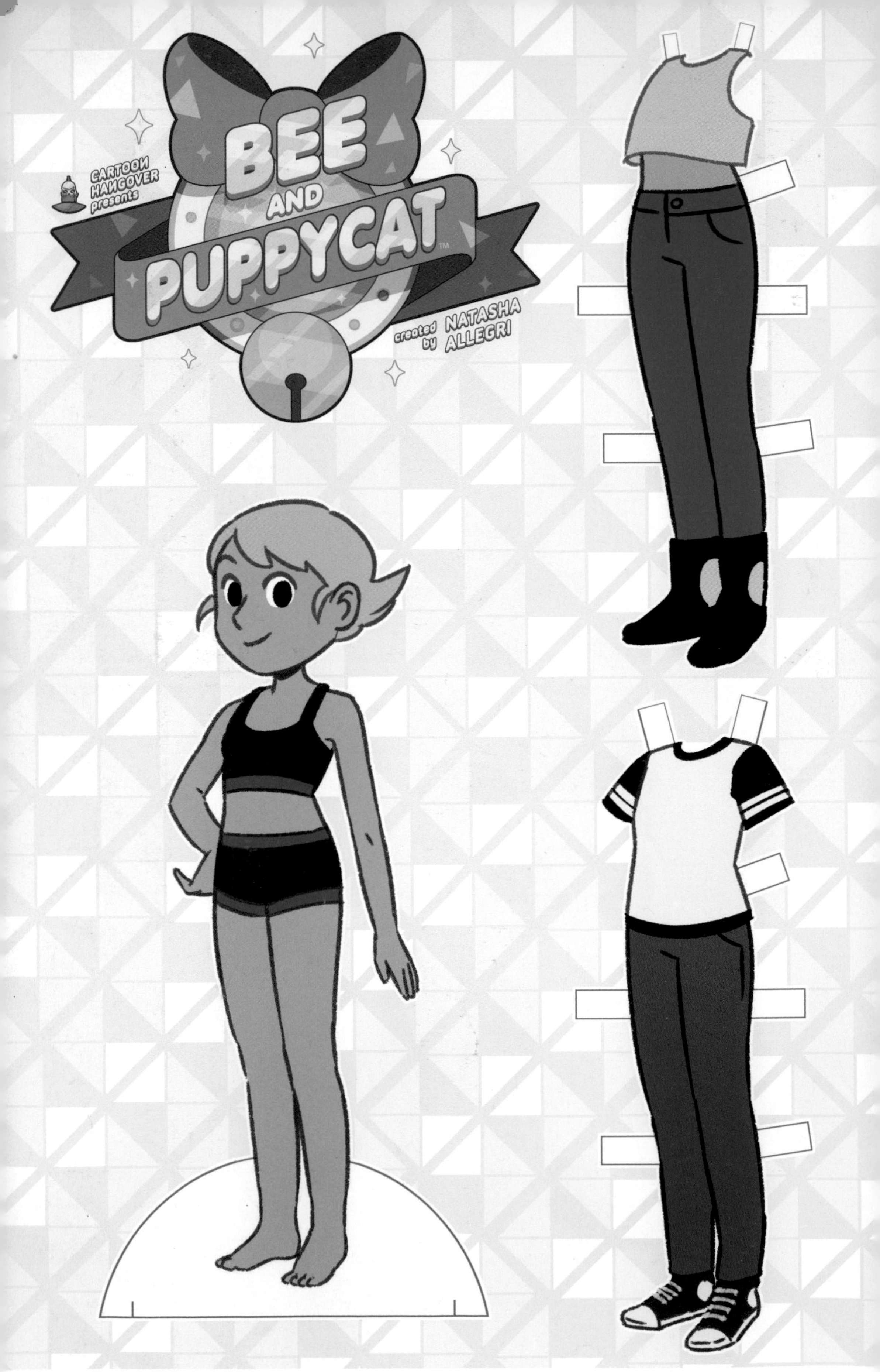
CARTOON HANGOVER presents
BEE AND PUPPYCAT™
created by NATASHA ALLEGRI

Issue Four Boom! Studios Exclusive by Stephanie Gonzaga

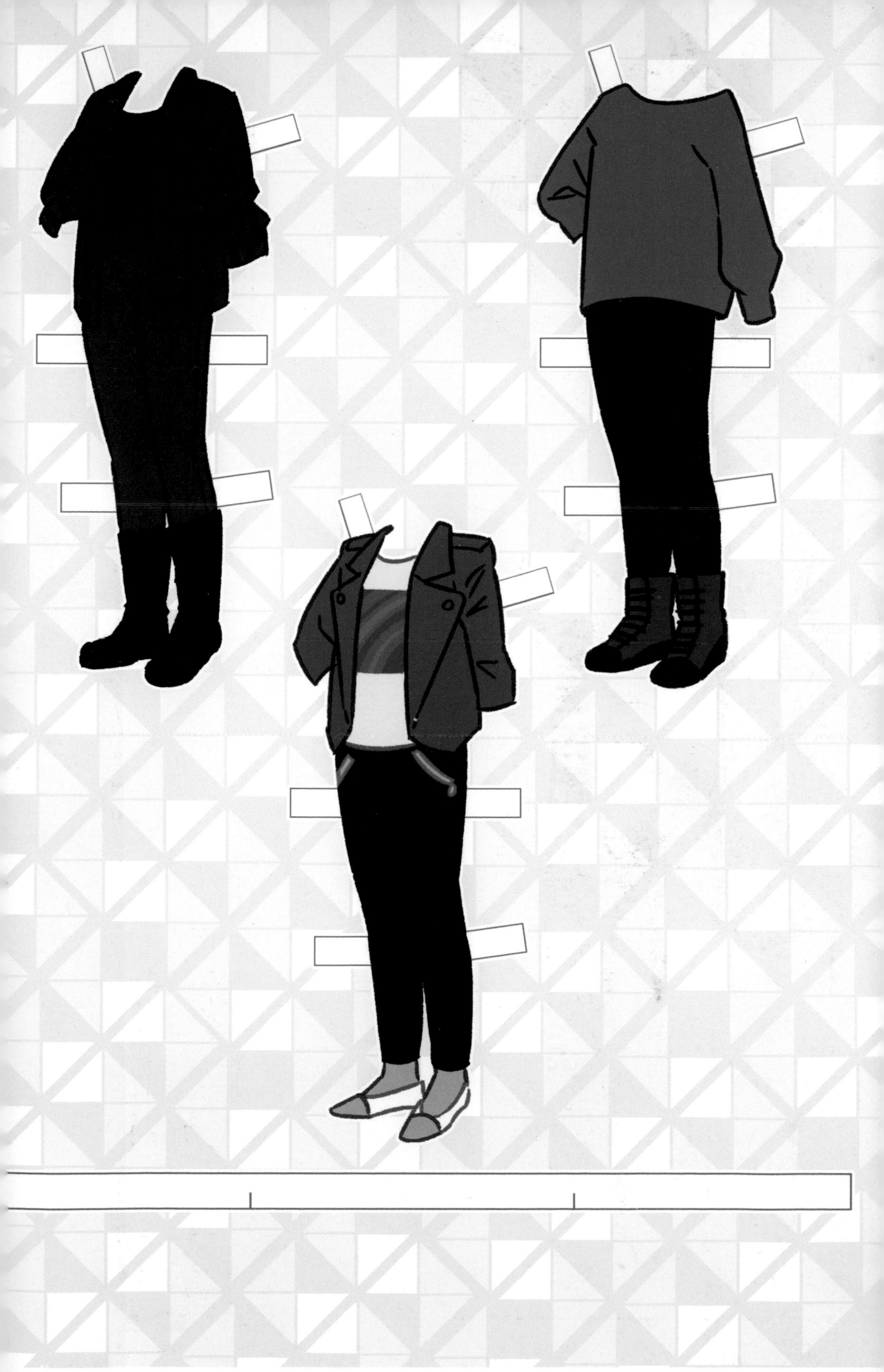